Who Desires Peace ...

James Emerson Loyd

Book One
of

The Great War Won
trilogy

*"Who desires peace should
prepare for war...
no one dare offend or insult
a power of recognized superiority
in action."*

*Publius Flavius Vegetius Renatus,
<u>De Re Militari</u>,
circa 383 A.D.*

The Great War Won

Book One:
Who Desires Peace…

Copyright 2011 – 2014

James Emerson Loyd

Cover design and maps by Sixto Juan Zavala Art Direction and Illustration.

Graphics by KibPrestridge.com

ISBN 978-0-9905763-6-5

Dreadnought Press

Foreword

Karlsruhe, December, 1954

When I was asked to provide an introduction to this book, I asked myself, *'What is this silly man thinking? That I, of all people, would lend my authority and gravitas to some dreadful revisionist history of the events of the last thirty or forty years?'* But, after consulting with Walter and Erich, and with Winston's blessings, I decided to have a go at it, read the silly book, simple as that.

To my great surprise and absolute delight! Did he not faithfully recall my bygone beauty at every turn? Clever, that, and not so silly after all, yes? Above all he captured the complexity, the contradictions, the tortured soul of my dear departed Dietrich. And the times and those who played such vital roles, many likewise now no longer with us.

I ramble, yes, truly I do, but I simply cannot forget those times, the brutality and terrors of the war, the intrigues and machinations and revolutions, my dear late brother's attempts to still the madness of the warmongers on both sides. And this writer captured so much more, many things I never knew, that Dietrich never recounted to me, like his and dear Walter's and that handsome Erich's escapade with the French, the gunrunning, much more, the conspiracy with my dear Winston, so much more.

I pause to reflect that since I had no children of my own, neither Richard's or Dietrich's, I have none to pass on my stories to other than my niece and nephew or my friends' children and grandchildren, all of whom look at me as that frightful, domineering Princess woman who comes to visit from time to time. So I give thanks to this author and his admittedly limited talents for giving a voice to my generation. A generation whose sacrifice and peril gave this age its liberty, its freedom from the demonic curse of Bolshevism, and, I must admit, from the Kaiser and all those horrid Hohenzollerns. But these moderns? They only care about their little transistor radios and their primitive music and this new blight of television, totally oblivious and thus ungrateful for all given them.

That sounds like the carping and grousing of an eighty-four year old woman, practically an old maid, yes? So, allow me close by thanking this fine fellow for bringing our tales back to life, not a moment too soon, I assure you.

Her Grand Ducal Highness CLAIRE

Author's Note

By way of confession, this and its companion volumes are my first works of fiction, certainly since my college admissions essays. In form, it is a mix of historical fiction, alternative history and nonfiction novel with enough romance and buddy movie script elements thrown in to keep it going. There, that should do it.

Why a long novel by an American about the First World War, told largely from a German perspective? After all, few today know anything about the Great War, save for snippets of *Downton Abbey* and *Warhorse,* and even after the centennial extravaganzas, few will still, in America, at least. A few years ago I resolved to re-read many of my history books – Tuchman, Shirer, Keegan, others – and realized while I thought I knew a lot about the Great War and its end (and I did), I did not know so much about the hows and whys of that end, known to us today as Veterans' Day, but until 1954 as Armistice Day. So, an unplowed field of uncertain fertility, the entire expanse a blank slate.

The books span 1918, the final year of the war, the year Germany lost the war and America entered the battlefields in Western Europe as Russia exited from the East. Why did Germany lose, what did America accomplish, and could the Bolsheviks have been thwarted, perhaps sparing the world from Communism? Those are the threads that run fairly true through the three volumes structured on the elements of Vegetius' famous quote, the first part being the beginnings of a quest to end the war (*Who Desires Peace...*), the continuation of the war upon the failure of those efforts (*...Should Prepare for War*), and finally, the entrance and dramatic impact of America *(A Power of Recognized Superiority)*.

Germany lost the war, having won it in the East, because it expended its energies and its most precious resource, manpower, in one final attempt to defeat the British or the French or both before the millions of untried and untested Americans could tip the scales against her. Britain and France had been bled nearly dry by four years of war, yet Britain, mainly, beat back the Hun. As Germany's armies faltered in their advances on the Western Front, the home front was hollowed out by hunger, the result of Britain's blockade, and by creeping discontent and finally, revolution.

America entered the war late, seeing less than six months of real fighting but looming large in 1919. Reluctantly pushed into the war by German miscalculations and provocations, she plunged in as enthusiastically and jingoistically as the other participants; Woodrow Wilson later said he could not believe how bloodthirsty the American people had become. Wilson considered his country at war with militarism and autocracy (the fall of the Tsar in the spring of 1917 had removed an impediment to that position), and insisted on an independent prosecution of the war on American terms. General John J. Pershing's orders and Colonel House's later instructions were evidence of that position, as was his insistence on his Fourteen Points as expression of America's war aims and his desire to frame the postwar order on his own idealistic terms. Pershing's memoirs from the field seemingly focus half on his frustration with British and French attempts to thwart this independence and half with the difficulties of simply getting his men and their horses and mules to France and the front.

Finally, this story is not about trench warfare, per se, but the futility of this war, especially the human cost, is not far beneath the surface. There were peace efforts from the very beginning, but positions had hardened by 1918, see Clemenceau's *"I make war"* and Lloyd George's "knockout" speech in January. Ludendorff's veto power, if not military dictatorship, kept German civilian leaders from following through with several peace feelers. So, if a few Germans knowledgeable of the facts of the war and desperate to keep their country from sliding into defeat and despair were to use their ranks and titles to sway those who could make a difference – enemies as well as friends – even small differences, what would have been the outcome? Versailles and its bitterness or a grudging standoff in the West, a far less grim regime in the East?

A few general notes:

- Winston Churchill was said to make his history with maps, and I can understand why and how. My office walls are covered with mostly 19th century political maps on which one can trace wars, conquests, creation of states and the destruction of empires. On one of those, of Berlin in 1861, I noted the suburb of Treptow which coincidentally was the name of a business partner in an earlier life. I then imagined the my protagonist's estate without having visited, although the Treptow of 1918 would have been devastated by the Red Army's advance in 1945 and fifty years of life under Communism. General Pershing's memoirs contain a comprehensive set of maps of the

Western Front and the campaigns of the American Expeditionary Force. To view any maps of the to and fro of the Western Front from 1914 onward, ground gained and lost, villages and towns destroyed first by one side, then the other, is to grasp the futility and agony of the trench war stalemate for which the Great War is known. Even Pershing's maps, with their daily or weekly lines of advance, drive home the frustratingly slow progress of the vigorous American style of open warfare, especially when one correlates each line reached with its staggering toll of dead and wounded.

- Plagiarism: I have studiously refrained from reading any contemporary war fiction such as <u>All Quiet on the Western Front</u> or <u>Good-Bye to All That</u> or newer works such as Ken Follett's <u>Century Trilogy</u> out of a desire to not even subconsciously adopt plot or phrasing. Any inadvertent lapses not explained in the notes and acknowledgments (see below) are regretted, but certainly not intentional.

- Acknowledgements: Notwithstanding the above, I quote directly and copiously from both primary and secondary sources where doing so solidifies the narrative, adding evidentiary weight. In some cases the truth, if not stranger than fiction, is more compelling and consistent with the narrative, too. In particular, Prince Max's and Winston Churchill's words cannot be surpassed in expressing events and opinions. When so quoting or adapting, I have taken care to acknowledge same in the *"Notes and Acknowledgements"* and *"Sources"* appendices.

- Characters: This period is rich and replete with colorful and dynamic personages, Churchill, Lloyd George, Clemenceau, Wilson and Roosevelt being merely the most obvious. Where these and others are in the narrative, I attempt to reflect their personalities and views reasonably accurately. Others, not so well known, are embroidered and enhanced: Rosa Luxemburg not just the revolutionary firebrand and Princess Claire, a completely fictional version of Max's (actually older) sister.

- Time shifting: While based fairly tightly on the actual course of events in 1918, some liberties have been taken. The most egregious of these are von Treptow's successful delay of Ludendorff's final offensive (although the push to Château Thierry happened as written) and Rosa Luxemburg's proleptic release from prison and involvement in the (real) demonstrations and strikes of January, 1918, whereas the actual Spartacist revolt and her death occurred in January of 1919. Some of Churchill's most stirring words were spoken later, as late as the Second World War, but have a certain resonance in this time, especially in the winding down of the war and the ascendancy of America.

- Conventions: Continental time is 24 hour; in England and America, 12 hour. Likewise, metrics on the continent, English measures in Britain and American usage. Military ranks, Field Marshals Hindenburg, Haig, and later, Foch aside, are American-style, to reduce confusion.

- Languages: The Continentals are assumed fluent in at least three languages and slip easily from one to another. As an example, Estelle and Dietrich could have been speaking either German, English or French, but not Dutch, and Rosa and Dietrich would have conversed exclusively in German. Churchill spoke no German and only a fractured French, so his German visitors would have used English, with ease. Also, there is a hierarchy in usage and syntax, German more formal, American more casual and slangy, the Brits and French in between. Note also an earlier age's familiarity with Greek and Latin, at least sources if not fluency.

- Cast: Added at my wife's request, seconded by several friendly reviewers. Can't tell the players without a program.

Finally, as I plunged headlong into researching and writing these 'works', I found I shared an experience recounted by Adam Hochschild in his book To End All Wars wherein he *"felt as if its subject matter were pursuing me..."* I researched as I wrote, and vice versa, and with uncanny frequency my ongoing research uncovered actual events or characters that I had already written about creatively, at least spontaneously, in some cases well over a year prior, totally unaware of the coincidence or whatever term one might choose. And I soon came to experience the wonder of seeing my characters not just take form, but take over the narrative to the point I was simply taking dictation.

JEL
San Antonio, 2014

Cast of Principal Characters (*fictive in italics*)

Germany
Brigadier General Graf Dietrich von Treptow, Army Intelligence
Lieutenant Colonel Walter Knorr, his aide
Captain Erich von Seeckt, his aide
Prince Max of Baden, honorary head of the German Red Cross
Princess Claire, his sister
Field Marshal Paul von Hindenburg, Commander, Imperial Army
Quartermaster General Erich Ludendorff, Chief of Staff, effectively military dictator
Crown Prince Rupprecht of Bavaria, Commander, Army Group North
Rosa Luxemburg, Spartacist leader
Major Ernst Bruckmiller, Military Police
Humbert Grosz, smuggler and con man
Loren Reifenstahl/Miss Lorelei, cabaret performer

Great Britain
Winston S. Churchill, Minister of Munitions
Reginald, Lord Elsmere, his aide
David Lloyd George, Prime Minister
Max Aitken, Lord Beaverbrook, newspaper proprietor

France
Pierre Laval, Socialist politician
Maurice Barton, industrialist

The Netherlands
Pieter van der Hoek, Naval Attaché, London
Estelle Vandenberg and her children

United States of America
General John J. Pershing, American Expeditionary Force Commander
Colonel Robert Wallace Emerson, Army Intelligence
Major Robert McCormick, his aide
Major George S. Patton, tank commander

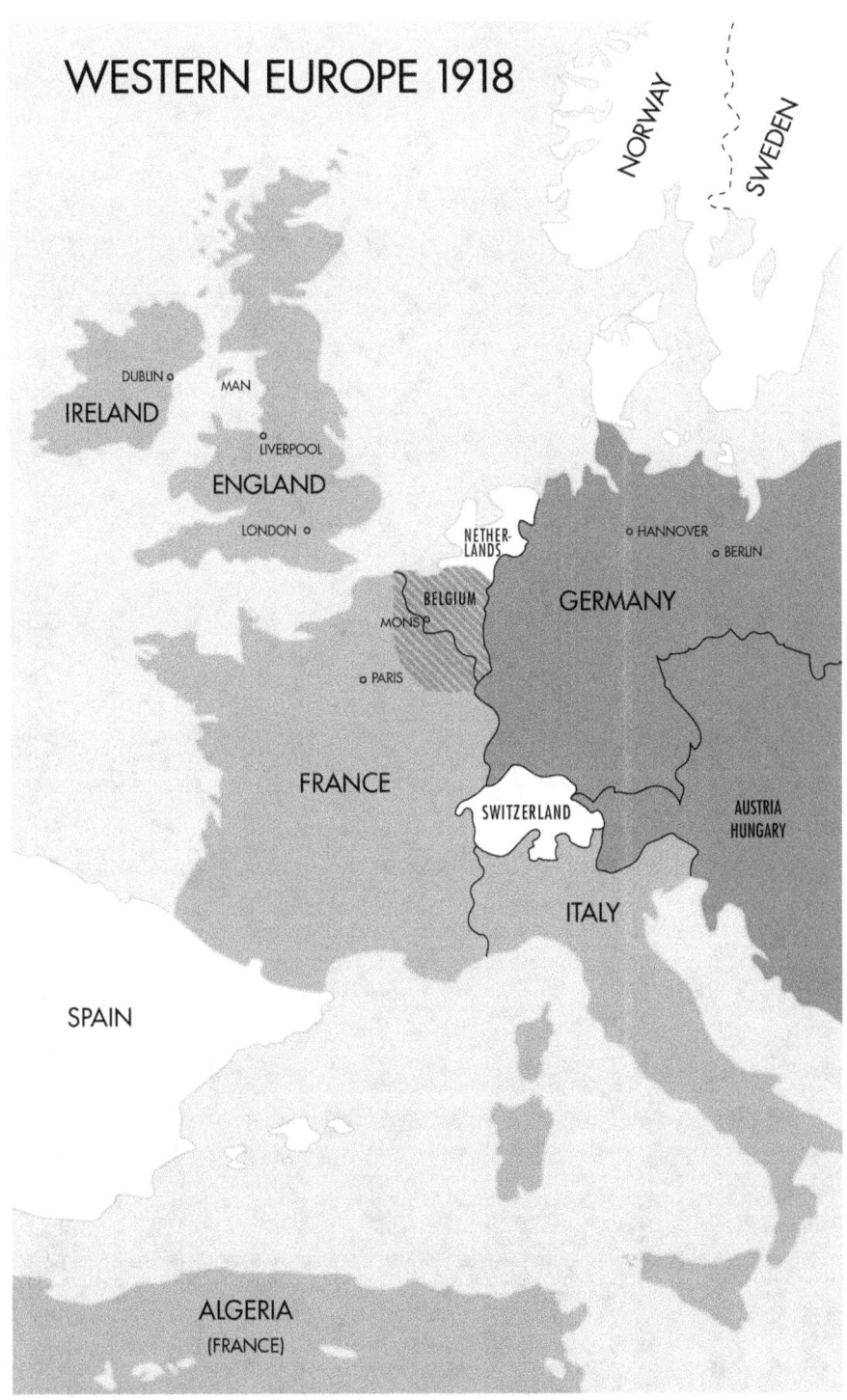

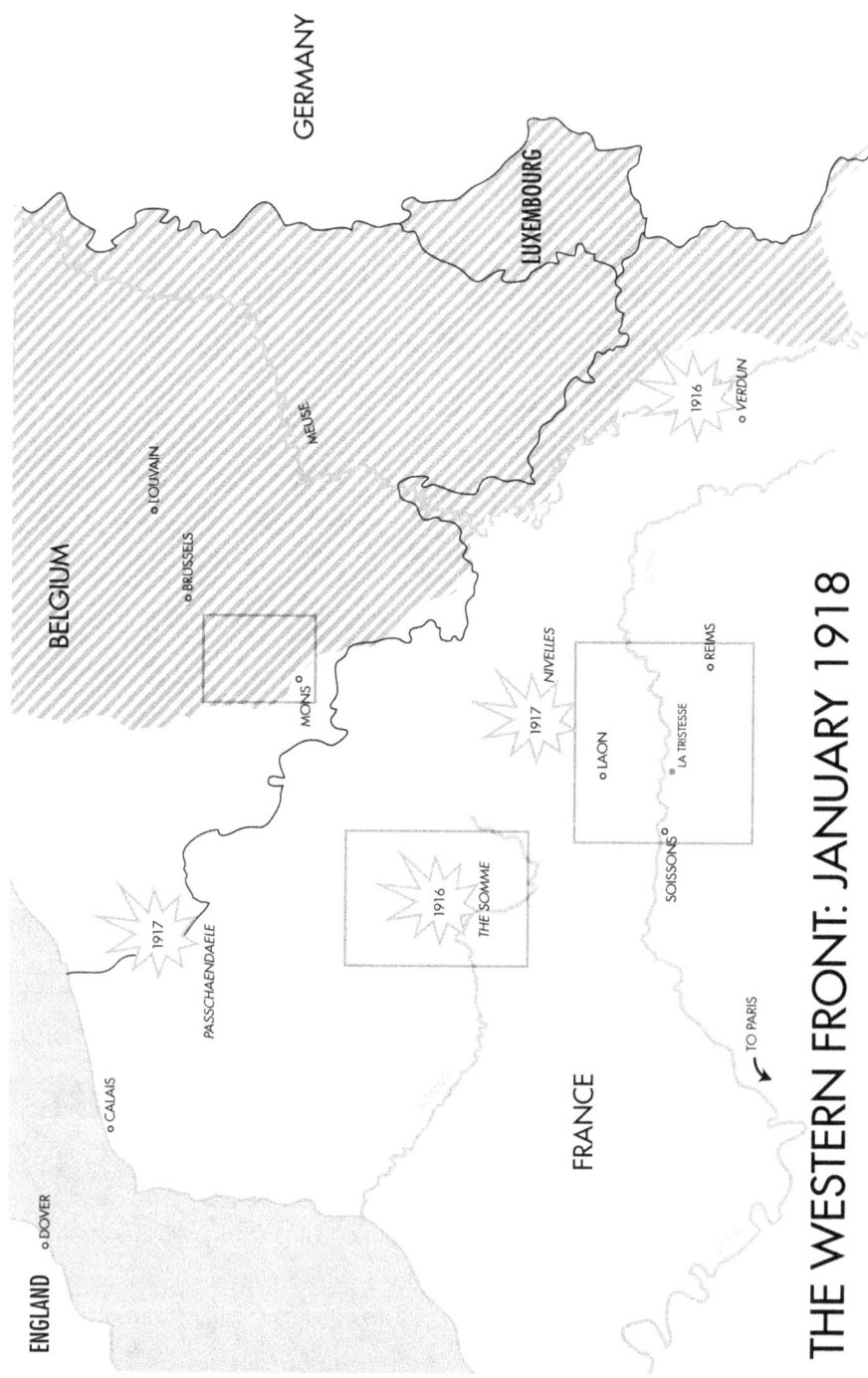

THE WESTERN FRONT: JANUARY 1918

THE HIGH WOOD
SOMME RIVER VALLEY
SUMMER 1916

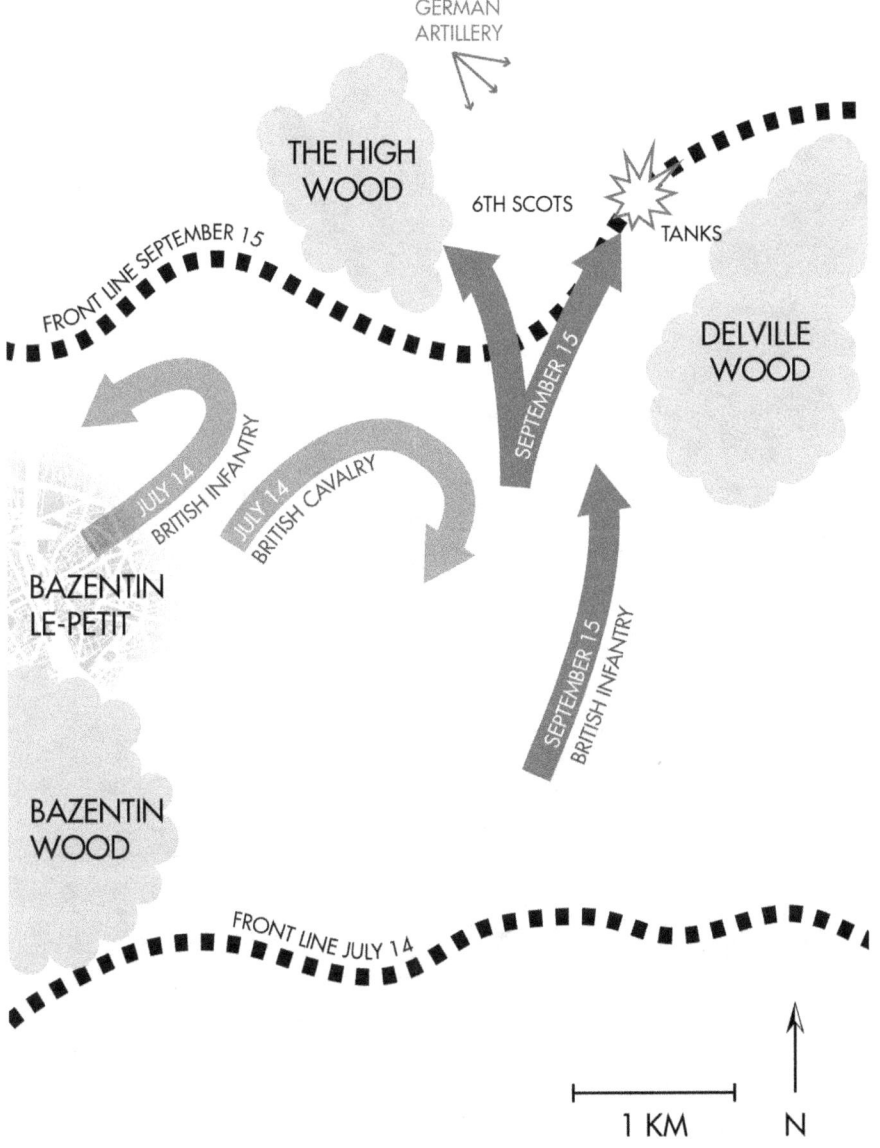

GERMAN
ARTILLERY

THE HIGH
WOOD

6TH SCOTS

TANKS

FRONT LINE SEPTEMBER 15

DELVILLE
WOOD

SEPTEMBER 15

JULY 14
BRITISH INFANTRY

JULY 14
BRITISH CAVALRY

SEPTEMBER 15
BRITISH INFANTRY

BAZENTIN
LE-PETIT

BAZENTIN
WOOD

FRONT LINE JULY 14

1 KM   N

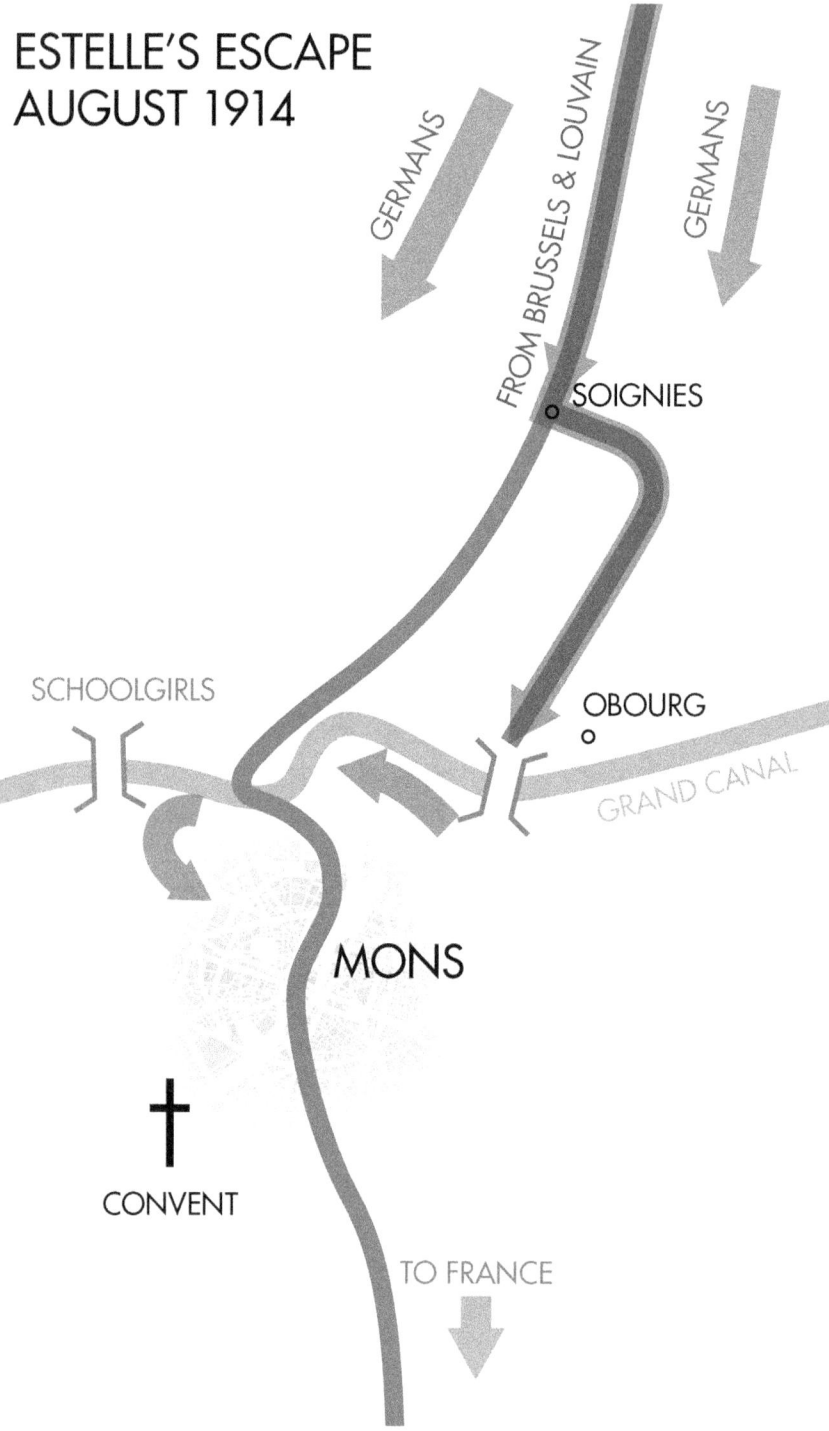

ESTELLE'S ESCAPE
AUGUST 1914

GERMANS

FROM BRUSSELS & LOUVAIN

GERMANS

SOIGNIES

SCHOOLGIRLS

OBOURG

GRAND CANAL

MONS

† CONVENT

TO FRANCE

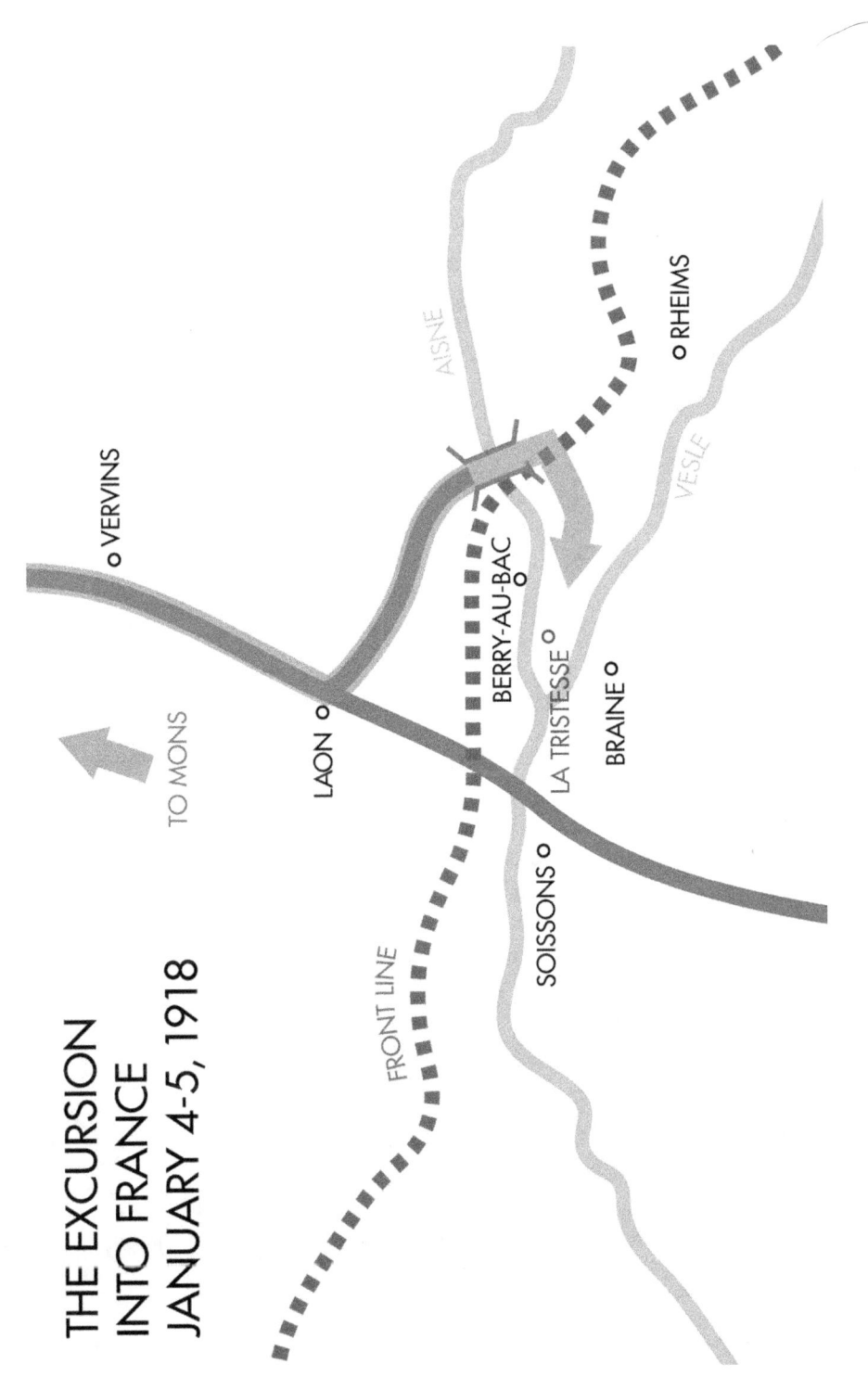

THE EXCURSION
INTO FRANCE
JANUARY 4-5, 1918

TO MONS

FRONT LINE

VERVINS

LAON

SOISSONS

BERRY-AU-BAC

LA TRISTESSE

BRAINE

RHEIMS

AISNE

VESLE

Book One

Who Desires Peace...

As *1918 opened the fourth year of what was already being called 'The Great War', the belligerents, while massively mobilized and equipped, were mere hollow shades compared to the bright, confident, idealistic nations that went to war in August, 1914. The war had brought unthinkable slaughter, the loss of brave young men beyond counting, it seemed, and the destruction of the peaceful lives and properties in the battle zones of Flanders.*

Succeeding years brought the world yet more horrors, 1915 and Gallipoli and Ypres and the searing acrid ochres and greens of poison gas, the pounding slaughter at Verdun and the decimation of the British at the Somme in 1916, the Nivelles mutinies and the utter senselessness of Passchaendaele in 1917.

Yet as the Allies, French and British, lost heavily, Germany lost as much or more, at home as well as in the field. Britain's naval blockade was strangling civilian life in Germany and Austria, even as the war subsided into the uncanny quiet of two behemoths staring at each other across No Man's Land.

All that was about to change in 1918, not in the tight deathgrip of the Western Front but at the margins, America and Russia.

Tuesday, January 1, 1918, 0800 hours
Imperial Germany Army Northern Group Headquarters, Mons, Belgium

"Good morning, Major!"

"For you, perhaps, a fruitful night?" Major Knorr's scowl slid into a grin as his aide shuffled in, trimly attired in tunic and decorations, but with a decidedly disheveled face. "Lieutenant von Seeckt and his lunatic band did some pillaging, did they?"

"But of course, Major, you expected less? Sadly, though, no raping. Were you equally active?"

This lieutenant had earned his right to a degree of cheek, and also to dispense with the obligatory stiff salute. His right arm could no longer be raised above shoulder level and his voice was still a bit hoarse, a result of his and the major's adventures together on the Somme in 1916.

"No, Lieutenant, I had a quiet dinner with your uncle and aunt and my friend Admiral Boecker and his daughter, Isabella – she would be a good influence on you, young hellion. The most excitement was in our winetasting – the general brought an 1900 burgundy I suspect previously resided in some Belgian manor house, the admiral a strong red bought in his Toulon stay from somewhere below Lyon, called Cote Rôtie, one I had not seen before. I, of course, brought the most impressive wine of all, despite my subordinate rank...."

"Insubordinate, you mean? Sir, I mean?"

"Only slightly so, from the dinner wine preceding. No, I brought a magnificent Schloss Johannisberg from Waelcker – no longer making wine – from 1870! My grandfather laid it down to commemorate our victory at Sedan. So, fittingly, a classic German wine from a great German year was adjudged winner, hands down. The general and the admiral were suitably impressed, I am pleased to say. And, by the way, your uncle is overjoyed to be back from the miasma, as he calls it, that is Turkey. Now, how are we starting off the New Year? Slowly, I pray?"

There were no holidays at Crown Prince Rupprecht's Army Group Headquarters in Mons, fifty kilometers from the fronts. "Reports from France – no action on our left, certainly good news, but still puzzling that the French have hardly moved since last summer. The Brits are scurrying about, but not advancing anywhere, not since Cambrai. And this telegram received yesterday midnight from a General von Treptow, saying he arrives from the East by train tonight, would like your time for a '*private luncheon tomorrow at the Major's discretion.*' Do you know this general, Sir?"

Lieutenant von Seeckt's rasp took on an even grittier tone. Officers from Military Intelligence were showing up more frequently, usually followed by some 'intensive discipline' in the form of gaol or even executions, making an example to the men. Every enlisted barracks was rife with talk of disillusion, of reluctance, in many cases of mutiny, with rabble rousers – Spartacists, Syndicalists, Anarchists – whispering and conspiring. Several units had threatened mutiny or defied orders, but the reaction was always swift, brutal and effective. Many agitators, real or suspected, were placed in forward reconnaissance or assault units, meaning death from mine, barbed wire and machine gun fire, from ahead or behind. Was this von Treptow another enforcer?

"Yes, Lieutenant, he and I were on Moltke's staff in the months before the war, but in different areas. We crossed paths again at Verdun, before you joined us, when he was commanding the 24th Brandenburg and my company had just stumbled into possession of Fort Douaumont. Sergeant Kunze, 2nd platoon, was literally carried through the air by the concussion of a shell blast, landing in the moat; when he came to, he peered inside a gun port and saw – nothing! The Frenchies had practically abandoned the place, we waltzed right in and set up house, cozy as could be.

"Colonel von Treptow, he was then, came up with his staff, boiling mad because my orders were to bypass the main fort on its north. When I explained matters, he was completely silent for a good two minutes, at least, then turned to his aide for a box, handing me an Iron Cross, Second Class to pin on poor Kunze whose hundred kilos were trembling like a child's gelatin on a railcar dining table! I thought he would collapse before God and Aristocracy, then what?

"Von Treptow then turned to me, conjured up another Iron Cross, First Class this time that you see here," pointing to his collar, "saluted, turned on his heels and led his entourage back to their cars, disappearing into the gloom, just like that.

"So five minutes, perhaps six, seven? That is all. I have no idea why he would want a private audience with a former Captain, last he saw me. Well, we will find out soon enough, will we not?" Walter Knorr looked up at young von Seeckt, seeing the consternation in his face, and continued in his command voice, "Lieutenant, have you any reason to believe otherwise? Is there any activity or attitude you should have reported to me? Out with it, if there is! I can indulge your carousing with your friends, but not in any unpatriotic conspiring!"

"No, Herr Major, absolutely not! I report everything I see and hear, just that..."

"What, Lieutenant? Just what?"

"Just that, well, last night, well, we rather took Monsieur Dumont's bar…apart. He threatened to present a bill for the damages, and I was afraid Command might have heard about it somehow, already."

Knorr, enjoying his normally cocky aide's palpable discomfort, let him roast himself until fully done, then said, "It appears we await visits from both Monsieur Dumont and General von Treptow. Anything else? Dismissed!" He watched von Seeckt slink out, closing the door behind him, then allowed himself a smile. Von Seeckt's exceptional heroism deserved him a safer billet than a slit trench in the bloody mud of the Devil's abbatoir that was Flanders.

Pouring himself a new cup of coffee, good stuff, straight from the Rotterdam docks to the percolator he had brought from home, he hoisted his sometimes balky left leg over to the footstool to gain the fireplace's heat, displacing Zig, who grunted and attempted to likewise displace Zag, with little success. The two shorthairs liked their creature comforts, too, and like the lieutenant, deserved them. Each wore a miniature Iron Cross hanging from a studded collar, earned for saving his life in that sticky Somme situation. They had the run of Headquarters, steadily fattening on treats, even from Rupprecht himself.

He turned to place the latest staff meeting notes on his lap to review, wondering what this von Treptow had to discuss with him so insistently.

* * *

Wednesday, January 2, 0900 hours
Headquarters, Mons

He could hear him that morning from a kilometer away, it seemed, the cavalry boots clacking and clicking in an irregular rhythm on the stone floor like boxcars traversing a railyard. Then through the door and into the antechamber, stopping short. "Lieutenant, what form of salute is that? Are you another of these Bolshevikii?" Knorr dashed through his open door to see the general shaking von Seeckt's hand and pinching his reddened cheek, saying, "Just testing you, young man. I know of your limitation and how honorably it was earned. Hans is very proud of his nephew, indeed. Ah, Major, good to see you again."

The two exchanged proper salutes and stepped into Knorr's little cloister, Walter steering his superior to the overstuffed chair right of the fireplace.

Zig and Zag had already jumped up to their version of attention, hackles raised, low guttural sounds with each breath. "The famous hellhounds? Come here, pups!" The general awkwardly knelt partway to the floor; the dogs came forward gingerly to sniff his offered hands. In due course their tails wagged, each gave a couple of licks and returned to their sentinel posts atop their feather beds.

Von Treptow stood stiffly and walked to the open chair. Knorr noticed for the first time the unusual gait, the right foot out at a small angle from dead ahead, dragging slightly at the heel.

"May I assist you, General?"

"No, no, quite alright, thank you. I am still a bit stiff from yesterday's long train ride. Next time I may accept a ride in a Gotha, despite the risk. You noticed my walk, I take it? I like to say I am the last casualty of the last French war! When my father's 24th Brandenburg came through Treptow in their victory parade, I naturally was on the reviewing stand with my family as he rode by at the head of the column on Diomedes, his black campaign mount. Unfortunately, both my brothers, older and younger, were with me, and being five and seven and three, we were uncontrollable except in the direct presence of our father and his strap. So, in our excited roughhousing it came to pass that one of us was fated to fall from the stand, and naturally it was me. It was not far, it did not hurt that badly, but I had a small pelvic fracture eventually causing this misalignment.

"I was more terrified of my father, since after all, we had disrupted the entire parade in front of the Mayor of Berlin and several high ranking Imperial Army officers. He pulled Diomedes up to within a hoof of my head, dismounted abruptly and then," he paused to raise his arms, "lifted me up, turning to the stand and his troops and announcing his little soldiers had certainly demonstrated their martial spirit! I nearly fainted, not just from the pain. As he laid me on the stretcher and saw my leg splayed out, he whispered that I was the lucky one, saved from the infantry and guaranteed the cavalry."

He sighed as he exhaled, looking to the ceiling, "That was Spring, 1871. A long time ago, now."

General von Treptow was now fifty-one, but like every one of his fellows in the general officer ranks, looked at least ten years older, maybe more.

He had the almost gaunt, hawknosed visage common to field officers, as if the sights and horrors of trench warfare had aspirated the padding from his skull. He removed his monocle, dropping it on its chain into his upper right pocket, his upper left festooned with decorations and ribbons. Taking a pair of horn-rimmed glasses from another pocket, he laid them on his lap, then rubbed his eyes and placed the glasses on his nose.

"Coffee, General? Javanese, fresh from Amsterdam." Both officers had forgotten von Seeckt's presence.

"Yes, please, sugar, if you would."

Major Knorr stepped over Zag and settled into the other chair. "General, I am flattered you even remember me, or was it the circumstances of our last meeting? And, please forgive my audacity, I am somewhat puzzled by your request for a meeting."

"Your audacity, as you call it, is in part the basis for my request. The Douaumont episode showed that audacity in combat command, plus a…a flexibility, an opportunism so lacking among our field officers these days. Your boldness at the Somme simply confirmed my opinion, but I do not know the entire story, I had only recently left command – perhaps you can recount it at luncheon. I prefer to discuss certain issues in privacy in a public place, if you follow my drift."

His 'drift' was clearly a reference to the increasing intrigues at HQ and in the government born of frustration and war weariness, but also an apprehension at the turn of events at home and further east.

Erich returned with coffee, and the general steered the conversation to what passed for pleasantries these days. Certainly not to the weather – Hainaut and Flanders were typically wet and miserable this mid-winter – but to common acquaintances. "Lieutenant, I know your uncle Hans from our days with the Kaiser Alexander Guards Grenadiers, before you were born. He then went to III Corps staff, and I to II Corps, but we kept up. Along came the war and Mons, a very, very difficult battle for us. He distinguished himself, I was fortunate to survive. Then, and good for him, Mackensen snatched him up for his staff, which at least was closer to home in the east. He made a glorious name for himself at Gorlice-Tornow, but he must have really pissed on someone's trousers to be seconded to Turkey, of all places!"

"He feels the same about Turkey, General, Sir – his favorite saying in his letters to Mother is '*The Ottomans are fit only for resting a Prussian's boots!*' Have you seen him? He is here for Staff consultations, Auntie joined him."

"Yes, my boy, I know. I know almost everything that passes from Petrograd to Riga to Berlin to Ypres. It is my job, after all."

He stiffened and clutched his right knee. Noting the tautness in his hosts' faces, he quickly added, "Apologies – it is sometimes difficult to remember which of my *alter egos* I am at the moment, staff officer or Military Intelligence. No secret, of course, just difficult to keep straight. At this moment, I am the former, so please relax. Major, our luncheon?"

"Of course, General, young von Seeckt here will drive us into town. Do you know Brasserie Colette on Rue de Nimy, just down from Saint Elisabeth Church? I know you spent some time here after the battle."

"Yes, I know this place, and it would do perfectly well, but I prefer the little Café Suzette off the Rue des Groselliers. Lieutenant, you know the way? Shall we?" He raised himself, carefully cantilevering his frame around Zag, who saluted the brigadier with one raised eyelid then returned to his meditations with a muted sigh, licking his lips in contentment.

The three stepped out of the corbelled stone doorway into the main hall, walking as briskly as their respective impediments would allow. But not far, as first Major Niemann, then Colonel von Lossberg emerged from a shadowed nook in the stony lacework of the old convent, hailing the general, barely acknowledging Knorr.

"General, allow me to introduce Major Heinrich Niemann, my aide-de-camp and main workhorse, I might add. You are here for this week's General Staff sessions, I understand, and, with your permission, we request an audience in advance, if your schedule permits?"

The colonel was practically wiping the floor with his grovelling, thought Major Knorr. Was this general so influential that the top two tacticians on the Staff were obsequiously begging for precious moments of his time? Von Lossberg was Ludendorff's golden boy on staff, with a record of tactical genius in several successful campaigns, if not actual combat experience.

"Certainly, Colonel, if you have something of vital importance to discuss?" Von Treptow's voice was altogether different than his almost avuncular tone, for a general, in Knorr's office, even more imperious than his mock upbraiding of young von Seeckt. "I have quite a full schedule here before I return to the Eastern Front, and Knorr, here, has monopolistic designs on my time. You know he is deeply immersed in the logistical planning for Operation Michael, do you not? Would your concerns be related to his work?"

Von Lossberg and Niemann glanced involuntarily at each other; were the heating in the drafty old stone pile not so feeble, Knorr expected beads of sweat to begin dribbling down von Lossberg's egg-bald head. "Only peripherally, Herr General," said von Lossberg, drawing himself up into a military mien, "but of the greatest importance, I assure you. Respectfully, though, we would request a more private audience," glancing sideways at Major Knorr.

"Anything you have for me can be for my new aide's ears, as well. He is now Lieutenant Colonel Knorr and has agreed to my request to be seconded to me as my personal strategist, with the concurrence of Marshal von Hindenburg himself, with promotion to proper rank. Please keep this to yourselves until a formal announcement is made. Perhaps the four of us could convene, say, tomorrow morning at 0800 in your offices, Colonel? Until tomorrow morning, then, Gentlemen?"

With that, he swung his right leg forward and began marching to the doors beyond. He stopped, pivoting to the left, and said, "Well, Colonel Knorr, are you coming? Lieutenant, I forgot my rattan valise by the door, please bring it along."

Knorr nearly stumbled on an uneven stone slab joint as he started after von Treptow, turning only to make a sloppy salute to the two officers. He caught up to the general who was surveying the gloomy morning overcast and drizzle from the shelter of the recessed doorway.

"General, now I have many questions."

"Of course you do, Colonel. Of course you do."

The two stood there in bare silhouette against the sky, their *feldgrau* overcoats shading them into the dismal grey beyond. At length, the lieutenant brought along the valise, and the three walked toward the new colonel's staff car.

Mons, 1130 hours

The café was was tucked between a warehouse and a dry goods store on the Rue de Groselliers east of and well away from the Grand Place. New

Colonel Knorr pulled the tarnished brass door handle for the taller brigadier who set down his valise, stripped off his gloves and banged them against the counter. Playing the arrogant *Boche* officer, he glowered at a plump middle-aged woman in a severe black dress and white apron who glowered right back as she led them away from the locals sitting inside to a table streetside.

The black and yellow and red awning overhead was tattered from age and wear, not war; the cobbles and gutter scruffy. Von Treptow levered the table awkwardly from the open windows to the curb. "Convenient and private, yet totally public – perfect! Even a hint of sun."

The menu was typical country Walloon. The general ordered for both of them in faultless French, to the surprise of the waitress used to the Huns arrogantly demanding she use her minimal German. Since the Schlieffen plan had sent hundreds of thousands of German soldiers through neutral Belgium, Hainaut and the other Walloon provinces had had a harder time than even the Flemish to the north, who at least enjoyed closer linguistic and tribal ties to their occupiers.

She had convinced herself to be thankful the town center and the restaurant had not been seriously damaged in the 'Battle of the Frontiers', when the unstoppable German advance had washed away Belgian independence and her only son with it. And thankful for the relative abundance of the local produce and chicken and pork; to the east, in Germany itself, shortages were becoming more and more severe.

Having German headquarters in Mons was thus a curse with a small consolation, the occupying regime encouraging local farmers and restaurateurs and paying them well. She knew it was the rich Junker and Berliner officers like these two at streetside who were funding the German largesse, such as it was, so a veneer of *politesse* was a small price. Still, she took pleasure in her furtive *schadenfreude* listening to the complaints of the officers about their rations.

As they spooned their soup, von Treptow began, "Please keep your voice no louder than mine; we have some sensitive matters to discuss and, of course, I am obliged to shed some light on my earlier comments.

"First, I have secured both your promotion and your attachment to my staff – your <u>are</u> my staff, as of now, you and your lieutenant. You are asking yourself, '*Why?*' Proceeding in a staccato voice, "I need an intelligent and experienced aide, but above all, one who could safely be deemed politically reliable, for reasons that will shortly become clear. Discreet enquiries about your capabilities confirmed my opinions formed from our earlier encounters, but there is more. Your uncle, that is, of course, your mother's brother and my father served together in the Austrian and French wars, long ago, to be sure. My grandfather and your great-uncle Wilfred were fellow generals in those wars as well, and longtime friends. But, you are Hannover, I am Brandenburg, and I am, what, sixteen? fifteen? years older, so socially we have not connected, but ties run deep.

"So, I have some confidence in you. I expressed my needs to both Hindenburg and Ludendorff who signed off perfunctorily, having no particular interest in the matter as I expected. Rupprecht, of course, is fully aware of my…requirements." He paused, squinting at Walter, "Hence, your new position. You rightly sense impatience and urgency, or I hope you do, Colonel."

Knorr nodded, laying down his spoon.

"Good. Then here is the crux, or will be shortly once we are served our main course." The waitress balanced their plates with unexpected grace, and turning sharply on her heels, left the two men alone. "The crux is simply this: we are on the precipice of winning this war and then losing it, totally, all within a few fortnights. At most, months. I cannot allow that happen, nor see our great nation ground beneath our inferiors' heels!"

"General von Treptow," Colonel Knorr began, "this is all coming rather fast, and I fear I do not follow you at all. What staff am I on? For that matter, what are you? Please forgive my insubordination, but who are you now?"

Von Treptow arched his left eyebrow and left it there for several seconds. "I am officially a member of Supreme Headquarters staff, advising Generals von Falkenhayn and von Hoffman on Eastern Front matters. I am also, somewhat less officially, a…part of Imperial Military Intelligence, reporting directly to Prince Max von Baden, who is, of course, not formally part of Military Intelligence." He smiled at his companion's befuddlement. "I have no administrative role, no office, no official public presence. I am simply there, an 'operative,' so to speak. But, everyone, by that, the entire general officer rank, knows who and what I am."

Knorr nodded, saying, "I am aware of your 'presence' and so, even, is young von Seeckt," proceeding to relate yesterday morning's trepidation. Then, "I still do not understand your purpose."

"I exist to keep damned fools from making damned foolish decisions, decisions which will destroy Germany. Call it bringing reason to madness, if you like. And, in that cause, a little fear is a very effective cover for my... movements. But, allow me to begin from a simple point. Communication in this war has been one of our greatest problems, paradoxically, as we now have telephone, telegraph, wireless, aeroplanes and Zeppelins. One would think we should command the battlefield with those assets, position our forces with precision and thereby force our desired outcomes. But every battle, every campaign, has been characterized by confusion and ignorance, a fog.

"But nothing compares to the intentional adulteration and sequestering of information at the highest levels, civilian as well as military. Adulteration in inflating advances, the enemy's strength, the state of morale, or in deflating – downplaying is the better term – our casualties, dissatisfaction in the ranks, anything reflecting ill on command. *'Truth is always the first casualty in war'* or somesuch, so said an American politician last year in their war debates. So true."

Von Treptow looked away at the ochre plaster and grey stone walls fronting the opposite side of the street, then turned again to Knorr. "No one, not even me, really knows where we stand, where our allies stand, where our enemies stand. Have you not wondered why the French have hardly moved but that once since their offensive failed at Chemin des Dames last year?"

Knorr nodded, trying to sound *au courant*, "The lieutenant and I were discussing that very point yesterday, as a matter of fact at the moment your message arrived. I say they are fatigued. Why, do you think?"

"Fatigue, yes, expressed as mutiny." Von Treptow faced his new aide's stupefaction. "When Nivelles failed so miserably, one hundred thirty thousand casualties in just five days, the poilu simply refused to advance. Those that did went bleating, mimicking the sheep they were, led to slaughter. The actual violent mutinies were few in number, and dealt with, but the officers got the message just the same, even Pétain himself, that lump of wood. They will not leave the trenches except to defend what is left of their country. If so, why should we attack them?"

More animatedly now, "The British cannot raise enough new men to fill their existing ranks, let alone expand their divisions and reserves. Did you know, Colonel, since 1914, the casualties in near every division exceed one hundred percent of original strength?"

Knorr, trying to keep up with his impassioned torrent, replied, "Then General Ludendorff's plan…"

Von Treptow cut him off, his fist striking the table, their plates jumping. "Idiocy! Do you not listen to me? Why throw away another half million of your countrymen against a foe that will not fight unless provoked? And for what? Another few hectares of trenchland? Even Paris – another quarter million dead – for what? Are you not considering those casualties in planning Operation Michael?"

Knorr looked around nervously. "Operation Michael is of the utmost secrecy, General. Should you speak of it so openly? Forgive me, but do you have the correct clearances?"

Von Treptow laughed sharply, but with amusement just the same, folding his arms and leaning back in his chair. "Do not fret yourself about clearances, my newfound friend. Who do you think arranges them?" He paused, looking down into the gutter at a bedraggled mother cat and two scrawny kittens crawling and cowering. Composing himself, he straightened and began tossing scraps of bread to the miserable creatures. The mother cat, her dark grey fur matted and eyes cloudy, mewed plaintively for more. The general sliced some of his sausage neatly into halves first, then quarters of one of the halves, which he handed down more gently to each feline. And again, once they had devoured the first serving. And again.

"What are you doing, Monsieur? We do not feed strays as they will infest us!" The proprietress had swelled to maximum indignation, cheeks puffed and inflamed.

"Madame, I am certain these poor creatures, despite their pitiful condition, remain true connoisseurs of rat."

At that, she flushed even more brightly, abruptly turning on her heels and stomping away as loudly as she could. The outburst had attracted the attention of others, however. Two officers, one portly in his general's greatcoat, were crossing the narrow street toward Knorr and his guest.

The general had just tossed a handful of scraps a meter away to the cats, shooing them with his hand, scolding, "You do not wish to end up in the pot!" He looked up. "Damn! Here comes that fool von Bruckow! Well, we cannot very well repel boarders now, can we? Quickly now, your Somme story."

Before Knorr could compose a few thoughts, the others were upon them. He and von Treptow rose from the table, much snapping of salutes, clicking of heels and stiff nodding of close-cropped Prussian heads ensuing.

Von Bruckow brayed, "My General von Treptow, what a surprise and a pleasure! A surprise to see you in these back streets of this miserable hellhole. Do you know Major von Rundstedt of the General Staff, here for the conference? He is an artillery man of exceptional genius even though he is my wife's second cousin, but I do confess he is perhaps too radical for me in his new ideas for the employ of our field guns."

"No, no, it is my pleasure, indeed, my General." The two were eyeing each other like cocks in the ring, two oversized fighting fowl squinting at the other through their monocles. Von Treptow's tone did little to dispel the chill. "Allow me to introduce my aide, Lieutenant Colonel Walter Knorr."

Knorr quickly saluted again, then extended his hand which was quickly enveloped in von Bruckow's fleshy paw.

"Colonel, you say? He's a mere major! Haw, haw, haw!"

"Not as of this morning; wartime promotions often precede the jewelry by a good margin. Do notice the jewelry, by the way, General – two Iron Crosses, one for his leadership in an episode he was just beginning to retell. Will you and the Major join us? You would help me justify some brandy to ward off the damp." He snapped his voice and fingers in unison, "Madame! Your finest cognac!"

Knorr was intimidated by von Bruckow's presence. Unlike von Treptow, who seemed to project his sinister aura at will, von Bruckow had the full-time air of an aggressive, blustering bully. "Not really so much of a tale, really…"

Von Treptow interrupted. "First, General, some background. Then Captain Knorr was the conqueror of Fort Douamont, commanding Delta Company of my 24th Brandenburg. Took it without a shot, nearly. Of course, we managed to give it back a few months later, not his doing as he had already moved north."

"Douamont? Really?" Von Bruckow seemed to deflate noticeably, slumping in his chair, cradling his brandy.

Knorr replied, "Yes, General, but not so dramatically as General von Treptow would make it, and one of my sergeants was the true hero then. You should ask the general what he truly thought of me at the moment," laughing a bit nervously.

Von Treptow said, "I thought sufficiently of him to hang that Iron Cross around his neck, but enough of the legend of the Armenius of Verdun. I know that story, but not the Somme."

* * *

July, 1916
The High Wood, Somme River valley, France

Knorr began, sensing von Rundstedt's intense interest, "After the Verdun action and an all too brief furlough, we were posted to the north, as General von Treptow noted. My company was billeted between Martinpuich and Eaucourt l'Abbaye. When the British attacked 1st July, we were held in reserve and I gave thanks with every dispatch totaling our casualties, enormous in defense of our lines.

"You recall, do you not, that this whole area had been quiet for well over a year, and our lads had dug in well, but it was still a killing field. My cousin's regiment, the 180th, lost about ten percent of its effectives killed and wounded on just the first day, despite being entrenched and with unbroken wire defenses. And that was against an entire enemy division with their casualties figured at more like fifty percent in that single day!"

He paused as his listeners nodded, then, "It was the same old story, barrage followed by troops stumbling across the surface of the moon, such were the craters and shell holes. Only to be slaughtered by our machine guns. But they persisted, day after day, driving us back to our second and even third lines. At which point my company was called up to relieve units of the 12th, taking a position on a ridge the locals called the High Wood, although not high enough to be proof against assault nor all that wooded anymore. There were some trees still standing with intact branches and even leaves, spared a year or so of shelling, toward the forward point of the finger of our ridge. A quarter kilometer along from our main lines in the rear was a partially intact farmhouse where we set up command and telephone. Further forward were two mostly ruined brick outbuildings, granaries or hay stores, perhaps, where I posted my machine gun emplacements.

"The ridge, such as it was, did have some elevation and command of the landscape below. The right flank was a steep and rocky slope, not easily scalable, but with a passable road alongside. Our left flank was lower, but still craggy save for a shallow ravine near the point, partly blocked by fallen trees, still a potential sally point.

"So picture us positioned on this finger of a ridge, maybe thirty, forty meters wide toward the front, projecting into the battlefield like the bow of one of our dreadnoughts. No artillery, though, Major, that was back at the base of the ridge. Our orders were to hold and protect our neighboring units' flanks.

"On the 14th, to our right a kilometer or two away, Bazentin-le-Petit was lost but was so exposed to our gunners that the Brits retreated to the rear of the village. That day's big excitement for us was an afternoon of skirmishes with enemy cavalry. Their horsemen came sweeping in front of us from behind Bazentin, trying to stay out of range of our machine guns, but not our Mausers. We took enough of them that they eventually withdrew, frustrating their infantry's efforts in the bargain. It was heartbreaking to see those beautiful duns and blacks struggling to find footing in the pocked ground – more horses and riders went down stumbling or sliding than were shot.

"We held this position for some time with only ten dead, and a few more wounded, repelling seven or eight probes. We were dangerously exposed on our little salient, of course, but were a small target for their artillery" – here Knorr was outlining his position with his finger, shifting salt and pepper shakers into enemy positions – "and we were protected by our field guns and topography."

Knorr leaned back in his chair as if to recover some strength or just to catch his breath. "Then one morning we saw more dust than usual at the front lines distant, and then came the smoke. Before ordering gas masks, as disabling as the gas, I had a private bring up Zig and Zag."

Von Bruckow interrupted, "Zig and Zag? Were we a circus detachment?"

"Sorry, General, they are pointers I brought with me, big thirty kilo boys. I had trained them to detect the slightest bit of T-stoff, phosgene or chlorine, well before any substantial danger reached us. The smoke was heavy and the wind was in our face but they were not perturbed in the least, so we were clear of that threat. I kept them with me as I moved forward to observe.

"At the point of our finger were three machinegun nests dug into old shell craters; the two granaries were further back covering the ravine," moving the salt shakers and a match striker to illustrate. "I brought up my three mortar crews and the rest of my riflemen. We had rigged an observation tower, a short one to be inconspicuous, and I climbed up to have a look.

"And what a shock! Out of the smokescreen came these clanking, smoking khaki machines – 'tanks' we now know the British call them – some with cannon in bulges on their sides, some with machine guns on their faces. Maybe a dozen, maybe more, crawling slowly up and down over craters and trenches, chasing our retreating infantry. The tanks then angled to our southeast toward the gap between us and Delville Wood, which the South Africans had taken ten days before. To our right, British troops were advancing from Bazentin, but without these machines.

"My runner came forward with a new dispatch: hold my position until 1300 to cover an orderly retreat of our flanking units! That was four hours away and the enemy was advancing minutes away. I sent orders back to artillery to concentrate first on the infantry to our right then move to hit the machines when they came into range in the gap to our left."

Von Bruckow snorted, "What do you mean, into range? No part of your front could be out of range."

Von Rundstedt opened his mouth for the first time, "General, this is the unit whose tactics impressed us so much, where we got the 'radical' notions which General Walter used to save us at Cambrai just these few weeks past."

As von Bruckow harrumphed, Knorr continued, "Just so, General, and thank you, Major. These machines were more like cavalry, very, very slow, to be sure, and direct fire works where barrage fire just lofts shells randomly in their direction. It still takes a direct hit to stop them, as we soon learned. My orders, a guess, really, were to fire at close to zero elevation, but only at fifteen hundred meters or so. You see, the tanks had to skirt the ridge at Delville which would put them at that range.

"Back on our right, the British infantry's advance wavered, then faltered under our combined fire. For the moment, I had concentrated my men on the right, as we were too short of manpower to spare by halves. The Brits retreated to regroup, so for the moment we had blunted that threat, and our boys below came back to their forward trenches to mask our flank again.

"It was the other flank that got my attention as Krueger's guns – Major, you knew Kurt, I am sure?" Von Rundstedt nodded and Knorr continued, "He started sharpshooting, the only way to describe it. From my post, I could see his crews manhandling their guns, setting up for what amounted to a rifle shot. As you know, the guns have a flat trajectory, more so with the new shells. Our gunners quickly learned to lead a particular tank and fire as they angled across the battlefield presenting their long flat sides to us. Within twenty minutes, our six guns had knocked out most of the tanks within range, mostly by hitting their tracks, which peeled off like ribbons. The remainder veered sharply toward Delville Wood, but even so, we hit several more. Their infantry regrouped behind the battered machines and held position, waiting for their reserves to join up. So, we had bought ourselves some time which eventually stretched to almost 1400."

Von Bruckow shifted his bulk uncomfortably in the hard iron chair. "Well done, Colonel, but thus far not nearly exciting enough for your decorations. What next?"

"Yes, Sir. Their infantry resumed their advance, now with reserves committed. Our units to our right began a slow withdrawal back to their next position as planned, but on the left, the Khakis were moving straight ahead, not yet bothering us. Lieutenant von Seeckt and I kept company notes, how long until our flanks were exposed so much as to cause us to be pinched off, he was calculating our retreat in meters and minutes. He called out, 'Now, Major, now!'

"Meanwhile, a detachment of Brits on our left had turned suddenly toward our ravine while somewhere on our right some mortar crews had apparently just set up. Then our left was suddenly enveloped in heavy smoke from canisters – I shot the dogs a look, they were alert, but not agitated – and our front and right flank erupted in incoming mortar rounds. I pushed the dogs into a shell hole and crouched in the shelter of the granary when a mortar round hit on the other side of the half wall, the concussion knocking me to the ground. I got up and looked into what was left of my best gunners, not much, I assure you."

By this time, Knorr's dispassionate, almost lecture hall tone had given way to a more agitated voice, hands trembling a bit. "Our front emplacements had also been hit and I saw von Seeckt – he is now my aide here, Sirs – running forward under fire, then coming back with a wounded man on his shoulder. He passed me, then moments later came running forward again.

"Then another round exploded somewhere off to my right, knocking me hard against the wall. I must have been stunned, because I saw von Seeckt running forward again, not having seen him pass behind me. Just then a Tommy came charging out of the smoke to my left, bayonet lowered, intent on skewering me. As I unholstered my Mauser, my dogs leapt in front of me, pinning him to the ground. He was yelling *'bloody hell'* or whatever it is they yell, Zig had pulled his left arm away from his rifle and was furiously shaking it like a terrier worrying a rat, Zag was clawing and snapping at his collar, trying to get at his neck.

"At that point, I was still dazed, I suppose, comes the most unbelievable sight. Out of the smoke trots John Bull himself – I swear – round ruddy face above a leather trench coat, cigar clamped in teeth, capped by a blue poilu's helmet. He was attempting to shoot the dogs, waving his Webley about, trying to avoid his man. I raised my pistol and called on him to halt.

"He turned to me and said, almost casually, *'Your dogs? I would hate to kill such splendid animals – release them*!'

"Surrender!" I shouted, to which he said, *'Never, never.'* Then he raised his pistol from the struggle below and pointed it at me. *'The dogs,'* he said.

"I called to the dogs, ordering them back. They released the tattered Tommy and retreated sullenly. *'It seems we have a standoff, Major,'* he said. *'Surrender now before more are killed.'*

"It then occurred to me there was shooting all around us. I replied, 'I will surrender my position, but not my men.' *'An acceptable bargain, Sir.'* We each shouted the cease fire, and I looked back to see his men in our old trenches, not ten meters from mine. *'You have ten minutes to retire, Major, gather your wounded.'*

"That was when I saw von Seeckt soaked in blood from his right shoulder down, gasping from smoke and staggering to stay upright, clutching another wounded man. I looked back to some riflemen, 'You men, go forward and help the lieutenant bring back the others.'

"At that I stood away from the wall where I had been propped and promptly collapsed, in real pain, I assure you. The blast had thrown me against the ragged brickwork, breaking my upper leg. The Englishman stood over me, calling two of my men to lift me, but then motioned them to lay me back down. He pointed to my now crimson trousers and reached inside his trench coat producing a long dagger, swiftly slitting my pant leg.

"He spread the fabric, probing with the blade, *'As I feared, compound fracture – cannot tell if it is the whole bone or merely a splinter. Hold this',* handing the knife to Berger, and then ripping the fabric further. He drew from his outside pocket a flask. '*Brandy, bad brandy. Will sterilize anything.*' He doused my wound liberally then took a swallow and put the flask to my lips. He was right – bad brandy!" The others chuckled.

"Berger handed back the knife, which had an ivory handle with an ornate crest. '*My ancestor received it from an Austrian general in 1704 as a token for saving his ass.*' My men then stood me up and started to turn me about. '*Major, your cap.*' He leaned down and picked it up, looked at it, paused and unbuckled his helmet which he placed on my head, plopping my cap on his round pate. '*You have ten minutes,*' looking at his pocketwatch. '*Go.*'

"On the way back, the helmet fell off. Conrad picked it up and handed it to me. A label inside caught my eye: *Lieutenant Colonel Winston Leonard Spencer Churchill, Sixth Royal Scots Fusiliers.*"

Von Bruckow fumed, "You let Winston Churchill go? Did not shoot him when you had the chance? The arch-warmonger? I should have done it differently, I assure you, and court-martialled you for cowardice!"

"Of course you would have, Hubert." Von Treptow's voice oozed honey laced with arsenic. "I have your dossier right here," tapping his case, "and it says precisely that."

Von Bruckow stiffened, his florid face descending into successive depths of vermillion. "General, you know what I am saying. This Churchill is the worst of the Englanders!"

Von Treptow responded evenly, "Agreed. But sometimes inaction is superior to action, the not doing trumps the doing. Your fiend, this Churchill, shortly resigned his commission, having been denied a brigade. He has returned to political life, sowing chaos in his every wake. Half England adores him, half think him the AntiChrist. We should be so fortunate to have him back in London concocting more Dardanelles excursions. Admittedly, his Munitions Ministry work does trouble me and my Irish friends." With that, the Oracle grew silent.

After an extended pause, toying with a new cigarette, he continued, "For his tenacity, then Major, now Colonel Knorr was awarded the Iron Cross First Class. His company's stand prevented the collapse of that sector and several regiments escaped entrapment. He then was seconded, after repairs, to staff duty, poor fellow."

"Major, Colonel, rather, my apologies for my outburst. Allow me to express my admiration for your courageous stand. Tell me, do you still have the French helmet?"

"Yes, General, in my office. I should be happy to show it to you."

Von Bruckow exhaled a belch. "Excellent! Major, look at the time! We must be back at Headquarters. General, forgive me my brusqueness and thank you and your Colonel Knorr for sharing this uplifting tale." His Ponderousness slowly ascended from his chair.

"I thought you would appreciate it," said von Treptow, tapping his cigarette pointedly on his attaché. "I shall see you tomorrow at staff?"

"Of course." More clicking of heels, saluting, nodding of heads.

When the interlopers were safely out of earshot across the street, von Treptow exhaled a cloud of blue smoke. "French cigarettes of course, we have none worth smoking. I do not tolerate the native Turkish. I have sources should you desire some. Well. Glad to be rid of him, at least for the moment. Come, we must go." He produced a two mark gold coin and placed it on the bill. He then opened his case and carefully extracted a small bundle wrapped in oilskin, then dipped his fingers into a pocket within, retrieving a Belgian one hundred franc gold coin. This last he laid on the table, placing the packet on top.

"Off we go, Colonel. Shall we walk through town toward the canal, so I might revisit the battle? That is, if you are able, your leg is healed?"

"Yes, General. I generally walk into town once daily as therapy, the injury does not allow me to forget, but I manage."

Von Treptow crushed his cigarette into the Suze ashtray. "Tell your aide to wait for us at the Hôtel du Roi."

Knorr strode across the street to confer with von Seeckt who had been idling in wait. He turned back to see the proprietress trotting and jiggling toward the general.

"Sir, Sir! You left this? What do you know of my Eduard? We have long since given up hope! Tell me, please! Please?"

General von Treptow turned to face her. He stood stiffly in the middle of the street, bracing himself, expecting the woman to throw herself upon him, beating her fists on his chest. Instead, she stopped short, breathing heavily, mouth agape.

"Madame, your son asked me to return those to you. He was in the defense of Liège as we advanced, closing rapidly on his unit. He could have escaped but chose to turn and fire to cover his fellows, narrowly missing me. One of our men hit him with a shot. As I advanced, I was forced to seek cover in the same shellhole where he had fallen. He was grievously wounded but already in shock, so I can assure you he felt no pain. He tapped his pocket, his diary, asking me with his last breaths to return it to his mother and father. I cradled him in my arms, giving him what little comfort I could, what with bullets zinging overhead, and he passed peacefully into another realm. He was a very brave man, a hero, and his last thoughts were of his family."

He gave her a small bow, "I found the gold piece in the pocket with the diary. There you have it, and my condolences, Madame. Good day."

With that, he made a sharp about-face, leaving her with tears streaming down her cheeks. Her husband, in black vest and white apron smeared with grease, stood dumbfounded in the doorway.

The two officers walked toward the industrial section past a perceptibly shifting streetscape, from the ornate Dutch-style brick gabled fronts with swept sidewalks and bare locust and plane trees to a scruffier working-class neighborhood a few blocks on with crumbling plaster and faschwerk. Mons itself was not a large town, even with its sizeable industrial works along the canal.

Von Treptow had been quiet for a block, then said, "Truth is, I shot him here" – he pointed to the spot where his trachea emerged from the sternum. "I did take shelter in the shellhole where he was gasping, spraying blood with each breath out of the ragged hole here" – pointing again –"dying gruesomely. I motioned for him to be still, then placed his rucksack on his throat and put my knee on it. Then I covered his mouth with my hand, said *'Be still, my son'* in French, and pinched his nostrils shut. He seemed to understand and closed his eyes, and just like that it was over. I found the coin and the packet but could not bring myself to pay that visit until now."

Again he was quiet. Their boots clacked away on the cobbles, the sounds of the town around them, the buildings passed increasingly shaded with soot. "He came to symbolize for me the idealistic, naïve young men who marched so eagerly to war in the early days, virgins to be deflowered by Mars. Such a waste..."

They had just turned a corner into a small square when they saw two *stahlhelms* accosting a young woman in local dress carrying a bundle. Typical young soldiers, Saxons, probably, thought Knorr. Something about the girl struck a chord and he knew he could not allow this to degenerate into rape, as all too often happened.

General von Treptow snapped him out of his righteous reverie, "Colonel, exert some discipline here! This not acceptable behavior for our Kaiser's soldiers!"

Knorr stepped forward quickly, shouting at the soldiers to halt. They turned, saw his rank and snapped to attention. "Let her go about her business and do not bother her again!" The girl scuttled into a dreary-looking café in the middle of the block.

"Yes, Major, Sir," slurred one, with more than a week's stubble on a sooty jaw. He had obviously just come from frontline duty, looking for some quick pleasure.

"Report back to your units immediately," said Knorr, noting the regimental insignia. "That general behind me is with Intelligence and I assure you he will remember your faces should more trouble follow."

Sheepishly, the two saluted and slunk away across the square. Suddenly, a loud crack issued from the upper floors of the café building. The unshaven private stopped, a sheet of blood flowing from his forehead, then he pitched forward, revealing a large hole in the top of his helmet.

"*Franc tireur*!" shouted Knorr. Several troopers across the square shouldered their rifles and peppered the windows above. Knorr pulled out his pistol, crouching exposed in the middle of the square. Seconds passed, then another loud shot from a brass-tipped barrel held by a shadowy figure within, ricocheting harmlessly off the cobblestones.

"You three, there! Go inside and bring everyone out! *Schnell*!" barked von Treptow, Luger raised as he strode into the center of the square. Seconds later another shot rang out, again errant.

The soldiers brought out some women and children and von Treptow had them lined up in the middle of the square. The gun barrel emerged in the darkened window then withdrew under a hail of fire.

"Cease fire, men. You up there, place your gun on the window sill and surrender yourself. I shall personally see to it you serve in a labor camp and do not swing from the gallows. I offer you the *brassard rouge*, not the black hood. I recognize you were provoked, hence my leniency."

Von Treptow was now strolling in full view of the gunman's window, reviewing the hostages lined up before him. The first, the proprietress, maybe a waitress, was a tall, worn, but faintly attractive woman. *In her mid-thirties?* Von Treptow turned her grease-smudged face with his pistol barrel one way then the other, then pushed aside her shoulder straps one after the other. She glared at him as he moved next to a stooped, palsied old woman dressed head to foot in black, mostly toothless, a vacant stare on her face, bloody urine puddling in the street.

"Your mother, Madame?"

"His," she hissed.

"I see. And this pretty girl? His?"

"No," through clenched teeth. "Mine."

He moved to the young girl, a winsome thing whose emerging beauty had not yet been beaten down by poverty and oppression. Younger than he first thought, but already her blouse was too small for her new body. "Yvette?" She jerked her head up, then back down. "Ah. Sweet on her, is he?" Her mother looked at him with a mix of hatred and puzzlement, then clenched her teeth and fists, saying nothing.

"As I thought. And these delightful children?" Two of them, the elder perhaps three, the younger just walking. He bent down toward the frightened urchins, catching their eyes with the gleam of some small silver coins he had slyly slipped into his palm. "Sergeant, have one of your men take these two around the corner. I believe there was a sweets shop or boulangerie or some such. Quickly, now!"

A corporal stepped up, took the coins, scooped up the infant and herded the other at a trot down the street. Once they were safely out of sight, General von Treptow strode behind the remaining hostages brandishing his pistol.

"You up there, you have one minute to lay down your gun before I begin executing your family. I know you hear me and the clock is running.

"Who shall be the first? Shall it be the young beauty? A shame it would be to have that comely face all over the cobblestones. Such a waste. Such a waste!" He paused for a length, curling the hair flowing from underneath her scarf with his free fingers, then jerking her head back, placing his gun-barrel at her temple.

"Thirty seconds now, Monsieur. Your beloved mother, will it be? Surely you are devoted to her?

He moved down the line, "Fifteen seconds. Your wife? Who would look after the café in your absence? Who would care for the little ones?

"Five seconds.

"Three seconds.

"No?"

A shot rang out, muffled by the skull the pistol pressed against. The old woman pitched forward into the wake of a shower of her blood, brains, bone and hair. Immediately another shot rang out and as Knorr wrenched his gaze away from the death scene, he saw the general's smoking pistol aimed at the window above. A moving shadow, a thud, a gunbarrel slamming against the peeling windowsill then coming to rest against the left jamb.

Briskly, von Treptow issued orders, "Sergeant, take your comrade. Post guards there" – pointing at the street corner beyond – "and there" – the row of storefronts behind him. "Let no one harass these people nor interfere with their business. Have the locals look after their dead."

He stepped over to the wife whose hands had not left her face. "Madame, that pig of a wife-beating husband is dead. Your daughter will be safe. Good day."

She swung her right hand toward his face, parried by his left arm. He jerked her hand down to her waist and loosened her fingers, pressing some-thing into her fist with his other hand. "For services."

He turned sharply toward the corner, Knorr doubletiming to keep up with him. Catching him, he started, "General, what…"

"What just happened back there?"

"Yes," said Knorr, trying to mentally parse the last several minutes. The two were a curious sight, Knorr limping a bit, the brigadier in his slight crabwalk.

"Colonel, when I devoted myself to my current mission, I knew little of intelligence – protocols, methods, spycraft. I found inspiration in none other than Sherlock Holmes. Not, mind you, that I affected a deerstalker and pipe.

No, I simply admired the powers of observation and deduction bestowed upon him by his creator. The curious case of the dog barking in the night?"

Knorr, his face a blank, said, "I am afraid I do not follow, Sir."

"The fact that the dog did not bark when a trespass was claimed to occur, you see? Small things, insignificant to all but the most perceptive and often the not doing, not the doing."

"I'm still lost, General."

Von Treptow cleared his throat and took a deep breath. "Very well, then. When I arrived yesterday at dusk my car took me from the station, six or seven blocks ahead, through that little square. As we passed, I heard snippets of angry voices, a man and a woman quarrelling, 'Leave Yvette...Shut your mouth, woman...' The voices drifted away to my rear and I paid no further attention. As we walked there just now, my observation came back into focus when I saw the young girl. I had never seen her before, but when the excitement began, I linked observation and deduction."

He tapped the colonel on the shoulder, "Tell me, when that unfortunate Saxon lad was killed, did you notice the size of the entry hole and lack of an exit?"

Knorr replied, "General, I must confess I only noticed it was not me that was hit."

"Understandable, but a modern rifle at that range would produce the opposite effect, a small entry, an explosive exit. As it was, the soldier was barely budged by the shot itself. Also, surely we have confiscated all the modern weaponry in civilian hands, yes? So, I deduced it must be a fowling piece, perhaps an old musket firing a heavy ball. In any event, inaccurate and slow to reload. You noticed the interval between shots?"

Knorr brightened a bit at being able to add an observation, "Yes, I did, but I thought he was just picking his moment."

"Perhaps, but I pictured a muzzle loader, tamping powder and ball, all the while with trembling hands. Trembling hands and an ancient weapon hardly make for accuracy."

"Certainly. Is that why you chose not to take cover?"

"That, and an officer should always show a cool presence, as you have experienced. And please know my offer of labor clemency was genuine as we desperately need men more than corpses. But as for the hostages, well, I thought that would work, truly I did. It failed and I soon realized why. The wife had a large fading bruise on her right temple and a swollen lip with a small gash, still red. Her shoulders were badly bruised, and recently, clearly from a strong man's grip.

"The girl, Yvette, reacted as I expected, as did her mother. But it was the wife's opinion of her mother-in-law that confirmed the situation. The old woman was expendable, clearly demented and ill, so for her it was a mercy killing." Von Treptow's voice showed no emotion whatsoever, clinical in its tone. "It produced the desired result, exposing her son to an easy pistol shot. And an excellent opportunity for a German officer to demonstrate his ruthlessness for the benefit of his men and as an example to the citizenry!"

He said the last in a bitter, ironic tone, gritting his teeth. "After all, we must give the conquered what they have come to expect. *Schrecklichkeit! The Hun!* We descended into barbarism in 1914 and dragged the world down with us!"

His voice quieter now, "Perhaps we do deserve a worse fate." A pause, then, "Forgive me, Colonel. I have wrestled with the Prussian Junker mentality all my career, the arrogance, the carelessly selfrighteous brutality. Von Schlieffen's strategy was intellectually correct, of course, and I myself could justify destroying Belgium to get at the French throat. Had Moltke not failed when success was in his grasp…But, the ready resort to terrorism was inexcusable and has branded Germany for all time as brutish, hobnail boots and all."

He stopped abruptly. "Did you know Louvain before we torched it? Did you know the wealth, the beauty, the learning there? All gone, thanks to another incompetent, this time von Luttwitz. But, after all, he owes his idiocy directly to von Clausewitz's terror doctrines, enshrined as they are in our academy."

He gave his aide a thin smile, "Enough of my quite useless moralizing. I certainly do not wish to disillusion you after a mere few hours of our renewed acquaintance. It grows late and we have been interrupted too often. Let us turn back to my hotel and I shall attempt to finish the introduction to my purpose."

They walked on in the lowering gloom, the buildings shaded on the sunward side of the grey streets. Mons was an industrial center in the coal belt running down to Briey on the French side, and the hard limestone faces of the warehouses they were passing were blackened with decades of sooting. Soon they reached and skirted the edge of a school and turned back toward the Grand Place through an allée of elms, elegant if leafless in dead winter.

"As I was saying, Colonel, we are approaching headlong a precipice, blindly. The precipice is the Western Front, the blindness is in our leadership, and we – they – are rushing away from the Promised Land in our rear. Had the Hebrews been led by Ludendorff, they would be in the Sinai, still. We have the war won, and my goal, and Prince Max's, is to declare victory and end the slaughter. And the deprivation at home. Have you heard from family recently?"

"Yes, and the news is grim. We, my household staff, are well fixed, fortunately, but it is hard on the common man and woman."

Von Treptow nodded in agreement. " *'Durchalten'*, they say. '*See it through*', by all means. But for how much longer? Britain's blockade strangles our western trade, and until recently Russia has not been in a sharing mood. Colonel, my two greatest fears are trouble at home and the advent of the Americans. The Bolsheviks and Mensheviks have their followers, particularly in Berlin and Munich, even if all they have on offer is the virus of revolutionary rhetoric to infect a disillusioned, deprived populace. We can inoculate against that plague only if we move quickly in the east to kill off the source and grab Ukraine's resources. We can do that.

"What we cannot do is prevail offensively in the West, now that the Yankees are here. Yes, they are amateurish – after all, a year ago, they had no standing army to speak of – but they will soon be millions, and they are well led. We need to preempt them and the Entente by establishing an impregnable defense line, probably along the Flemish frontier, Luxembourg and Alsace – I would toss Lorraine as a sop to the French, just to be done with those pests.

"This is the one thing we can do, that we can control, and that will work. The Flemish will agree, I am sure – we have their Front Party in play as we speak. We have the manpower to hold defensive positions forever, and most of all, we have French and English war-weariness in our favor so long as we manage our own."

Von Treptow paused to offer Knorr a cigarette, who declined. He lit his, took a long draught and continued, "I said earlier we were winning. Did you believe me? Truly, now?"

Knorr was the dog caught with the Christmas fowl, having no choice but to come clean. "Truly? General, we have fought in the last three years over the same twenty or thirty kilometers of depth of front, and for what? What is the point, after all? And I realize I am speaking defeatism, if not treason, to an Intelligence officer."

Von Treptow beamed. "I knew I had chosen my aide wisely, Colonel. Exactly the assessment I expected. You do understand my reasoning, then?" Knorr nodded and von Treptow continued, "The basis for my claim we are winning, or will win in the West? The numbers, purely. We have bled France for a generation to come, perhaps longer. However large our casualties, theirs are greater on a much smaller population, one that has long since ceased growing adequately. Well over a million young men dead, well over another one million permanently disabled, never to farm or work in a factory again. We have gutted France. She will never again challenge us in Europe, militarily or politically, so long as we preserve our might. England has suffered less, but still grievously, except in their Navy, which, after all, is the Briton's heart and soul."

He crushed out his cigarette. "Think of France, she still drives the omnibus here. It is her territory that has been lost, Belgium is emotion, not consequential, and a curious amalgam, at that, and it is France's soldiers that are dead, maimed or mutinous. France will strut and posture but will not assault our new line, so long as it does not change their border *ante bellum*, with the exception of Lorraine to their advantage and a temporary occupation of Briey-Longwy."

"Why that area?" asked Knorr innocently.

"You will soon learn to think strategically, Colonel. One of France's richest iron ore regions. Had those deposits been exploited before 1871, we would have included it with Lorraine when we wrested her from Louis Napoleon. No matter, we own it now. We shall occupy for some limited time, say a few years, as hostage to France's good behavior.

"The other factor, paramount, even, is public opinion in the true democracies, a thing truncated in our Reich, but you must understand how vital it is. If we declare victory as I propose, certain...undercurrents...will begin circulating. There are publications in France, England and America that may be, shall we say, disposed to be friendly toward our new 'pacifism', and will eagerly beat the drum for an armistice to avoid further bloodshed.

"The Americans, ironically, are the least vulnerable to these overtures, partly due to Hearst and Pulitzer and other newspapermen, but mostly because the coffins have yet to come home in great numbers. France and England, on the other hand, are thoroughly disillusioned, no matter how supportive seems the public."

He clapped his hand on the colonel's shoulder, "The British units you faced at the Somme, not Churchill's Royal Scots, but those on your right flank? Those were part of Kitchener's new volunteer army, the 'chums' and 'pals.' Churchill's Scots were old Army, with some NCO's having served in the Boer Wars, tough and experienced. At Mons, they handled their Enfields as their ancestors handled their longbows and proceeded to handle us as roughly as they did the French at Agincourt. Had they more men in the field, they might have celebrated a new Saint Crispin's Day and it would have been a short war. The Kitcheners, the others, these are new units raised among fellow towns-people. When you hit them hard, you created many casualties in a single market town, friends and neighbors as well as family.

"Until then the professional army had taken most casualties, so the pain was spread widely and not very deeply. Now the reverse is true and being highly painful, is not popular. The coffins come home to England in the dead of night, in darkness. Did you know that? The Somme cost them half a million killed and wounded in five months. Third Ypres, the same. We shall exploit that."

The two men walked along in silence for a while as von Treptow caught his breath and Knorr tried to process these new ideas. As good a field soldier and as thorough a staff officer as he was, he realized he had been confined in his thinking to the immediate. He had shown admirable initiative in the field, especially in his response to the new tank threat, but was a functionary at staff, calculating field pieces per kilometer of front or the number of horses and limbers needed to move artillery or the sheer density of Maxims needed to neutralize a given number of enemy troops.

Now, for the first time, he had a dim glimpse, an inkling of a world beyond the stratification of rank and the bitching of his fellows over beers. *Careful, Wally, this shit could be addictive.*

Little did he know.

By now the weak northern sun was losing its warmth, the bare trees casting eerie, Grimmlike shadows across their path. They turned a corner to the left and Knorr pointed out the general's billet down the street. "Just in time, Sir, I was beginning to tire a bit."

"As was I. Good – there is your aide. You are in one of the farmhouses around the convent, I take it?"

"Yes, General, von Seeckt won it at cards. We keep it quiet as it was destined for a brigadier who does not yet realize what his subaltern lost."

"He will be valuable in our efforts when he comes with us."

Again, Knorr drew blank. "When, where will he come with us, General?"

"We shall see, shall we not? Flexibility and initiative, Colonel, flexibility and initiative are to be our guides." Approaching von Seeckt who was slouching vertically in the car, "Lieutenant, have you any confessions to make to your Aunt Mathilde when I dine with her tonight? Nothing I could possibly say could ruffle your uncle, but…I wonder, have I any messages from a Monsieur Dumont?"

Lieutenant von Seeckt shot a glance of betrayal to Colonel Knorr, who shrugged his shoulders and raised his forearms, palms up. Taking his cue from the look on Knorr's face, he said confidently, "General, Sir, I am proud to say I handled that matter diplomatically. My comrades and I apologized to him and promised to forget where his teenaged daughters attend school if he would forget the damages issue."

Von Treptow convulsed with laughter, the most overt emotion on his part all day. "Excellent lad! Colonel, I told you he would be useful!" With that, he saluted and took his leave into the hotel. Knorr and von Seeckt were left at the curb looking at each other with bemusement.

"Well, Lieutenant, what are we and the dogs having for dinner tonight?"

* * *

Thursday, January 3, 0730 Hours
Mons

General von Treptow arrived early at Knorr's office. "I encountered General von Bülow in the hotel lobby this morning, and he kindly offered me a ride in his staff car. The other passenger was Ludendorff who I am sure was struggling to conceal his distaste." He gave a low chuckle, "Of course, it is not a laughing matter, but still…Colonel, allow me to fill you in on some particulars for our meeting this morning, and some background for Staff."

At 0755, Major Niemann announced himself, saluted and offered to escort the two to von Lossberg's meeting. The general replied, "Colonel, you go with the major. I must make a stop at the water closet and the lieutenant here will lead me from there."

Knorr thought, *Great, just great. He leaves me alone with him. One question from Niemann will expose my ignorance totally. There goes my new authority, such as it is, or was.*

Niemann led, casually, "You know General von Treptow well?"

"Not so well, really. I served under him until coming to staff, but well down in the ranks, at company level. Our families have ties, according to him." The last he threw in as a diversion.

"Oh? You are a Berliner? I do not believe I know your family."

Knorr relaxed. "I doubt you would. My family are bankers in Hannover, not part of the Junker landlord set." Hannover and Prussia had a strained relationship since the latter defeated the former in 1866, Knorr's comment revealing a kernel of that animus.

His gambit worked. Niemann also was outside that aristocratic circle else he would have polished his 'von' and worn it in brass on his sleeve. Only a few meters more to von Lossberg's anteroom.

"How is it, then, that you served in a Brandenburg unit with the general at Verdun and the Somme?" Knorr's fame had obviously been spread widely at headquarters the previous afternoon, by one, at most two likely suspects. No one had expressed any interest in his exploits over the last year or so, but naturally his pointers were celebrities for that one episode with the Tommy.

"I was traded, Major! When I regained my commission from reserve in 1912…let me see if I can retrace this for you…the uncle of a banker in Berlin was a Brandenburger divisional officer in need of a finance officer. The Berlin banker was a correspondent of my late father at our bank. My father coveted a particular trade and letters of credit expert in the Berlin bank, so he traded me. Even up, fair and square. For a brief moment I felt like a star association player, but that soon passed. My deficiencies as a financial bureaucrat were soon revealed and I was sent off to General Staff, in logistics. When war came that position was less in demand than command officers. Destiny, of course, brought me full circle to staffwork."

They stopped at the doorway, a carved ogee arch three meters high, replete with demons and gargoyles. *Appropriate,* thought Knorr. *Abandon hope all ye who enter here.*

Several stern-looking general officers marched past them, retinue in tow; the two juniors snapped to attention and saluted crisply. As that group veered right into the corridor perpendicular, Knorr's own *vons* appeared to the left.

"Here we are, General, Sir." Lieutenant von Seeckt glanced furtively into the office. "I shall remain outside should you require anything."

General von Treptow gave the young officer a casual salute, then craned his neck around the doorjamb and retracted it with a smile. "I should think you would, young man!"

As the lieutenant flushed, Colonel Knorr walked into the anteroom, smiling as a very pretty young woman looked up from her typing. Knorr glanced at von Seeckt, eyebrows up. Erich smiled, rolled his eyes upward and shrugged his good shoulder.

"Hello, Isabella! May I present you to General Dietrich von Treptow? General, this is Isabella Boecker, Oswald's daughter, and a lifelong friend, since her infancy – you know Oz, our Admiral of destroyers?"

"Thank you, Walter, you are too sweet. General, it is an honour." She glanced inquiringly at Knorr. "You know my father, do you?"

"Indeed I do, young lady, although Army and Navy are not meant to mix, except in barrooms and ballrooms. I met him in the former, in a brawl, and have cultivated his friendship in the latter over the years. Sadly, I just missed him this trip."

"Yes, it was nice of him to come down from Zeebrugge. I miss him, too, particularly ever since he volunteered me to stenographic duty here. It was his idea of combining national service and hunting noble husbands, I should think."

Von Treptow laughed, then quieted, "Too many noble prospects are not coming back from the front, sad to say." He realized he had trespassed somehow, and for the first time since his arrival was distinctly discomfited, even awkward. "I apologize, my dear, no need to be so macabre on first impression, nor inadvertently piercing in any way. Forgive me."

"General, your candor is well placed." She left it at that, with a small grimace. "Well, Gentlemen, Colonel von Lossberg is waiting. My duties include coffee and tea service – not that I ever had much practice at home!"

She took orders as she ushered the three men into the colonel's office, a high coffered ceiling rising from triplet pilasters and corbelling, fireplace and mantel blackened from several centuries' use, the blacking making even more vivid the orange and red and gold flames.

"General, Colonel! Thank you for coming on short notice. I assure you our discussions will be on matters of the utmost importance. Please make yourselves comfortable."

Knorr mused to himself. *All I would need to live in this place would be a sleeping pallet and a coffeepot*, looking around at the spacious room, plush chairs, Persian rugs. *His? Certainly not the Army's. The Sisters'?*

"Colonel, perhaps you did not hear me? Congratulations again on your promotion. And just perhaps on your association with our noted general." Von Lossberg's voice startled him out of his thoughts.

"Thank you, Sir." He could not read von Treptow, whether he appreciated von Lossberg's attempt at humor.

Isabella walked in with a bowl of sugar and a spoon. Like a trained dog, von Seeckt trailed carrying a tray, balancing four cups of coffee. "Thank you, Isabella, and you also, Lieutenant...?"

"Von Seeckt, Sir, my apologies for not saluting, Sir," as he tried to keep the tray level. He lowered it onto the round table between the four officers, stood at attention and gave his half-mast salute. Von Lossberg started to sputter.

"That will be fine, Lieutenant," interposed von Treptow, "Your salute is unique, and in any event unnecessary in this company."

"Thank you, Sir," said von Seeckt, turning about face neatly and marching through the doorway.

Knorr caught a glimpse of his aide beyond the closing door, leaning over in Isabella's direction. Von Treptow gave him a wink. "My aide has been holding back. I did not know he had made Fräulein Boecker's acquaintance, at least not yet."

"He skulks about here regularly," laughed Niemann, "a good man, and brave, too, it seems. A general's nephew and nobility, to boot!" All four laughed, ranging from the general's restrained chuckle to von Lossberg's hooting.

"Now, to business, my General." Von Lossberg attempted to take charge, von Treptow choosing to lay in wait. "As we know, the Kaiser Offensive is

tentatively set by the end of March. We are to have our strategic plans finalized in two weeks, tactics and orders within the month after. General, you
have not seen this." He went back to his ornate desk and took a wirebound
pamphlet from its center. "One of my brightest young officers, Captain
Hermann Geyer, prepared this under Major Niemann's direction. Our most
advanced tactical plan, titled '*The Attack in Position Warfare*', it incorporates
the new shock troop techniques. Within, Niemann and Geyer have refined
von Hutier's infiltration approach, so successful at Caporetto, admittedly
against Italians.

"The problem is, it is <u>too</u> good. I have no doubt that everything in this,"
he slapped it against his palm, "will work, at least to the extent of our
resources and field leadership. If we present this tactical plan in its fullest,
the March offensive will be impossible to stop as Ludendorff will take it as
the new Gospel to dispel any lingering dissension."

"So you have created a monster, have you?"

"Yes, my General. Geyer is a good man, for a Bavarian, and we can
keep him and this work under wraps for a few weeks longer but no more.
You see my, our, predicament, General? This office is expected to deliver
this plan according to schedule. To do otherwise would be to disobey a
direct order, and if I may be so bold, even you, Sir, could not keep the Major
and me out of irons. Particularly, no, especially if its existence became
known."

Von Treptow turned to Knorr. "Colonel, I owe you an apology. I did not
expect to ensnare you in our conspiracy so soon."

"Conspiracy, Sir?"

"Yes. I call it the 11 November conspiracy, hatched the very evening of
last year's staff meeting in which Ludendorff announced the Wooden Titan's
vision of the all-or-nothing offensive to conclusively win the war. Welcome
to the Eleven-elevens!"

Knorr turned to the other staff officers, "Sorry, Gentlemen, I have yet
to learn my superior's ways."

"No need to apologize, Colonel," said von Lossberg in a surprisingly
good-natured way. "We often seem to find ourselves in the same leaky
boat!"

"That's the spirit, comrades." Von Treptow stood up and began to pace
the floor, finishing his coffee. "Pray let us maintain this attitude all the way

to the gallows, if need be." He skated quietly to the door, unlatched it and startled the chatting couple, prompting much leaping about. "Do I merit another cup?"

"Certainly, General." said Isabella as she brought the pot, pink cheeks even rosier.

"Thank you, Fräulein. Lieutenant, carry on."

With that, he closed the door behind him and resumed pacing. He adopted a more formal tone. "For the benefit of my new aide, allow me reprise the strategic situation. We have consolidated our defensive positions in the Hindenburg Line behind the Somme front. The map, Major, please."

Niemann leapt out of his chair to fetch a large map bonded to a thin piece of plywood, laying it on the table facing the brigadier's chair.

Von Treptow returned to the table and began tracing with his index finger a line starting from the North Sea below Ostend then on an east-west line along the Flemish provinces on to Luxembourg, dipping first down to encompass Briey-Longwy, then around the north of Lorraine and then to Alsace. "This will be our armistice line to be heavily fortified by midsummer in the north; it has already proved itself in Alsace. Keep this in mind, Colonel, as the visual manifestation of our goals in the West. We discussed Lorraine, Briey and the rest yesterday, no need to repeat. Easy to chart, difficult to achieve.

"I have been negotiating with the Flemish since early last year. We and they have created a 'Council of Flanders', the council members amply subsidized, of course. In Brussels, the public anticipates the return of King Albert, the Flemish would be happy to shed their Walloon burden. The back room reality is a semiautonomous state within the Reich with independence, but full economic dependence, maybe ten years on.

"The West, then, calls for a strategic retreat to our new borders. The real action comes in the East. That is not Colonel von Lossberg's concern but will soon be yours, Colonel Knorr. Our concern, here and now, is to prevent this final offensive. Those of us who have dealt with the *Generaloberst* class, particularly Hindenburg and Ludendorff, know well that a frontal assault has as much chance in the War Room as it does at Ypres. How would you accomplish this, Colonel?"

Now you have done it, General! On the spot – the Somme was no worse than this. Knorr parried, buying time. "Outflank the enemy, of course, get into its rear. But that is a tactical answer – what is the strategic key? That one thing which would swing the balance? How do we reach checkmate?"

"A concise assessment, Colonel. It is our task to do the flanking, move the bishops back and forth." Von Lossberg raised his hands. "General, I know you well enough now to expect you have the crowning move in mind."

"So I do, Fritz, so I do. But I shall keep you three in the dark and thus harmless, until Staff this afternoon. You two just waltz around the subject. Colonel Knorr, I will need your latest logistical calculations – you will be joining us." He motioned Knorr to follow him out of Lossberg's office.

"Come along, Lieutenant. Fräulein Boecker, as incredible as it may seem, he actually does have work to do." Von Treptow bowed, then took von Seeckt's good arm, and with a smile ushered him into the corridor. "Please stop by Signals, bring me my latest dispatches."

Off went the young man in the opposite direction, casting a last backward glance. "Colonel, I have given your man a message for the cipher clerks who receive all telegrams from Colonel Walther, Department IIIb, Military Intelligence. He will then be cleared to discreetly deliver such messages. Please emphasize to him the utmost need for secrecy."

The two continued down the corridor, saluting or nodding at groups of officers as they passed. "By the way, Colonel Knorr, is that grand society ball still held in Hannover this time of year? What is it you call it? Something avian, yes?"

"Yes, Sir, the Swan Ball. On the twentieth this year, but I do not expect to be free. Why?"

"You and I shall attend. You can, of course, arrange the invitation? And perhaps Fräulein Boecker might be persuaded to invite Lieutenant von Seeckt?"

"I will wire my brother today to see what he can do, but the reason? Why the interest in our provincial affairs?"

"Oh, just a small, bright respite from this bleak winter. And this war." By now they were back in Knorr's office. The general was at the leadglass windows, surveying a light snowfall just beginning. The scene was like an old engraving, the treeline in the distance still largely intact, dusted and frosted as were the haystacks, a few cows grazing, lending the whole a traditional sense of peace and plenty. "There will be naval personnel there, no?"

"Of course, sir. It is Wilhelmshaven's only social diversion other than the grogshops and bordellos."

"Ever the humorist, Colonel? No, there are several navy types I have need of consulting. Besides, it will be a convenient stop on our way to Berlin and points east."

"I am sure the General will further enlighten me at the appropriate time." Knorr shook his head and went back to his calculations. "General, Sir, not that I am nervous in the least to be presenting my analysis to the assembled General Staff of the whole damned Imperial Army, I assure you, but are these truly the numbers you wish to see?"

"Yes, as long as you preface the presentation attributing to me the numbers from the Eastern Front. You are well prepared. Trust me. Carry on, Colonel, I am off to luncheon with Count von Wittenberg, my intelligence superior." With that, he was out the door. Zig and Zag, hearing the magic word, rose and followed him expectantly.

"Back, boys," barked Knorr.

"Please, Colonel, allow them to accompany me. They will give me something to talk about."

Von Seeckt stepped into the antechamber, looking first at the general, then the pointers.

"Ah, yes, Lieutenant. Please send a wire to my man Reittimann at my home in Treptow, instructing him to ship a set of formal attire and kit to Colonel Knorr's home in Hannover. Here is the address," scribbling on a sheet of paper. "What have you here?"

Von Seeckt handed over a sheaf of telegrams and decoded messages. Von Treptow flipped through them, stopping at one, reading it carefully, then reading it again. "How is your French, Colonel?"

"Passable, not completely fluent, Sir."

"And yours, Lieutenant?"

"Reasonable, Sir. I try to keep it up here with the locals."

"Of course. Always use the *lingua franca* when ordering beers and wenching." Knorr and von Seeckt looked at each other, then at the general. Von Treptow snapped the dispatch in half. "We shall make a little excursion tomorrow night." Then he and his canine retinue disappeared into the corridor, their toenails beating a soft snare to the irregular rhythm of his boots.

Knorr looked through the anteroom to the corridor beyond, listening to the crisp staccato fading away. *I wonder what other secrets this one holds. All the generals do, one sort or another. But, I suppose, so do we all, in our own ways. Well.*

1400 Hours

The staff conference was held in the convent's refectory, a narrow chamber with high clerestory windows below a beamed pitched ceiling. A long wooden table a meter and a half wide was set in the center with chairs and pews along the perimeter. Hindenburg and Ludendorff made their grand entrance, Hindenburg plodding ahead, short salutes and nods left and right, Ludendorff clutching his papers, eyes down, all business.

They seated themselves opposite one other in the center. General von Treptow took his place well down the table, on Ludendorff's right, next to von Wittenberg. General von Kuhl, Chief of Staff of Crown Prince Rupprecht's Northern Army Group, had the honor of presiding, the Crown Prince at the head opposite. The beautiful Flemish tapestries that once lined the walls were long gone leaving nothing to muffle the general's stentorian voice. "If there is no new business to discuss, let us begin..."

General von Treptow raised his hand, index finger pointed, and stood up. Knorr, in the corner away from him, shot a glance at von Lossberg and Niemann opposite. *What is he doing?* Two pairs of shoulders shrugged in response.

"Gentlemen, let us be the first to congratulate our leaders on new honors soon to be bestowed by our Kaiser. While we generally hold our Navy in the highest regard" – much laughter and pounding on the table – "in their more lucid moments..."

Ludendorff suddenly slapped his palm on the table, silencing the group. "Have you something to say, General, or are you merely practicing your cabaret routine?"

"But of course, my General, please forgive my impertinence. Very simply, Gentlemen, Admiral von Holtzendorff shortly announces the Kaiser's decision to name the second of our new battlecruiser class after General Ludendorff, joining General Mackensen so honored." The room rose together, applause thundering in the stony chamber. Letting the moment linger, von

Treptow carefully watched Ludendorff stroke the end of his mustache, an expression of his unease.

"Thank you, Sirs, and all honors to General Ludendorff. But, there is more. The next two battlecruisers, even more powerful and superior to anything the Englanders have, are to be named *Tannenberg* and *Teutoberg*, commemorating the great forest battles defining our great nation."

Again an eruption echoed through the hall. Ludendorff, less perturbed now, even allowing a smile, said, "Thank you, General, thank you. Let us hope our new offensive in the West will be as decisive as Hermann's victory over the Romans in days of old."

"Or the Old West, as the Americans would say," slipped in von Treptow, his meaning clear to all through the humor.

"Of course," said Ludendorff stiffly. "How come you by your information? You have privileges the rest of us lack?"

"The curse of the intelligence officer, Sir. I assure you I have the proper clearances to make this announcement."

"Very well, General von Treptow, very well. Enough of this, now. General von Kuhl, please proceed."

The chamber began filling with tobacco smoke and smells. And warmed... Knorr, trying to be inconspicuous, loosened his tunic's collar. The meeting droned on as each Army Group commander or his Chief of Staff gave condition and readiness reports, each more upbeat than the previous.

Von Treptow noted Hindenburg's square crew cut head nodding and signaled von Kuhl with a finger. He, in turn, waited for von Below to finish, then suggested a break.

"A timely suggestion. Let us air this room in the interval." Ludendorff stood and strode out without another word.

Von Treptow stood, bending his back in a stretch, hands on hips. As he turned to walk out, a *sotto voce* in his left ear said, *"General, yours is a precarious position."* He made no acknowledgement as General von Seeckt passed by.

He has seen something. Have I pushed too far?

Von Treptow exchanged pleasantries with several officers on the way to a cigarette in the cloister's court. A few puffs, then back to Knorr's anteroom where he found Hans von Seeckt chatting with his nephew as the latter pinned a Lieutenant Colonel's insignia on a grimacing Knorr.

"Ah, these came just in time," said von Treptow, picking out the next piece and handing it to the younger von Seeckt. "General, a word?"

He shepherded his fellow into Knorr's office and closed the door behind them. Von Seeckt wasted no time, "The big boys, von Kluck, von Bülow, the rest, know of your...reluctance...toward the offensive. They also know of your contacts with Fritz von Lossberg. They are just intelligent enough to put two and two together. You will be challenged today, just be aware. Your royal ties, a mystery to all including me, will save you from otherwise certain impeachment, but those powers are hungry for more war and more glory." He allowed himself a small laugh, "A brilliant diversion, Dietrich, those battlecruisers. Problem is, your opponents will want their family crests on the next set of bows. I must go." He exited quickly, slipping out into the corridor with a wave.

"I am afraid to ask, General."

"Hmmm? Oh, he was merely alerting me to obstacles I already expected, just more so." *'Hungry', he said,* lost in thought, leaving his aides in their now customary befuddlement.

Staff resumed, the proformas finished, the main event about to begin. General von Kuhl first called on Colonel von Lossberg to brief the assemblage on his tactical proposals.

Von Lossberg and Niemann stepped to von Kuhl's corner of the table, the major holding the map from their office. "We are adapting the infiltration tactics General von Hutier used to such good effect at Caporetto." That battle was barely a month old, and few of the generals were familiar with the details. "Our German-Austrian army group used these tactics with such force as to penetrate deeply into the Italian lines, causing massive breakdowns in discipline and positions. A few units at Cambrai also used these tactics, helping turn the British back, along with General von Walter's new anti-tank artillery." He waved toward the latter, who smiled and nodded. *Every ally we can get.*

"Our task is to determine if those tactics can be incorporated into a massive offensive. It is one thing to spearhead a few divisions in a narrow valley and quite another with nearly two hundred divisions over a two hundred kilometer front. Operation Michael's terrain is the old Somme battleground, truly a lunar landscape. Training is another matter altogether. Finally, the Italians are hardly comparable to the British and the French, and these last are securely dug in."

Von Lossberg took a deep breath. "Those, in summary, are the challenges we face." *Now comes the tricky part.* "Despite those factors, there is potential with these new tactics. We are examining aerial photographs of Operation Michael's planned advance literally with a jeweler's loupe, identifying where rapid penetration will be most effective, and where mass will prevail. This is painstaking work, but will be completed on schedule. We will then meet with each Army group to assign individual units to each opportunity, and give advice, if not extensive training. More time would be invaluable, but we understand the urgency, I assure you."

Von Kluck spoke up. "What exactly are you proposing? Describe these new tactics so these old wardogs can understand."

"Yes, General." Turning back to the map, he paused, then pointed to an area around Saint-Quentin. "This area I am familiar with. General, Sir, if I may ask you to move aside." Von Bruckow grumbled as he worked his chair away from the table.

"So. To the immediate north we control this area here," pointing. "Just here is a marshy area where shelling has ruined the drainage systems. Not easily passable for a regimental or battalion frontal assault. Please, Gentlemen, that would be suicidal. But a smaller group, company size, carrying rifles, light as well as heavy machine guns and flamethrowers, can advance on the run, here, and break out here." He traced a lily shape on the map, a slender stem flaring out to the right and left. "Here we attack the flanks on either side, eroding them as we go. Keep in mind this is a small group, so once there we must move more troops here," pointing, "and here, or the advance group is vulnerable to counterattack or being stymied."

Ludendorff, losing interest in von Lossberg's minutiae, said, "We will punch a hole...For the rest, we shall see. We did it this way in Russia. Thank you, Colonel, continue to work your wonders. General von Kuhl, what is next?"

Von Lossberg breathed sighs of relief as he collected his things and returned to obscurity.

"Logistics, sir, limiting ourselves to Operation Michael for the moment. Lieutenant Colonel Knorr has been tasked with determining the resources we require." Von Kuhl was not about to raise the issue of Knorr's promotion or his new mentor, trusting Ludendorff to be disinterested.

"Thank you, General. I have prepared a summary of my findings on this chart," which he draped over Niemann's map. "The figures are gross, that is, calculated according to benchmarks set from past experience. For instance, we have averaged one hundred artillery pieces per kilometer of front; using the breadth of front here," now pointing to the British positions on the map, "we would require seven thousand five hundred pieces. However, as the chart shows, we have available five thousand pieces in the West, with another sixteen hundred yet be to be transported from the East, leaving the reserves General von Treptow recommends." Several heads turned, some abruptly, toward von Treptow.

Knorr continued quickly, "Accordingly, we are a thousand pieces short, but with production from Krupps and Skoda adding four hundred per month, we should have adequate resources on schedule. Those new pieces still have to be sighted in by General Bruchmüller's group. A typical day's preliminary barrage alone would require up to two million shells, which are not in short supply for up to thirty days' sustained action. The same analysis carries through each category, down to the last, manpower. Here is the concern: even with repatriation of most of our forces in the East, we lack the divisions to impose a three-to-one correlation versus the defense. I leave it to the strategic and tactical planners to determine their dispositions."

Hindenburg sputtered, "We shall field two hundred divisions, battle tested and rested!"

Knorr let his adrenaline crest, then recede, "Of course, Sir, depending on the East's requirements, but the Allied forces still can field nearly as many. And in …."

"And the Americans will soon be adding a quarter million men per month, nearly ten of their huge divisions, twice the size of ours." This was von Treptow, coming to Knorr's relief.

Von Treptow continued, "Of course, as Colonel Knorr was about to say, we can easily concentrate two or three attack divisions in any sector to one in defense, probably at several points. However, our total manpower is a concern since we are sure to commit our reserves, yes?" Several heads nodded in agreement.

"Also, General von Hoffman recommends we retain more strength in the East, for a short time, to advantage ourselves of the turmoil there. I concur for reasons I shall discuss. But first, there is another pressing issue. Hunger. Literally, Gentlemen. Each of you hears from home how bare are the shelves, but admittedly, we here at headquarters are hardly starving. At home, another matter entirely..."

Ludendorff simmered. "General, we are discussing Army matters here."

"An army travels on its stomach, my General. The British blockade affects us as it does the homefolk. Our troops are ill-fed, beyond question. A question: has anyone in this room surveyed our enemy's rear?" No one spoke. "Well, I have, and recently." This set the room abuzz. "General, spare me five minutes?"

Ludendorff, exasperated at losing control of the spectacle, said, "Five minutes, but make these five worth our while."

"Thank you, Sir. In October, a letter reached my agent in Geneva. In it was an American newspaperman's accreditation and clearances. I trained down, changed into civilian garb, and with a forged American passport took a train into France, then up past the Marne to an area twenty-five kilometers behind the front at Rheims. Farmers still farm, fresh meat and milk abound, the poilu lives in relative luxury.

"I went further north where the British were still pressing us at Cambrai. I saw your gun flashes in the distance, General Walter. Yet, it was the same, abundance. The trenches themselves resemble their Fortnum & Mason emporium when compared to ours. The Tommy has a ruddy complexion and a healthy posture. Compare that to your frontline troops, any of you."

Seeing Ludendorff's frown, "My conclusions, then, are twofold. First, our troops are clearly less fit for intensive combat than the enemy's, and second, when we overrun their lines, as we most assuredly will, do you not think our boys will not stop to eat, and of course, drink? Sheer numbers, division counts do not tell the story."

Von Treptow paused a few seconds, then continued, "To the French. General Ludendorff, I respect your decision to attack the English, but allow me one argument to the contrary. Colonels von der Schulenburg and Wetzell argue for an attack on Verdun, with the aim of breaking the French spirit. I agree, not with Verdun again, but because the French are already broken."

This last caused an uproar. "Please, please, Gentlemen, allow me continue. Last summer after Nivelle's failure at Chemin des Dames, their front went quiet until their brief and perfunctory thrust in November. Why?"

He leaned over the table, "Mutiny! The French Army is paralyzed by war weariness and a refusal of the common soldier to fight. We will see no major offensives, but I suspect they will defend to the last. They themselves describe it as renouncing their doctrine of 'rupture' in favor of the 'nibbling' of November, but even now have given way to mere holding, so say documents we have captured. If so, why bother shedding more good German blood?"

"You are mad as well as insubordinate!" bellowed von Bülow. "What gives you the right to challenge the General Staff, concocting these tales?"

Von Kluck began to chime in when Hindenburg raised his hand. "Do go on, General. I find this interesting."

"Thank you for your indulgence, Sir. This is not some fiction I have composed. Thanks to Count von Wittenberg's network of informants, and my own contacts, I have a very clear picture. My 'newspaperman' trip confirmed it, I spoke at length with many common soldiers, and they are done. But, like a hornet's nest in the early morning, once they warm up they will be fierce defenders. The British, on the other hand, are still fighting cocks. And, of course, General Ludendorff's concern about the Americans is well founded and frightening, indeed."

"So, General, what do you propose?" Hindenburg adopted the impatient tone of a grandfather to a rambunctious grandson. "Are we to fight, or not?"

"Yes, General, we shall fight, and we shall win." *I am in this deep, I might as well go all the way.* "First, as a tactical matter as much as strategic, we must finish the business in the East. Chaos reigns among the Russians. The Tsar is gone, now Kerensky is gone, replaced by feuding revolutionary factions. This past March, I accompanied one Vladimir Ilyich Ulyanov – he calls himself Lenin – from Zurich to Saint Petersburg. Who is he? Now the most powerful man in Russia, that is all. He immediately organized his thugs into *Soviets*, they call them, a network of terror, murder and iron fisted control.

"Why would we ship him there, and support him to the tune of five thousand goldmarks a month?" Several in the room whistled. "He is a virus infecting Russia, disabling her. But he is dangerous, and we will have to deal with him, the sooner the better. In the meantime, the Russian Army, our nightmare, is dissolving. Lenin begged us for the armistice we soon negotiated, saying, *'the Russian soldier has voted for peace with his feet.'* The serfs, the peasants, rather, have gone home leaving just the skeleton of the bear, and the Tsarist elements, the officers, mainly, are beginning to coalesce in opposition to Lenin's revolutionaries, his 'Reds'.

"I signed that armistice for a ninety day period, on 15 December, before coming here. Do not take that agreement as justification for shifting our best men west, however. Lenin and his Red Army chief, Trotsky, are the vilest, most dishonest and untrustworthy scum I have ever encountered." He passed his gaze over the assembled generals, making his small point. "Trotsky is particularly loathsome. Lenin has ordered him to stall on finalizing a peace agreement, thinking our workers will rebel against their masters and subscribe to their revolution. We are done with them. If they do not come to agreement upon my return to Brest-Litovsk at month's end, we finish the job."

He stopped to catch his breath, then plunged in, "That is why Generals von Falkenhayn and von Hoffman and I request deferring redeployment until we finish this business."

Ludendorff pre-empted several of his generals in objecting, "You have just told us the Russian Army has crumbled, but at the same time, you need more men? To fight whom? Phantoms?"

"Sir, there are still capable Red Army units. No, the lesson to remember here is Sun Tzu's maxim, *'The lion spares no strength against the mouse'*, or something to that effect. We must have our full forces for no more than six weeks – that would be no later than mid-March – by which time we can take all of Russia to the Urals and the Caucasus. We can then hold all this with *Landsturm* and *Landwehr*.

"Think of that, Gentlemen. One month ago, we faced the prospect of a continuing war with Russia, a slow, difficult, costly war, pinning down a million or more of our best men. One month later, the field is clear. Never have we seen such a strategic reversal, not since Napoleon's retreat from Moscow.

"But to my earlier point, hunger. When we succeed, we will control the Ukraine's agriculture and industry and Ploesti's and Baku's petroleum as well. The Black Sea will be a German lake. The British blockade will be broken from the other side of Europe. Without compromising my operations, we shall have agreements with an independent Ukraine and Finland in four or five weeks. There are other forces, as well..."

Hindenburg interrupted him, "General, this is most encouraging. My experiences with the Tsarist Army never gave me the hope of such a decisive conclusion. You shall have your Eastern Army until 15 March. The trains west will be waiting the next day. Agreed?"

"Of course, Sir."

"Now, that was your first point. What is next?"

"Sir, I have stuck my neck out this far, might as well place it squarely on the chopping block."

Von Bruckow muttered loudly enough, "Hear, hear!"

Hindenburg retorted, "Pay him no heed. Proceed."

Thus emboldened, von Treptow cast the die. "It is no secret I have questioned the Final Offensive. Actually I oppose it, most vigorously."

This was more than most could take. Several senior officers rose, shouting and shaking fists. Ludendorff's face grew bright red, mustache twitching.

Again, Hindenburg imposed his will, "You realize it was General Ludendorff and I who proposed this offensive? You realize your impertinence borders on insubordination? Why so inflammatory?"

"Yes, Sir, I was in this very room last November with the Quartermaster General. And yes, I realize the gravity of my comments. My...position... requires me to take a look at the larger situation outside this headquarters, beyond this front. With what I know or think I know about the East, I look to the West and see a war that we have won, but could still lose. Some minutes ago, I spared Colonel Knorr the discomfort of presenting the final statistics in his analysis, casualties, two hundred thousand dead, wounded or missing per month of offensive, more if the Americans effectively enter the fray."

Having regained some control of his congregation, he continued, "Think of that, Gentlemen. What has our strategy been since unification, Sedan, Bismarck? To neutralize France on land, Britain at sea, and Russia in the east, allowing us to take our place among the great empires of the world. Well, we have neutered France. Two and a half millions killed or disabled. Two million pairs of lost testicles unable to create new soldiers. A third of their youth, many of them their finest. And their people, war-wearied and mourning. And the gold, do not forget the financial cost."

He leaned back, creating a caesura for effect and breath, then, "We are poised to meet our war aims, exceeding them vastly in the East. My proposal is very simple: declare Victory and retire to impregnable defensive positions of our choosing, daring the Entente leadership to explain to their exhausted citizenry and brutalized soldiery why, how, they can justify more sacrifice."

Now I have truly done it. Did I let my own passions rule my head?

This time, the refectory virtually exploded in argument and fingerwagging. It took von Treptow several moments to realize it was not all directed at him – the spectacle of senior generals, Army Group leaders, shouting at each other, papers flying in the air was beyond belief.

Then, as a shrill whistle pierced the room, the grey-green mass stopped boiling and began to subside. The whistle came from none other than Crown Prince Rupprecht of Bavaria, who was now standing, leaning forward, fingers arched on the table.

"Sirs, this is the most cogent argument I have heard in the last three years. Marshal Hindenburg, you, of all, understand the sweep of this discussion. Please, you and General Ludendorff" – a friendly nod and smile to the table's center – "reconsider your plans along these lines. The East as you said, Paul. The West, rethink the French sector, and above all, maintain strategic flexibility. If our renegade here is able to deliver on his claims, our outlook is very different than a mere few days ago. We cannot disregard this changing correlation of forces, or we now do so at our peril." He looked over the table. "It is late. This meeting is over."

As Colonel Knorr gathered his charts and files, the Crown Prince approached him. "Congratulations on your promotion, but my deepest sympathy on your association with the general from Intelligence, here," beckoning von Treptow over. "That was courageous, Sir. Whatever possessed you?"

"Idiocy, sheer idiocy, Excellency."

"Hardly. You did us a great service. Even should not one iota of the plan change, you will have forced a much needed review. I feared a rigidity was setting in, an ossification fortified by fear of authority. I am much more confident in our course. Max will be pleased."

He turned, placing an arm over Knorr's shoulder. "Where have you been hiding my hounds? I miss the beggars."

"As the Brits would say, that was a close run thing, *nicht wahr?*"

Knorr watched the Crown Prince stride from the room. "I would agree, General, if I knew how it happened."

"Sometimes one's powers of observation fail. Mine did. I had no idea that last outburst would take on the character it did. Nor that Prince Rupprecht would ride to our rescue as he did. I just blundered forward – perhaps our generals sensed a kinship with that tactic." He laughed. "It had to come out sooner or later, and sooner is better, as we now have been given a deadline."

"Excuse me, General." Major Egon Jacobs approached and saluted. "Colonel, when will you be prepared to brief my staff on your work? We are at your service."

"Jacobs here has been appointed, no, anointed, to take over my planning and assume custody of these toxic documents." Knorr looked at von Treptow. "When is our appointment tomorrow?"

"Late tomorrow afternoon. I suggest you two confer first thing as we will have some preparations to make later in the day."

"Very well, Colonel, my office at 0730?" Jacobs saluted and turned on his heels without an answer.

"What preparations, Sir?"

"A good nap. Lieutenant Erich, as well. We shall be in need of one. I think I shall take my dinner at the hotel, Colonel...Yoicks! Von Bülow and von Kluck approach! Make your escape while you can!"

Knorr saluted and clicked his heels, executing a brisk left face and an orderly retreat, leaving the oncoming *Generalobersts* behind.

Cornered, von Treptow stood to salute from afar, adding a friendly, or so he hoped, wave.

Von Kluck started in on him from several meters away, "Do you think your protectors can save you every time, Dietrich? What signal did you give the Crown Prince? I did not detect it. Or are you so close to royalty you use telepathy?"

Before von Treptow could muster a defense, von Bülow took von Kluck's sleeve, restraining him but slightly. "Yes, General, what can you say for yourself after upending our plans? Is there some pacifist solution to our current dilemma, perhaps mobilizing your friends Luxemburg and Liebknecht?"

He had by then slowed the bullish von Kluck to a stop. With a sly wink, he went on, "Seriously, Sir, even our friend here would thank you for highlighting our troops' material deficiencies in front of the Most High. Neither he nor I could do so without facing retirement. I have just now taken Ludendorff aside and pressed him privately on the matter. He agreed to have someone look into it."

"If you mean me, Sir, I respectfully decline as my cup runneth over with other duties. And it will take much, much more than just 'looking into it.' 'Looking into it' does not change nature's harvest schedule nor Britain's blockade. No, Generals, it is insoluble in the short run, unless we further deprive our civilian population which already approaches desperation." A wry smile faded aborning, "My friends, as you call them – I consider them useful idiots – are weak, but so is the cowpox virus, yes? Their fitful, fanciful cries of '*Revolution*', '*Workers of the World Arise*', and such amateurish drivel are useful vaccinations against the smallpox of Bolshevism. As of now, the people reject them. But should the screw turn much further, their red star will rise. Already I am seeing reports of action, general strikes and the like in the next months."

These generals, for all their bluster, were genuinely unafraid of their military foes but privately terrified of the unknown and unquantifiable threat of the masses. Their rank, their social positions, their estates, their very world, all were rooted in the old order and its stability. No one knew where a new tide might sweep, but the omens from Saint Petersburg and Moscow were truly frightening, to their class most of all.

Von Kluck was the first to speak. "Even I am aware of these matters, but our task is to defeat the enemy. If that means better feed and more rest for our men, so be it. But it remains to defeat the enemy, and after three years, I am determined to crush them."

"So, General, how do we do it? How do we beef up our troops and march to victory in France?" This was von Bülow, almost pleading, "If it is food, are we not feeding a million Russian prisoners? Why not starve the bastards and ship that food west?"

"A good point, Sir. Aside from violating the Hague accords? Confidentially, I have given much thought to a final solution, but as yet have no answer short of Bolshevik barbarism. At the moment, we are happy to be their *hôteliers*. Keeping them out of trouble, you see. But as you note, we must feed them, not nearly as much as our lads require, but still…" Von Treptow drummed his fingers on his cheeks as he pondered that angle. "Hmmm…"

Von Kluck, recovering his bluster, barked out, "Let us declare a truce, a temporary one. We each have our factions, our backers, our orders. So, we rest our men, you help us find more food, you create your *Lebensraum* empire in the East, we march to victory in the West. Agreed?"

"In that order?" purred von Treptow.

"Yes, yes, of course, damn it. That is the way I said it!"

"Agreed, with one coda appended to the last: '*as deemed necessary for the survival of the Reich.*' "

"This is not one of your fancypants treaty negotiations, von Treptow! Of course, damn you, it is for the Reich's survival."

"A small clarification, only. Agreed. One final point. I shall prepare a brief monograph on these and other issues of interest to inform you both further of matters not to be discussed publicly. Delivered tomorrow. I would appreciate, no, I require, your comments. Good day." He saluted and walked away.

1800 hours

"Hello, Dietrich! How fares the Red Knight of Brandenburg?" The bellow echoed down the long corridor leading to the motor court. Von Treptow turned to see Falstaff himself, reincarnated as his old childhood friend and, now, General Rupert von Spandau.

Von Treptow sized up his girth and retorted, "Rupert, how many times must I tell you to leave some victuals for the troops? Is there a beeve or a boar left in Germany?"

"Oh, mine friend, you cut me to the quick! You know how trying it is to be food taster to the Imperials! I understand you played the revolutionary this afternoon. '*To the barricades, Comrades! L'état, c'est moi!*' Oops, wrong historical allusion."

"Illusion, you mean. As you are a welcome illusion to tired eyes. How is family?" Von Treptow had genuine affection for his old friend, roly-poly since birth and mischievous, as well.

"Not so good. Father has cancer, a rare kind. Of the lungs. Doctor Boehme has only seen one other case in his forty years' practice. Father is still comfortable, though. Mother is distraught. Sister is inconsolable since the loss of her Fritz." His brother-in-law had been killed in October at Third Ypres, or Passchaendale as the Brits called it. A truly senseless battle in a war long since passing all understanding.

"My regrets all around. You, professionally?"

"Managing. Plenty of munitions, bullets, shells and the like. Have any spare mutton on you, perchance? Or squirrel? Rat? Provisioning is increasingly difficult with each passing week."

"As always, your timing is beyond reproach, my friend. I just finished conversing on the very topic with certain high personages. I had planned to be a hermit and take dinner at my hotel, but perhaps I could persuade you to join me?"

Von Spandau raised an unkempt hedge of an eyebrow. "Are you buying?"

They took their dinner at the Brasserie Colette, von Treptow having passed on it for lunch the day before. Mindful of the writing he had promised, he begged off on the dessert tray, the port, the brandy and the last nip or six von Spandau indulged in, shamelessly.

At least they had been able to discuss the provisioning problem. Von Spandau was quite resourceful, using his shipping company connections to great effect in the Atlantic and Baltic. His forebears were founders of several of the first Hanseatic trading houses. His great-grandmother was the first to marry outside Lübeck, to a minor prince west of Berlin.

He had managed to keep a steady flow of American wheat and Argentine beef through Stockholm and Rotterdam. It seems the middlemen were not particularly fastidious about end users and in any event did not compare their totals with their competitors. If they had, they would have noted each month's combined shipments would feed the entire Scandinavian peninsula for over a year. The shipping companies, Dutch and Norwegian, were similarly 'uninterested.'

But not the British. It had taken them a while to grasp the worldwide nature of the war, at least in this regard. Now, cargoes were given more scrutiny, agents in Oslo and Stockholm and Rotterdam were totting up crates and barrels more intensely. Ships were being boarded and inspected at sea, in the distant blockade, and neutrality was increasingly being eroded.

So, supply had steadily been strangled. Geography was the main culprit, along with the Royal Navy, of course, and there was little to be done about that. Sweden, Denmark and Holland were the only contiguous access points to Germany, in the entire world. Spain was blocked by France, and Austria, Bulgaria and Turkey by the British Mediterranean Fleet controlling the Straits of Gibraltar and exits from the Suez Canal. South Asia was under British control from Iran to Afghanistan, India, Burmah and Malaya. And that was it.

Except for the Trans-Siberian railroad.

2100 hours

Von Treptow took his leave from his friend as he was dropped off at his hotel. He asked for messages at the desk and finding none, scuttled to the lift, not noticing a figure in black sitting in front of the fire, its back to his path.

Once von Treptow was safely away, the figure rose and walked to the desk. "That is the general. I do not know his name, but I owe him a debt I should like to repay. May I have his room number?"

The clerk, an Army sergeant, declined, "You can understand our security concerns, Madame. No."

The figure removed its veil and shawl exposing a pretty face and uplifted bosom. "Surely you can see I mean no harm?"

The sergeant suddenly adopted a different approach to security. "Madame, I will have to frisk you. Thoroughly."

She nodded, and draped her coat, veil, and shawl on the desk. She submitted silently to the sergeant's groping and regroping. "Can't be too secure, you understand."

She understood all too well. When he was finally done, he summoned a private to escort her to von Treptow's room. *Fine figure,* he thought. *I wonder how much?*

The two ascended in the lift to the general's floor; the private led her to his room and knocked. Von Treptow opened the door, removing his hornrims and rubbing his eyes. "Yes, Private? What is it?" Then he saw the figure wreathed in black. "Yes?"

"Sir, this…woman…has requested to see you. We have searched her."

"I am quite certain our sergeant has done so. May I see your face?"

As she removed her hat and veil, he said, "Thank you, Private. Please stand guard in the lift lobby. Do come in, Madame."

The general waved her in, closing the door behind her. "To what do I owe this visit? And please excuse my attire. I was not expecting guests." He was down to his dress shirt, suspenders slung, boots off.

"General, I owe you a great debt. Unfortunately, I have but one coin with which to repay you." At that, she sat on his bed, removed her hat, veil, scarf and gloves, placing them on the nightstand. She began unbuttoning her short jacket from the bottom up.

"Please, Madame, before you go any further, what is this about? The… incident…yesterday?" *Surely she cannot be an agent? That would be coincidence beyond belief. And we were the cause, so it could not have been a trap. Or could it have been?*

He gathered up his papers, placing them in the desk drawer. When he turned to face her, she had finished undoing her jacket buttons. She was naked within, the curves of her breasts pressing the lapels outward. He dragged his gaze upward to her face, lightly rouged and quite pretty, quite pretty indeed, far from the grimy, tired washerwoman he had first seen. Her golden blonde hair was tied in a bun which she deftly loosened, letting her curls cascade over her shoulders.

"Yes, General, for that I find myself in your debt, gladly, I assure you."

Von Treptow sat on the chair opposite. He waved, "No more, please. At least until I understand," he smiled slightly. "Pray tell me your story."

She sunk a bit, interlocked her fingers on her knees and began, "My husband and I have, had, lived in Louvain since we were married. Yvette is our only child, after her I lost one in infancy and one to a miscarriage. He was a director of the Bank of Louvain, a prominent position, really, in our town. We had a lovely life, a nice house, a circle of friends.

"Then came the war. Then came you bastards, like locusts – no, like hyenas. You know what happened. You may have been there." Her cheeks were now flushing naturally and brightly, her hands clenched as yesterday.

"The first days were calm enough, I suppose." *Henri had time to send the Bank's gold and our holdings to Brussels and then on to Antwerp and London. He does not need to know that.* "Then there was an incident, a stone thrown, a shot, perhaps, I do not know. A bank clerk called to tell me Henri was one of the ones taken away. Your soldiers kept me away from the square, but I could hear the shots. When the soldiers cleared, we rushed forward to the most horrid sight. Fifty bodies, some still alive, writhing on the cobbles.

"I found my Henri, a bullet in his face. I vomited all over him, I am ashamed to say. Then the soldiers returned and chased us away, killing those resisting. I had to get to Yvette." Her voice and torso were trembling, rage mixing with the horror of that day.

"I had kept her from school out of fear of your soldiers; was I not justified?" Von Treptow looked on impassively. "I had just time to grab Yvette and some clothes, and the contents of my household allowance tin, and escape out the rear door. Another Bank director and his family had their car in the alleyway waiting for us. He, Willem was his name, planned on driving first to Brussels, to gain news of the German advance, hoping to drive on to Antwerp and book passage to England.

"The drive was short, only thirty kilometers or so, but slow as the road was crowded with refugees. And cyclists and soldiers. We arrived to much confusion in Brussels. Willem got us to the Brabant Bank in the city center. He disappeared inside for some time then came out with another man. *'Estelle, Frank here thinks we can get to Antwerp ahead of the Germans, but just. Will you come with us? He is preparing to leave for France, and can take you and Yvette, if you so desire.'*

"No one left in Holland in my family, any more. I know no one in England, but my husband's uncle lives in Lille. If we can get to France, perhaps I can contact him. Surely the French will not let the Germans in? *'Not in a thousand years,'* said Frank. *'We will be back home in two weeks when this dreadful affair is over, but must first stay alive. Come, our car is around back, let us hurry. Good fortune and Godspeed, my friend,'* he said, embracing Willem. *'Send word to Barings when you can,'* replied Willem.

"With that, we went to his car with his wife and three children. It was crowded but we cared not. He knew a way out of town to the south. *'We will* go through Bergen' – Mons, here, she said – 'it is the shortest route to the border, and a good road. I go there frequently to meet clients.'

"Again, the road was clogged, but we made our way. Less than a hundred kilometers, but it took hours. Finally, nearing Soignies, only twenty-five kilometers to go, the car stopped, steaming. Trying to be cheerful, Frank said, 'We'll have to let it rest a while. I will walk to this next village to see if I can find some fresh water – it is thirsty!'

"I decided to walk with him, taking Yvette, to find a drink. His oldest son was eighteen and could guard the car. It was not too far to the town, and Frank found a pump and scrounging around, a bucket. He filled it, then turned back. 'Stay here in the shade and we will come for you.'

"We waited, then decided, why I know not, to begin walking. Our cases were in their car except for my purse. We had not gone far when we heard distant thundering. An old man passing said, 'Cannon.' I glanced back at the road behind us. The car was just over a hill, alongside a stand of poplars. Then a cloud, then another. When the smoke cleared, the poplars had been stripped of leaves, and some were down. That was all I could see. And then, flames. And people running, some aflame.

"I asked a group passing where they were going. 'Mons,' they said, 'We hear the French are coming to rescue us.' 'And the English,' said another. The old man said, 'We should get off the main road. Up here is a side road, about two kilometers over to a market road I knows, gets us to the back door of Mons, along the Canal. Ain't on their maps, I'll bet.'

"We joined the flood, walking most of the night. We rested several hours either side of daybreak, then walked another few hours until we could see the hill of Mons from a rise in the road. So we felt we were fairly safe.

"Then it was as if the world had come to an end! From behind us came this thunder, this eruption," she said, gesturing with her hands in a fountain above her shoulders, her breasts falling from her jacket. She covered them and continued, "The sky behind us was on fire, as far as we could see along the hills. Then we heard this rasping sound, a hoarse roaring, above us. 'Them's the cannonballs,' said the old man, 'Watch.'

"He turned, looking towards Mons. Suddenly, in a line to the town's west, was a cloud rising, the colors of earth and red clay and coal with sparks and flashes, added to by more and more puffs of smoke. A few seconds later we heard a low rumbling coming from the smoke.

" '*Best get moving,*' said the old man. '*Look yonder,*' pointing to the west, where another cloud was rising, this time soundlessly." She was deeply in her story, looking past von Treptow, not at him. " '*Boche,*' he said, '*marching. Where we was.*' We saw some horses and riders going first forward, then some came back.

"The road then dipped down into a little valley, lined with poplars. We stayed close to those for shelter. We were far enough ahead of any pursuing soldiers, that with some running and trotting we passed through a village, Obourg, I think, and approached the Grand Canal first. Two men in tan uniforms suddenly rose from behind a barricade, rifles pointing. One whistled and beckoned us over to him. '*There's the bridge. Make it quick!*'

"We did, and quickly, indeed! Then the thundering started again, a different sound, more a crack and whoosh!" She was gesturing again, uncovering herself again. This time she made no attempt at modesty, von Treptow noticed. He noticed something else. *More bruises than I first saw.*

"Please, General, stop me if I am going on."

"No, please, continue."

"Then a wave hit us from behind, knocking some of us down. Not all got up. The old man who led us was face down. I started to help him, then the back of his coat got red, and blood began seeping from beneath him. I backed away in horror. I looked back to the men in tan and there was nothing, just smoke."

She stopped to catch her breath and her composure. "Cigarette?" asked von Treptow. He went over to the bureau and took two cigarettes out of the gold case with the family crest engraved.

"No, thank you," she said, head down. Then, "Yes, please," looking into his eyes, "Please tell me to stop, do not let me go on."

"No, no, no," he replied, "I believe you need to talk."

She paused to smoke a bit, then continued, "Very well, then. Another soldier in tan, British we now saw, said they were going to blow up the bridge. He directed us down a side road, would bring us closer to the town center, he said. We ran. And ran. We were running past fields and houses, following the curve of the canal, although we did not know that.

"We stopped for breath at a corner where we could see past a warehouse to the land across the canal. Here came the Germans, marching like a parade. Suddenly a 'rat-tat-tat' rang out from the tan soldiers hiding on this side.

Your soldiers dropped straight down by the scores, it seemed. Then they started kneeling and firing, bullets flying high, so we dashed past a field to the shelter of the next block of buildings.

"Once we started into what I thought to be the town, but the cannonballs were crashing in front of us, so we cowered a while. And so on, running for our lives, we kept on along the canal, from one group of Britishers to another. Every time we found a quiet spot to rest, more shooting and cannon fire chased us onward.

"Finally, we had to stop. We had fled kilometers by then, it seemed, and were exhausted. I peeked around another corner building and there was another bridge. I could see the tan soldiers hiding again, then along came a hundred horsemen, maybe more, some with flags flying. The British started shooting and hit a dozen horses and men, then a dozen more. The horsemen turned away except for one who must have been their leader – he was in front. He spurred his horse to the side of the road and got off and disappeared into a ditch. He came back, now waving something white from his sword's tip, with fifteen or twenty schoolgirls in jumpers and pigtails following him like baby ducklings. He had taken off his spiked helmet, I think it might have scared the younger girls. He ushered them to the head of the bridge and pointed, saluted the British, turned and got on his horse and rode off."

She had been gesturing, embellishing the scene, but now dropped her hands into her lap. "The British had stopped their shooting, of course, and that gave your Germans time to get out of danger, I suppose. That was a brave man, but I was surprised to see any compassion for the little ones, he could have just left them there to die. Perhaps he was just using them to save his men."

"Both," said von Treptow.

"What?"

"That was me, trying to save both and probably die in the effort."

A long silence followed. Von Treptow leaned back, finishing his cigarette. The woman held her jacket closed, trying to regain some modesty.

"Estelle."

"What was that?"

"Estelle Vandenberg. My name."

"Dietrich Rheinhardt Ehrenburg von Treptow, Margrave von Brandenburg und Mittelmark. My friends call me 'General' or 'General, Sir.' Please call me Dietrich, or hyena, or filthy bastard, as you please."

"I am so sorry, General…"

He cut her off, "Dietrich, and no further apologies. Are you able to continue? Of course, if you prefer…"

"There is not much more. A lorry full of British wounded approached us as we huddled next to the canal. The driver's passenger hailed us and they took us to the Hôtel de Ville in the Grand Place. They loaded more wounded, there was no room for us, so we sat on the pavement until another one came along and carried us to the convent, where you Germans work now. It was their hospital, and we were given a little food by the sisters. They did not have much and had many patients, but we were safe.

"The next morning, we awoke to much noise. The Germans had broken through and taken the town and now were at the convent. I think the sisters were afraid for the soldiers, but the Germans treated them decently, at least as far as we could see. I think, though, that several of the sisters were shot…"

She broke off, trying not to cry. Von Treptow winced.

"Anyway, I was afraid for Yvette, so we slipped away through their dairy, then through the fields but kept running into your soldiers. Finally, we walked back to town hoping to find someone to help us. I had brought some money, as I said, but not much. Everyone was hiding inside, I think. We chanced upon the café which had a '*Waitress Needed*' sign. I had never waited table but was desperate for a place for my daughter. I met Gaston inside, he seemed pleasant enough, and so it was I donned the apron. Once the fighting stopped, things were almost normal. Then Gaston…" She started choking, then recovered, waving off von Treptow who had started to rise.

"Then Gaston started taking me. He threatened to sell Yvette to you Germans or kill her. She was only eleven then, and scrawny, so he was not yet interested in her. We tried to get away once, but one of his brothers, a true brute, found us in Saint Elisabeth's and dragged Yvette out by her hair. That was the last time I dared. Next, I got pregnant with Etienne. Gaston seemed indifferent, but when it was a boy, he treated me better for a while. Then came Sophie and he got even worse. He accused me of bringing four mouths for him to feed. He became very abusive. I was constantly bruised.

His mother was as bad, with her words, like the evil stepmother in the fairy tale until her mind snapped last year, mercifully.

"Then Yvette began to grow up, just this winter. He lost interest in me, thank God, but started staring at her, intently. He tried her last month but I managed to fight him off. Then again the day before the...incident. And, then, you." She looked at von Treptow, pleadingly, "Thank you. That is the debt I came to repay. And to beg for your protection, please, please, I beg you, for my children, if not for me. Please? This is all I have to offer." She wiped a tear and started to open her jacket but von Treptow waved her off again.

"What will you do now? What about the café?"

"I was not his wife. Besides, I am Flemish, Dutch, actually, not Walloon. His two brothers and their shrews came before the dirt was heaped, taking over. They have given me until tomorrow to be out."

Von Treptow stood up abruptly, picked up the telephone receiver and barked, "Give me Headquarters Signals – now!" He stood waiting, then heard the other end. "Who is this? Lieutenant Glazer? Get a runner over to Colonel Knorr's farmhouse now, tell Lieutenant von Seeckt to bring the car to the Hôtel du Roi, *schnell*! How long? Ten minute walk? How about a two minute run? Now!"

He turned to his guest, "Your carriage arrives shortly. Tell me of these brothers and wives – their names?"

"Oh, please, no more trouble, please. They will hurt Yvette!"

"No trouble, I assure you." Von Treptow's voice was cold as ice. "They will not hurt your daughter. I merely add them to our list of the usual suspects when a demonstration of our will is required." She recited names and he wrote them in his little book.

"You will kill them?"

"I have killed one, two, may as well do them all. Mere numbers."

Estelle recoiled at his casual cruelty. *Maybe he is just like the rest, just like the Germans that killed my Henri.*

Seeing her face, he continued softly, "Madame, I have no patience for the brute in men's souls. There is not enough time in creation, certainly not in this war, to correct, to palliate, to make whole these people. Easier to simply be rid of them. And just."

"But, you are a soldier, a brute yourself!" she blurted, regretting it instantly.

"Do you really think so? Would you have brought yourself here had you thought thus?"

Estelle looked down.

"Do you still think so?" He raised her from the bed, buttoning her jacket from the top down. He reached for her hat and veil, then turned, empty-handed. He raised her chin and kissed her gently. She reached expectantly toward him for more, but he placed a finger across her lips. "Not now." He then gave her the veil.

"I no longer need this," she said, holding it over the bed.

"May I keep it as a talisman? Excuse me, I must get dressed myself." He looped one suspender over his shoulder and Estelle helped him with the other. He took his tunic from the armoire, slipped it on, then his boots.

"One other thing, I just realized," she said quietly. "The little ones. I thought of them as Gaston's children, not mine. Now, they are all mine. Thanks to you." Tears welled in her eyes. "The greatest gift to a mother, love for her own."

"Please?" He opened the door and escorted Estelle down the hall to the lift. "Down, please." *Of course,* thought the private.

Once in the lobby, they had only a few minutes to wait when von Seeckt came screeching to a halt in the staff car. "What is it, General? What goes?"

"Lieutenant Erich von Seeckt, Madame Estelle Vandenberg. Please take her to her…residence…and bring her and her children to your and Colonel Knorr's farmhouse. They require quarters."

"But, where will we…? Away in the manger?"

Von Treptow nodded, "Only for a day or so, until we arrange something more permanent. Take two men with you, drop them back here on the way out."

Von Treptow led Estelle out to the car, taking her hand as he helped her over the running board. *She carries herself with more elegance than one would suspect from a provincial hausfrau. Is that good or bad?*

"Good evening, Madame. Lieutenant, do try and get some sleep."

Erich drove through deserted streets to the café. He stopped the motorcar in front and Estelle alighted and knocked on the window. The curtain parted slightly as Yvette peeked out, then unlatched the door.

"Quickly now, child. Gather the little ones and all your things." She and her daughter ran up the stairs.

Von Seeckt stood in the open doorway. One of the sentries approached. "Lieutenant, Sir? We were ordered to stand guard here by a major. Any instructions?"

"Yes. You are dismissed by orders of General von Treptow. Return to your unit and so inform your officers. And, Private..."

"Yes, Sir?"

Von Seeckt enjoyed the pleasure in giving orders and seeing them obeyed. "Well done, man, well done."

At that moment a whirlwind of swishing dresses and bedclothes and bundles of clothing enveloped him. He looked down to see a young boy standing straight, saluting. He saluted back with his left. *He is too young to understand.*

He felt a tug on his trousers. Little Sophie raised her arms. *"Up? Up?"* He reached down and picked up the child then took the lad by the hand to the car. A good thing they did not have much more as the car was soon fully laden, even with the two privates moving to the running boards.

Fifteen minutes to the farmhouse, driving more carefully than usual. At the door, the light within silhouetted Zig and Zag like lion sentries before a beehive tomb. Seeing their lieutenant, they did not bark, ambling forward to greet him. Von Seeckt gingerly placed the young ones on the ground and the dogs stopped abruptly. Each side eyed the other warily, neither having seen their kind before.

Sophie broke the ice, toddling forward. Zag gave a small growl and backed up. Zig moved to sniff the little hand, nuzzling it, then sniffing her chest, then a good chin lick. Sophie giggled. Etienne advanced on Zag, who held his ground, then sat, suffering the child to pat his head and tug at his ears.

"New friends!" chimed Yvette.

"Better. New sleeping companions," replied von Seeckt.

By this time, Knorr was standing in the doorway surveying the scene. He looked at Estelle in the flickering of the oil lamp, then Yvette. "From the café, then? Welcome to Versailles. Lieutenant Colonel Walter Knorr at your service. Shall we make some room for you?" He took Estelle aside. "Please keep your daughter close. There are many soldiers here who have not been with their girlfriends for a long while. I should not wish to make matters worse."

"Thank you, Sir. I feel badly for displacing you."

"Quite alright, I assure you. Lieutenant and I have slept on haystacks before, and we have turned out rather well, I should say."

* * *

Friday, January 4, 0700 Hours

Colonel Knorr dressed for his early meeting, straightening his epaulets and collar with their new insignia. Von Seeckt had gone to mess early, bringing back some sausage and bread and a rare bottle of milk which he placed out of reach of the dogs.

Knorr knocked softly on the bedroom door, cracking it open. "No need to get up, Madame, your breakfast is in the cupboard."

Estelle sat up, gathering the blanket around her. "Thank you so much, Colonel." Knorr waved, then looked at the floor where the little ones were on a sleeping bag with one pointer on his back, limbs up and folded, curled next to Sophie, the other letting Etienne use his chest as a pillow. Bliss.

"Off we go, Lieutenant. Can this day get more bizarre?"

"It is early yet, and we have yet to see our general, Sir. No foretelling what is in store, not least his excursion this evening."

Knorr went off to his meeting with Jacobs. Lieutenant von Seeckt leafed through a couple of messages before making coffee. One was from General von Treptow. *Make sure the car is fueled and tires in good condition. Get some bread, sausage and such enough for dinner and breakfast. Provision your guests for another two days. Pistols and carbines.* "A long trip?" he muttered out loud.

"Where?" asked Isabella as she disappeared from the doorway, trailing her fingers across the frame. "With whom?" Her voice faded away, "Is she pretty?"

Erich stuck his head out to see her receding down the corridor, turning slightly with folders held across her chest. He called after her as she vanished around the corner, "I do not know where or who. And who is pretty?" He started after her but was brought up short by the traffic enjoying his blush. Slinking back to his desk, he picked up the telephone to reach the cook's helper to call in some of his gambling loans.

The day dragged on. General von Treptow arrived around 1100 having met briefly with an almost cordial von Kluck to whom he entrusted his monograph. He commandeered Knorr's office, the latter still in his staff consultations.

"Lieutenant, where are the dogs? I shall hazard a guess. Playing with the children?"

"Yes, Sir. Either that or napping with them."

"You are spoiling them, totally. Have you no shame? Please come in that I might brief you on your role tonight and tomorrow."

Lieutenant von Seeckt stepped in smartly and sat opposite the general. "I shall give you both the full background on the drive down, but we are to be impersonating French cavalrymen tomorrow morning. I have arranged suitable mounts from Second Cavalry."

"Shall I bring my blanket and saddle, Sir?"

"Only if they are French issue, Conneau's Corps, to be specific. No, we are to be as authentic as possible. When the colonel returns, we must go to Count von Wittenberg's area – they have several uniforms taken from prisoners and the dead for precisely such an adventure. Your French – academic or colloquial?"

"Probably in between. Shall I practice with you?"

They spoke of other details for a while. Von Treptow decided the lieutenant spoke with a passable Picardy accent. "Where did you serve on the French side of the border? Arras, perhaps Lille, even better?"

"In the field, Second Ypres, Arras, Saint-Quentin, the Somme, of course."

"Arras, it is. What do you remember of it?"

"Aside from devastation? Not much."

"That will have to do. We must get you out of France – you are too unfamiliar, could be tripped up by a question." He tapped his cheek a few times, then, "Very well, you attended boarding school in Switzerland, Saint David's, Lausanne. A discipline problem."

"Sir?"

"Your boarding school, of course. You fabricate the rest."

"Yes, Sir, as you say, Sir."

"I am quite serious, Lieutenant. Should we arouse suspicions, the easiest thing for an inquisitive cavalryman, or worse a *Deuxième,* is to ask an innocent question, '*Do you know so-and-so? He would have been attending there.*' So, how do you answer? If yes, he says no such person – caught! If you say no – you could not have possibly gone there and not known him – caught! No matter that the name is wholly imaginary, you are off guard and vulnerable. How would you answer that question?"

"Let me see, now. What about, '*Was he the one kicked out for fucking the Senegalese chambermaid? He would have been gone pretty quickly, then.*' Or, perhaps, '*Was he a Red or a Black?*' He stared aggressively at von Treptow. "Well, General, was he a Red or Black? Do you actually know this man? If you do not know whether he was a…"

"*Kamerad, kamerad*, Lieutenant, I surrender. Very good, you shall do well at this." A pause. "What are Reds and Blacks?"

"Rugby teams, if it comes to that. Or houses. Or clubs. I do not know, just trying to catch the other off guard, as you advise. Or, maybe…'*He might have been there when I was asked to take a year's leave at my uncle's farm near Arras. The school did not appreciate my defending my sister's honor by beating the shit out of three fellow students. Hospital for two of them. Might he have been one?*'"

"Pray do not get carried away, but that is the general idea. Ah, here comes our colonel. How is the inn?"

"Booked solid, Sir. The Holy Family has taken to the stable."

"Without the animals, I hear."

At that moment, Major Bruckmiller of the Military Police stuck his head in, then remembered to salute. "General, I heard you were here. Welcome back!"

Von Treptow introduced him to his aides. "Ernst, here, is the most accomplished police detective in Berlin, now our connection to the Police. The newspapers were full of his exploits before the war."

"Yes, Gentlemen, now reduced to dreary cases of petty theft and drunkenness." He looked curiously at von Seeckt. "Have we met, young man?"

Von Seeckt squirmed, having missed the general's eye signal. "No, Sir, no, Sir, I assure you. Always on the up and up!"

"General, methinks he doth protest too much. A blanket pardon is hereby granted."

Bruckmiller was the classic big city detective, a frame at once taut and burly with a face and nose that had seen many a fistfight, uncomfortable in any uniform, equally at home with the cream and the dregs of society, but truly at his best on the streets. "Well, Sirs, off to a meeting, my favorite thing. I have no new news, specific, at least, from the Berlin ragtag, except for that steady undercurrent of meetings, posters and the like. The numbers are increasing, and there have been a few small clashes between Socialists and Bolshevists – jockeying for control, most likely."

"Sounds like the calm before the storm, then. Keep me posted wherever I am, if you would, Major."

"Certainly, Sir. Wouldn't mind mixing it up with those scum myself."

"Oh, Major, one small matter, if I may?" Von Treptow reached into his pocket for his little notebook. "In the event of another incident, please add these names to your list. They will be found in the industrial quarter approaching Nimy. And any able-bodied young males, might as well be thorough." He tore out a page and handed it over.

Bruckmiller raised a scarred eyebrow. "As in, make an example of them, Sir?" He made notes in *his* book.

Von Treptow's voice was frosty, "Yes, Major, acting on my authority. Make them the first."

"Yes, Sir!" The policeman saluted, then wheeled and marched out.

Knorr took the initiative, holding up his hand, "No, Sir, we do not wish to know."

"No, you do not. Back to business. Lieutenant, please take care of the provisioning. And ask Madame Vandenberg for the name of her late husband's uncle in Lille. Bruckmiller may be able to help us find him, they cannot stay here forever. Tell her we are off to Kreuznach, back tomorrow late. Among ourselves, I find something unsettling about her, so please be circumspect. We leave at 1800 hours. Now, excuse me, I lunch with the Crown Prince and must come up with a reason for the absence of his hounds." He took his cap off the rack, saluting on the way out.

Erich smirked, "It is still early yet, Colonel."

The rest of the day passed without further surprise or dramatics. Both men managed to take a brief catnap per the general's orders, but then had to hustle to their French cavalry uniform fittings.

"Ah, yes, my traveling companions arrive." Von Treptow introduced his men around to the costumers, as he called them. "Does this make me look more or less gallant? Frantz, I think this," pointing to a bullet hole near his heart, "probably will not do."

And so it went, until the three were a reasonable facsimile of a French cavalry patrol. "See here, now, we need saddles and blankets and harness to make this masquerade complete. And armament. What else have you in your macabre inventory?"

Finally outfitted with a full kit of Ninth Cavalry Division accoutrements, the general oversaw the loading of the staff car, the ersatz costumery hidden in duffels. He had Franz add an extra set to each duffel.

As they began to pull away, Major Bruckmiller hailed them. "That fellow in Lille Lieutenant von Seeckt asked me about?"

Von Treptow was impressed with his efficiency, as always. "Yes?"

"Yes, Sir, an industrialist, middling, still in business. Jew Not exactly friendly, but not exactly uncooperative, either. Leather goods, gloves, cases, some harnesses and saddles. A reliable supplier. No known association with resisters or politics, keeps his nose clean. We have seen no reason to, uh, appropriate any of his property, so no acrimony."

"Excellent." Looking at his aides, "Did I not tell you he is the best? Now, how to broach the subject without tainting her or revealing ourselves? Colonel, your thoughts?"

"Straightforward is best, Sir. I suggest Major Bruckmiller, here, have his counterpart approach Monsieur Uncle, tell him his niece was caught up in an incident and she gave the Police his name. We are attempting to confirm before shipping her and hers to a labor camp. That should do it."

"Fine with me. I will have my man put his hand out at that point. We will split whatever we earn." Bruckmiller looked around. "We must stay in character!"

Von Treptow shook his head. "The chaff with the wheat. Very well, please proceed, Major, and report day after tomorrow. Oh, and would you please have one of your men, a discreet one, please, look after Colonel Knorr's farmhouse tonight and tomorrow. From afar. I do not wish to be the cause of any temptation."

"You intrigue me, General. I may accept that duty myself."

"I suspected as much. Well, we are off, Major. Thank you for your assistance."

"It certainly beats trailing von Seeckt and his knaves." He saluted, waved and was gone.

They drove north toward Mons, then turned onto the main road south, toward France. "We're about eighty kilometers to Vervins, Sir, two hours given the road," said von Seeckt. "Your people will contact us there, or do we go elsewhere?"

"Elsewhere. Below Laon we will meet our cavalry friends, saddle up there and cross over. Then somewhere through the lines."

Knorr asked, "Should we expect a welcoming party?"

"Not certain, we will see what our scouts say. We arrive early for that reason. We will assume our French identities on our side, in case we encounter their scouts right away, then change back somewhere in No Man's Land so we can cross our lines as Germans. Safer that way."

He leaned forward to smile at his 'staff'. "Once across, we take a lei-surely ride toward Braine, east of Soissons. We will be meeting with Charles Maurras, Maurice Barton and a politician named Laval. Maurras is a poet and newspaper man, publishes *Action Français*. Deaf as a post. Barton is an industrialist with holdings everywhere, have known the man for some years. Both are monarchists, supporting the Orléanist pretender, but in the main, they despise the Third Republic. Make no mistake, they are no friends of Germany. They are merely opportunists seeking to take advantage of what they see as the coming calamity of France. If we can assist, so be it. Well, Barton, he wishes to prevent it, credit him that."

He leaned back, searching for a cigarette. "Pierre Laval is the interesting one. Left Socialist, pacifist, he met with our own Socialist friends in Switzerland last year to fantasize over a negotiated peace. A supporter of the Russian Socialists and Bolsheviks, tried to meet them in Stockholm. So, if he has any influence in opposing the war he is a potential asset. Why he is consorting with the other two, rabid Rightists both, is the mystery.

"My sources say he is a greedy bastard despite his lofty Socialist principles, so I have brought along an Epiphany present for him." He jangled his saddlebags. "Call it an honorarium. The meeting place is Barton's hunting lodge in his private forest. A half day of talking. We wish Maurras to support our 'peace' initiative, Barton to continue managing his production, this Laval, I do not know what he wants. They called the meeting, let us see. I do know Maurice felt it a matter of urgency."

Anticipating his aides, "Yes, it could be a trap."

The drive south was uneventful. In the dark, the scorched earth was less noticeable and signs of life – lamps in windows, the lowing of cows and barking of dogs – were everywhere. Like the Somme, this area had not been disputed for some time, and the earth had begun to heal itself as it had since time began. But this was still Belgium, then France, and the three were thankful to be traveling in the dark, not having to acknowledge the glaring eyes of the conquered.

At least the road had been well maintained by the labor battalions. Presently they came to a checkpoint on the approach to Vervins, a crossroads village. A bulky sergeant approached swinging a lantern, rifle slung casually on his shoulder. His men were lounging around an open fire on the roadside beyond, faces flickering as if on a cinema screen. The sergeant leaned into the open car, looking at Lieutenant von Seeckt. "Where are you going, boy? Stealing chickens, are we?"

Before he could reply, a voice came from the rear seat, all quiet steel, "Sergeant, show me your lamp. Do you recognize these?"

Von Treptow pointed to the insignia on his collar, the sergeant jerked upright to attention. "That is better, man. Is this the way you guard a key road?" Pointing at the fire ahead, "Could you possibly give your position away any better than with that signal beacon?"

Out came the notebook. "Name, unit?" The sergeant replied, eyes darting to the scribbling general. "Clean up this slovenly mess you call a squad and make your position secure. I expect to observe your compliance upon our return. Now make yourself useful and get out of our way."

As the car motored along toward Laon, von Treptow lectured his companions at length on slipping discipline and declining preparedness. They hardly noted the burnt out shells of villages, heaps of cobbles and soil at the curbs.

At the Laon checkpoint, a car was waiting. Major Reinhard Zimmer stepped smartly out to greet them, saluting as he came. "Gentlemen, we will drive another twenty-five kilometers southeast down this road, there we have your mounts ready for you." He pointed to the French-held Chemin des Dames ridge looming to the south, then placed slit covers over the headlamps. "Time to be discreet from here on."

The country road was rough, uneven at the edges. The larger shell craters had been roughly filled but had subsided over time, leaving axle jarring dips. It was a slow twenty-five. Finally, the cavalry campsite came into view, but barely. No fire was visible, just the jack-o'-lantern eyes of a few holes in the barrels used as a fireboxes, wisps of hot gas escaping above the rims. The whole encampment was hidden behind a hedgerow and a clump of trees to which the horses were tied.

Major Zimmer stopped, turning his car to the north, away from the border and von Seeckt did likewise. The travelers emerged from the car, stretching and twisting tired muscles. "General, the Aisne is only two hundred meters south. Seventh Army controls this section of front on both sides of the river. We will use our bridges to get you across river and canal just east of the French lines. We do not have any reports on activity there, but we have no assurances. Then you have another twenty-five or so kilometers to Braine."

The Aisne river was the frontline in the Rheims sector. Wide and braided along most of its course, paralleled by a canal, its bridges had not been blown in the great advances and retreats of August, 1914. Nivelles' failed offensive against the Chemin des Dames in 1917 still left a stretch south and west of the river from Berry-au-Bac in French hands. Von Treptow and crew would need to pass below the river in that area, between the smaller Vesle river and the Aisne. Barton's hunting preserve was in that wedge with frontage on the Aisne, under French control.

At least they could stay dry.

They changed into their French cavalry uniforms, gathered their gear and saddled up, their mounts all blacks. Major Zimmer said, "We will accompany you across the river here, then west to our trench lines. You have chosen your insertion well, General, Sir – this sector is the least entrenched and fortified along the entire Western Front, and the breathing space between us and the French is more than a kilometer. There is a wood, mostly intact, half a kilometer from the line that could serve to insinuate you, if you can get there unseen, into the open country beyond as if you belonged there. Your best cover is to be heading back to Soissons from furlough. You have papers?"

"Yes, our printing presses are excellent – Gutenberg himself would be pleased. I am just thinking, though, where to hide our change of clothes. If we cannot find our way back here through the lines, we may find trouble instead. Well, we shall carry them tied up as if a bundle of leave clothes." Von Treptow was pensive. "How hard would it be to ford the Aisne?"

"Difficult for a skilled rider, at best, Sir. This is not *dressage* territory, General. Your horses would have to swim. Remember, both sides of the river are French where you are bound. That might not be the worst of it. Getting through two armies may be."

Colonel Knorr noted von Treptow's silence as they rode on. In his brief acquaintance, he had not seen him at a loss for words. "Major, how long to daylight once you leave us?"

"Comfortably several hours, Sir. We can get you in sight unseen as far as we can go. The French are also not terribly diligent in their watches, either, as we surprise them regularly. Again, it is the getting out will be the issue."

Von Treptow finalized matters, "We have an appointment to keep. That much is certain."

They approached and crossed a pair of narrow bridges, acknowledged by the guards, then turned right toward the lines. The night was dark, the waning moon's sliver not yielding enough illumination to betray them to watchers. Then on at a comfortable pace until they reached a series of blockhouses and dugouts, with a field full of artillery and limbers. A horse or two, smelling the new arrivals, neighed from a corral. "Third line, Sir. Footing gets a little tricky from here. Best let me get a pilot to guide us." Zimmer dismounted and entered the largest of the blockhouses, coming back with a corporal, this one's eyes and face bearing marks of gas attack.

The rest of the patrol dismounted and proceeded quietly and carefully afoot, following the corporal who knew every path, every shellhole, each dugout and trench. Soon they came to the front line, mostly observation posts and several rows of barbed wire. The corporal jumped down a ladder into a trench and quickly came back with a lieutenant and several privates. Major Zimmer conferred briefly with the lieutenant. "He suggests we go several hundred meters north where his wire is more mobile; it is also more nearly line of sight with the wood I mentioned versus the nearest French posts."

At the designated point, the party greeted the duty staff in their dugout. When von Treptow was announced, the dozen scruffy trogdolytes jerked to near attention, shocked to see such a high rank at the front line, much less in French dress. "At ease, soldiers," said the general. "We are merely off for a moonlightless ride. How is life here?"

The highest rank was a sergeant. "It's not too luxurious, sir, but it's home."

"When was your last relief? How are your rations?" General von Treptow peppered the men with questions, avoiding direct mention of morale, but listening carefully. "How competent are your officers?"

A three man patrol came in from No Man's Land, dumping arms and kit on benches in the dugout. Their commander, a captain, stared in shock at the three French cavalrymen conversing easily with his men. "What gives here? Where did we find these prisoners or are they more deserters?"

The major explained the situation sparingly. Captain Lockemiller nodded, "Well, then, General von Treptow, Sir, let me offer you a little guidance. Willy, the map." A private brought a large map over to the table, unfurling it as he came. "We are here," pointing to a smallish salient in the line. "Here is the wood opposite, and as of just now the French posts are yonder, no Frenchies in the wood itself tonight," pointing five hundred meters beyond the wood's edge. "The French move their scouts nightly rather than man each post, maybe short of men, I cannot tell. Here and here" – pointing – "they have sentries. Here, not. Your best bet is to move to the northeast edge of the wood opposite that point, then ride down this little wooded swale until you reach this road, here. No trenches directly behind the wood, seems they appreciate our artillery's range. Then you will belong in France. Then the trenchlines start. I suggest you keep going on this back road, just fields either side, bends to the south then on to the Soissons road, here. Fewer eyes, yes?" He pointed at a spot on von Treptow's little map. "Next checkpoint is a kilometer up, so said the last aeroplane observation. Then straight on, road to your appointment angles right a few kilometers or so before you reach Braine. When do you return?"

"Tomorrow afternoon, probably around dusk," replied von Treptow. "Same route?"

"If you can. You will be able to spot the sentry posts as you go. Tell them you are going on to Berry-au-Bac. When, if, you get back to this swale, you should be pretty well shielded from prying eyes until it flattens out up above. You will then be but a hundred meters or so from the trees. Come back the same way, but please change into our gear in the wood. Do you have a torch? Good. Flash SDL, my initials, wait for a response. Then be prepared to ride like hell. We will have the doors open for you."

Knorr spoke, "And if we cannot get back this way?"

"God be merciful upon you then. It gets more difficult the more you have to travel south into French territory, and you have the river to your north."

Knorr heaved a sigh, "General, we better go, then. We should need to reach that road before first light."

"Major, Captain, thank you for your assistance. And you, too, Corporal...?"

"Hitler, Sir. Adolf Hitler."

* * *

Saturday, January 5, 0430 Hours
Below Berry-au-Bac

The crew opened a narrow path in the wire and the three mounted men moved through slowly. Free of the last wire, then a curving approach at an ambling pace to the wood's edge. Von Seeckt dismounted to reconnoiter. "There is a game trail going the right way, it seems, over here. Let us try that."

Mounting up, he led the group, carbine across his lap. Picking their way in the dark, it took an hour or so, but they could see the wood thinning in front of them. He dismounted again to scan the wood's edge. "We are a half kilometer short of that ravine, Sirs, not as straight as I thought."

They turned north and in twenty minutes were descending into the shallow, twisting rocky swale, partly shielded by mixed scrub and wood. They crossed over the road to Berry-au-Bac without detection, waking a crew at a machinegun post, then onto the quiet country lane, pacing themselves as they trotted, then cantered, stopping to listen from time to time, reaching the main road with time to spare before dawn. "Might as well get going, Sir," said Knorr, "but perhaps we should go the other way a bit and light a fire. Anyone who comes along, we have been bunking by the roadside and are just making our coffee. Then we can be seen as coming from further down the lines. More credible?"

Von Treptow looked up and down the road. "Yes, but be discreet. Keep the fire low, or in the gutter, even better."

The three tied their mounts in a stand of trees ten meters off the road, then made their bivouac amid piles of road spoil, nicely shielded from long views.

The lieutenant nodded off, capable of sleeping on a bed of nails. As dawn broke over the German lines now far behind them, he started awake, then put his coffee-making gear to work. In a few minutes the three were having coffee along with cold sausage and bread. They finished their breakfasts quickly and broke camp. As von Seeckt retrieved their horses, a platoon-sized infantry unit could just be seen coming from the east, first by their dust, then by their Lebel rifles spiking into the air, then the mass of dusty blue uniforms, silhouetted grey in the early light.

Three imposters stood by the side of the road, holding their mounts' reins. Von Treptow hailed the sergeant leading the unit, "Do you know the location of C Company, Fourth Normandy? We thought they were bivouacked back there at Cormicy, but they have moved on, apparently."

"No Sir, Major, Sir," replied the sergeant, eyeing von Treptow carefully. "Not familiar with that unit, least not in this area. Where're you coming from?"

"Rheims originally, then up the line to Berry-au-Bac, now on to Soissons. Couriers with orders and messages. Well, we shall find out where they are when we get there, do not wish to double back. Where are you bound?"

"Soissons, also, for reassignment."

"Well, may see you there. Any messages?"

One of his privates, securely anonymous in the middle rank, shouted, "Tell Clemenceau we're ready to go home!"

"Shut your mouth, *poilu*! Sorry, Sir, we're a bit worn down, it seems."

"So is everyone, everywhere I go." Von Treptow approached the sergeant and murmured conspiratorially, "Sergeant...?"

"Breaux, Sir."

"Is it so bad with yours? I thought matters were improving at the front. As we go back and forth, I do not see so much improvement."

The sergeant walked to the other side of the road to get out of earshot. "Food, leave, yes, better. But the boys are reluctant to fight. My company's lost a tenth to desertion I'll guess. But let *les Boches* get near us and they'd have a big fight on their hands!" He gestured vigorously, smacking his fist into his palm, his bottlebrush of a moustache shaking, then wilted a bit, "So long as we don't have to go over the top again. But, Sir, the big anger is at the shirkers and the politicians and the profiteers comfortable in Paris or Nice or elsewhere, drinking champagne and chasing girls – their sisters, probably," jerking his thumb over his shoulders at his bedraggled little column. "Can't forget the officers, either, no offense, Sir, but that's no longer so bad since the troubles."

"Sergeant, I know how your men feel. At this Christmastide past I visited my sister and her family in Paris. We are strolling the Avenue Montaigne and see that traitor, Caillaux, at a café, chomping on oysters and guzzling champagne. How is it a rat such as that has not been crushed?"

"The Big Boys always come out allright, it's us common folk that end up with the shit duty. That bastard Barton, got himself a fancy place somewhere around here, he's one of 'em. My brother, foot shot off at Verdun, goes to work at his ballbearing factory in Tours. Gets hurt in one of the machines. Tossed out on the pavement like trash. No help, no nothing. Unions bought off. Wife and three children, while Barton and his friends gouge the rest of us. Someone will pay when this is all over."

"If it *were* all over...Sergeant Breaux, if the *Boche* said, '*We have had enough fun, we are going home*', would you chase them? Would your men? What I mean is, if we could make it all go away, would you still fight? I am not sure I could, anymore."

"I can tell you these boys wouldn't. They'd be off to home and girls before the ink dried or the last Hun pissed on Belgium on his way back. Me, I'm career. Don't have no place to go but the Army. But Saint Joan herself would have a tough time persuading me to fix a bayonet ever again, I tells you true."

"Well said, Sergeant. We could only wish our superiors were so wise. Now then, good fortune to you and your men – perhaps Saint Joan feels the same way. We have messages to deliver, so we shall be off." Von Treptow turned to walk back to his stallion, frisky in the early morning chill but held tightly by von Seeckt. The sergeant followed. "Thank you for listening, Sir. Ain't many officers that'll do that. Are you hurt, Sir?" noticing the major's stiff gait.

"Shot near Maubeuge on a sweep, in '14. Bullet went through my leg, second bullet kills my horse, down I go. My comrade to my right takes one through the skull, he and his horse go down atop me. A year in hospital and recuperation. Now all I am suited for is the Pony Express. Such is life in war, Sergeant."

"The Good Lord is mysterious, they says. Let me help you up." He gave von Treptow's right leg a boost over the big horse's back. As he did, von Treptow realized with horror he had somehow left his black Uhlan boots on, and in the dark no one had noticed. He saw the sergeant inspecting his left boot and spur.

"These is German boots, Major."

Von Treptow tried to recover, "Yes, my man, I took them off a Uhlan after I ran him through with my saber at Soignies. They are much more comfortable than my old ones, and I think they are quite the trophy. They remind me of the old days when I was still useful."

"Well, they is nice looking, Sir, I gives you that. Off with you, then, and we'll catch up in Soissons."

The three gave suitably cavalier salutes to the platoon, and headed west at an easy trot, trying to put some distance between them and an inquisitive sergeant. "That was incredibly stupid on my part. All this costuming and I put a German General Officer nameplate on. Damn! I have placed us in danger. Well, we shall see – if we can get out of it, that is."

As Captain Lockemiller promised, the first checkpoint was not far down the road. They produced their identification and Colonel Knorr pulled some official-looking papers out of his saddle bag as evidence of their role. Without any ado they were waved on. Twenty kilometers on, having passed only a few formations without challenge, they came to the cutoff angling off to the right between hedgerows and briars, once an old cartpath that had been ground down and sunken over the years. Their heads barely reached the top of the hedges, and their trailing dust easily topped those.

"Nice place for an ambush," said von Seeckt, uncomfortably.

Von Treptow spit into his right hand, then leaned over to daub the ankles of his boot and his spurs with spittle, repeated it twice, then did the same to his left. He dropped back to the end of the little column, hoping the dust would stick to his boots, covering the distinctive insignia. "Perhaps that will offer these a touch of camouflage."

Another two kilometers on, von Treptow recognized a roadside shrine then an abandoned mill or workshop at a crossroads. "Getting close, now, these are the landmarks I was told to watch for."

Two more kilometers and they entered a gentle bend to their left, the right side of the road displayed before them, changing dramatically from unkempt hedgerows and scrub to manicured privets behind a stone and wrought iron palisade. A massive stone corner marker was inscribed *'La Tristesse'*; the same motto was repeated on either side of the twin pillars marking the entrance to Barton's estate.

Two armed men, not soldiers or at least not dressed as such, stopped them at the entry. Von Treptow waved the telegram he received yesterday and the men admitted them without further question. The horses clip-clopped down a seemingly endless drive bounded by an *allée* of teardrop-shaped dark green, almost black poplars backed by gravel sidewalks either side bounded in turn by a row of towering plane trees at ten meter spacings, now bare of leaves. The entire effect was that of a theater backdrop painted with a dramatically forced perspective, the mottled trunks and branches of the tall planes receding out of view almost mechanically, as if on a conveyor. Majestic, yet spooky.

At the far end of the drive was a cream-colored building slowly coming into view, still nearly a kilometer off. "Nice little place your friend has here. Good to see the war has not affected it," said Knorr.

"It was off the direct path of our 1914 advance as there are no bridges within several kilometers either side, and he has built himself a significant detour, to boot." Von Treptow looked around as their mounts' hooves clicked and clacked on the cobbles. "We concentrated our attacks on the left and right, Soissons and Rheims, shelling the cathedral there in front of the newsreel cameras. Priests were armed with holy water, I suppose."

"We have a welcoming committee, Sir." Von Seeckt handed over the field glasses, "Look friendly enough."

"Yes, Barton, Maurras and two others I do not recognize from here. Well, well, the gang is all here and ready to parley."

Finally they reached the building, a foursquare bulk of cut stone atop a rusticated base. The wings were medieval, Norman brick and faschwerk topped with slate roofs. *A true folly*, mused Dietrich.

Knorr checked his watch: not quite 1000.

Their host was standing above them on the portico of the first floor. Two grooms came to take their horses to the stable marked by a rampant stallion weathervane above a thatched roof a quarter kilometer away. The Germans began to shake the dust off their uniforms only to have a valet and two chambermaids come at them with mean-looking whisks, brushing them down like overheated horses, wiping the caked dust off their boots with once-spotless cloths.

Von Treptow paused at the base of the stair and hailed Barton, "Do we gain admittance?" Barton gave a weak smile and waved them up. At the top of the stairs, Maurice introduced his guests before entering the double doors. "Maurras, you have met, General. This is Pierre Laval, Member of Parliament. And this gentleman is Jean-Louis Malvy, lately Minister of the Interior."

"On personal recognizance, I take it?" Malvy had been accused the past August of treason for supporting a defeatist newspaper. Von Treptow's voice was as cold as Knorr had yet heard, colder even than with Bruckmiller. He trafficked with traitors such as these and supported the same publication as part of his operations. That did not mean he enjoyed their company or admired their character, and he was not shy about letting them know.

Barton intervened as Malvy stepped forward to confront the much taller German. "Come, come, Gentlemen, I realize this is not a club meeting nor our class reunion, but let us not murder one another, at least not at the outset." Barton released the general's sleeve, noting the dust on his fingers, and turned to his butler, "Perhaps we shall take our luncheon on the terrace, Gerard."

The group strolled through the salon, decorated in fine tapestries, rugs and surprisingly, some Art Nouveau furniture among the more traditional pieces. Von Treptow stopped to admire a particularly fine secretary. "This is a beautiful piece, Maurice. Is it from Majorelle's atelier?"

"No, Dietrich, actually one of Guimard's finest works. I commissioned it especially for this spot. You have a good eye, Sir. I have some of Majorelle's in the library which I would quite proudly show you after luncheon."

Malvy muttered, "Now we are in a furniture showroom with two sales-clerks. *Bon.*" Neither principal paid him any attention.

"Here we are, Gentlemen," gesturing through the open doors. "Thank you, Gerard." The terrace had a sweeping view of the Aisne valley. Straight ahead, the view was picturesque, mostly heavy wood, evergreen pines and hemlock spotted among bare deciduous skeletons. Several clearings could be seen, some with farmhouses and outbuildings. Von Treptow strode to the balustrade, ridding himself of the mouse Malvy. Looking first far to the left, then to the right, he could see the scars of war in the distance. Oaks and chestnuts and sycamores, once tall and spreading, were now stunted palm-shaped sculptures; large areas were totally treeless, and even at this distance, tumbled and pocked, a bad case of acne on Mother Earth's face.

"Yes, General, the war passed us over. Must have been the lamb's blood over the doors. Gerard, here, and the staff saw the whole thing, from your sweep to the retreat. No one either side wanted to be pinned against the Aisne at this point between bridges, so we escaped. A little shelling was all. Most fortunate."

"Fortunate to have had General Joffre's orders protecting you."

Barton started at this comment, backing up, nearly stumbling. "How, what...? Are you accusing me?"

"No, no, of course not. Merely a small fact that just popped into mind. No offense meant." Von Treptow bowed, clicking his heels.

"None taken," said Barton, clearing his throat. "Ah yes, now, let us eat. I am sure you are hungry from your ride."

The round table had been set at the edge of the terrace receiving the most sun at that hour, just enough to dispel the winter dreariness. The seven were seated around the table, the Germans in an arc clockwise starting at 0600, lieutenant-colonel-general, with the four Frenchmen completing the circle with Barton at the top, keeping von Treptow at bay from Malvy, then Laval, then Maurras at the 0400, able to read lips across the table. The seating arrangements suited von Seeckt, exempting him from conversation.

Likewise, Knorr was at ease. He surveyed the hosts: Barton, robust, auburn haired, clean shaven and well-dressed; Malvy, small, with fine eyebrow arches, heavy lids and a downward crescent of a moustache – tinted?; Laval, faintly oriental in visage, well-dressed for a socialist; finally, Maurras, the oldest, with a greying vandyke, in tweeds, the intellectual of the lot, one would be led to believe. Von Treptow and Barton were in cordial animated conversation about art or something, to the total exclusion of the others, then he heard, "Breaux...a sergeant...his brother...Tours factory...hire..."

Malvy interrupted, "We did not come to discuss your affairs of commerce, Monsieur Barton."

"Yes, yes, of course, but let us at least enjoy our soup in peace. General, Sirs," as the soup was being ladled, "please enjoy this wine from my Graves vineyards. I shall not be insulted if you limit your intake, but I would be most offended if you do not take at least a sip."

"You first, Monsieur," laughed Knorr. Wine was his mother's milk, and he 'sipped' at every opportunity.

"Poison? Let me show you!" Barton took a generous draught from his glass. "Poison?" he laughed genially. Knorr followed suit, but more reserved. "An excellent dry white, Monsieur. Delightful. Even to one baptized with Rheinwein."

"General, he is a good one. May I have him?"

"He is but a few days in my employ. You may see him yet."

They finished soup with small talk, Von Treptow, Knorr and Barton, with Laval and the others in silence, sullen or grateful. A fish was served, then the main course, boar and venison from Barton's forests.

Naturally, Barton had a wine for every course. "This one, Colonel," bypassing von Treptow, "is from my Pauillac vines, now twenty years grafted. The oldtimers say the old vines made better wines. I cannot tell the difference."

"Heady bouquet, yet balanced body. Very fine, indeed. Thank you, Sir." Knorr generously complimented a pleased Barton.

Who, in turn, now conscious of his countrymen once again, cleared his throat. "General, I asked you here in view of the, er, changes that have occurred since our meeting last spring. The military situation has not evolved to our advantage as we had hoped. Our manpower situation at the front and at home has become perilous. I am even scrounging for cripples like your sergeant's brother. Politically, we are now in the hands of the firebrand Clemenceau…"

"The warmonger!" shouted Malvy, abruptly.

Laval interrupted, suppressing Malvy's hand and its wagging finger, "You can understand his animus?"

Von Treptow started in cooly, staring at Malvy, "Of course. And you," glancing at Laval, "can understand mine. Fifty thousand goldmarks to support *Le Bonnet Rouge*, ten of which to support him," a thumb at Malvy. "His protégés, editor Almereyda and director Duval, get caught red-handed with our money, the fool Almereyda with our bank cheque in his pocket! Fifty thousand for a few meek editorials? Animus?"

Waving off Malvy's protests, he continued, "Maurice, I presume this is why you have brought Monsieur Maurras here under such urgency?" He looked straight at Maurras, speaking slowly.

Barton nodded. "Just so, General. This newspaper business is most unfortunate." Von Treptow glared at him. "Yet, in view of circumstances, perhaps there is an opportunity to…cement…a more substantial relationship?"

"Certainly, Maurice, were Charles to undertake a robust program aimed at undermining the Third Republic and dissipating the public will to continue this mad war. Not just in his pages and poems, but in the streets? Energize the *Camelots du Roi*, the *Croix de Feu*? Turn them out into the streets? More to the point, infiltrate and influence the ministries? Monsieur, do not the leading Army officers still receive your newspaper each day, *gratis*, even in their trenches?"

"You are bold, General, especially for one so deep in *la France*." Maurras spoke with the remembered diction of one who had lost his hearing thirty years before. "That is a long list of desires. Here, your arrogance is for nought. Your *Boche* artillery and gas and infantry mean nothing here," tapping his finger on the table, "so perhaps you should consider your place?"

"My place? My place is at a table of traitors to their own country, their own government, their own people. I come here as a patriot, seeking a conclusion to a tragic conflict, for my people's benefit, to be sure, but also on terms advantageous to all those in front of me. Your insults mean nothing to me, Maurras. You are an ant, a worm, in a universe beyond your feeble understanding."

He paused to scan the red faces of his adversaries, save for Barton, who seemed curiously unaffected, even amused. "But, such talk achieves little, does it not, Gentlemen?" Von Treptow took out his cigarette case, offering it to Malvy, Laval and Maurras, each accepting to his satisfaction. Barton slid carlotas to von Treptow's aides, then lit his into a bonfire and smoke screen.

Von Treptow leaned back in his chair, arms crossed, cigarette aloft between two fingers. "Yes, Gentlemen, we hate, despise, and wish the other a slow and painful death." He took a long drag at his cigarette, then exhaled, blowing the smoke upward at an angle through pursed lips. "So, we are perfect partners, yes?"

Maurras took the lead, "I admire your cockiness, even as I question your self-assurance. Very well, what have you in mind?"

"Yes, Herr General," hissed Malvy. "What have you to offer us, and France?"

"You, Sir, we offer a comfortable exile, safe from extradition. Preferable to the guillotine, I should think. Your goose is cooked. My sources say you and Duval are bound for perdition, like the unfortunate Almereyda. The only question is whether you have the balls to honorably do yourself as did he, or will you be led mewling to your fate?"

Having discarded Malvy, he turned his attention to Maurras. "Monsieur Maurras, I outlined our 'desires', as you so casually term them. You presumably require finance to satisfy those desires. So be it. You shall have ample resources, but please be more discreet than your predecessors. But, let us talk of philosophy, even if I disadvantage myself in your august presence. You have an unmistakable vision for a new France, the *pays réel*, or a return to the old France, I should say."

He twirled his cigarette hand, "What stands in your way? The Third Republic, its very existence, for a start. The Radicals and Socialists, for another," turning away to look straight at Laval. "Not the Army, it would rally to your side, particularly if you brought Pétain into your fold. Which you already have, I understand."

Maurras started at that. Von Treptow continued, slapping his forehead theatrically, "Of course, I forget one other trifle. The Tiger. How will you deal with Clemenceau?"

"You and they will leave that to me." This was Laval speaking, waving his hand dismissively. "I gain his confidence daily and were it not for the fossils at the head of the Socialist Party, I should now be a leading influence in the Government. Soon enough I will shed those ties and assume my right-ful place in power."

"And use your influence and power to do what, exactly?"

"I shall begin by ratifying the common soldier's wisdom. Enough of the doctrine of the offensive. *Offensive á outrance? Élan? Le Cran*? What have these notions brought us but disaster, tragedy? No, we will consolidate our defenses, fortify our lines. Would you dare cross the *poilu*, General? Would you?"

"It seems we have several times, and have yet the forces to do it again. And again. That is not the question, Sir. Will they fight, after last summer? Shall I recite the names of the fifty-five?"

The Frenchmen looked at each other uneasily except for Laval who thundered, "Martyrs, not mutineers! Socialist brothers who dared challenge the corrupt bourgeoisie officer class. When the workers of France link arms with the workers of Germany and Russia, your whole rotten, tottering struc-ture of empire will come crashing down around you. Mark my words."

"Lovely sentiments, Sir. Please, tell me how is it you are associated with these two creatures of the Right? Barton is the very exemplar of the oppres-sor class, and Maurras," von Treptow waved across the table, "well, Maurras is the hyper-reactionary. Surely the only thing you could possibly share with these is a blood type. Truly, I am puzzled."

Laval smirked, "Despite being so obvious, that is a perceptive ques-tion, General. I am sure they asked themselves that very same question when I inquired into attending this event. You, yourself, provided the overarching answer – our mutual abhorrence of the Republic itself. What replaces it is yet to be seen, yet to be determined in the arena of ideas and power. Yet, clearly, it must go. When this war ends we will doubtlessly be at each other's throats, but the war must end to allow that entertaining spectacle. The war must end, honorably and victoriously, but the war must end!" He turned to the head of the table. "Monsieur Barton's enterprises

– I will not call him a war profiteer, yet – will be affected, dramatically. Monsieur Maurras' dreams of restoration and Boulangism will prove illusory, I am confident, but he breathes the fire of a glorious new France, which I share. Regardless, I am quite certain they will adapt to the new order, General."

"A new order led by yourself, of course. Now it becomes clear. And with ample leeway for your accomplices, here. Or do they simply sell you the rope, literally and figuratively, with which you will hang them? Charles, I understand your eagerness to…engage…Monsieur Laval's ambitions, with vigor and violence, most likely. And the Army, your pet. Maurice, you, I confess, I do not understand. This man would mean your end, would he not?"

"He and I have discussed certain, ah, accommodations, shall we say? In the new order of which he speaks, private enterprises such as mine will be supported by and harnessed to a more ordered, more scientific management of the economy. Excessive competition will be eliminated and labor relations will be…managed…jointly by industry and government. Favored interests will do well, less favored, not so well." He showed von Treptow a mischievous grin. "It is the way of the future, Dietrich. Just look at Germany's war economy, and envision something similar in peacetime."

"Must I? You might as well commence to melting down those statues of *Marianne* dotting your *départements* and *arrondissements*."

Maurras spat, "Marianne? The Whore of France? She shan't be missed, I assure you."

"General," Laval, again, "look to your own parliament. Mostly Socialists of one stripe or another. And my comrades of the new left are breathing new life into your politics. You are looking at the future in your own land, can you not see that? Perhaps a little too much *Liberté*"– Maurras harrumphed his assent – "but we can manage that, as well."

Von Treptow turned to his aides. "Gentlemen, you are present at the foundation of *La Nouvelle France*, the birth of crony socialism. Remember this to tell your grandchildren!" He toyed with the idea of grilling Laval on the role of the 'new left', the Bolsheviks with whom he so sympathized. To do so would give away too much, better to present him with a *fait accompli*, too late to affect events, both East and West.

"My, my. Look at the time! We must dash!"

The seven rose from the table with varying degrees of vigor. Von Treptow thanked Barton lavishly for his hospitality and even took Malvy aside with a friendly handshake and arm around the latter's shoulder. "Mistakes were made, such things happen. I could recommend a very good attorney, the expense not an issue."

Laval interrupted, "I represent the minister, General. Please do not insinuate yourself into this matter with your slimy tactics any further."

General von Treptow released Malvy's hand and withdrew his arm, looking intently at his palms for the least bit of oleaginous residue. "Very well, Sir. He is all yours. *Bon chance.*" At that moment he began plotting a *revanche* toward both men. He turned to Maurras and said, "Maurice here handles our financial matters out of his Swiss offices. He will keep you informed. Maurice, you will continue our arrangements on munitions and materiel?"

Barton looked nervously at von Treptow, "Which arrangements are those?"

Maurras interceded, "Those that are well known in certain circles. Say nothing further," looking sideways at the two Socialists.

Barton's face flared, but only briefly as he came to realize the opening von Treptow had made in his relations with Laval.

Barton and von Treptow detoured to spend a few minutes in the study, admiring the former's taste in Art Nouveau furniture and exchanging confidences while the remainder were left together in the gallery outside in awkward silence. Presently they were rejoined by their host and guest of honor, and the assembled group strolled toward the front entry.

"Here come the grooms with your steeds, Gentlemen. It is a beautiful day for a ride." The Germans descended the stair followed by their French hosts. Von Treptow reached into his saddlebag to fetch an old leather binding secured with a clasp. "Monsieur Laval, when Barton, here, mentioned your name, I looked into a suitable gift of introduction. I understand you are fond of Baudelaire, and we found this edition of *Les Fleurs du Mal*. Please do not ask where. I trust you will enjoy it." He extended it to Laval, making sure the other could feel the tome's unexpected weight before he released it. Laval shot him a glance full of shock, then relaxed and tucked the volume under his arm. "Yes, yes, I am sure I will. Such a thoughtful gesture. Thank you."

With that, the three mounted up. "We shall meet again, but none can predict the circumstances. Maurice, thank you. And wait a week with that Breaux business, if you please." Waving, they turned and began their trot down the long entrance drive.

"Such a strange man," opined Maurras. "So contradictory. A military man offering peace, despite his dominant position. And the risk at coming here."

"Not so strange, really, if you would allow yourself to look at him through the lens of historical dialectical materialism," Laval countered. "He is thoroughly a creature of his class. He can no more escape his nature than can we escape the dawn. His world is doomed, to be succeeded by World Socialism, and he knows it – he is doing his best to stave off the inevitable, a Horatius at the bridge, fated to be overcome by the sweep of history!"

"You really do believe such Marxist nonsense, do you not? Maurice, tell me again why you brought us together?"

1300 Hours
Soissons, France

Sergeant Breaux and his weary platoon dragged into Soissons. Finding a tent full of officers, he announced himself and saluted. The officers were indifferent to his presence, turning back to their maps and wireless telegraph. *Rich shit officers*, he thought, *care not a whit for the common soldier.*

"Excuse me, Sir," stepping in front of a lieutenant, "we are from D Company, 28th Orléans. We are to be reassigned, but were ordered only to show up in Soissons, no address."

"What unit? Never mind, your best bet is Brigade command at the Hôtel du Ville, four blocks down." He eyed the dusty sergeant and even dustier rabble outside, lounging and smoking. "Where have you marched from?"

"Courcy a while, then back at Hermonville and Cormicy, Sir. Before that, Épernay."

"I see. Skirted the German lines?" Breaux nodded. "See anything interesting over there?"

"No Sir, all quiet. We did run into a peculiar major, with two others. Cavalry, don't remember the unit."

"Peculiar?" asked the lieutenant. Across the small tent, another pair of ears perked up.

"Yes, Sir, the major was wearing German boots. Said he pulled them off a dead Hun at Soignies, I think, or Maubeuge. Liked them better than our own, he said. And he spoke posh."

"Posh? Like Paris society, you mean?" This was Colonel Theroux coming over from his eavesdropping. "High and mighty sounding, like that?"

"Not so much that, Sir, just that he spoke perfect. Before the war, I worked me some as an usher at the Opéra, so I seen and heard that type. No, Sir, not the ones that looked down their noses at the common person, but like a professor, or a poet, maybe. Posh, like."

"Where was this posh major going, did he tell you?" Theroux was not sure why he pursued this, just something instinctive, coming naturally to an officer of the *Deuxième Bureau.*

"Here, Sir. He and his were couriers, coming from Berry-au-Bac, before that, Rheims, I think that's what he said. They were cleaner than us, though – it's dryer and dustier here than further back in Champagne country, but they were cleaner. They had stopped the night before on the roadside, maybe they cleaned up."

"Or they did not come from Rheims, after all," mused Theroux. *He would not be wearing German boots in France, though. No one as obviously intelligent, at least educated, would make that mistake. It is the 'posh' business. Cavalry are elites, after all, and more likely to speak an educated French, so, perhaps, it is nothing. Then again...*

"Sir? Sir?" It was the sergeant. "Will you be needing me anymore? We need to find our new assignment."

"No, and thank you, Sergeant, for your alertness. This could be important. Lieutenant, please run over to HQ and see what you can find out about couriers in from Rheims today. I will be at the stables. We may need to rustle up a posse." *Zane Grey would be proud*, he thought.

"Colonel, Sir?" It was the sergeant, doubling back. "I didn't want to talk about this in front of the rest, 'specially my men. He asked me about morale, and whether my boys would fight and such. Like he was my new best friend. Just seemed…peculiar for an officer. Please don't take this for no mutiny, Sir." The sergeant was distinctly uncomfortable with his confession, and would have been more so if he knew the colonel was in Military Intelligence.

"Not at all, Sergeant Breaux, is it? You have performed patriotically. This is very valuable information. Oh, one more thing – what color were their horses?"

"Black, Sir, beauties, Sir, gorgeous things."

Theroux turned to his aides. "Let us go, men. We need to saddle up."

Before they reached the gateposts, Von Treptow had von Seeckt pull out his French boots, donning them and returning his Uhlan pair to his kit. "No sense in compounding my error, unless we see the same sergeant. Time to change our identities and ranks as well, men."

They waved to the guards at the gate and started off to the east in a canter. Knorr checked his watch – *1300, plus four easy hours to that roadside spot. Just about right.*

"Are we on schedule, Colonel?"

"So it appears, if we are not interrupted."

"So, Gentlemen, what think you of that little *soirée?*"

Lieutenant von Seeckt led, "Strangest group of unlikely bedfellows. I will take wagers on how soon they rat out each other. That Laval is especially…I cannot finger the word …"

"Untrustworthy? Disreputable? Overly ambitious? And, let us not forget arrogant. He is a lawyer, after all, but that hardly begins to describe the political animal."

"But why would Barton bring them together, in front of us?" Colonel Knorr was wondering the same thing as von Seeckt. "Why not separate *tête-à-têtes?* First Left, then Right?"

"Barton plays the rich scion of an industrial empire. His grandfather started with metalworking – in partnership with old Krupp, actually – then his father built and expanded the business. Maurice, though, is the brains and the energy, now, has increased their total output tenfold through building and acquiring. But he acts the playboy dilettante in public, ensures he is seen with the most beautiful women in the most fashionable spots. All to deflect attention, to depict him as a lightweight."

Knorr nodded, "Which he most assuredly is not. But, what is this arrangement he bristled at?"

"Very simple. We pay him, franc for franc, for 'lost' production. He is operating about seventy-five percent of capacity in his key works, such as ball bearings and large forgings. Sufficient for the defense of France, so says he, but not for attack. His calculations, not ours. He publicly blames labour unrest and material shortages, harassing the Clemenceau government constantly. In fact, he shrewdly manages his spider web of inputs, shielded by his reputation as the carefree hedonist."

"And we pay him to deprive his own soldiers?" Von Seeckt was having a hard time digesting that possibility. "Knowing they may run short of bullets or tanks or aeroplanes at a most inconvenient moment?"

"Indeed, but back to the first question. Barton was enjoying the left-right armwrestling, if you noticed. An excellent observation, Colonel. And, Lieutenant, he is hedging his wagers. He is already linked with the Right, Maurras and that crowd, by class and social circles. But, if they do not win out, he needs an alternative.

"Laval is a very shrewd choice, as I reflect. Sufficiently prominent in Socialist circles, but not yet a leader. That chafes him, clearly. His ambitions are being stymied by the existing structure and I am now certain he would have no qualms about discarding the fossils athwart his rise. Plus, he is greedy, today proved that. The book of poetry, hollowed out, held ten thousand francs in gold coin. He realized from the heft it was not mere light verse, yet made no protest.

"Maurice is no fool, however, and will never commit unless he absolutely has to, so I pushed him over the cliff. Now Laval has suspicions, thinks he has something on Maurice which he never will be able to prove. Maurice's staff only saw French cavalrymen today – no witnesses, credible that is. Malvy is degraded. If, then, Laval were to make a public accusation, Maurice would destroy him with his resources and connections. Or, Laval now sees a fellow traveler in the Peace front, to be sure with very divergent methods and goals. And wealthy beyond counting. So, he has two choices: attack or cozy up."

"Heads, Maurice wins, tails, Maurice wins." Von Seeckt loved his gambling metaphors. "He is the house."

"I could not express it better myself," said von Treptow.

By this time, they were approaching the cutoff to Braine and Soissons. Von Treptow stopped them. "Something tells me we make one more change here."

There were several artillery-made breaks in the hedgerows. Their mounts lurched up and over the edge of one such and led them into an adjoining wood. There they shed and hid their French livery and adopted the khaki which von Treptow had added to their packs at the last minute. With their ties and Sam Browne belts and crushed caps, they certainly looked the part of British cavalrymen. Von Seeckt's English was the least polished, so he wrapped a gauze around his neck, pricking a finger to add a little blood for effect. "Ow!"

"Poor baby," Knorr chided his aide. "Bullets and shrapnel, yes, a pin-prick, no. This younger set!"

"Well, we are saddled with him. Cannot very well leave him. I am told some of the French colonial troops, from the Cote d'Ivoire, I think, perhaps they are Senegalese, are cannibals. Lieutenant would make a tasty addition to their stewpot." Von Seeckt was a fine specimen, two meters tall and a hundred kilos, muscle, all of him. Still, he shuddered at the thought.

Von Treptow released him from his fears. "Off we go, then. Colonel, degrade your English a bit, as you are now a mere 'Leftenant'. I shall attempt to monopolize any conversationalists we might encounter."

They turned left onto the main road and von Treptow led them in a decent trot. "Let us see what these boys can do for the next ten or so." They slowed once to let a full company pass, von Treptow faking a pidgin French to address the commander. Then off they went again.

"How much farther do you reckon, Colonel?"

"Less than fifteen klicks to the lane, Sir. No more than hour and a half at this pace or close to it."

"General, you might want to look behind us, Sir." Von Seeckt was in the rear. "Could be trouble, based on their hurry."

Von Treptow craned his neck, then swiveled in the saddle. "Yes, Lieutenant, I believe you are right. Look lively, then, no abrupt moves. Have your blades at the ready." Behind them and closing fast, dust trailing behind, was a cavalry squadron at a gallop.

As their pursuers approached, von Treptow led the others to the side of the road as if to let the formation pass. Colonel Theroux pulled abreast of von Treptow, now Colonel Godfrey Wilberforce of the Fifth Dragoon Guards Regiment, Third Cavalry Division, British Expeditionary Force. "Good afternoon, Colonel," Theroux saluted, von Treptow/Wilberforce returned the gesture with a sharp, palm out salute of his own. "May I inquire the reason for your journey, your destination and purpose, that is?" Theroux's English was passable, not fluent.

"Certainly, Sir." Von Treptow responded in the Queen's English taught him by his Cambridge-educated tutor years before. "Liaison detachment seconded to Division Headquarters, Rheims. First, though, touring the front from Berry-au-Bac with," he retrieved and opened a folded paper, "a Major Dupree's detachment, then down to Rheims. Then two months with General Conneau's staff, observers, champagne, what?"

Theroux turned and murmured to his lieutenant alongside, who offered a brief translation.

"Apologies, Colonel," Von Treptow adopted a fractured, halting French. "I am afraid I was not in the top form in French at school."

"Quite all right, Colonel Wilberforce, I appreciate the effort. May I see your identification and orders, please?" Von Treptow and the other two fished out the desired documents, the forms for which had been collected over time from the captured and the dead. Theroux could find nothing to question on either form, written in a particularly dense military argot, barely English. "Thank you, Colonel, soldiers," returning the papers. "These are beautiful mounts you have. Did you bring them from England?"

Von Treptow instantly realized the sergeant had done his duty and quickly formulated a response. "No, Sir, they are yours. We just now traded horses at Soissons after our first day and a half from Amiens. These three, and two more like them, were the only ones to spare. One of them is a bit tired, though – I would be exhausted toting Private Armstrong back there, I dare say," loosing a hearty laugh. "They are splendid, are they not? Some sports-man must have been quite sad to see them enlisted. Too big for polo ponies, though, would you say, Armstrong?"

Von Seeckt forced a whisper, "Yes, Sir, entirely too big, not nearly maneuverable enough. Racing, maybe, or stud?" He was holding his throat as if every syllable was tearing it apart.

"Please forgive him, Colonel. We made a little night foray across the lines last week, and he was grazed by a parting shot, as it were. Slow to heal, though, try not moving your throat for a week."

"Only hurts when I breathe, swallow or speak, Sir."

"Enough, Armstrong. Hurts me just to hear you."

The French colonel remained suspicious, even with translation. He could not pin it down, everything was in order, but the horse story was just not right, somehow, and Berry-au-Bac, a coincidence? "Well, then, we will just ride along with you, going on to Rheims ourselves."

"As you wish, old boy. By then we will teach each other our native languages. Jolly good!" Von Treptow was grasping. The country lane was not that far away. Was there another way through the lines?

They rode on for an hour or so, the two colonels bantering and laughing at the other's malapropisms, like newfound friends, poking and picking. Then they approached the checkpoint from this morning and von Treptow's and Knorr's veins chilled. The same guards were still on duty, lackadaisical as ever, but would they recall the faces or the mounts? *We will have to trust to the British masquerade,* thought Knorr. *The general made the right decision – we would not have gotten this far as Frenchies.*

By this time, Colonel Theroux had dropped his guard somewhat, more satisfied than before at his charges' authenticity. Von Treptow's linguistic subterfuge had its desired effect, distracting Theroux from the 'posh' business. After all, he had made a quick decision to head this way seeking his quarry. *Perhaps they doubled back toward Braine, or even beyond Soissons. Perhaps there was no quarry to seek after all?*

The group dismounted and the privates took the horses off to a trough at roadside. Theroux offered von Treptow and Knorr a cigarette, both accepting. He left them with their smokes and approached the checkpoint, conversing with the commanding officer, a lieutenant, tossing a thumb in the Germans' direction. The guard officer looked briefly at the three, turned and shook his head.

Von Treptow allowed himself to exhale. "That was close, lads."

Theroux was not finished. He pointed to the watering horses, the blacks standing out among the duns and whites like ebony on ivory. Again, the lieutenant evinced no recognition or even interest. He was stuck with a boring duty commanding a boring squad on a boring road where nothing exciting ever happened. His ennui had infiltrated his sense of duty and, crucially, his sense of observation.

At length Colonel Theroux rejoined them as the horses were being brought back to the road. The group rode on another kilometer, passing the back road, then veering southeast. Von Treptow and Knorr exchanged nervous looks, but neither dared glance at their maps. Another two kilometers to Cormicy, a half-ruined village, sad in aspect, a few women in black, a pack of four curly-tailed mutts rooting in a small trash midden. The *Deuxième* colonel waved his hand about as they trotted on, pointing to the destruction, "Germans, Sirs, they did this." He turned to one of his men, saying something quietly in a French dialect von Treptow could not make out.

The sergeant dismounted and trotted into a somewhat tattered chateau in the village center, a large and equally tattered tricolor attempting to flutter away from its pole. Ten, then fifteen minutes passed, then the man returned. "Colonel, my earlier orders are remanded, as my sergeant here handed me a communication to return to Soissons." Pointing across the village shells, "Colonel Wilberforce, you take that road north, yes? Nice and straight, I think you might say. So we leave you here, enjoy your travels." He saluted, turned back to his horse and mounted up. "Save a little champagne for us, will you?" At that, he ordered his men to about-face and they began at a trot westward.

Von Treptow murmured under his breath, "That was too easy. Look sharp, Lieutenant, eyes in back of your head." Two kilometers north, they could just see the ravine in the distance as it traversed a low area in the road. Von Treptow dismounted and fiddled with his strap, releasing it, lifting his saddle, rearranging the blanket, all the while giving orders. "Lieutenant, come to the other side of my horse to help me and turn about so you can see behind us. Good. Any dust? Any movements?"

"No, Sir."

"Good. Was there not a high point back there, somewhere? An observation post?"

"Without using field glasses, I cannot see anything. But no sign of a post, or sandbags or the like. If there is someone there, perhaps he will be careless enough to catch some sun on his lenses."

"Very well. I think, Colonel, we will make it to the ravine, then a hundred meters past. If we are to take these horses with us, we need to dismount there, and lead them back, heads down – only way to keep low."

"Still too exposed to my liking. Need more cover."

"We shall see."

General von Treptow remounted awkwardly, and the imposters moved down the hill toward their exit, then on along the flat stretch of road curving just to their left. Fifty meters into the curve, von Treptow called a halt. "Let us dismount here, watch and wait a bit. Maybe even until dark?"

Knorr measured the sun and horizon with his fingers, comparing his observations with his watch. "1600 hours, Sir, sundown not for another two, two and a half hours. The long shadows will begin to help in an hour or so, though. Lieutenant, make as if you are attempting to dislodge a pebble from your horse's hoof in case someone comes along."

There they sat for a half hour, von Seeckt checking all the hooves, methodically and leisurely. Then came their deliverance in the guise of a large formation marching south from Berry-au-Bac, two companies strong. As the men tramped forward, they rose a mighty cloud of dust; the second company was lagging a hundred meters behind to let it settle rather than breathe it in straightaway.

They exchanged bilingual pleasantries and good-natured jibes with the passing *poilu,* almost as khaki as they were, such was their chalky dusting. The second company's commander stood aside to salute and greet, offering to let the Germans trot along in front, but was declined. "We shall just follow along as we have a long ride back to Amiens."

Quickly the three saddled up and turned their mounts into the Army's wake. As they reached the ravine, a sergeant happened to look back and von Seeckt put his handkerchief to his face, waving them on. The sergeant laughed, poking one of his men to look back, prompting several others to do the same. Taking pleasure in discomfiting the British, and officers, at that, they returned to their plodding. None bothered to look back to see that the interlopers had vanished.

Minutes later, however, someone did. "Colonel, they are gone! One minute they were there by the side of the road, now they are nowhere!" After sending half his squad back to Soissons, Colonel Theroux had taken the back road through little Gernicourt at a steady gallop, trying to gain an advantage on the British. *Well, we have some time here...* He had taken a position on a wooded rise along the country lane to see if his quarry was true to their word. Then the troops marched through, *obscuring everything with their accursed dust*, thought Theroux, and then they were nowhere to be seen.

He and his squad abandoned their vantage point and galloped toward the troops. They choked their way through the columns and the billowing dust, then pulling on their reins, looked for signs of the mysterious three. He sent two riders on around the curve to pick up a trail, if one, while he and the remaining cavalryman sought signs high and low.

"Colonel, they went this way, up this draw." In the dust were unmistakeable hoofprints laid atop one another as the horses were wheeled around to their left. As the dust petered out, so did the prints, but the direction was clear. Theroux blew his whistle to attract his other men's attention.

The shrill of the whistle alerted the Germans to danger nearby. While the lower end of the winding ravine offered excellent cover, it flattened out closer to the safety of the wood, and the riders would have been clearly visible if only Theroux had not abandoned his lookout. They spurred their horses to scrabble over the uneven ground, strewn with large and small stones. Von Treptow knew they would not make the safety of the wood before they would be vulnerable to gunfire, shots in the back. He waved von Seeckt up and over a knoll, looking up at the lieutenant, who glanced at the small dust cloud below. He raised three fingers, then closed his fist and raised four.

The general gave Erich a hand message: *Wait for any others.* Then he looked back at Knorr, gave his shoulders a little shrug and wheeled about, dashing breakneck down the ravine and around the bend concealing them. Knorr followed suit. *Here we go.*

Sabers out, they surprised Theroux and his mate who were picking their way through the stones, unprepared for the downhill momentum of the assault, unable to unholster pistols before the Germans were upon them. Out came their swords and a confused melee ensued, horses and riders crashing into one another, blades flashing. Von Treptow engaged Theroux, quite a competent swordsman, neither gaining immediate advantage.

Knorr, meanwhile, was doing his best to parry the savage strokes of Theroux's companion, a burly sergeant, not terribly skilled but strong and energetic. As they careened, Knorr pushed his steed against the other's, causing it to rear up and smash its rider against a treetrunk leaning into the ravine. Down he went, but before Knorr could take advantage, the rearing stallion's forelegs came down across his saddle, tumbling him to the ground.

Both were momentarily dazed but then the sergeant leapt upon Knorr like a beast. He quickly pinned Knorr's saber hand to the ground and was attempting to stab the German with a bayonet. They rolled on the ground, the sergeant maintaining the advantage until Knorr broke his saber hand free and pummeled the other about the head several times with the hilt, only enraging the Frenchman more.

Meanwhile, von Seeckt had seen the remaining two cavalrymen gallop toward the ravine. From his elevation, he was able to charge downhill unseen and begin a pursuit of the two from the rear. The noise of the fight up above and their own mounts' hooves on the stony ground drowned out his approach. He drove his horse full speed between the two, striking to the left at the base of the neck and on the backswing slashing the throat as the other turned.

Knorr was tiring as the sergeant continued to batter him, now with a free fist, the bayonet having been lost. Fending him with his left forearm, he still could not free his saber arm. Suddenly the sergeant's head jerked up sharply and paused like a ball in midflight as his eyes rolled into the back of his skull. Then his head dropped, unnaturally.

Knorr looked up to see von Seeckt's bloody sword, then lifted the Frenchman to one side, seeing the slash through his spine, his windpipe and throat muscles all that kept the head attached. Revulsed, Knorr tried to push the corpse off, but the lieutenant just gave it a kick and rolled it off to his right.

Then they heard von Treptow, "Gents, come help me truss this one up!" There was the general with his saber at the French colonel's throat, the latter bent backwards over a fallen tree trunk. "Quickly now, and gag him." Knorr did the honors while von Seeckt retrieved the horses. "Let us depart *La Belle France* posthaste."

Off they went with four horses in tow, one carrying the French Intelligence colonel slung like a lamb over the saddle, the other three carrying corpses. By now the shadows were favoring them as they hugged the sparser tree line until they entered the safety of the wood. Von Seeckt found the game trail and an hour later they approached the verge.

They dismounted and quickly changed back into their German uniforms in front of the furious Frenchman. It was just nearing sunset now as the lieutenant eased up to the wood's edge and signaled – $S – D – L$ – and again. A light flickered in response. They mounted up and made ready for one final dash, but slowed to a trot when it was clear there was no challenge from behind or their flank.

"Best to be casual, inconspicuous, as best we can with this caravan." Von Seeckt was already embellishing his tales for the poker table.

The same trench crew welcomed them back, opening a small gap in the wire as they trotted up. Captain Lockemiller surveyed the little entourage. "Did some shopping, did we? Nice horseflesh. Oh, this one's alive? So hard to get them fresh these days," pointing at Theroux convulsing in his bondage. "Come, lads, let us help them unpack."

Three pairs of privates hauled the corpses down gingerly. "Please give them a proper burial, Captain; they did their duty commendably. This one," pointing at Theroux, who was rubbing his chafed wrists, "let us see who he is." A bayonet jabbed at the Frenchman's ribs as von Treptow searched him. "We have broken the bank at Monte Carlo, Lieutenant! A genuine *Deuxième*! These are most difficult to come by, intact, at least. He will make a fine trophy."

Addressing Theroux, he continued, "Colonel, I am prepared to grant you freedom of movement and personally guarantee your safety as long as you agree not to make an outcry. I will not ask you to eschew thoughts of escape, as that would be unnatural, but I will kill you myself, instantly, if you compromise my men's safety in the slightest way. General Dietrich von Treptow, Imperial German Army Military Intelligence." He made a dramatic bow and loudly clicked his heels, holding his salute.

Theroux was too stunned to make a move or say more than a muttered, "Thank you, Sir."

"Very well. Captain, he and we will need a medic's attention before we continue on. And please telephone Major Zimmer to meet us wherever you deem appropriate."

"Closest field hospital is two rows back, about a kilometer. We can head straight back, I will assemble an escort. Corporal, raise Major Zimmer at Cavalry and so inform him."

"Excellent." Von Treptow stretched and groaned, then grabbed his left arm in discomfort. "You winged me, Sir. Allow me a look at your collarbone. Hmmm. We are even on points, it would appear. Off we go, let us walk, shall we? Good for the joints, good for the steeds."

Twenty minutes later the caravan ambled into the camp, going directly to hospital. All but von Seeckt had been cut or bruised in several places. Theroux had taken a nasty, but shallow, slice to the collarbone and shoulder, von Treptow's saber coming just short of his neck. Von Treptow, in return, had been slashed in his left bicep, a deeper wound requiring sutures. Knorr was just plain battered and bruised, front and back, top to bottom.

As the medics were finishing up, Major Zimmer and a mounted platoon rode in. Saluting, he walked straight on to von Seeckt, fishing two five mark coins out of his pocket. Wordlessly he placed them in the lieutenant's out-stretched palm, shaking his head. "Glad to see you back. I confess I was not at all sure you could do it."

Von Seeckt rolled the coins in his hand loudly and ostentatiously. "I, for one, will never bet against the general, Sir, not after this escapade."

"Major, I am shocked, shocked! Shocked, that a wager could be placed on our safe return, such a serious matter. Shocked, that is, that Lieutenant here bet on us, not against us."

Von Seeckt was the very image of false contrition. "Sorry, Sir, I allowed emotion get in the way of considering the odds."

"Well, we are here, and we have a long ride home tonight. I brought you a present, Major, treat him well. Please house him in solitary in the brig, not the prisoner's compound tonight, then arrange to have him delivered to Mons tomorrow. He is to speak to no one." He stood from his chair, rubbing his arm gently, and approached Zimmer, whispering, "Very important not to let him get loose. Kill him if he makes the least move. Very important."

Zimmer was taken aback at the almost nonchalant ruthlessness. "Sir?" he whispered back.

"Kill him," was the answer.

The major called for a Military Police patrol, giving his subordinate some very clear orders. Presently, the MP's arrived, cuffing the colonel and escorting him to an *ad hoc* brig, a concrete pillbox, double guards posted.

"That should do nicely, thank you. Let us go home, Gentlemen. It has been a long day."

The drive back to Mons was uneventful except for von Seeckt's occasional nod at the wheel of the staff car. "More danger than a whole host of Zouaves," muttered Walter. After delivering von Treptow to the Hôtel du Roi, Knorr and the lieutenant motored back to the farmhouse. Major Bruckmiller met them at the farm gate and took his leave. Von Seeckt killed the Daimler's engine and coasted the last twenty or so meters to the front of the house. Since the little ones had come, the dogs were alternately fiercely protective of, or fast asleep with their charges. Asleep they were, as soon were the two officers.

* * *

Sunday, January 6, 0700 Hours
Mons

Lieutenant von Seeckt made his provisioning trip early next morning; Colonel Knorr slept in a bit longer than usual, but was in his office by 0800. They had not missed much, nothing out of the routine. The dogs had risen to do their business outside and today they returned to the convent with their master.

Crown Prince Rupprecht and another high officer dropped by looking for von Treptow. By way of excuse, Knorr recounted an abbreviated version of their adventure. The Crown Prince looked him over, bruises, dried blood and all, or at least attempted to, with two large dogs jumping up on him, nosing in his pockets. Knorr finally corralled the two and saluted to the laughing generals as they left.

0950 came and von Treptow walked in, his arm in a sling. "It was throbbing last night, so I had it re-dressed. Not so bad now. Allow me a look at you. Please tell me you did not let the children see you like this. They would be scarred for life at the terror."

Just then, Major Bruckmiller walked in, whistling. "Damn!" He stopped abruptly and saluted, jerking to attention. Resuming his whistling, he sauntered over to Knorr's desk and with a last tweet of satisfaction deposited a small packet in front of the others.

"This cat has eaten several canaries, I would surmise by that face." Von Treptow's eyes brightened, forgetting his arm, "Please do not tell me you also organized a sweepstakes on the outcome of our trip?"

"No. Should I have?" A pause, "Yes, I should have. Next time, then. No, General, I have the result of our inquiries in Lille."

"Before you commence and I forget, Major, we have a prisoner of war coming today from France, a Colonel François Theroux of the *Deuxième Bureau*. Please show him every hospitality, but keep him well secured and separated from any other prisoners. *Incommunicado*. He and his knowledge cannot be allowed back to France, under any circumstances. My orders."

"Yes, Sir, understood, Sir." The policeman knew the meaning of those orders. "Now, if I may, as to the Lille issue, my counterpart Hilje paid a visit to your boarder's Jewish uncle yesterday morning. And may I compliment you on your choice of aunt and niece back at the farmhouse? Quite attractive, particularly when they did not realize they were being observed."

The three, on an eye signal from the general, reached for their sidearms.

Bruckmiller was not the least bit impressed with the theatrics. "A mere jest, Gents. Back to business. Hilje sat down with Monsieur Lang at his office and explained the predicament. He said it took the old gentleman a good five minutes to even respond. Here is the gist. The family is Jewish, of course. His younger brother went and married a Gentile, moved to Belgium. Family enraged, excommunicate him and so forth. Our friend, not so much – mostly the women and the local Rabbi. He stayed in touch on the side, you see. Brother has a boychild, they raises him Christian, he marries your houseguest, she being Christian, too. Doted on Yvette, did not know about the others.

"So, his dilemma. He would take the whole brood, but the rest of the family wouldn't have it. The old man showed Hilje a big family picture. Mean looking women. He asks him to get them somewhere safe until he can figure a way different. Dips into his cash drawer, pulls out that" – pointing at the packet – "three hundred gold francs and a hundred English pounds. He wraps it up, Hilje takes the packet, sticks his palm out, the old Jew sighs, gives him another fifty francs. Hilje stuffs those coins into the packet, the Jew smiles, that's it. Came in on an overnight motor lorry convoy. No commission on this one, Sirs."

Von Treptow slumped back into Knorr's chair, overwhelmed. "Is there nothing you cannot do, Major? And thank you and your Hilje fellow for your generosity. Please sit and have a cup of coffee. Allow us a few moments to think. She cannot stay here, at least not forever, and she has now more than ample funds to travel to safety. Major, could you escort her to Switzerland or Amsterdam if we can find a place? Colonel, any other ideas?"

"She may not know anyone in Switzerland. Holland, I do not know. Hard to set up like that. If she cannot stay here...I have a large, empty house in Hannover with a full staff with nothing to do. Since Rosalie, I have kept on the whole lot, she was so fond of them. We could send them there, it would be safe, the Handley-Pages cannot reach Hannover, at least not yet."

Von Treptow looked at Bruckmiller, who nodded vigorously. "Goes without saying I can arrange some extra security for them. No worries about Bolsheviks, General."

"Excellent! Colonel, that is very generous of you." He thrummed his fingers on the desk, looking away to the window. "Hmmm..."

"General, what scheme are you concocting now?"

"Your Swan Ball, of course. She is a beautiful woman, considering what she has been through. Neither of us merit an escort among your society ladies, unless you, too, have been holding out, Colonel," winking at Erich. "She would dress both our arms, would she not?"

Bruckmiller grinned. "Certainly the rose between the thorns."

Knorr was concentrating hard on balancing his fountain pen upright on his palm. "I shall surprise you, General. I agree."

"What? Please do not deprive me of the opportunity to browbeat you into submission," pleaded von Treptow. "Why?"

Knorr snatched his pen in mid-air. "Since the war, but really since Rosalie, I have fallen away from that icy menagerie. Time to rebel. Why not?"

Laughter echoed down the stony halls of the convent, in and out of death's drafting rooms.

Lieutenant von Seeckt brought two days' worth of messages back to the office. He had placed two in particular on top, priorities. "Seems you were ordered night before last to appear yesterday morning at 0800 in the Crown Prince's office. He came by this morning, but Colonel explained your absence. Now you are commanded for luncheon, dogs expected."

Von Treptow leafed through the rest. "I shall be busy the rest of the day with these, and His Excellency, but we should devote a few minutes this morning to discussing our plan with Madame Vandenberg. Lieutenant, please bring the car around. We will leave the dogs here – if we take them, we will not get them back, much to my misfortune!"

As they approached the farmhouse, the little children came squealing to greet them. Etienne and Sophie were smitten with the huge but gentle von Seeckt, who waved the others to go inside while he babysat. Yvette, too, was already under the handsome lieutenant's spell and brought out her laundry to fold under his supervision.

Von Treptow and Knorr knocked and Estelle greeted them, dressed in the same waitress dress and apron as the day of the Incident, as they still called it, certainly much prettier than that day, or in the dim light of von Treptow's room. She made a huge fuss over Knorr's sad sack face, black eye and all, and the general's wounded wing. He, in his turn, was struck silent by Estelle's appearance, so Knorr relayed the story of her uncle Monsieur Lang, laying the packet in her hands.

Estelle was pensive, looking at the packet, unwrapping it, her eyes widening at the gold therein. There also was a note on a small sheet of paper which she unfolded and read, then closed, tears in her eyes. "Uncle Isaac is such a kind man, was so good to Henri and Yvette and me. He is trying to do the right thing. Thank you so much, Gentlemen, for the first time since this war began, Yvette and the little ones will be safe. Thank you." She gave each a lingering, rather passionate hug.

General and colonel then looked sheepishly at each other. Von Treptow found his voice, and in turn, conveyed Knorr's offer of housing, not yet mentioning the society ball scheme. "Then it is settled. We shall arrange an escort to Hannover on the next convenient train. There is one other matter." He looked at Knorr for support, but got only a mischievous grin in return. "The colonel, here, and I, well, we…well, we would be honored if you would allow us to escort you to Hannover's Swan Ball in two weeks' time. If, of course, you have any interest in such affairs. Or would even wish to go with…"

Estelle laughed out loud for the first time since they had encountered her, holding her sides. "Men! They have no idea of what is involved. Just another party to them! Dress up like princes and strut about swiping champagne glasses off silver trays, telling lies to their hunting chums."

Laughing again, "You have no idea! Look at me – Cinderella! What dress? What shoes? This hair?"

She paused for effect, looking first at one, then the other, enjoying their discomfort. "Of course I would go. What girl could turn down such handsome, or once handsome" – a glance at Knorr – "gentlemen? I loved the Swan Ball, but obviously have not been in a position to send my regrets the last few years."

The officers looked at each other, then at her, then at each other again.

"There are many things you do not know about me, yes? My parents sent me to Heidelberg in 1899, once the University allowed women. There I met my Henri. While there, I attended your ball twice. A long train ride, but first class, great fun. And not so far from home in Arnhem. After we married, we attended, not every year due to my pregnancies, for several years, up until, I think, 1911 – no, 1910 was the last. Then, we just had more domestic responsibilities, I suppose. It is still held, Colonel, the war and all?"

"Suspended in 1916 and last year, no. Renewed this year for morale. My brother tells me every effort is being made to recreate it."

Von Treptow began, loftily, "Madame, you have outwitted us or we have outwitted ourselves, one or the other. I, myself, harboured the suspicion…"

Estelle's face suddenly transformed itself into a Fury's, "The suspicion that I was some mere waitress to be rescued by gallant knights and transformed magically into a Princess? That I would be overwhelmed, overcome with gratitude at the thought of entering your society? That I would give a damn? That I could forgive you for what you did to Henri? What you probably did to Arabella in Dinant? That I would ever want to see another German in my life, even those I knew in Hannover? Why? What do you want of me?"

She turned away, sobbing, "Go away. Leave me alone." Knorr started to reach out, but von Treptow held him back by his sleeve, nodding his head back toward the outside. The killers of men tiptoed backwards out of the house.

Knorr was genuinely downcast, "God, what a fool I was to forget what has happened to her. Sending her to the heart of Germany? To live among the very people who caused her misery? Idiot!"

"And my presumption that somehow we would be doing her a grand favor, granting her the privilege to glimpse our high society. Pygmalions shaping their Galatea?" Von Treptow paused. "Bah! Colonel, we are much better at planning war than the lives of others. Perhaps we should remember that."

Meanwhile, all was well in the rare clear winter sunshine outside. Von Seeckt had surrendered, collapsed in a heap with the little ones tumbling all over and about him, Yvette clutching rather than pouncing. He attempted to rise, trying to shake off one, then another, then finally, Yvette. "Colonel, I could use some assistance here."

Knorr sidled over while the lieutenant grappled with his attackers. "Boooo!" he roared at close range. The little ones, startled, turned and shrieked as one seeing the colonel's battered face. They clung even tighter to Erich, bawling uncontrollably.

"Now you've done it, Sir. Look, children, it's just Uncle Wally. Dressed up like the bogeyman. Look!"

Etienne turned his head just enough to take another peek, then buried his face in the lieutenant's trouser leg, then stole another glance. Knorr was squatting down, eyes level with the boy's. Etienne released his iron grip and stuck a finger tentatively to the colonel's face. He poked and prodded the bruises, the puffy cuts and the black eye, all fascinating him.

Little Sophie still was not convinced and continued to cry until Yvette picked her up. Estelle watched from a window, a handkerchief to her face.

The general broke it up, "I must get back, lads." The two aides stood up, shaking off the dust. "Until later, then?" He abruptly turned about face and strode to the car. The others followed and soon were back at the convent.

Colonel Knorr started to say something as they walked as briskly as they could down the corridor, but von Treptow abruptly cut him off with a wave of his free hand. The general retrieved his other messages and with a snap of his fingers summoned the pointers to follow as he walked away, silent save for the dogs' accompaniment.

"Colonel, Sir?"

"Let us concentrate on our duties today, Lieutenant. I have much to do." He closed his office door behind him.

1300 Hours

Luncheon was in Rupprecht's office, the convent's former library, the jewel of the complex. The sisters had evacuated the Flemish school portraiture, priceless illuminated manuscripts and irreplaceable diaries and journals to another convent in Rouen, the last truckload just eluding the German gunners. Even as the books were being removed, British soldiers were being brought in on litters and tended to by the whiteclad nuns. By the time Staff selected this place as a Headquarters, the library was full of wounded and dying.

As ranking field commander, Crown Prince Rupprecht earned the privilege of the office. He had the remaining books and effects crated and shipped to the Rijksmuseum in Amsterdam for safekeeping and now it was a bare, yet still majestic space, perfectly suited for its austere occupant.

Three rather austere occupants at the moment. Crown Prince Max of Baden had arrived without ceremony the night of von Treptow's sortie. The three of them constituted a conspiracy, legally, but more importantly, in fact. Each had his constituency, Max, a more liberal, yet still traditional regime; Rupprecht, preservation of the Army and order; Dietrich, a geopolitical strategy. The three saw no contradictions, indeed shared the same vision of a more democratic regime encompassing a Greater Germany protected by a strong military. They shared the same fear – an Army command effectively controlling the nation, squandering all in an avoidable *Gotterdämmerung*. And they had few qualms about the means and methods to achieve their objectives.

"Here they come now, Max." Rupprecht held a small mutton bone in each hand. Zig and Zag knew exactly where to go for their treats and retreated to the edge of the rug, close to the fire, chewing noisily.

"Sounds like the Eastern Front over there – the crushing of an army." Prince Max was a cat man, but he agreed these were fine dogs. He took a few steps forward to shake von Treptow's hand, then led him to the table. "So, off on another adventure, were you? Let me guess – bloodshed?" Von Treptow nodded. "One of these days, Dietrich, you will come to understand the notion of peaceful discourse."

"Oh, there was ample discourse, Max. It is just that the *Douane* treated us rudely at the border."

"Of course they did. Please brief us as we dine, then."

The Barton & Cie. encounter took quite a while to spool out between bites, with nuance and analysis accompanying each stage of the account.

Questions, too, from the royals, well versed in von Treptow's intelligence operations. "So, General von Treptow, do you still subscribe to the poilu's dissatisfaction, his reluctance to retake the offensive?" This was Rupprecht's particular interest as a tactical military matter. "And is this Barton fellow sufficient to starve them if they do?"

"Yes, and yes, Sir. The sergeant we encountered was freely candid, the proof of that being the cavalry hunt." Prince Max started to question him but was waved off. "You see, Max, the *Deuxième* would not have come after us had the sergeant not reported us, guilty at having spoken so, the French colonel implied as much.

"And, as to Barton, yes, on the margins, but key margins. Ball bearings, for instance, and larger castings for the Renault FT tanks are falling behind other components. Instead of twelve units per day off Renault's line in Berliet, they may only get five or six, and cannot increase." He sketched the tank with its top-mounted revolving turret, showing the missing components essential to its operation.

"So he confided to me. Barton is not going to risk his neck for us, so he is being very careful, laying blame on labour and suppliers, relying on his protégés to accept his rationales. He is protected at many levels, partly by blackmail, partly by force of personality, partly by wealth and class, but almost always by coin." Von Treptow rubbed thumb and forefinger together. "Our coin, of course."

"Very well, Dietrich, I am satisfied." Max was impatient. He wanted results. "What is our next step?"

"At the end of the month, I meet with Max von Hoffman in Berlin to map out his Russian offensive. Then with Trotsky on 1 February. He has only a few days. If the Bolsheviks continue to refuse to negotiate in good faith, I unleash Max. He says six weeks; I say six months. Knowing him, it may well be a matter of weeks. Russia-in-Europe and the Caucasus will be in our hands."

Dietrich lit another cigarette and continued, "My personal priority is Saint Petersburg and this Lenin monster. I intend to have Trotsky already in hand.

From Riga, we can be there within two months, less. Investing it may take longer, but the Finns will be eager to help. Diplomatically, Your Excellency," smiling at Prince Max, "Romania, the Baltics, Finland, Ukraine, the Czechs, the Slovaks, Georgia. And, of course, the Hapsburgs. Your field, Sir."

"Those discussions are well advanced. Not necessarily popular, but when the correlation of forces in the East is clear, there will be…understandings. If you and von Hoffman succeed."

Von Treptow turned the tables on the Prince, "Max, we will be liberating a million prisoners of war, as early as the middle of the month. The Poles and Czechs and Slovaks will surely not rejoin the old Empire, and the Hungarians are at best doubtful. Best we have progress by then, Sir."

"Well said, Dietrich. I accept the challenge. Matters will be fluid, to say the least. What else have you for us? I shall be here through the tenth, reviewing my Baden regiments."

"Yes, Sir, there are some other matters. I received this morning a message from our Dutch friend in London. Seems there now is mounting talk in high circles of the Bolshevik threat to the English way of life. Labour strife, you see, is alarming the elites. Also, word is Lloyd George is at odds with his generals, will not commit British reserves to more trench warfare. Very promising, but we must find a champion within His Majesty's Government."

Smiling at the Princes, "And our Irish friends are restive, in want of guns and funds. Gunrunning, again. I shall requisition the regular advance. A new conduit apparently must be established, the banking types are pursuing that."

He lit another cigarette. Through the new curls and wisps of smoke, "It would appear I have some calls to pay in the British Isles."

* * *

Tuesday, January 8, 0700 Hours
Mons

The night before, Colonel Knorr had worked late sifting through the logistical information von Treptow had laid in his lap concerning the upcoming Eastern offensive. He walked back to the farmhouse alone, lost in his thoughts, and headed straight to the barn where von Seeckt was already half buried in his haystack, fast asleep.

He and the lieutenant rose at reveille, Knorr hoping to slip away without disturbing his houseguests. It was not to be. Estelle looked out from the farmhouse door in the early light, calling softly, "Colonel?"

He walked to the door and held up his hand. "We, General von Treptow and I, and Erich, are glad to be of help. But what we did Sunday was foolish. We forgot ourselves. I apologize. If you desire, we have made arrangements. The next passenger train to Brussels and thence to Hannover is two days hence. Lieutenant von Seeckt will escort you as will the dogs. If not, we shall seek safe passage for you to someplace less offensive. Please understand, we are fully aware of the tension created by our proposal."

"Walter, please. My life ended in 1914. You people ended it. There is nothing I can do about that now. I have three children depending on me. I must begin a new life for their sake, and would do so among the Hottentots and Mohammedans if I must. And you three have been the angels of our deliverance. What is so difficult is facing a ballroom, no, a whole city full of Germans. How do I say, *'Oh, you killed my husband, maybe my sister – you knew them well, danced with them here – but let bygones be bygones and have another glass of Champagne?'* Help us get to Lille, and my uncle will help us, in his way. We shall not trouble you further."

"As you wish, Madame. I will have the lieutenant inform you of the arrangements."

"Colonel?"

"Yes?"

"One more matter. Erich, Lieutenant von Seeckt. He has been the perfect gentleman, but does he have a girlfriend? Yvette is in the throes of her first girlish infatuation. I should hate for her to be let down hard, first time."

Walter brightened, "Yes, I myself just discovered, just this week, that there is someone. She is actually a great friend of my family, a Hannoverian, works here at Headquarters."

"Perhaps I could meet this someone? There may be a female solution."

"Of course, Madame. Good day."

"Colonel, please, one last thing." She touched his sleeve. "Yesterday, if just for a moment, you and General Dietrich made me see a possibility of a better life. Perhaps when this war is done, we may reconcile, one to another, nation to nation. Not yet for me. I am sorry. So very sorry." She placed her hand on his cheek, then let it fall and turned back into the house.

On the brief ride to the convent, Knorr let his aide in on it all. When he had finished, von Seeckt pleaded, "Would it be possible to excuse me from this for the next few years, Sir?"

Arriving at their office, General von Treptow and Major Bruckmiller greeted them. "Just in time to join us for an interrogation. Our French fencing friend awaits."

The interrogation center was merely a room in the Military Police wing, formerly a storehouse. Colonel Theroux was seated in the center of the small room. The major's tableau was complete down to the bare bulb hanging from the ceiling, the dirty ashtrays on the small table, the metal chairs, the stench of stale tobacco and frightened men.

The four Germans strode in with the arrogance of the conqueror. Theroux feigned indifference, "Do you not offer the condemned a cigarette?"

Von Treptow slid his gold case across the table. "Gitanes? Help yourself, there are more where those come from."

Theroux lit one, took a draught, then said, "Francois Theroux. Colonel. 1587964." He folded his arms, moving only to take another puff, then another.

"How is the shoulder, Colonel? My arm is still quite tender. I believe you had the best of me in our match."

"Well enough to be sent home, General. And why am I being held in confinement away from my fellow prisoners of war? In violation of conventions?"

Major Bruckmiller started in on him, harshly, his very crude French amplifying the effect, "No other POW's here, just common criminals. Consider yourself privileged I haven't thrown you in with that scummy lot. Most of them are Germans, not our finest, you might imagine. They would find a gentleman from Gaul the source of endless amusement."

Theroux was not happy at that thought, but maintained his composure. "That would be a war crime and you know it. You would pay dearly for such a breach."

Von Treptow took over, "Once this damned war is over, feel free to press charges. You know my name. You can find me, I shall certainly still be found in the Berlin telephone directory. Of course, you need not talk. That is your right as a prisoner, and your privilege as a fellow officer. So, not wishing an awkward, unproductive silence, I shall talk. Your Sergeant Breaux, I believe was his name, expressed the sentiments we, my merry band and I, heard over and over the last three weeks in your fair country."

"Three weeks?" sputtered Theroux.

"Yes, actually a bit longer. We ranged from Paris as Swiss businessmen to Verdun as American artillery observers, to Amiens as the Englander horsemen you encountered. Only you among your countrymen saw fit to give offense. But, we are glad to be…home." He waved his cigarette hand around the room.

"I preferred Paris, your ladies…,"

Von Seeckt was cut off by the general. "Ah, youth," he laughed.

Knorr, whose role was observation and deduction, noted Theroux's perceptible relaxation at this bit of buffoonery, hastily rehearsed on the way over.

"Yes, Colonel, we enjoy regular furloughs in Paris as we please. Can you say the same?" Theroux glared sullenly at von Treptow. "But, aside from giving the lieutenant here several opportunities to lose his virginity, we were on a fact-finding mission. We found many facts. Sufficient to corroborate the reports by our agents in France."

"And what facts, what reports might those be?"

"*Percée, gringnotage, tenir.* Have you heard those words?" Translating for Bruckmiller, "Rupture, as in an offensive, nibbling and holding. The decline of the once grand French strategic posture since the mutinies last summer."

Theroux bolted upright. "Lies! The French Army is as determined as ever to exterminate you Boche!"

"Yes, yes, of course you are. So long as it does not require a sergeant to order his men over the top. Nibble, yes, a feeble probe here or there, but mostly holding position. Your French Army was built around the audacity of advance, always the offensive. Now you are glorified border guards, nothing more."

"I demand to be returned to my cell!" shouted Theroux. "This minute!"

"Sorry, no treaties require us to do so. We shall continue. You shall listen." Von Treptow circled his prisoner, dragging fingers along the tabletop.

"As I was saying, it seems the *poilu* has lost heart. We know the names of those executed last summer, the regiments and divisions involved, all the details. My judgment is the French Army is weakened from within, not to mention the losses it has suffered to us. To be sure, we have suffered grievously in this senseless war," – Knorr saw the Frenchman's knuckles regain their color – "but not so much as you. And we are much, much larger. And certainly much richer."

Dietrich leaned across the table, his hands and face a few centimeters from his captive. "So, my fencing partner – oh, one more thing. We are bringing west a million and a half seasoned fighting men, having destroyed Russia. Have your high command, your government, your newspapers reported that? No? So, would you fight? The overwhelming response from our…interviewees…is…no."

Theroux looked down. His hosts allowed him to remain silent for a minute or more. "What do you desire of me? Surely, my personal observations are of little value, and I somehow doubt you will send me home if I win the sweepstakes. So?"

"Gentlemen, did I not tell you he was a *mensch*? No, Colonel, there is no brass ring for you to grasp. Only an honest exchange of views. You shall not be going home any time soon. I have given orders to kill you at the slightest indication of escape, so please do not tempt us. You see, we and other influential types are actively pursuing the rescue of our familiar world from the very brink of destruction. My task is to persuade some blockheads my theories are correct. I would appreciate support from inside the enemy's camp, support that would persuade the Kaiser to end this war. But, we have inconvenienced you sufficiently. Major, please escort him back to his quarters. Dinner is supposedly edible – you dine with us tonight, Sir, that is, if you wish." With that, the general walked straight out of the little room, retinue in tow.

Bruckmiller placed the cuffs on the French officer. "Sir, you have met the most extraordinary German I know. Take him at his word, Sir. Off we go – Sergeant, see to his every comfort. Dinner is at 2000 hours, Sir."

The Germans walked through the corridors toward their office. "Colonel?"

"You are almost there, Sir. I suspect dinner with the high personages will turn the tide. He released his white knuckle grip – a proxy for his self-control – when you admitted to our losses. I deduce that comment made you somewhat more human in his eyes. Then, not pressuring him, you further lowered his defenses. Most importantly, he knows he will not go home until war's end but he will remain alive to be repatriated, so what is to be lost?"

Von Treptow stopped in his tracks. "Lieutenant, from this moment forward, please afford your Colonel Knorr the utmost respect for his insight and deduction. Learn from him, except in matters regarding the opposite sex, of course."

As if on cue, Isabella Boecker appeared around the nearest corner. The officers stopped and paid their respects, Erich's white cheeks ablaze.

Colonel Knorr took the initiative, "Dear Isabella, we have a...situation you may be able to assist us with. It requires a feminine intelligence we obviously lack..."

Isabella stared back at him, hands on hips. "Uncle Walter, please get to the point. What on earth are you talking about?"

The others, particularly Bruckmiller, were delighted at her spunk. Seeing her foot tapping, Knorr surrendered, "Lieutenant, your serve."

"Um, well, you see, we have, um...some guests...um, at our house, and one of them, well, is younger and..."

"And thinks you hung the moon, are the incarnation of Adonis, the cat's meow? I welcome the opportunity to burst her bubble. Where do I find this ingénue? Of course. The two beauties I have just heard so much about. One older, the other barely into puberty. They are at your farmhouse? Shall I go on? So, Erich, you have been seducing a child?" By this time, she had the big soldier, all two meters of him, pinned to the wall behind her jabbing finger. "And you want me to make it right? Just like that? And let your accomplices off the hook at the same time? Men!"

"Yes? Please?" Lieutenant von Seeckt had just killed three Frenchmen in particularly brutal fashion not two days ago.

General von Seeckt attempted to rescue his aide. "Please, Fräulein, my doing, entirely. I just did not realize the young lady would succumb to his charms, as have you?"

"Wally, you have the strangest taste in friends. Bold to the point of, well, I should not say." She paused, glaring at each one in turn. "Very well, let me call my handsome gambler's bluff," pinching von Seeckt's cheek, hard. "No time like the present."

None were prepared for such precipitous action. Each protested, claiming pressing matters at their respective posts.

Isabella would have none of that. "I am available as we speak. Beyond that, I cannot make any guarantees. Gentlemen, we will proceed as a united front, or not at all. Make your decision."

No decision, only capitulation. Off they went, a motorcarful, Bruckmiller riding the running board. By the time they reached the farmhouse gate, Isabella had been briefed on yesterday's debacle and declared them all idiots.

Zig and Zag thundered to greet them at the gate, the little ones running to catch up. Estelle and Yvette were at the front door. Isabella saw Estelle turn to say something to her daughter who nearly dropped the pitcher she had been drying.

Isabella had long since quit pretending she was not beautiful, accepting it simple fact, Mendelian luck, as she had learned at university. And she knew how to use her beauty. "Gentlemen, I am about to meet your sweethearts. How do I look?" She took off her broadbrimmed hat and pitched it to Bruckmiller, then pulled several long pins from her piled-up hair, handing them to Erich. Down came her hair, a meter's worth of rippling, shimmering mahogany. She gave it a shake. The men stood slackjawed. *Works every time.* "You stay here, amuse the children. That is all you are good for in this instance." With that, she unlatched the gate and marched straight to mother and child.

Estelle stepped off the porch to greet her visitor, both hands outstretched. Yvette cowered in the doorway, fighting back tears. Isabella led, "I have heard so much about you, and also your children and the troubles you have faced. I am so very sorry for everything this war has done to good people like you. And, now it seems my Junker Apollo is causing more heartbreak?" She looked over Estelle's shoulder and gave Yvette a little wave.

"Not his doing, at least not this time. He has been the perfect gentleman and the children adore him. Yvette is, well, she is coming of age, we know how that goes, do we not? You cannot blame her, after all, a handsome young man rescues her after everything she has endured."

"And a little fantasy helps her fly above her drab surroundings, forget her uncertain condition. Of course. May I speak with her, alone?"

"Certainly. Yvette, this is Isabella Boecker – did I get that right?" Isabella nodded. "Lieutenant von Seeckt's…friend."

Yvette was paralyzed, stock still at the door. *Good, I do not have to chase her into the house.* Isabella walked over, said a few words, then took her by the hand to the low stone wall of the corral. They sat, Isabella talking, Yvette finally opening her mouth. The young girl shot glances at the men, mainly the lieutenant, but also Knorr and von Treptow, at whom she pointed, then broke down into tears. While Isabella comforted her, the general murmured, "What have I done now?"

Estelle joined their little group, absent von Seeckt who was being chased in slow motion around the yard. There were only so many pleasantries to exchange that did not involve Germany, or Louvain, or the Swan Ball, or the war, so it was an awkward twenty or so minutes until Isabella and Yvette rose.

Walking toward the group, Yvette was smiling and animated, now laughing at something Isabella said. "She will be a great beauty herself," whispered Colonel Knorr to Estelle, who took his hand.

"Lieutenant, front and center, please! This young lady was under the sadly mistaken impression that you were perfect, free of faults. I have now informed her to the contrary. Please inform Colonel von Lossberg I have been called to other duties the balance of the day and shall not be returning to my desk. Well, what are you staring at? Dismissed!" She and her company, toddlers and canines included, turned and disappeared through the doorway.

"You heard the boss!" Major Bruckmiller barked, "Let's move!"

2000 Hours

Von Treptow and Knorr escorted Colonel Theroux from the Police section to the refectory for dinner. As the roomful turned to stare, the general introduced his guest, adding for effect the story of his sling. "An honorable man and a good soldier. We should all be so valorous."

Several generals and colonels introduced themselves throughout dinner, shaking hands, repeatedly chiding Theroux for not finishing the job on von Treptow. Dinner was adequate, not terribly sparse, but turnip-heavy. The Frenchman made a gallant effort.

As they rose after coffee and cigarettes, Von Treptow was handed a dispatch. "Sergeant," waving to one of the guards, "please escort our friend back to Major Bruckmiller at Police. You shall require four strong men to contain him. Thank you for joining us, Colonel. Until tomorrow?" He shook hands, saluted, then was off in a flash.

He pulled Knorr down the corridor to Signals. "Important," was all he said.

At Signals, the duty officer was sorting stacks of incoming messages, then looked up and held out one sheaf, "From the Swiss Embassy in Washington to Foreign Office then to us. Not encoded, Sir, it is in the clear, but is a long one. Seems the American President said something interesting this afternoon. Also received is some commentary from Berlin. To begin, here is the Swiss Ambassador's advance letter, Sir."

Von Treptow scanned the letter. "If the speech is as he says, this is the opening we have awaited. Captain Koehler, please send a runner to find Prince Max and Prince Rupprecht. I, we, request an immediate meeting." He handed the ambassador's letter to Knorr and started on President Wilson's speech. He sat down hard on the nearest chair. "Colonel, you think we have acted the fools the past few days? Well, here before us is the greatest fool of all. And the most powerful man in the world. All in one supercilious donkey of a political type."

The runner came back, breathless. "Sir, you are wanted in the Crown Prince's office immediately."

As the pair made their way, Knorr queried his superior, "General, what does this mean for us – Ludendorff, for example – and the Allied Powers?"

"In our case, as little as HL think, until we demonstrate otherwise. Abroad, I imagine our adversaries cannot be happy with this proposal, at least not initially. Frankly, it is too favorable to us."

Prince Max greeted them at the door, "Here they are! What is this news?"

"I am still reading, Sir, but it seems President Wilson's idealism – or his naiveté – have made the best of him. He has announced a vision of the postwar world not unlike ours." A runner from Signals interrupted to deliver another message, this one decoded. "From Berlin. Highly Confidential, et cetera, et cetera. Foreign Office's summary of private comments from privileged sources within our enemies' embassies. Seems Wilson forgot, or did not bother to consult his Associated Powers before speaking. I can imagine what Lloyd George and Clemenceau are saying at this very moment!"

"General, I am new to this. Please explain?" Colonel Knorr was lost in geopolitics, and not reluctant to admit it.

"Quite allright, Colonel. We ourselves often do not follow his cartesian reasoning at first." Rupprecht continued, "This Wilson fellow runs what will be the richest country left standing after this sorry conflict and his allies will be looking to America to finance their recovery, particularly as we shall never agree to reparations. Second, he is speaking as leader of an Army that has not yet been blooded, in stark contrast to the opened veins of his friends. There is presumption there along with his idealism."

Prince Max had been reading the full text, "Extraordinary. I should take him up on the entire proposition except..."

"Yes, except for Russia. His timing is excellent in every other regard. Hoffman and I must accelerate our marching schedules. But, his language is categorical in its renunciation of occupation and thereby our plans. Please read again that final sentence?"

Max ran his finger down the dispatch. " '*The treatment accorded Russia by her sister nations in the months to come will be the acid test of their good will, of their comprehension of her needs as distinguished from their own interests, and of their intelligent and unselfish sympathy.*' Not much room, Dietrich. We need to plot this very carefully. And our response. Today's words are battles, surely as much as those in the field."

"Yes, we will. May I?" Von Treptow took the dispatch from the Prince, rereading its Point Six. "Independent determination of her own political development...Max, what exactly do you think America knows of these Bolsheviks? After all, it has been less than two months since they consolidated power, and precious little news has escaped. I doubt they yet recognize them for the chancre they truly are."

He continued with that thought, "If we can engineer that '*independent determination*', then we might even meet the letter of his statement. Particularly if we divide to conquer – a separate Ukraine, Baltic states, Poland – yes, here we are, number Thirteen –'*establishment of an independent Poland.*' All within our grasp within a month's time, Sir?"

"I shall redouble my efforts. Mister American President shall be presented a *fait accompli* that will be part genuine, part Potemkin village in proportions altered over time as we, and we alone, see fit." Max paused, putting up a hand up to still the discussion. "Dietrich, that cinema man you know, Walgener, Walrusser?"

"Yes? Paul Wegener?"

"Yes. Not that his work is to my taste, but a moving picture from Warsaw or Kiev celebrating new nationhood?"

"Excellent idea. I shall look him up when in Berlin later this month. Back to this agreement – would we trade Alsace and Lorraine for control over the Ukraine and the Caucasus? And while we are at it, do we really need the Cameroons, Togoland? Giving up those would meet Point Eight, except for this vague '*invaded portions restored*' language, which diplomats can argue over for years. Austria, Italy – bah! Restoration of Belgium, we should have begun that regardless, a sop to public opinion. All told, favorable. How, though, to persuade those truly in control to see things our way?"

"That is the nut to be cracked," said Rupprecht. "Let us sleep on it and reconvene tomorrow morning."

"Yes, Sir. Oh, one more consideration, this adds impetus to our anti-Bolshevik proselytizing in London. Which may well be the key to our success."

Both Princes nodded.

Knorr simply exhaled, "London?"

* * *

Wednesday, January 9, 0700 Hours
Mons

Colonel Knorr and Lieutenant von Seeckt found Isabella Boecker waiting for them at the office door. "Shall we talk?"

Erich got the coffee going, the pointers elected to wander the corridors looking for adventure, and Knorr guided Isabella to a fireside chair. He put on some kindling, then some logs, coaxing the firebox alive.

Coffee came and Isabella began, "First, Wally, this poor woman is very fragile, emotionally, very fragile. Think of what she has been through." She stopped. "No. You cannot possibly understand the degradation, the fear, the desperation. You never could. It was hard enough for me to listen to her story and a man could never fully understand.

"Second, you and this peculiar general of yours – my words, not hers – have been her deliverance, and it frustrates her that she cannot express her gratitude more completely. When she tries, her emotions erupt and she loses herself to her anger and hatred. Did you know that when she came to General von Treptow's hotel room with the intent of giving herself to him in return for protecting her children, that she also concealed a sharpened knitting needle in her hair? Had your general not been such an honourable gentleman, he might now be dead. Think on that. Her sole focus in life is keeping her children safe, yet she would have forsaken them, abandoned them to seek her revenge on Germany.

"Yet she will survive. Her will is as strong as her emotional foundation is weak. Yesterday, after many tears, she made the decision to face her demons directly. She will go to Hannover with us and will attend the ball. I am not nearly convinced this is a good idea, but at least she is confronting her turmoil, seeking a catharsis, an emotional release, an intense realization of some truth. Something she needs dreadfully but may not be able to handle. The other complication, complications, rather, are you, Walter, and the general. She is in love with both of you, just as young Yvette is in love with Erich. Or was, until I showed her the folly. No, that one, she will be fine, it is her mother I worry about."

Knorr had missed the last comment. "In love?"

"Yes, Uncle Walter, you handsome devil. But not as you think. Do not commence your preening just yet. She is in love with her ideal saviours, not the men themselves. She hates her husband's killers. Please keep that in mind if a...a situation...ever arises between you and her. It could be dangerous, for both of you. That is the limit of my perception, the best I can do. I will take her and Yvette into town, if a certain handsome chauffeur is available, to help them find some feminine basics and some traveling clothes. We have already made an imaginary shopping trip to Frost's to outfit her for the ball."

As she gripped the arms of her chair to rise, "Oh, one more thing. She asked about your bank, Walter, and something about Barings in London."

She rose, gave the lieutenant a peck and waltzed out with one last look behind. Turning, she almost collided with von Treptow, who was looking back at von Bülow and von Kluck.

"Fräulein Boecker! Truly a relief from these grim stonecarvings," waving the smiling generals away. "You spoke with our guests after we left?"

"I did, General, and have explained matters as best I could. I must return to my desk as I lost too much time yesterday. Your aides will inform you. Please excuse me."

When she was gone, von Treptow raised his palms, asking, "What have I done wrong this time?"

"This time? Nothing. It seems we have a complicated woman on our hands. You were right, Sir, there is something unsettling about her." He debriefed him on Isabella's psychology exercise.

"Hmmm. Keep our guard up, then. Not so high, perhaps. Well. You two will join Princes Max and Rupprecht and me at 1100 as we do battle with Ludendorff. Lieutenant, go do your duty, but do return in time. Take the dogs, Ludendorff does not tolerate them."

"General, to change subjects, but what is in London? Not another cavalry charge?"

"No, no, no. Nothing so dramatic, I expect. But not just London. We have to get to Dublin, first, then the Isle of Man. Then London. Then home. The worst of it is, mostly by ship. I do not tolerate the sea very well."

"What costume this time? How do we tease the spies and risk our necks, I might add?"

"Details, details. We shall be properly outfitted, I assure you. Cannot be too English. Probably Canadian businessmen traveling from Rotterdam to Ireland. There, I have not given that much thought. The finance types shall tell us who we are to impersonate on Man. We shall deposit funds at a bank there. England, London, we rely on the Dutch to arrange that."

He tapped the desk top, "The Irish want more guns and money. They are a hotheaded lot, very divided among themselves, united only by their hate of the English – and Protestants. We attempted to run Russian rifles and machine guns over in 1916, were caught, ship scuttled. Poor Casement fared even worse on the try before that. Our Ministry of Smuggling and Piracy claims to have refined its methods. We shall see. All in all, four or five days. Must return in time for the festivities!"

A messenger interrupted his travel planning, "Sir, some dispatches for your attention."

"Thank you, private. Dismissed. Ah, here we are, some insight into the American mind. New York *Herald Tribune* news article dismissing Wilson's Fourteen Points, demanding more fighting. Another," glancing from sheet to sheet, "another *Tribune*, this time, Chicago, pushing the plan, bring the boys home by Easter, 4th July at latest. These here, confidential notes on

State Department deliberations – seems Lansing, the American Foreign Minister, is upset Lloyd George was not notified in advance. Probably got a Welsh earful! Significant support for forcing this on the Allies, not merely proposing something. Excellent!

"Lastly, a private message from their parliamentary party leader to Colonel House, Wilson's confidante. It is an election year at parliament level, and he is concerned about our American fellow kin grasping the Fourteen Points and demanding a peace. Seems the Germanic vote is considerable in their Midlands and big cities. Hmmm. In their General Pershing's Texas, too. I did not know that."

Plucking from the stack one message he had overlooked, "From the English. Their Wilson, General Henry, that is. Quoted in indiscreet company, it would appear, *'Everyone angry and contemptuous of Wilson. A vain, ignorant weak ASS!'* Emphasis in the original, I should add. So, good news. And, we have yet to begin our campaign of persuasion. Excellent!"

"Sir, your enthusiasm is lost on me. All I can contemplate is a gallows set up at the Tower of London."

1100 Hours

The time came for the big powwow. The lines were clearly drawn, the Princes and von Treptow on one side of a table, Ludendorff on the other, aides in the background.

"General, are you not satisfied with your victory the other day? Rupprecht, is this just another excuse to delay our mighty offensive? I am offended and angered at having to fight harder in my rear than at the front. Am I understood?"

Ludendorff's salvo reverberated off the walls of his office but had no effect on the Royals. "General," Prince Max started in on him, "I represent the Kingdoms and Principalities and the people of Germany, not to mention the Kaiser. You will listen to us. Do you understand?" He was not entirely convincing.

"You know I effectively have the ultimate power..." Ludendorff replied in his best bullying tone, but was immediately cut off by Rupprecht this time. "One telephone call to Berlin and you will be a former general, a wartime hero, retired with full honors and the gratitude of the German people, but retired nonetheless."

"I shall not stoop to call your bluff. Why have you called this meeting?"

"Very well, Sir." Alone among those at the table, Von Treptow's neck veins were not bulging. "I have here a translation of a remarkable proposal made by the American President, Herr Wilson, yesterday afternoon in an address to their Parliament. As you read it, you will see it is a framework for a favorable peace settlement, with modifications, of course, that we shall discuss. Clearly it would not remain on the table in the face of a massive offensive. Our task today, this week, is to ascertain what and how much of this with which we can live."

"If any," snorted Ludendorff. "We have seen this claptrap before. This Wilson and his Americans are amateurs, on the world stage and the battlefield alike. Why should we even acknowledge this drivel?"

"Precisely, General, because it is drivel." Prince Max attempted to employ some reverse psychology, as the Viennese would describe it. "You know as well as we that Britain and France would never agree to this dog mess. But if Germany did, even if only as a ruse, a feint, think of the world uproar that would ensue. If the Kaiser, or you, Sir, were to say, in American, *'Looks good. We accept. Where do we sign?'*, then what? How do Wilson's allies reject it?"

Max continued, "You heard General von Treptow's assessment of the European military situation. We take Russia. We set up new nations under our control or influence as you already have proposed in Estonia and to a lesser degree in Finland. We write new agreements that seem to meet Wilson's definition of self, self whatever he calls it, there and in Ukraine, Georgia, Crimea. An expanse of German control never, ever contemplated."

"Meanwhile," Rupprecht added his weight, "France is well bled, Britain nearly so. Our lines can resist any assault, so long as we husband our resources prudently."

"Balderdash. You admit the Englanders and French would not agree to this. And these things in the East will take time. I know the place."

"Yes, General, you are exactly right. It will take time in the East. Three months. 1st April, mid-month at latest, we have what we want. The West is your domain. Respectfully, Sir, forget for a moment the offensive," von Treptow held up his hand to stay Ludendorff's inevitable explosion. "How would you interpret this proposal, in terms of the most favorable establishment of an armistice line?"

"Were the German Army to plead for permission to draw such a line?" Ludendorff was unexpectedly calm. "Well, this says, and we know, that we must leave Belgium. It may surprise you, but I admit to our failings in regard to their cities and the populace. Mistakes were made. By others. Those mistakes have made the conduct of this war and the prospects for peace very, very difficult. I say these things in the strictest confidence."

He looked around the room collecting nods of assent. "So difficult, the only way to extricate ourselves is to win, to smash the French, the British, or both. Before we bloody the American nose. Negotiate with the Entente? A fool's errand. Remember your Thucydides, Gentlemen. We now find ourselves in the position of Sparta facing a strengthening Athens, this time, America. We must strike, we must prevail before this new Athens overwhelms us. I must maintain that posture. If you demonstrate otherwise, Field Marshal von Hindenburg and I will listen."

Ludendorff lowered his voice, "Excellencies, General von Treptow, I am most concerned about our homeland, and our soldiers, both. Hunger and sedition make a powerful cocktail, one that I have tried to deny, to ignore. No longer. Gustav, the Opel brothers and the other industrialists have begun to implore me, and your comments second their views. Again, my only solution is to win the war before we collapse into revolt and treason."

Von Treptow said, quietly, almost in a whisper, "General, you are a great actor. We never would have expected this from your public persona."

"Do not deceive yourselves. If you falter in the least, I proceed as my brain tells me. I have no heart, you know that!" Ludendorff laughed out loud, the first time anyone in the room had seen such an outburst. "You have until 15 March, as agreed, to give me my troops. See that you do not fail. Is there anything else? I have an offensive to plan. Good day."

"Shall wonders never cease?" Crown Prince Rupprecht stroked his moustache as he strolled jauntily toward his office.

"Temper your confidence, Cousin. He can yank the rope around our neck at any time. Our bluff and bluster had little effect, certainly much less than the facts. He will not soon or easily forget our effrontery."

"No, Max, you are correct. We have bought ourselves some time, but no lessening of the pressure. We must not fail." Rupprecht was a man less of diplomacy, more of action. "He will not stop unless we stop him with results. General, your thoughts?"

"Merely marveling at being still intact. Yes, yes, all true. We must shorten the time frame in the East – it is too thin as it stands. Max von Hoffman will be happy. Max, we have sixty days to neutralize the new countries. Not a day more."

"Why? These things take time, Dietrich." Max was now somewhat peeved at von Treptow's impertinence.

"We cannot allow this opportunity slip from our grasp. The longer it lingers and festers, the more the British and French will pressure Wilson, nibble away at the best parts of this new inititative." Von Treptow stopped in the middle of the corridor. "We cannot do it."

"What do you mean?" Max's face reddened. "This has been all for nought?"

"Those months in Russia, if they delay our response to Wilson, could be fatal. We must resolve Russia, first."

"No, Sir, we need not do these things simultaneously." Knorr had screwed up his nerve. "We only need to appear to do so."

The three senior officers and von Seeckt crowded around Knorr.

"How, pray tell? With a magic lantern show? Some miracle of electricity?" Rupprecht prided himself on his neophobia, except in matters military.

"Of sorts, yes. Excellency, you mentioned earlier the cinema man, a moving picture director. What if we gave the world a moving picture of our version of events in the East? Just long enough to mask our movements across Russia?"

Von Treptow corrected him, "Borders are porous, Walter. News hardly knows any limits. Someone, the embassies, businessmen in Russian ports, any number of sources can contradict whatever we say."

"Sir, telephone and telegraph lines can be cut. Ports can be blockaded. Roads blocked. Our movements will be dictated by communication, not merely lines of advance. Use our infiltration techniques in a new way."

Knorr rapidly rattled out his ideas, "All of this springs from my planning for General von Hoffman. We count on a rapid advance using Russia's own railroads. With the railroads go the telegraph and telephone wires. His plan is to go from station to station, commanding all communications. You say we only have ten weeks. Accordingly, we have only to maintain the charade for ten weeks, perhaps less."

"Actually, much less." Prince Max was stroking his chin. "I like your thinking, Colonel. For once the fog of war may work in our favor. Let us say we commence this…miscommunication…on 8 February, only thirty days, General. We announce the independence of the Ukraine to great fanfare in Kiev. Your cameraman records it for the newsreels. Thence to Riga, Tallinn, Vilno, Warsaw, Helsingfors. Much rejoicing. Newspaper photographs of German generals embracing new Presidents and Prime Ministers. All smiles. Their liberators, our good Germans, in the background with flowers around their necks. Max starts the same day, the 8th, Dietrich?" Von Treptow nodded his assent. "A month, two to surround Saint Petersburg?" Another nod. "A friendly embassy or our agents map the key communications lines. We seize the rail lines back to Moscow, blockade Kronstadt, we already occupy Riga, of course."

"Colonel, how fast are you planning to move?"

"Assuming the rails remain intact, as much as fifty, sixty, seventy kilometers a day, more. Landwehr occupation troops right behind, depending on rolling stock. Ten days could put us to Moscow's door, but that is just logistics. The actual fighting will be different. Figure three, four weeks to surround Moscow. Weather improves by the day, we hope, but we are done before the mud slows everything."

Prince Max clapped his hands. "At which time, we will have recognized a new government composed of former Tsarist elements, more amenable to our political requirements. With a smattering of Socialists and the like, including Kerensky, but quite devoid of Bolsheviks. By that time, that breed should be nearly extinct. The rest of it, the dirty work, no one will pay attention. No one ever does. We just keep moving. Present the new Eastern Europe to Herr Wilson 1 March, with Ludendorff's signature on a copy of the Fourteen Points. Two weeks to spare."

"Sounds easy, Sir." Von Treptow was now the skeptic. "Too easy?"

Rupprecht closed the discussion. "It is all we have. Let us make it work."

1750 Hours

"Message from a Herr Tomas Masaryk in Geneva, General, Sir. Wire through Berlin, Sir."

"Thank you, Lieutenant. Colonel, just to make matters more interesting, another new front to explore. Bohemia and Moravia. Any familiarity with Prague or Bratislava? Slovakia, for that matter?"

"Prague, yes, both banking and military. Brief staff liaison, 1913 during the Second Balkan War excitement. Banking over the years. Friendly with several at Wenceslas Bank, if they are still there. This Masaryk, is he inside or outside?"

"Most definitely outside at the moment, but we plan to make him President or Premier of a new Czech or Czech and Slovak-speaking state. Our Austrian friends need not know that, please. He is one point of a triangle, we are another and a rather dubious, but capable fellow, Radola Gajda, is the third. Gajda is commander of the Czech Legion, a Russian Army unit composed of émigrés and former prisoners. Rabidly anti-Bolshevik. Tough unit, sixty thousand or more, very good fighting force. We want it on our side. Masaryk wants it. So does the Entente. The Reds want it out of Russia.

"When we move into Russia, we promise them the moon, sun and stars. We shall clear a corridor for safe passage from their positions somewhere in the east into Moravia. They become the new Czech army. We install Masaryk as leader of the new nation – whenever he tells us what borders he wants, that is. We do not expect gratitude, but demand neutrality and cooperation in our new order.

"Did I mention we plan to dissolve Austria-Hungary?" He scanned the message from Masaryk. "This fellow has shopped himself from Paris to Moscow to Washington. He could have found everything he needed closer to home, he now realizes. He is canny, give him that. He expects us to be the high bidder for his, and the Legion's services." Reading on further, "Lieutenant, you are forbidden to play at cards with him. You would have his entire treasury by evening's end."

"Sir?"

"A cumbersome analogy, my apologies. He has no idea of his real worth. He asks pfennigs when he could have marks. So be it. We need a little extra for Gajda. No, his gold is our agreement to excise his country from the old Empire. Easily done. Lieutenant, take this down, if you would, "Herr Masaryk: financial terms are acceptable. Stop. Must have Legion's concurrence. Stop. Expect our transport to Prague by…Colonel, add to your list of Max's objectives. I want those thousands home for Eastertide…where was I, Lieutenant?

Ah, yes. Prague by 20 February – that should shock him – Stop. Totally confidential. Stop." He stopped abruptly, sighing, "No, no, no. This will not do. Just tell him terms acceptable, meet us in Berlin last week January to finalize. We provide transport and security. Respond immediately. Let us see if he bites." He grinned slyly at von Seeckt, "Lieutenant, how is your Ukrainian?"

"Sir?"

"Your Ukrainian? Are you fluent or not?"

"Not fluent, Sir. Never heard it spoken. Polish, yes, not Ukrainian. Sorry, Sir."

"Very well, my Russian is so poor, it could be mistaken for Ukrainian, will have to do. Perhaps the peasants will understand my *syurzhyk*."

"Sir?"

"Yes, Lieutenant?"

"Is this another adventure?"

"I certainly hope so, young man, I certainly hope so."

"General, whilst you two plot more mayhem, what about this London business? How are we to get there and back, intact? This time?"

"All in due course, Colonel, all in due course. This next memo addresses exactly that, would you but allow me the moment to read it." Von Treptow's features sagged as he read, "Oh, my. This is positively ghoulish. Simply ghastly."

"What is it, Sir?"

"The guns for the Irish? Fifteen hundred rifles and assorted ammunition? Shipped in coffins. With bodies exhumed from temporary graves in the northern sector. Unembalmed bodies? Can you imagine...?" The general was growing greener by the moment. "And on a ship, for God's sake."

"With us on board?"

"Sadly, yes. Hmmm. Embark from Dunkerque. That will be difficult, and Providence may not smile twice upon us in France. Lieutenant, please take this back to Captain Waldemar. Have him coordinate an itinerary whereby we depart Rotterdam, link with the mortuary ship in Portsmouth or Liverpool or elsewhere. Or, go separately, my preference."

"Sir, how are the guns meeting the coffins? Who is doing that?"

"There is a fellow, we may meet up with him at some point. Extraordinary. A smuggler, confidence man, swindler. Comes to us courtesy

Major Bruckmiller, in fact. Straight from Berlin gaol. Humbert Grosz, by name. Looks like his name, as I think on it. We deliver the guns somewhere near Ostend, he gets them across the lines. The coffins are coming from…Lieutenant von Seeckt, tell Waldemar we travel separately. I do not wish to be part of this shipment. There is no need for that risk. Or discomfort."

Colonel Knorr persisted, "Who are we this time? And where?"

"Woolens and fur dealers, businessmen, someone else in London, I do not yet know."

"Woolens and furs?"

"Yes, probably Canadians. Representing sheep growers and animal catchers."

"Sheepmen and trappers, Sir."

"What?"

"Proper terminology, Sir. One cannot go traipsing about northern Europe talking about sheep and beaver improperly, Sir."

Von Treptow stopped his pacing. "Really?"

"Yes, Sir." For once, Knorr had the upper hand, "And you may be a Canadian, Sir, but if we are to be from the West, I shall be from Laramie, Wyoming." He folded his arms, grinning smugly.

The vons looked at each other. "Wyoming, Sir? The Wild West? Cowboy and Indian country?" Von Seeckt was instantly attentive. As a child, he had avidly read Karl May's Winnetou stories and seen several traveling shows purporting to be authentic depictions of America's old west, folding all into memory along with the Brothers Grimm and Nativity scenes.

"And why Wyoming, this place in particular? Do we have the time this day for a full exegesis of some five pfennig novella?" Von Treptow was amused for the moment, but on the alert for more foolishness.

"My great-uncle Wilfred, of course. Your father's colleague. Spent his last tour before retirement as Attaché in Washington. I was sixteen and a handful, begging my parents to let me go with him. Uncle being a bachelor welcomed the company until I began pleading with him to let me be a cowboy or one of Roosevelt's Rough Riders. This was 1898, you see.

"Finally, a politician he had met, a Senator Warren, arranged for a spring and summer as a vaquero – Spanish for cowboy – with two constituents on their ranches outside Laramie. The happiest days of my life, single life, that is. Once I got comfortable in those big saddles, I could easily keep up with the others, learned to rope, herd cattle, castrate and brand them, the entire Western experience. Living outdoors a month at a stretch, a marvelous time.

"A man, do not recall the name, came through Laramie on his way to the railroad at Cheyenne, recruiting horses and men for Roosevelt's Cuban expedition. Picked up two of the wranglers – cowboys – and some horses. Had me signed up for about ten minutes until my host pointed out my short-comings – underage and German!

"Some years later, after my wife died, Father and some other bankers made a trip to America, meeting with Morgan and Drexel and others. He took me along, not for my banking expertise – I never was cut out to be a banker – but as a holiday. I took some time out to travel back west to see my old friends. In just those few years – this was 1909 – the place had changed. No more bank and train robbers, the buffalo herds had disappeared, the Indians hemmed in by the farmer's barbed wire, that infernal invention we have lost so many men to in Flanders. Finally made my connection with Roosevelt. He was visiting my hosts, friends of his and fellow ranchers, and he invited me to hunt with him in Yellowstone. Spectacular. Someday before you die, you must see it."

Lieutenant was impressed, "Sir, I think he passes the examination."

"So he does. You shall lead this expedition, Colonel."

* * *

Thursday, January 10, 1000 Hours
Mons

The next few days were hoped to be almost uneventful, logistics for the Irish trip, plans for whisking the Vandenberg family to Hannover, more meetings and more meetings, but Major Bruckmiller could always be counted on to unravel the knitting. Late morning he came to the colonel's office where Knorr, von Treptow and Captain Johann Waldemar, their travel agent from Intelligence, were trying to pin down their upcoming trip.

"Sirs," without knocking or saluting, "a few matters for your attention," making himself comfortable in a fireside chair. "First, your Frenchman is getting frisky. Might be ready to talk some. Second, Herr Grosz comes this afternoon should you care to speak with him. And, any more thought to sending your girlfriends off to Lille? Hilje cabled me, says Uncle has a place he can stash them somewhere in town."

"Always to the point, are you not?" Von Treptow welcomed the break. "Well. For the moment, our 'girlfriends', as you so unchivalrously term them, are set to go to Hannover as planned. But I shall not presume on Colonel Knorr's hospitality so the Lille option may yet be required. I confess I would rather not let them depart our company, as maladroit as we have been, as we have already grown attached to them. Honourably, Major, honourably! Agree, Colonel?"

"Yes, Sir. Certainly. I am not sure I care to reopen those negotiations, Major."

"Fine. I'll have Hilje tell the old man to stand by. Grosz? Johnny, you're meeting him anyway, correct?"

"Yes, but with him, no telling the time. When did he say?"

"He didn't. We'll see him when we see him. I'll add you two to the guest list. Now, our friend François. We can keep him here forever but I'd rather let someone else deal with his dietary demands. What do you want to do with him? He'll talk, like I said, but only to get out of his hole, I bet."

"He knows too much. Can we find him a room at Spandau? Problem is, he is smart, can, probably has put two and two together, which might jeopardize our French friends. Perhaps not, but a chance I rather not take." Knorr was speaking for his superior, too, but also projecting onto the prisoner his own behavior.

"Why not let him go?" Waldemar dealt more with informants and go-betweens, generally unsavory, in his clandestine operations. "If he really is such a burden. What have you told him so far?"

Von Treptow gave a quick summary, which Waldemar immediately grasped, "Well, let him be stuffed with false information, just off axis enough to let him think he has something valuable. Drop him off at the Swiss border, it will take him some time to get home."

"Damn!" Von Treptow slapped his cheek. "Breaux. Damn!"

Waldemar asked, "What, General? Who is Breaux?"

"Sergeant we met. Brother had been fired at one of Maurice Barton's factories. Attempting to be compassionate, I mentioned his plight to Maurice, who agreed to rehire him. If Colonel Theroux is as sharp as I think, he will investigate the circumstances of that day. If he finds Breaux for further questioning and Breaux mentions his brother... Well, you would make the connection, would you not, Captain? At least grasp the hint?"

"Persons, time and place. Hard to miss, Sir. Can you prevent Barton from carrying through?"

"A cable will take two days. Yes, just possibly. In the interval, he goes nowhere. Yes, Captain, he will be well fed with matters spurious. And please remind me not to be sentimental, compassionate, ever again."

Later that afternoon, Bruckmiller and Waldemar returned with a curious figure. Short, disheveled, no shortage of warts on a crumpled face, Humbert Grosz carried himself as if he were a Greek god. "No salutes, Gents, none of that crap. Got a cigar, a good one? You," pointing at Knorr, "I'll sit there." Bruckmiller put a finger aside his nose, Walter got the message.

Dropping his compact frame into Knorr's vacated chair, he looked around. "Damn sight better than Bruck's quarters. I could get comfortable."

Von Treptow sat quietly at Knorr's desk, arms folded, observing, not visibly reacting.

"You, big shot. Going to Ireland, but don't want to ride along with the dead? Pansy. Well, I don't get paid for chaperonin' you, just for the rifles. Pretty good idea, huh? You smarties didn't think of it, did you? And those Irish twits, such big friends of yours, they didn't either. Took Grosz to show you how it's done. Got some brandy?"

The general's amusement was growing. He opened a desk drawer, pulled out a bottle and a short glass, tossing them across the room one after the other. The little man caught the bottle with his lap, jerking up in his seat, then the glass with his left hand.

"Fuckin' servants. Can't fuckin' do nothin' right." He grinned at von Treptow as he poured into his glass. "He's a good one, Johnny."

"I am honoured, Sir."

"Shit. A sarcastic pansy, the worst fuckin' kind. Will he whinge, Johnny?"

"Yes, I will. Whenever I am with you."

"Shit. All right, then. Here's the square. I gets the guns at a spot I knows inland from Ostend. I'm takin' 'em over in a hay wagon. Just me. Don't have to split the pot. In the Portuguese sector. I got some boys over there I get some nice things to. They owe me. Hell, they like me. Don't everybody?"

Knocking back his glass, "Coffins from a crooked Frenchie. Didn't ask why I wanted false bottoms, he's paid enough. Ships 'em to the cemetery at Poperinghe. False bottoms sit on little pegs just high enough to fit the rifles. Key to the whole thing? My idea. Brilliant, even for me. Well, do you want to know or not?"

His audience shouted as one, "Yes! Yes!"

"Bunch of fuckin' jerks, you jokers. God, the things I do for a mark. Here. Irish priests, of course...and Irish crews...Catholics!"

The Germans were a mixed lot. "So?" asked Knorr, a Catholic.

"So they keeps the fuckin' Brits away, idiots. It's a high religious service, the whole thing. There's a horse barn there, for the hearses, see? My hay wagon goes in, we unload the hay and hide the rifles. The coffins come, get stacked in the barn to keep 'em dry. The coffins are loaded five by five inside the barn, with all that Latin and incense and crap. Father Mulcahy, Army chaplain but an IRA man, is in charge. Ain't no Brit gonna look past a shot up, moulderin' body to search for contraband. Yes, you can say it, Grosz is a genius." He smiled triumphantly and tossed back another tumbler.

"Then the Micks truck 'em to Dunkerque, board ship for Dublin or Wexford. No way I'm going to Belfast, Johnny boy. Long as my deal don't pay in full 'til delivery." He turned to von Treptow and Knorr. "Bastards! Don't no one trust no one no fuckin' more?"

"Excuse me, Sir. Why not Belfast?" Von Seeckt was the innocent in all this.

"Now there's some class you fuckers should imitate. 'Sir' and all. Reason, laddie? Protestants, shit on 'em. Come to think of it, shit on all of 'em. They won't let the Catholics bury in Ulster, probably would set fire to the whole lot, just for spite. Cook off the ammo, then what? No, gotta stay south, with the rest of the Romans. Got it?"

"Yes, Sir, Herr Grosz, Sir."

"I think I'm gonna cry."

* * *

Friday, January 11, 1100 Hours
Mons

"Well, Colonel, are your accommodations here to your liking?" Crown Prince Rupprecht offered a cigarette to François Theroux who was seated between Erich Ludendorff and von Treptow, then leaned back against his desk. This mid-morning meeting was the last opportunity for an interview before the London trip. Major Bruckmiller propped himself against a column in plain view just in case the Frenchman needed a reminder of an alternative interrogation style.

"I suppose they are superior to the Iron Maiden or hanging from chains." With the boldness of the condemned, he continued, "When am I to be transferred to a proper prisoner of war camp and allowed Red Cross access? And your food constitutes a war crime on its own."

The half-dozen German officers broke into laughter, surprising the Frenchman. "Please make that complaint to our Kaiser, my good man. He has not listened to our carping thus far." Ludendorff had reluctantly let himself be coached into an unthreatening role, encouraged to doggerel and derision.

Theroux was taken aback, "I did not mean, General, Sir..."

"Of course you did, Colonel. As did I. I will have you know I have ordered my underling here," – pointing to von Treptow – "to provide you with proper cuisine from the local bistros. Far superior to turnip soup disguised as *vichyssoise*."

"General, Sir, thank you, Sir." Theroux took a few moments to compose himself. "But I must protest at the conditions, the violations of conventions..."

Rupprecht cut him off. "Colonel, we enjoy your company, but you survive at our sufferance. Do not press us. In any event, your incarceration will be of a temporary nature. By that I mean no more than two or three months. Brandy? It is rather chilly in here."

A tray of glasses was handed around, a bottle placed back on the Prince's desk. "Very well, then. Our days are as short as yours are long, so allow us proceed. Despite your uniform, you are an *espion*, an espionage officer, subject to summary execution at our whim. Do not bother to argue the point." Rupprecht had assumed the voice of authority. "We respect your right to silence, and in any event, we have no need of the usual information on troop dispositions, trench locations and the like, most likely already out of date. You have before you the most senior command in Germany – think of your Foch, Pétain, Joffre and Clemenceau, combined." After a lengthy pause, he leaned forward, "We want to end this war."

Rupprecht and Knorr scanned Theroux's face. The latter's conflict was plain to see.

Rupprecht pressed on, "Surprised? We are in control, in the strongest position, after all. Yet, we are ready to cease fire. General von Treptow mentioned developments in the East, I believe." Theroux nodded. "We see no need for additional bloodshed in the West."

Von Treptow picked up the thread, the Frenchman jerking abruptly to his right, "Unfortunately, your people are not possessed of such wisdom. The slightest hint of weakness would provoke the atavistic urge to conquer, to revenge, to prance on the prostrate bodies of *les Boches*. So, we cannot simply disengage."

"Which means we have no choice but to attack. With two million more men from the East, we will prevail. But consider the cost." Ludendorff was doing his best at the conciliator role, not entirely unconvincingly. "Regardless of cost, we will prevail. What then of France?"

"The Americans…" Theroux stuttered.

"Too little, too late, my friend." Von Treptow made the French head swivel back his way. "By the time they are in the field in numbers, we will have crushed you. And your *frères* will see the British sitting idle while we turn our entire fury on you. What do you think they will do? Do you think the Anglo-Saxons, both, will come to your rescue? This time? And less than a hundred kilometers and we are at the gates of Paris. Recall we allowed no more than three months for your release – you will be sent home to a nation at peace. Whether prostrate or prosperous, that is your decision."

"Mine? You mean Clemenceau's, Foch's. Not mine."

"No, my dear François, the decision is yours." Ludendorff patted his wrist. "May it be the right one. Well, I must take my leave. I have an offensive to plan." Ludendorff bolted from his seat to the door without a backward glance.

As Major Bruckmiller led the baffled Frenchman away, back to his cell, Von Treptow turned to Captain Waldemar standing in the shadows. "Well, Johnny?"

"He is confused, of course. Completely. I could not tell which was more disconcerting, the peace talk or the high ranking personages catering to his whims. Were we to insert him back at the *Sûreté National*, he would be considered mad, or worse, turned. He needs to ferment, though, Sirs. The best course is to keep him here, let him mingle, dine with us, the like. Tight leash, of course, and ours need to be briefed. But with a little time, congeniality and guilt will set in. Congeniality in the sense of identifying with his captors, guilt at his cushy treatment while his chums are dead or about to be." Waldemar was a psychologist by training. "Then it remains to see how best to use him. I am not convinced he has any value to us. But it is up to our imagination to create our Frankenstein's creature, is it not?"

Von Treptow and Knorr walked through the corridors to the costumery where Frantz met them at the door. "Always the last minute, Gents? Do not pretend you had other matters more important. Come, we have some things for you."

"Do not be so full of yourself, Frantz. My tailor in Berlin treats me far worse, and I am paying him."

"The same for me, then my housekeeper starts in on me, on my taste, the fit, the rest." Knorr was laughing at his own mental images.

"I am sure you both deserve all the opprobrium heaped upon you. Very well. We actually have a nice little haberdashery here, and fortunately you two are fairly normal sizes. When we broke the British positions at Mons and elsewhere, their retreat failed to rescue the billets of any number of their officers, up to General levels. You would not believe the arrangements they brought with them across the channel. Recreated their estates, they did, complete with baths, wine cellars, silver and china settings plus several changes of civilian clothes. Be assured their batman was their valet from Merrie Olde. You, General, Sir, need a baronet's business suit. Here, try this, Carney, Goodwin and Locke, Savile Row. Very nice. Excellent fit, I think, considering. Good. Take two suits. Same officer, a nice set of tweeds. Help yourself to cravats and shirtings. John Lobbs, but may not be the right size."

Sizing Walter up, "You, Colonel Knorr, a little stockier. A bit harder – the Brit officers tend to either the wasp waist or the blimp. These will have to do. Fiddle with the braces to make your trousers hang straight. Hunt around in here for your *accoutrements*," waving at a trunk.

Frantz fiddled with the shoulders of von Treptow's tweed coat. "Well, that was easy. Much better than certain officers who treat this office as their very own rummage sale. Colonel, can you even tie your own bowtie?"

The two took their prizes with them, packed in proper British luggage. "Can you see why I abhor shopping, Sir?"

"This is why God created uniforms, my good man."

* * *

Saturday, January 12, 0800 Hours
Enroute to Rotterdam

Two now tweedy gentlemen entrained early for Brussels and on to Antwerp station where two men in German uniforms, one holding a sign saying '*Herr Gleisen*', met them. They were Waldemar's contacts, Dutch Military Intelligence, here with full knowledge. "Hello, General, Colonel. We will be driving you on to Rotterdam this afternoon. Beautiful day?" They introduced themselves, Knorr promptly forgetting their names.

Approaching the border, the Dutch shed their German tunics and caps in favor of their own versions, waved at the guards they had dealt with earlier and then were in North Brabant. The roads were excellent and they made good time, covering the ninety kilometers to Rotterdam's outskirts in less than ninety minutes. Knorr marveled at the landscape, rich and almost lush even in midwinter. The weather was just pleasant enough for the dairy cows to be out sunning themselves, pictures of contentment amidst the haystacks.

Then into Rotterdam, another visual altogether. Wharves, cranes, warehouses, bales of this and crates of that, all in a beehive of noise and activity. Coal smoke and soot everywhere mingled with the smell of heavy fuel oil. Von Treptow leaned over to his Dutch escorts, "These smells remind me of how miserable I will shortly be."

"Sir," said the senior officer, "these smells remind me of why I am in the Army, not the Navy!"

"That is the spirit, my fellow!" said the general, clapping the man on the shoulder. "If only I shared it…," slumping back into his seat.

Presently, they stopped short of a quay where a British freighter, *S.S. Culloden*, was moored. "Here we are, Sir," said the senior Dutchman. "We drop you at the freight forwarder's office there. He speaks English, handles the passenger bookings. Your papers in order?"

Captain Waldemar's staff had produced a handful of passports, identity cards, business cards, invoices and the like. Knorr grimaced, "Tall enough to stand on at the gallows."

The four gave nervous laughs, then took their leaves. Mister Smithgall from Calgary, Alberta and Mister Stansfield from Laramie, Wyoming sauntered into the office as if they knew what they were doing. "Yes, may I help you gentlemen?" The clerk was a small man, the very picture of a clerk, indeed. Balding, eyeglasses, green eyeshade, garters on white shirtsleeves. They explained themselves and the clerk motioned them to some tall backed chairs against the wall opposite. "All on schedule, Sirs. Will be letting you on in, oh, about an hour and a half. Fancy some coffee or other diversions, I can give you directions," he winked.

Walter answered, "Coffee, perhaps. May I inquire something?" The clerk nodded. "We came in on a Dutch flag. We are now sailing on a British ship. Is that not riskier? Submarines and all? We came over from America on *Olympic*, absolutely flying we were, but this one seems unable to dodge its own shadow."

"Safer than you might think, Sir. She enters dangerous waters only well after dark, runs blackout. Only two hours until she sights the English coast and the safety of the Royal Navy. Besides, that jack will be coming down, and Norwegian going up. The Norsies won't be happy, but we don't care. We just book 'em."

"That certainly is comforting. May we leave our bags here with you?" Knorr kept his lawyer's valise with him.

"Of course, Gents. Coffeehouse two blocks down on the corner," pointing. "The ladies are upstairs. Tell them I sent you."

The two partook of some coffee, but not the ladies. The Dutch newspapers were incomprehensible so they simply took in the sights, the smells, the bustling, surprisingly polyglot nature of the commercial hub of the Dutch Empire. Indonesians in batik, Arabians in burnooses, Africans in all manner of garb, sailors of every conceivable origin and uniform.

Spies, too. At least two had some interest in the tweedy types. Knorr nodded to the general, "That one across the street, over there, is British, Army Intelligence, I wager. Note the fold to the paper. Vertical, peeping past it constantly. The other is Dutch, watching him more than us. Our guardian angel."

"Preposterous! How come you by these conclusions?"

Knorr made a little gesture at the 'Britisher' who instantly retreated behind his paper. "Observation, my dear General, and deduction. Neither place was taken when we arrived. They arrived in sequence, the Dutchman following the first. The Brit paid in advance, the Dutch not yet. Finally, compare the shoes." The first man's were nicely shined, the other's rough.

Von Treptow looked casually at each. "You may be on target. Shall we have some fun? I ascend the stairs as if to engage in the business above. You approach the Dutchman. See what happens and I shall be watching from the staircase window."

They rose simultaneously, moving as agreed. The vertical paper twitched, then twitched again as the head looked first at Knorr crossing the street with valise in hand, then at the coffeehouse. Clearly conflicted, he finally rose and walked across the street toward the bordello.

Knorr, meanwhile, passed the Dutch spy, murmuring in German, "Briton. Following us. Help?" Looking back over his inside shoulder he saw the seated man make a slight hand signal. A movement across the street in response, another agent now tailing the Brit.

Knorr reversed, passing the seated man. "I am going to walk around the block, old man." He crossed the street shielded by a passing horsecart, then quickly down the alley, then right, then right again, almost toppling the thoroughly surprised suspected secret agent. He winked at the Dutch follower, not stopping when he heard the cries of protest from the fellow as he was accosted and hustled to a waiting car.

He returned to his seat, to the waiting von Treptow. "That was quick, Colonel."

"Sir, I was about to say the same of you, General."

The Dutch agent came to their right, taking a paper from a newsboy. "Good eyes, Gents. Not a Brit, South African, same thing in the end. They know their Dutch from our Boer brethren. It was time to take him in, way too nosy. Let Pieter know we are looking out for his friends."

Von Treptow asked, "Hold him a week or so?"

"As you wish," he said, turning and disappearing into a convenient crowd of sailors and seamen.

1645 Hours

Boarding was routine, document checks cursory. Knorr did not know what kind of contraband could be coming from Rotterdam to Britain, nor did he care, but the whole air aboard had a bit of the pirate or smuggler ship about it. *Johnny presumably knows what he's doing.*

"Gents, this way. Cabins are spacious for a tramp such as this. We must be popular as we are full up." The First Mate led them below the weather deck down a ladder into a corridor. "Sir, yours, and yours next door. No cabin services, Sirs, but the wardroom is available to you. Back up that ladder, then up the next ladder back. Takes you right there. Captain will welcome you on the bridge once we're clear of the harbour. Oh, yes, we're traveling black. No lights, no cigars or cigarettes on deck, keep your portholes draped. Violators will swim home. Seriously, Gentlemen."

Time passed, as did the daylight. Toward dusk, the freighter was eased away from the quay, shepherded by a little tugboat. From time to time the two captains shook fists and exchanged expletives, ending in laughter. Finally, the ship reached the outer harbor and the tug cast off, leaving matters in the skipper's hands.

Once they worked their way to open water, von Treptow and Knorr ascended to the bridge. After meeting the Captain and several other passengers, von Treptow felt the North Sea swells building when a series of wakes of a larger ship rocked the little freighter. "My apologies, Captain, Gentlemen. I shall be indisposed a few moments." He made it down one deck, then to the railing just in time, vomiting violently over the side. He straightened up just in time to see another set of wakes approaching on the starboard side, their foamy crests faintly illuminated in pink by the setting sun, prompting another round of retching. *Enough. To the bed.*

Knorr chatted with the captain and crew for a while until it was too dark to see anything of interest and nearly too dark to use the outside ladders. He made it back to their cabins, knocking gingerly on the general's door.

"Come," was the pitiful answer.

"Sir, may I get you something?"

"No, I am slowly getting used to it; going faster helps, it seems. My personal plague, Colonel, this *mal de mer*. The slightest rocking, swaying, sets it off. Started when I was posted to Southwest Africa. Had to ship around the Cape from Tanganyika, in a rusty thing not much different than this boat. So sick I had to be lifted off. The sensation lasted for several minutes on land, then I was a new man. Hence, my reluctance to sail. I shall survive, somehow. Help keep me distracted from the idea. We have not shared our histories yet, would you care to do so? Aside from the generalities about ancestors and such? But, first, I might be able to stomach some tea, if you would be so kind?"

A few minutes later, Knorr returned carrying a tray with two cups and a pot. He filled the general's, then his. He settled into the chair opposite the bed in the cramped cabin. "After my cowboy days, I came home, finished highschool, then to university at Cologne. Father was determined both his sons would be bankers, of course, their portraits alongside his, his father's and grandfather's. My brother Wolfgang thrived, having the necessary combination of numbers sense, judge of character, and *bonhomie*.

"The *bonhomie* was fine with me, but ledgers and accounts were fatally boring. I should have been an engineer, it seems, at least I enjoyed understanding our clients' business far more than the lending. The ship-yards, construction sites, all were more to my liking. Father, bless him, understood and allowed me enter the Army. That was 1905, just when the Algeciras matter was bubbling. Joined as a lieutenant in engineering and loved it. My first posting was in Vienna in a liaison role. There I met Rosalie, my wife. She is, was, the most beautiful creature when I saw her the first time at a ball. We soon became inseparable, and despite two fathers who enjoyed twisting each other's whiskers, were married in March, 1906.

"We bought a house in Hannover that summer, so she could have a stable base and some family support. In 1908, with the Serbian situation I was posted again to Vienna, and she naturally accompanied me. I then was assigned to Rome – not bad duty – for three months, and she came with me. We took a short holiday in the *mezzogiorno* – Abruzzi and Sicily – but by the time we returned by train, she was ill. It was cholera. She was a little frail to begin with and she was unable to fight it. She died three days after our return to Rome.

"It was hard." He paused, looked around, poured himself some more tea. "Very hard." Another pause. "Very, very hard." He was thankful for the minimal lighting in the stateroom.

Sighing, "So, I requested a return to the Reserves and rejoined the bank. About that time I made that trip back to Wyoming. I muddled my way along at the bank, but clearly my heart was not in it. So I regained my commission, and ended up in Berlin on von Prittwitz's staff." He quickly recounted the 'trade.' "Then to General Staff, then to war. That sums me up. Boring, do you think so?"

"Not at all. Not so dissimilar from mine. Always the Army, much time in Africa, managed to survive the native bacilli and avoid contracting malaria. Like your Yellowstone, Tanganyika is beautiful – Kilimanjaro, the Serengeti, the wildlife. Too beautiful to shoot, in my opinion.

"Was married, a lovely wife, a handsome boy, Gregor. Louisa died when he was ten, when I was posted abroad, in Windhoek again. Her death, my frequent absences on duty, all took a toll. When Gregor was ready for university, he finally broke away. Renounced me, my name, everything. Then joined the Army in the first flush of enthusiasm. Then died in the first flush of the brutal reality of war.

"His commanding officer? Von Bruckow, the pig. Sent the youth units straight to their deaths." He stopped, the pause lasting and lasting. A look came over his face. "Douse the lamp, I must open the porthole." He stuck his face as far out over the sea as he could, retching nothing but tea, then retching again.

"I think I will rest now."

An hour or so out, running dark, Knorr sensed a buzz or a bustling above him. He slipped on his trousers and stepped into the passageway, nearly run over by a hustling seaman. "Life jacket, Sir. Huns a'hunting." The sailor disappeared through the watertight door, clattering loudly up the ladder. Knorr reached inside for his tweed coat and the life jacket, then headed topside.

He reached the bridge and was about to enter when the First Mate brusquely dragged him inside, stashing him in a corner. "Sorry, Sir, trouble afoot. Two U-Boats sighted a few miles away. Warning from another freighter."

The first swerve of the ship's new zigzagging course threw Knorr off balance and he crumpled against the outside wall. "Careful, landlubber! Keep a hold." The Captain was smiling, but meant business. "I think we're far enough away, can't say the same for the rest of the chappies. Might want to get your seasick friend into his vest, matie. Next turn in five…four…three…two…one…now!" His helmsman spun the wheel counterclockwise and the ship lurched to port. "Now – you'll get three minutes."

Knorr clambered down the ladder back to his passageway. He found von Treptow with lifevest on. "One of the sailors rousted me. Oddly, stomach feels fine with all this jerking about. Shall we take a look?"

The two stepped out onto the deck, looking away toward the rest of the little fleet. The thin crescent moon was just another wisp among the wisps of cloud, faintly illuminating one ship a kilometer away and barely glinting off the funnel and slab side of another somewhat beyond. There was another, larger ship aft, hard to tell how close. Knorr started to say something when the next course change sent their feet sliding from underneath them, still holding fast to the railing. Then a flash and a red and white discoloration of the sea beyond the more distant of the ships abeam. The unfortunate ship's bulk masked an explosion's glare and much of the noise, a growling felt through the railing as much as heard. Then an eruption of white and yellow from the stern, followed a half second later by a sharp crack and aftershocks.

"She's gone, Gents. *SS Molucca*, Jack McIntosh's little collier. He's a good one, though, he'll get his boys off." The Captain called down to them, shaking his head. "We ain't out of the woods, yet, but least we knows where the Germans are. Already telegraphed for some destroyer help, shoulda had it miles back, but that's what the Hunsters is waiting for. We don't amount to nothing, but a destroyer? Look sharp now! We won't be fishing you out if you swing over the rails on the next change."

The next zag was handled more gracefully by the Army men. Knorr looked up at the bridge, an open affair, to see the Captain with his binoculars. He looked back and saw a faint luminescence, pencil thin, emerging from behind the nearest ship. Then another. Then a very audible explosion followed by another column of flame and smoke from their neighbor. He looked back at the glowing pencils and realized they had covered half the distance to their own ship.

The lookout above the bridge shouted, "Torpedoes! Bearing Zero Eight Zero!"

"Damn! Second sub." The Captain shouted, "All ahead starboard, reverse port engine. Hard over to course Two Six Zero!"

The little steamer groaned and creaked as it heeled over to port. It seemed to the Germans like the turn took forever, not at all like a sailboat or a motorcar. Finally, as the list leveled out von Treptow pointed aft, "Look! One of the torpedoes – almost upon us!" He was bracing himself when he saw it was running just wide and nearly parallel to the starboard beam. As it came on, they could see it was diverging slightly, and sure to miss by a good ten meters or more. Then the ship shifted to starboard and the two were lucky to maintain their grips.

The bubbling phosphorescence of the wake was now leaving them behind, dimming gradually as it passed as if the sea was calming its anger. The Captain hailed them, "That was close, Gents, port was even closer. I doubt they'll trouble us again at this range."

"That is very reassuring, Sir," said von Treptow, not at all convinced. Then to Knorr, in mixed German and French, "Cured my *mal de mer,* for the moment, at least."

Only then did they realize several fellow passengers, a dozen or so, were sharing the deck with them further aft. "English, Sir."

Soon a Royal Navy destroyer was blinking messages to the little merchant fleet. The cavalry had arrived, too late for some. Captain Elwood leaned over to the passengers crowding the rails, "Drama is over, Sirs. Should be in Hull only a bit behind schedule. Count yourselves among the lucky few to have escaped a torpedo attack. I do."

* * *

Sunday, January 13, 4:00 p.m.
The Midlands, England

To von Treptow's immense relief, the trip's schedule had been altered the last minute by Captain Waldemar, sparing him the misery of the long sea trip around Portsmouth to Wexford. Instead, the two disembarked at Hull and stayed overnight, then took a train through Leeds on to Manchester and finally to Liverpool.

Seems the heat was being turned up on the two Irish Republicans the Germans were to meet, Lynch and Collins, the former by the British, the latter by his fellow countrymen. The two needed a little holiday and a country house was the answer. One of the movement's most generous clandestine

supporters was a Manchester businessman and Member of Parliament, Ronald
Colmar, who owned a large home fronting the Irish Sea on the Serpentine
in Great Crosby just north of Liverpool.

At Lime Street Station, the two officers waited the better part of an hour
for their contact. Eventually, a tall ruddy redhead approached them. "Fancy
a drive in the country, Gents? I have a car outside, stocked with corned beef
and wurst." Von Treptow and Knorr looked at each other and debated the
merits of the offer. "No corned beef, my man," said Knorr. "Perhaps something else?"

"Something else it will be, then." Passwords having been exchanged
and verified, the Germans rose from their bench, stretching and rubbing
away the slat marks on their rears. "Let me help you with your bags. We'll
be right out here, Sirs."

They ambled casually out the main entry to a car parked a dozen yards
down the curb. The driver tumbled their cases into a bustle-like boot, then
opened the door for his fares. "Eoin's the name, Sirs. No last name needed."
Leaning his head out to check for traffic behind him but more to check for
surveillance, ahead and behind, he continued, "Sorry to leave you so long
in that drab place. The Brits have Army Intelligence types all over Liverpool
these days. Had to loll about a bit to get the measure of them here. Clear, I
think."

"Thank you, Eoin. Your diligence is much appreciated, as we would be
lost lambs here without help." Von Treptow continued on, "Tell my colleague
here about this Colmar fellow, and our other fellow guests, if you would be
so kind."

"Not much good to tell about your host. Industrialist of the blandest,
most careless type. Collieries just east of here in Lancashire, bloody awful
places to work and to see, for that matter. Got a hardware factory and plating
shops in Aston-in-Makerfield. Not renowned for his generosity to his workers, let me just say that. But, he's been helpful to the Cause. Born in Ireland,
sentimental attachments, I think. And an up-by-the-bootstraps type, so's
been shunned by the local squires and landed nobility, shares our hatred of
that class. Bought his constituency in Manchester, pays it little attention.
The other guests? I believe you know our Michael, General? Liam Lynch
you have not met, he's the hothead of the crowd, makes Collins look like
milktoast."

"Then, there's the ladies. Gad! Charlotte Despard, all piss and vinegar. Emmeline Pankhurst – at least she's still a bit of a looker at her age, and got a good head on her little shoulders. Them's the two main attractions but there's a few followers dropping in from time to time."

"An odd grouping, but perhaps not as odd as our last one, Colonel," said von Treptow. "Madame Despard is sister of none other than General Sir John French, Haig's cashiered predecessor. Miss Pankhurst is the Queen of the British suffragettes, violent confrontational methods. I cannot be sure why they are here, but it should be interesting."

Eoin added, "Your Grosz fellow sends his warmest regards. I had a pint with him in Portsmouth. The transshipment went smoothly. The cargo was getting a little rank, so the stevedores made quick work of it. Grosz made sure I told you the evidence of his genius – no British officer would get within nosing range."

Von Treptow and Knorr laughed at the image and shared a few anecdotes of their introduction to Grosz with their driver. "Yessir, that's him alright, Sir. Better to have him, I guess, than have him agin ya."

"Yes, I suppose so, Eoin." Knorr was looking out at the grey skies and matching grey seas as they passed clusters of grey cottages and shops. "Reminds me of Peenemunde, Sir. A mischievous God's idea of a summer holiday spot."

After the longish train ride, the wait and now the motor drive, the sun was growing dimmer in the west, spilling a quavering puddle of yellow and white across the Irish Sea. Soon enough they arrived at the Serpentine, a coast road with houses and sand dunes either side. Seaward the houses were uniformly larger, but uniform, too, in design and construction, clearly some builder's notion of the model seaside mansion repeated often for effect. Colmar's was somewhat larger and equally bland, but at least the landscaping was more generous on a double or triple lot, it appeared.

As they rolled up the gravel driveway, a sandy-haired fellow in a military outfit appeared in the doorway, hands cupped against the breeze, lighting his cigarette. "That is Michael Collins, Colonel. He is an important leader of the Irish Republicans. Am I saying that correctly, Eoin?"

"Yes, Sir. He is prominent in both Sinn Féin and the Irish Volunteers, to be precise. As is Lynch. Those two are more often arguing than not, and it isn't

just Irish tempers. Lynch is deadset against any type of agreement with the
British. Collins is more diplomatic, yet no less belligerent – proved that at the
Post Office two years past. The rest of us, the rank and file, we don't care, just
get the British out of Ireland, even if we have to give 'em Ulster to do it. Last
thing we want is a fight amongst ourselves. Well, then, here we are."

He stopped the car with a lurch, and trotted over to greet Collins. He
pointed back at the car where von Treptow and Knorr were climbing out.
Von Treptow gave Collins a formal salute, which was returned a bit less
crisply. "General Collins, a pleasure to see you again. My aide, Lieutenant
Colonel Walter Knorr."

Collins gave each a hearty handshake. "Eoin, you have delivered them
just in time. The ladies' arguing is giving me indigestion and worse. Come
in, laddies. General, sharpen your wits and tongue is my advice."

Colmar came to greet them as they entered the foyer, an arcade ending
in a sea view at the other end of the house. As they walked along toward the
salon, women's voices were rising. "You, of all people, Emmeline! Siding
with the oppressors against the working poor? After all you've done and
seen? How is this possible?"

Von Treptow and Knorr entered the broad room spanning the rear of the
house, stopping short to survey the scene: two women, one older in black
Victorian garb, a black lace mantilla atop her grey head, the other somewhat
younger, more stylishly dressed, trilling away over their shoulders as they
sat in wing chairs angled away one from the other. Despard, the elder, was
reading the *Guardian*, Pankhurst a book. Colmar threw up his arms in mock
despair. Out the French doors onto the terrace was another man reading,
reddish hair, bulkier than Collins. "My other guest, Lynch. Taciturn at rest.
Not much of a conversationalist until he gets agitated. Which is often enough.
Ladies, may I introduce these supporters of the cause?"

Emmeline Pankhurst looked at Collins, Colmar and his German guests as
if the four were caryatids and turned to hurl more insults at her neighbor.
"Madame Despard, I have seen the future in Russia and it is a dismal prospect.
Have you seen it, as it truly is? You may well forget the entire notion of women's
suffrage and equality. These will not transpire with those beastly men in charge,
and they show no inclination to change, much less abdicate."

"My dear, I am simply saying you are an ignorant wretch. The Communist
movement is the only hope for mankind. Do not let your misanthropy blind

you to the immutable march of history toward the revolution of the proletariat. And each and every day you slide toward the Tories is a day lost on that march."

"A death march, dearest Charlotte. Do you really think your idols, this Lenin, Bukharin, that crowd, would give you the same freedom to protest you enjoy under the present regime? Granted, our men are every bit as benighted, but at least we have a prospect for change..."

Colmar escorted his guests through the salon without the least interruption of the distaff exchange. The shrillness trailed away only as they stepped out into the sea breeze on the terrace, crisp and salty in their faces. Liam Lynch rose from his deck chair to introduce himself, setting aside his Yeats. "These be the Germans you been speaking of, Big Fellah?" directing himself to Collins. "Bringing lots of pounds, I am hoping."

"Always charming on first impression, is he not? He only gets worse with familiarity, Gentlemen. You have been warned." Collins wasn't exactly apologizing for his compatriot.

Lynch planted a solid ham fist on Collins' shoulder. "Aye, he knows me all too well. Not nearly so good with words as the motion picture star here, English or Gaelic, but I have my ways. Best behavior this point forward, I promise."

"I am holding you to it, Liam." Colmar was expecting the worst. "Whisky, Gents? How do you have it? Irish or Scotch?"

Knorr replied, "Let us give the Irish a try. We are here on their account, after all."

Von Treptow nodded his assent, "Quickly would be nice, if I am not too bold, Sir."

"Not at all, General, I am in your camp on this one." Colmar snapped his fingers and raised five fingers to his butler who quickly rematerialized with a tray. "Now, let us retreat to the windbreak and the fire before I am chilled." The windbreak was a double row of trees, much like aspens they seemed to Knorr, that did the job of deflecting the gathering breeze.

"So, Mister Colmar, kind of you to spare us the passage to Ireland. I am not much of a seaman, I willingly confess. Eoin tells us the shipment is proceeding as expected?" Von Treptow could not hide his amusement at the thought of Grosz. "He met our...export specialist...and had nothing but admiration for his abilities, it seems."

"Just so he delivers," said Collins. "Now, General, let's get to particulars before the harpies in there get their talons into us. We appreciate your giving us the guns on credit, as it were, and the funds as agreed come at a critical point. But your communications were vague as to your expectations of us. Honestly, we expected more of you at Eastertide two years ago, and I'm sure you expected more of us with our lads in Flanders. So, where are we, General?"

"At a crossroads of sorts, Collins. Our discussion was not fit for wires and messages, hence our little rendezvous. The next few months tell the tale for all of us. For us, whether we can extricate ourselves from this conflict on terms to our advantage. If not, well, you would not be able to count on our future largesse.

"And, it is a curious conundrum..." Lynch started to interrupt the general, but Collins restrained him, von Treptow continuing, "Thank you, Michael. Mister Lynch, no philosophy here, just pragmatism. The puzzle for your consideration is this: if we lose this war, of course the British will then turn their full attention to you. If we win this war, the British do the same, weakened to be sure, but even angrier. Do you see the answer?"

"Of course! The war goes on, forever!" Lynch jumped on the notion. "The Brits get even more worn down, we bring more of our lads home, or somehow keep 'em from fighting. We just keep low and get stronger until the time is right. Michael, you and Eamon just keep on talking to whosoever the English send up."

"One problem with that scenario, Mr. Lynch. To wear down those English, we must perforce be worn down even more. That is not part of any bargain Germany will entertain."

Colmar then spoke up, "Like the peeling of an onion, then. So, General, what is the next layer?" He poked at the fire, generating some welcome radiation.

"See the fog creeping in?" Von Treptow pointed out to the Irish Sea, now shrouded in a light mist. "Something not unlike that."

"Liam, he is inscrutable as our poetry. We need to introduce him to William." Collins was smiling. "Seriously, Sir?"

"Seriously, Mister Collins. We benefit from a conclusion, you do not. You benefit from a stalemate, we do not, at least not in the form of perpetual trench warfare. So, we create an ambiguous conclusion that is a benign stalemate. Everyone is happy. The stalemate is the fog, a state of neither peace nor active war, at least not fighting. That stalemate is, for us in practical terms, a conclusion – I am thinking of the Western Front here, of course – which suits our purposes as well as a peace treaty. If you were to contemplate a major rising in Ireland in, say, April, could the English afford to divert either their home reserves or their frontline troops to deal with same?"

"No more than they could today, that's clear." Collins was indeed contemplating.

"Correct. So we, you and we, that is, keep them in that state of limbo. At sixes and sevens, as they would say. I cannot divulge too much of our strategy in theater, but it revolves around the movement of over a million men and their equipment from Russia. By springtime, we shall have an irresistible force in the field."

"So why not use 'em, dammit, and crush the Brits?" Lynch was insistent, "Don't tell me you expect us to rise and get bloodied just to make things easier on you. Fight on to the last Mick, that sort of thing?"

"Yes."

Lynch bolted from his chair and grabbed von Treptow by his lapels. "Not you, not the bloody English, no one will ever, ever do that to us, ever again. Do you understand me? Do you?"

"Yes, of course I do."

"Liam, let him go." Collins was as red as Lynch. "General, he was just quicker to his feet than me. Explain yourself, or let's all go home."

By this time, Knorr was standing over the crouching figure of Lynch, stripping Liam's arms away from the general. He spun the Irishman around, locking his arms rigidly behind his back. Lynch gave him a shocked look, then smiled. "This one's all right, Michael. He can come with us. This other one…" Knorr released him, Lynch adjusted his jacket and sat back down, a wide grin on his face.

Von Treptow was irritated but remained calm, "Please, please, spare us the histrionics. No, I do not expect to bleed you. But I do expect you to make a show. Let the Brits think so. Can you handle their troops on the island? With some heavier equipment, were we to furnish same?"

"We could handle them now, Sir. With this shipment, that is, we should be able to. Not in a pitched battle, but with our tactics, yes. We won't play by their rules, ever again. We'll invent our own."

"Bloody mayhem!" blurted Lynch, then softer, "We've got good at it."

"And they are distracted, we are building our strength." Collins' tone was more measured, "But, as you know, it is only a short ferry ride from Liverpool and Scotland, and they can bring as many troops as they want to Belfast. We can't stop them."

"You cannot, but your friends can."

"How? You?"

"Mines and torpedoes. The Royal Navy has every advantage – a narrow sea in the way of Belfast, hundreds of ships, aircraft, every advantage. Except knowledge. Knowledge of when the rising will begin, knowledge that we can position in advance a half dozen submarines, knowledge of the minefields our other submarines can lay. Their Navy is looking to the east, to the channel, and to the west, to the approaches. Not so much out there," waving to the Irish Sea. "Mind you, I could never persuade our Navy to sacrifice itself, but if they are in and out, so to speak, quickly, just that one time, we can give the Englanders pause. Considerable pause. A surprise which leads to panic which spawns paralysis. Just sufficient to advance your cause."

"Do we feel better now, everyone?" Colmar looked at his watch, then at the setting sun. "Not getting warmer out here, Gentlemen. I have laid on an early supper in the probably vain hope of dispatching the ladies sooner than later."

"I cannot control my curiosity, Sir," said Colonel Knorr. "Why the guest list as it is?"

"I take only partial responsibility, Sir. I had invited Miss Pankhurst to speak at a suffragette event at one of my plants in Manchester, so naturally I extended the invitation to join me here. She knows Collins and Lynch here by reputation, I thought she might as well get the Irish gospel directly from them. They run in parallel of sorts, or so I thought. Madame Despard?"

"She heard we were coming, latched onto us." Collins rolled his eyes, "Cannot spurn a major contributor, you can understand."

"No matter how unpleasant," said Lynch.

"Agreed. Now let us go in. Edmund just gave me the high sign."

Dinner was ample and delicious, the company another matter. Collins, Colmar and Lynch had managed to maintain the fiction that their guests were in fact Canadian and American sympathizers, not Imperial German Army officers. While Madame Despard would have been thrilled by their identity and mission, Emmeline Pankhurst was a devoted patriot, having set aside her revolutionary suffragism to support the war effort, placing the patriarchs ruling Great Britain on notice that she would resume in full force her campaign for women's rights upon victory.

So the general and the colonel had some breathing room. None of the guests had much knowledge of North America, at least past the Hudson River, so Knorr was free to try out his Western stories.

Lynch in particular was entranced by the cowboy lore. Miss Pankhurst, too, found the images romantic. "Were that Walter Scott were still with us, what he could have made of all this! Stevenson just scratched the surface in his California stories, but the majestic sweep of the plains and the mountains, these magnificent bison creatures and, of course the Indians against the Cowboys. It sounds so grand! Tell me, Mister Stansfield – that is not a particularly Irish name, is it?"

"No, Miss Pankhurst, thoroughly English. But out West where I'm from, and California, Texas, all those places, we seem to intermarry without any problems. My mother is a Malloy, her mother was an O'Malley. Political family in Trenton – that's New Jersey. So many cousins sharing similar names! Seriously, though, the segregation of the races is so much more pronounced in the big cities. I think it's the politicians on each side, playing one against the other. Out West, we haven't the time for such shenanigans."

Von Treptow marveled at his aide's quick wit, "Tell her about the stampedes, George. George?"

Knorr jerked, then said, "Oh yes, certainly. Best way to describe it – you have all seen the first flood of a creek or a stream – when the water comes tumbling and rising around a bend, maybe then spreading out as it goes? Not so dissimilar. When you have three or four thousand head of cattle milling about, and lightning strikes nearby, or maybe just one of them gets rambunctious, they start running, like a school of fish, that's a good image. Nothing to do but get out of the way, try to police the edges. Sounds like thunder, rolling thunder. Eventually they'll slow down and go back to their grazing, unless they hit a gully or a river. Then it gets ugly, and you can lose hundreds to drowning and trampling."

Charlotte Despard sneered, "What about fencing? The horrid barbed wire your country gave to Flanders, that my brother sent ours by the thousands to die upon?"

"Like a few thistles, M'am. Gone in a matter of seconds. It'll tangle them up some but those unfortunates end up trampled. It's funny, on reflection. Even the biggest bulls stay away from it in pastures – a few nicks, they don't like it much. Unless there's a heifer or a rival bull the other side. But in a panic, it is as nothing."

"Not unlike men in war," Collins said. "All a matter of motivation."

"And the Indians, their women? What is their life like?" Emmeline continued her fascination with Knorr's tales.

"I hate to disappoint you, Miss, but the 'Noble Savage' is a myth. The men hunt and ride and smoke the pipe. The women work, bear children, all the burdens and cares. They are typically somewhere between a possession and a servant. Maybe a Russian serf is close. And there are slaves, captured in raids on other tribes. The only ones I've known well enough, and that seem to be more like English ladies are the big chiefs' daughters. Otherwise, it's pretty grim. Their whole existence is grim, brutal even, at least to us. What most people don't realize is, in the days before the white man came or at least took things over, the tribes fought each other constantly. Savagely. Blackfoot against Cree against Sioux, others against neighbors."

"Protestants against Catholics. Ulster against Éire. Ever the same, Mister Stansfield, no matter where you are. Tribalism knows of no boundaries or distinctions, sadly." Lynch was well liquored, getting poetic, " '*I imagine new races, as it were, seeking domination, a world resembling but for its immensity the Greek tribes – each with its own Daimon or ancestral hero – the brood of Leda, War and Love; history grown symbolic, the biography changed into myth*' We cannot escape our fates, friends. The gyre turns with or without us."

Collins interceded, "He is under the spell of our friend and compatriot Yeats. Especially with whisky. Please continue, Mister Stansfield, please continue."

"Yes, then. In any event, those days are over. The Plains Indians, some of the finest men I've ever met, great warriors, hunters, are now herded into reservations. Dishonored, idled, they turn to drink and fighting amongst themselves. It is a pity, a miserable existence. Our world has changed, not all for the best, at least not for everyone."

"All of which will change, even, I daresay, in my lifetime." Madame Despard lunged into the conversation. "World Communism will be the saviour of the oppressed, the workingmen and women, the poor. Even your reserved Indians. Some fail to see the inevitability of the proletarian revolution being unleashed upon the world, to their everlasting peril. Would you not agree, my dear?" She held up her glasses to peer at Madame Pankhurst.

"You know I would not, not in the least, dearest Charlotte. You know nothing of which you speak other than parroting the evil dreams of a failed philosopher, not even worthy of the specious title of intellectual. You believe everything Eleanor told you as gospel, even twenty years on, without experiencing first hand. Stand down from your ivory tower, Madame, and see the brutes for what they are. Liam, you know your poet:

'...and what rough beast, its hour come at last,
slouches toward Bethlehem to be born?'

"These are rough beasts, indeed, and no good will come of them. Their gaze is certainly as blank and pitiless as the sun. I have seen that gaze in person, face to face, those cold, heartless eyes. Have you? Of course not. They will destroy an entire people, peoples, just to remake them in their own warped images. They should be killed in their cradles, stillborn, whilst we have the chance and time."

"Now we speak of murder. Are we the Saducees and Pharisees, Emmeline? Are we to crucify these great men? The redeemers of the workers, the poor?"

"Now you blaspheme, you wicked woman. Enough!" Emmeline stood abruptly, throwing down her napkin. "Discard your life, your station, your liberty, such a weak thing as it is. But not mine!" She stormed out of the dining salon.

The remaining guests looked at each other. Their host rose, saying, "Gentlemen, cigars and brandy? Madame Despard, since you seem to have lost your conversation partner, would you care to join us?"

Charlotte tilted her chin. "Of course. Thank you, Mister Colmar."

After an eternity of speeches and Marxist slogans, it seemed, Madame Despard took her leave. Colmar was exhausted. "I have finally met a banshee, Collins. I now believe in them. Spare me another such." The only antidote was more whisky or brandy. Ireland was in the lead with Germany not far behind. Lynch was singing softly, slumped in his chair. Collins and von Treptow were engaged in serious, if slurred, conversation.

"General Collins, then, pray let us turn to practicalities. Can you assure me of a significant diversion? A diversion, within your means, planned to turn Britain's attention away from the Continent even if only momentarily? I do not expect you and Lynch to take on the entire British Army, merely remind them of the threat in their rear."

"If Germany does its part, yes. Otherwise, we won't be doing the sacrificial lamb thing for your benefit. I have to think on it, but with a few field pieces we could change the terms of discussion with the English, if we can get them. Pick our spots, you see, then fade away. Keep them off balance. The pitched battles at the Post Office and Saint Stephens Green showed we could not face fifty thousand Brits, not head on."

"You may not need face them at all, Michael, certainly not all at once."

"Are you daft, man? First you speak of building up our forces, then what? Forgive me my skepticism, it is born out of great distrust of any power that would use us as fodder. We've been used that way too often in our sad history. Show me sincerity as well as cunning, General."

"Allow me both, General Collins. Suppose you pick your spots, as you say, just one or two. A demonstration of possession of heavier firepower. Then hide away. Then, a week later, say, another spot or two, hide and repeat. Assuming the populace would not betray you? Then your everyday irregular attacks would take on a more threatening aspect. Never knowing where the cannon might fire, you see?"

"Easy for you to say. And how are we to get these field pieces? And training?"

"We shall arrange their delivery if you can secure docks. Not sure where, which coast. Not that many, in any event – only so much can be hidden, after all. The number is irrelevant, their mere existence is what counts. The threat is the key, the strategic crux, not so much the use."

"More riddles, man?"

"No riddles, Sir. Here is the proposition. We deliver a dozen or so eighteen pounders captured in Flanders, with ammunition. You bring back a few of your artillery lads, on medical leave, deserters, as you choose. All you need then are some strong, fast horses to haul the limbers quickly into place and back into hiding. Now, to you. How long do you think you could keep up this cat and mouse escapade? A few months, at most?"

"Maybe."

"That's all we need, both of us."

"Wonderful! We tweak the English nose, you hightail it back to the Continent. We face them alone after all!"

"Damn it all, Collins! At some time you will have to wean yourselves off us. There will come a time when your peasants' revolt has to become a real nation, with a real military. So, yes, you will have to face them, on your own, in the main."

Von Treptow leaned back in his chair, taking off his glasses and rubbing his eyes. "Let us rephrase this conversation. In a few months – by June, let us say – we expect to force the British government into a ceasefire, but by peaceful means." He saw Collins' quizzical look. "Colonel, help me with this one. Please explain our goals to Mister Collins. I fear I no longer have my tongue or his trust."

Collins started to protest, but Knorr said, "Easy now, Sir. It is really very simple in concept. Perhaps execution will be another matter." He grinned at von Treptow, who merely nodded. "We plan to free up a million or more men in the East and their gear by, say, April first. Those men then come to the West and hover over the British and French, and the Americans, too, like vultures, harbingers of death. All along we will have been undermining the Associated Powers' will to wage war, politically rather than militarily.

"Part of that is a revived threat in Ireland. Pinpricks, but with artillery heralding an escalation, a much greater threat. What does Lloyd George do? Yield to Haig and commit his reserves to Flanders? Or hold them against your threat? We already spoke of using submarines to complicate their reinforcements. The key, which General von Treptow was approaching, is time. We do not need much. Again, April. Three months from now. We will propose to end this war. A ceasefire, an armistice, a treaty, the form does not matter. Would your fellows in France not then clamour to come home? Would they not find a way home? Particularly if we declare the seas free from threat?"

Von Treptow added, "Between the pinpricks and your repatriations, in the well-trained thousands, even the Conservatives would blanch at full scale suppression. Clearer, now?"

Collins shot back, "The obvious risk remains, if we harness ourselves to you, and you fail, we sink."

Von Treptow rejoined, "We shall have sunk before you. That is the only comfort you shall have."

Collins beckoned to his host to sit beside him on the sofa, "Colmar, what d'you think?"

"It is a business decision, Michael. Either you stand pat, status quo, as-is, and wait for events, as hostages, or you change your mode of business to seize an opportunity. Their proposal rests entirely on their success on the Continent. How much do you wish to risk on that success? If they are right, you will have an independent and free Irish nation by yearend. That is the opportunity. If they fail, it may take years of war with the English. That is the risk. I do not know the correct counsel."

Collins turned toward the Germans. "General von Treptow, the only basis I will consider is a more substantial investment on your part, of arms and munitions. If your continental schemes fail, then, at least, we are well-armed. And, as I think on it, if you do fail, our boys will come back soon enough. We win both ways?"

"I shall not discourage you in that train of thought, General Collins. Your success hastens ours. Our success buys you time and distracts the English. Our failure delays your men's return, freeing your enemy to gaze your direction."

Colmar interceded, "The essence of risk, Gentlemen, is uncertainty. The certainty of the sun's rising tomorrow," looking at his watch and the loudly snoring Lynch, "all too soon, it seems, renders it a riskless proposition. This gambit, on the other hand, well, it is uncertain, no? But such is life. We Irish, paramount above all people, understand that, do we not?"

"Our little deposit that Colonel Knorr is carrying will be evidence of our confidence and goodwill. We have explained ourselves as best as we can. Sleep on it, Michael, speak to de Valera and others. The money will be on deposit day after tomorrow, your guns arrive the same day. We will expect an answer before the funds are released, but the guns are yours. If you can keep them. Goodnight, Gentlemen, this has been an exhausting day." Von Treptow embraced Collins, shook hands with Colmar, and disappeared up the staircase.

"Well," said Collins.

"Yes. Goodnight, Sirs." Knorr stumbled, weaved, then straightened himself and departed uncertainly.

* * *

Monday, January 14, 8:30 a.m.
Great Crosby

Collins and Lynch vanished before dawn, taking separate paths to ship back to Ireland in small craft, avoiding unwanted observation. Mesdames Despard and Pankhurst likewise shipped separately, at a more civilized hour, Charlotte by train to London, to her Battersea women's shelters, Emmeline back to Manchester by car for another round of speeches.

Colmar greeted his thickheaded guests as they marched into a late breakfast. "Well now, Gentlemen, the wages of drinking with the Irish is a trying morning after. After breakfast, please join me on a meager shoot. I lease two hundred acres the far side of Sniggery Wood this time of year. Not nearly to the standards of my Scottish estate, but it will have to do, given your circumstances. The birds will be frisky in this weather, at least. Shall we?"

The change in their travel schedule had left a rare uncommitted day for von Treptow and Knorr, as their banking appointment had not been changed, nor their following engagements in London. The day passed agreeably, the shooting was better than expected, and Colmar and the German officers developed an unexpected rapport. Colmar was all business, to be sure – his postwar aim was to expand free of the restrictions of Imperial Preference, and his base would shift to his nascent Irish operations. He was intimate not only with the military types such as Collins and Lynch, but also with the leadership, de Valera above all. In any independent postwar Ireland, Colmar's star was sure to shine.

So his interests were aligned not only with the Republicans, but with his German guests, as he was sure their triumph would hasten Ireland's freedom. He would hedge his bets, of course, playing it both ways, but he shared von Treptow's strategic vision and the humbling of England was an especially delicious prospect. He also had the means, in connections as well as finance, to assist. The previous evening's discussions had elicited but few comments, but he had listened carefully.

"General, with all due respect, your plan presents unnecessary complications to all involved. I expected as much upon hearing of this current gun-running scheme. Your man certainly seems intrepid, but there are inherent risks that could be avoided. Though, I must admit, smuggling under the very noses of the British is music to mine ears."

After a sip of coffee, "I would simply concentrate first on the men, not the machinery. Collins was loath to admit it, but he and his Republicans are woefully short of combatworthy men and cannot command the undiluted allegiance of the populace. Perhaps sufficiently to carry out your sporadic scheme for the few months you propose, but not much longer. Bring thousands of the National Volunteers and the other Irish regiments home, however, and the game is afoot. Strangle the British reinforcement movements, as you so generously propose, and the calculus favors our lads even further. If they could bring their playthings with them."

"How would they gain leave from the Army to head for home? In such numbers, certainly?" Knorr's natural skepticism was at work.

"Politics, Colonel. Politics and old-fashioned desertion, disguised as demobilization and rotation. Remember these are volunteers, truly, and deserve more flexibility, if that is the word, in their leave arrangements. For every man granted leave to return home, another man deserts alongside him. We have sympathizers in the steamship business, and the Irish have a clever printing business, so identities, orders and transit vouchers will be available. I have finally persuaded de Valera to start the process, slowly enough to avoid raising the alarum, but on pace to return, oh, upwards of several thousand a month, in small groups.

"Then the politics. Our Members of Parliament, Irish and others friendly, will agitate on behalf of specific units, not on an individual basis. One division's equivalent a month, in mixed regimental and battalion increments, are due to be rotated. As long as things are quiet at the Front, as they are now, the need to bring them back to action can be countermanded by political pressure. Lloyd George can hardly press the issue, holding the reserve divisions here. It can all be done quietly, or as quietly as possible with the muckrakers on Fleet Street skulking about. Your peace initiative, if it merits such a label, hastens the process. Combined, easily forty, fifty thousand in a few months. Perhaps that is all, who knows?"

Knorr continued probing, "And equipment? Surely the returning regiments will not ship home their artillery?"

"Correct. You and I have much work in that regard. I do not have a solution at hand, but I assure you it will demand more than your man Goss, Gross, whatever his name is. Here, before I forget," he handed von Treptow a business card. "My man in Copenhagen. Our contact. You seem to have some ideas, General. Make them work."

* * *

Tuesday, January 15, 9:15 a.m.
Liverpool

Colmar had arranged for Eoin to spirit them out of the house late that night, just before dawn, for the motorcar ride to Liverpool harbor. In the dark they were of course less conspicuous, and since Rotterdam had not concerned themselves with counterespionage tactics. Eoin thought otherwise, arranging for each to slip to adjacent houses, to be picked up by separate cars, then reunited in the jumble of a warehouse district on the outskirts of the harbor. Once so sanitized, they made straight to the outer Mersey docks, to a steamer named, ironically, *Éirinn go brách*, flying the Irish tricolor below the Merchant Jack.

Colonel Knorr shook his head, "Really, Eoin? Was this necessary?"

"Met your schedule, Gents. I take a later ship, will see you there." At that, he waved, smiled, and left them to their fates.

* * *

Tuesday, January 15, 10:45 a.m.
Ministry of Intelligence Department Five, War Office, London

"Colonel, Sir?" Lieutenant Abercrombie knocked tentatively on the jamb.

"Yes, man, what is it? Can you not see I am engaged? Important matters, I need not add." The Colonel was stabbing crowsfeet-like notations with his pencil, much like a modern-day Sumerian scribe, on the *London Morning Post's* football page.

"Yes, Sir. I just rang off with Mortimer over at Six, Sir. He had several most intriguing tidbits to pass along..."

"Yes, yes, I am sure he did. Cumming told him to share some quotidian crumbs on the pretext of Cooperation and Coordination. Bah!" He turned again to his form. "Well? Get on with it, man."

"Yes, then, seems one of their agents was detained by the Dutch in Rotterdam…"

"For whoring or drunkenness?"

Abercrombie quaked slightly, "No, Sir, he was observing some suspicious characters. The whole thing was observed by his partner, Roseworthy, I believe is his name. Your know him from…"

"Lieutenant, along with your story or along with you." The Colonel scowled as he shifted to another match.

"Yes, Sir. They were observing some men, two of them, they believed to be Germans, Sir. Spies, Sir. Took passage to Hull that day. Roseworthy stayed with the assignment, observed just that."

"What day, again? Or did you say?"

"I did not, Sir. Saturday afternoon, it was."

The Colonel slammed down the manila folder concealing his association papers. "Saturday? Saturday. That would be three days ago, young man. Those horses are well and good several counties escaped. Had he no notion to contact us, or failing that necessary and proper course, some other authority?"

"He did, Sir."

"And was that authority this office? No, I wager not."

"No, Sir, it was not."

A sigh. "And who, pray tell? Allow me a guess. The Embassy. Who did nought. I am correct, am I not?"

"No, Sir, they then contacted Naval Intelligence, of course."

The Colonel's stiff mustache twitched and bristled.

Abercrombie continued, "Who contacted Hull Constabulary, who contacted the harbormaster and the railways superintendent…"

"All of which we would have done. We would have, would we not?"

"Yes, Sir."

"And?"

"Nothing, Sir. No one, no one thing suspicious on the ship's manifests. Ordinary business travel by rail to Manchester, Leeds. Final destinations unknown, Sir."

"Nationalities of the shipping passengers?"

"British, Dutch, of course, Canadian, American. Several of each. There were six ships made the passage safely."

"Safely?" *Another club fails me.*

"Yes, Sir. Three ships lost to submarine attack."

"And Naval did nothing else? Very well, nothing actionable. Is that all, young man?"

"Something else, Sir."

The Colonel looked up at his wall clock, then down at his folder. *Drat! Missed Queen's Park Rangers. Drat! Sure to prevail over Watford, were they not?* "Yes, Abercrombie? Succinctly now, if you please."

"That publican in Portsmouth, the one we found so useful with that German ring last spring?"

"Yes, yes, Bartlett, Bartlesby, what?"

"Barnett, Sir."

"Of course, Barnett. What?" *Spurs lost? Good God, and the Yids did not even have the courtesy to cover. Drat!* He tossed the paper into his wastebin. "What about this tavernkeeper Barnacle?"

"You will recall, of course, this Eoin Kenney fellow we have traced to Collins and de Valera? A handyman sort, if you catch my drift?"

The Colonel neither recalled nor caught, but nodded, "Go on."

"Barnett had him in his pub. The *Wandering Ram*, you recall?" The Colonel waved him on, so Abercrombie continued, "Having a pint or two with a short weatherbeaten sort of fellow, he says. Spoke with just a hint of Germany, hidden beneath a layer of coarse talk, but distinct enough. The subject apparently was guns, Sir."

The Colonel looked at him blankly.

"Guns, Sir! Do you see? Guns for the Irish! From Germany, Sir!"

"Quell your enthusiasm, young man. Yes, of course I see. What good does that do me or us? Have you more?"

Abercrombie wilted against the doorjamb. "No, Sir. Only that a man answering the Irishman's description was noted on the Mersey docks this morning, shipping to Man. Mortimer again, Sir, just now, Sir."

"The Isle? Why?"

"No Man knows, Sir."

"No man?"

"A punnish jest, a slight one, it would seem, Sir. From *The Odyssey*, Sir."

"Punishing indeed. You Oxford types…" He groomed his mustache absentmindedly. "So, what do you make of this?"

"A gunrunning scheme, but how these other two mesh is far from clear, if indeed they do. I shall make some enquiries if that meets with your approval, Colonel d'Eyncourt?"

"Yes, yes, and be snappy about it. Now close the door as you make your exit, as you will shortly, if you please."

Damnation! Down twenty quid to Ladbrokes and still an hour until lunch!

* * *

Tuesday, January 15, 11:00 a.m.
Douglas, Isle of Man

Von Treptow and Knorr disembarked from their small steamer at the port of Douglas. A rickety Renault cab took them to a salesman's hotel near the town center, one street off the main esplanade. They checked in with their old identities, paying in advance, and rested a bit in their drab room. At noon, having changed into more stylish business attire, they slipped out a rear door, crossing an alley into the service vestibule of the Empress Hotel, one of the better hostelries on the island.

They took a leisurely luncheon in the hotel's restaurant, eyes carefully tracking every passerby from behind their *Times* and *Telegraph*. At precisely 1:15 they rose, Knorr leaving a one pound note on the bill. The doorman asked, "Taxi, Gentlemen? Going to the bank?"

"Yes," nodded von Treptow, acknowledging the signal. "If you would, my good man," handing him a shilling. The cab arrived immediately, having been idling for the last few minutes. The two climbed in, and the driver made the turn back toward the town center. A short drive to the Bank of Man, then the two strolled up the granite steps into the grand banking hall.

"May I help you gentlemen?" piped a portly, middle-aged clerk, obviously impressed with their suitings and demeanor.

"Yes, please direct us to Mister Dillon, if you would be so kind." Knorr thought his Scots accent came out allright, and apparently so did she, smitten with him, it would seem.

Dillon rose to greet them, saying, "Such a pleasure, Sir William! And this would be Mister Reynolds?"

"Yes, thank you, and thank you for making room in your busy schedule. Is our transaction in order?"

"Absolutely, Sir, and let me thank you again for entrusting our bank to handle these...sizeable funds."

"You come highly recommended, He-, Mister Dillon," said von Treptow. "May we execute the documents? We have a steamer to Glasgow within the hour."

"This way, Sirs, and I will have you on your way in a few minutes. May I offer you the use of our car, Gentlemen? We are quite pleased and proud of it, a new Silver Ghost with Hooper bodywork – extra cost," he winked.

"That would be most kind of you. Now, what do you require of us? Here are our corporate resolutions, executory authorizations and passports. And the funds, of course." Knorr opened his briefcase then removed his Montblanc from his vest. "I shall sign, Sir William shall attest."

"A fine instrument, Sir, did you come by that here?" Was there the slightest hint of suspicion?

"A gift from the House of Julius Baer in Zurich, our main banking relation on the continent. You know them, have you dealt with them? First class, I assure you." Von Treptow peered down at Mister Dillon through his monocle.

"Of course, of course, fine bank, fine bank."

In a matter of minutes, signatures were affixed, authorizations confirmed, seals stamped, and two hundred thousand pounds began their journey through a series of middlemen in England and Jersey, on their way to twenty-three bank accounts in Ireland and Switzerland, most remaining in Douglas.

"Thank you, Mister Dillon. That was quite painless. I do so detest the normal rigamarole of the bureaucrat," said 'Sir William' to the bank officer, who considered himself the consummate bureaucrat.

"Again, Sir William, my pleasure. And the Bank of Man's, as well! Our car should be waiting for you out front, if you will follow me, please." Knorr's new admirer took the banker aside. He straightened, "My apologies, she tells me it seems our driver has chosen to sit in the carriage court – I will have him bring the car around."

"No need, my good man. Just lead us on, what?" Von Treptow was beginning to have some fun with his Sir William persona.

"These Irish," said Dillon, "an incorrigible lot, but with so many of our men gone to service…"

"Yes, my good man, qualified help is frightfully hard to find. You can scarcely imagine the difficulties my estate managers have at finding beaters and cleaning boys. Beastly situation, it is. Can hardly put on a decent hunt. And farriers? Hmphh!" Von Treptow was laying it on.

Dillon, now thoroughly intimidated, hustled the two through the court-yard entry and into the waiting Rolls-Royce. "Thank you, Gentlemen, and good day."

"To the port, Eoin. No need to take evasive action."

"Will do, Colonel. Enjoying your stay?"

"Yes, such as it was. Any news?"

"No, Sir. Nothing new. Your arrangements in Liverpool are still as you made them." In minutes, they arrived at the quay. Eoin carried their bags to the gangway, pocketed a token tip and waved goodbye.

* * *

Tuesday, January 15, 6:30 p.m.
Dutch Embassy, London

SS *Kandahar* was comfortable enough for the short float back over to Liverpool. The two stayed in their cabin, napping, von Treptow admitting to some queasiness.

In Liverpool they made their connection at Lime Street, settling into their First Class compartment, every bit the modern English businessmen. Their four hour train ride was timed to arrive at dusk; stepping out of their carriage at Victoria, a Dutch embassy clerk escorted them to a waiting car, unmarked, no diplomatic plates.

Von Treptow could not be certain, but he somehow felt they had escaped surveillance from the Bank of Man on. Even so, he had the driver make a wrong turn or two on the way to the Embassy. He could see no obvious tails, and hoped he was right. Tomorrow would be dicey enough.

Pieter van der Hoek met them in the Embassy's motor court, shielded from Hyde Park Gate. He embraced von Treptow warmly, then shook Knorr's hands with both of his. "Come in you two, we have a light supper waiting. Alexandra, please show these gentlemen to their rooms. Dietrich, do come down while supper is still warm."

Down the pearl marble floor, between the silver marble walls to the lift. All three fit snugly with their bags, but Knorr minded not a bit. Alexandra told them she was a Hamburger whose parents had moved to Amsterdam for her father's furs business. She also had attended college at Cologne, worked a few years in the family business, and obtained her current position in 1914 through her best girlfriend, van der Hoek's niece. Her parents were relieved to have her out of a potential war zone – being German, they had no faith in the Kaiser's guarantees of Dutch neutrality.

"Now my father wants me back home, in the business with him and my brother, but I like the culture and the people here. It is really not that bad – the Zeppelins and Gothas make a big show with the searchlights and guns, but the damage is light, in the City, at least, and I have yet to meet anyone who has lost family in the raids."

She went on, "Things have been a bit tight since last year, at least outside the Embassy – food rationing started just this month, you know – but that seems to have eased for us considerably. Dinner will be satisfactory, I assure you." They reached their rooms and she took her leave. Knorr took a lingering, admiring glance after her.

"Down, boy!" Von Treptow whispered as he disappeared into his room.

Van der Hoek sent the servants off to other duties. The three men seated themselves at a round table in a bay window nook overlooking the Embassy's interior courtyard. Supper was anything but light, soup, sole, ham, cheeses, potatoes, salad of greens and carrots with French wine and Sumatran coffee.

"Well, Pieter, I am relieved to see you are not starving here." Von Treptow surveyed his plate. "We seem to come up short at home."

"So I hear, Dietrich, so I hear. How bad is it? How long can you hold out?"

"In strictest confidence, of course?"

"Of course," replied Pieter.

"Without a large fall harvest, not just from our fields, next winter will be very difficult, indeed. Thousands are stressed, but not yet starving in our cities. The effect on our factory workers and their families is debilitating. Our soldiers are not much better placed."

"Not just from your fields, you say? *Drang nach Osten*?"

Von Treptow nodded, "The subtext of our meeting tomorrow."

The men ate in silence for a while, then van der Hoek started on tomorrow's plans, "I have arranged for the two of you to assume the identities of our military attaché and his aide, down to dress uniforms and caps. Our meeting is scheduled at 1000, after our host's midmorning staff review. I am told the subject is wagon wheel production, so let us plan on being there early, say, 0945. Your exit arrangements will have you out of the City immediately thereafter. You do realize the risks here?"

"I do, Pieter, and I am indebted eternally to you."

"Anything in the pursuit of peace, my friend."

* * *

Wednesday, January 16, 9:00 a.m.
London, West End

Next morning, the three met for coffee and pastry in van der Hoek's office to escape general notice. Pieter explained in detail the morning's plan of deception, should anyone be watching. Then it was time.

The motor court had a canopy to keep off the mist and weak rain, but also to conceal the 'attachés' from the servants and any other interested eyes. The Netherlands being neutral, there was not a keen interest in the Embassy's doings, but as Intelligence station chief as well as Chargé d'affaires, Pieter took no chances.

The driver, also a Pieter, cautiously edged out into the London traffic. "Sir, there is no sign of any increased guard activity around Trafalgar Square, nor any of the normal surveillance spots in the surrounding buildings. There is, however, a parted curtain on a third floor well down Northumberland Avenue, but easily within sight by spyglass. I will stop first, then back up slightly just past the Metropole entry so your backs are to that observer, if he is there."

"Well done, thank you. See, Dietrich, we are rather careful here."

Knorr started, visibly jerking, having been deep in thought as they drove through the streets. "Sorry, Sir, just trying to prepare myself."

"Here we are, Gentlemen," said the driver, casually. He maneuvered the big Daimler to the curb as planned, then eased back to a stop. He stepped out sharply and opened the door for his passengers, taking Knorr's barrister's case for him, returning it at the curb.

"Don't turn, Colonel, straight ahead now." Pieter, however, turned to face the invisible observer, then guided his charges to the black lacquered doors and presented his credentials to the Highlander on duty, waving back to his two companions. The tall kilted infantryman ushered them through the former hotel lobby into the foyer of the office of the Minister of Munitions.

Shortly, a slender, very well-dressed young man came traipsing in, clutching Pieter's hand, gushing, "I say, old man, it has been a century since you dropped by last! Surely our Dutch friends are twiddling their thumbs awaiting the end of this ghastly war?"

"Reggie, there is a gracious plenty of trivial matters preying on us poor public servants, constantly! But you look well – new tailor?" he asked, fingering a well cut lapel.

"Perceptive as always, my friend. Yes, indeed. Sadly, Robert perished at Passchendaele," glancing at the visitors. "Perhaps you can lunch with me today or sometime soon, we can pay my new one a visit. Jermyn Street."

"Unfortunately not today, but I now have something to anticipate eagerly. Allow me to introduce Colonel Gunter Vanderslice and Captain Albert Huipel. Gentlemen, I give you Reginald Saint Vincent d'Eauclair Collingwood-Tyndale, known to his friends alternately as Reggie or Lord Elsmere, depending on our libationary status. Reggie is the Minister's private secretary."

"My pleasure, Gentlemen. Allow me to show you in, but I warn you our Former Naval Person is in a charcoal gray, if not completely black, mood this morning."

Reggie knocked twice, a muffled grunt issued from within, and he opened the door, showing them in and immediately withdrawing.

"Reggie! What in the hell are we...well, well, Pieter! What have we here? Do thank your lovely new bride for accompanying my Clementine to those dreadful diplomatic luncheons and such. I should prefer to be sunbathing nude amidst scorpions in Gallipoli in the mistral to sitting through one of those affairs."

"I shall pass along your kind words to Hilde, but perhaps not the imagery. I know she enjoys her company. Winston, I have brought these military gentlemen to discuss some important matters…"

Churchill rose from his chair, reaching across his desk to shake hands. "Cigar?"

Von Treptow shook his head, but Knorr nodded, looking at the artillery piece puffing away in Churchill's jowl. "Perhaps a smaller one?"

"Not a dreadnought, then. Perhaps a sloop? A nice Cohiba, Cuban, very mild. A snack cigar." He clipped the end, handing it to Knorr, producing a flaming match.

As Knorr lit his cigar, Churchill went on, "Always first things first, introductions can always wait on cigars and brandy. Brandy? No? Then introductions."

Pieter started to speak, but von Treptow intervened, "Minister, I am Brigadier General Dietrich von Treptow, Imperial German Army Military Intelligence. My aide, Lieutenant Colonel Walter Knorr."

In a millisecond Churchill had pushed his chair back from his desk. "Pieter, you have brought assassins? I am to be assassinated in my own office?" He reached forward to his righthand desk drawer, fumbling with the butt of his Webley, trying to shake it loose from an overgrowth of pencils, cigar ashes and rubber bands. Then he stopped, and with a comic theatricality, pressed his palms to his torso seeking bullet holes. Finding none, "Well, then, this *is* an interesting state of affairs."

Knorr had kept Churchill's brandy tumbler from falling off the desk, catching his attention. "Well done, man, in the face of death keep your priorities straight." He peered closely at his guest, "You look familiar, Sir, but I cannot seem to place you."

Knorr smiled brightly and leaned over to his lawyer's case. He unsnapped it, reached in and produced the blue helmet, presenting it wordlessly.

Churchill picked it up and turned it over to inspect his label. "Major, was it not, then? The High Wood?" Knorr nodded. "And those dogs, those fierce things, splendid animals. Still with you?"

"Still with me, Sir, wearing their own Iron Crosses, but getting fat and lazy as Headquarters mascots."

"Pieter, this man…it is a story too long…Major, Colonel, rather, there is your cap hanging on the rack. Fancy it back?"

"No, Sir, you may retain it as a souvenir, a reminder of our reunion."

"Well said, old man, well said." Churchill paused, leaning back in his chair, crossing his arms over his oval waistcoat. "Reunion's over. Now what?"

"Mister Churchill, we have come a considerable distance at great risk to discuss a critical matter. And our mutual friend here," a slight nod toward Pieter, "is risking career and perhaps more..."

Churchill interrupted, "I can have you marched to the Horse Guards Parade and shot as spies within the hour. You have also placed me at great risk. But you have taken your risk, which impresses me immensely. And which intrigues me even more. It seems I am known in these precincts for my infatuation with intrigues." Van der Hoek attempted to disguise his guffaw as a cough. "Even the Dutch know that."

Churchill scanned his guests' faces. "There are now four of us privy to your forthcoming admissions, more than constituting a quorum for conspiracy. So, we are all doomed, me for consorting with the enemy. We therefore might as well be familiar with one another; please do call me Winston."

"Thank you, Sir, Winston, Sir. Understand I must be guarded in my revelations, I emphasize none of which concern the Western Front. My main area of interest is the East." Churchill's eyebrows lifted. *A good sign.* "I am primary...military-political adviser to *Oberbefehlshaber Ost* Prince Leopold of Bavaria. I also report to certain highly placed personages..."

"Blast!" interjected Churchill. He picked up his telephone receiver, stabbed at a button and shouted, "Reg, old boy! I need you in here this instant!"

Pieter responded to von Treptow's raised eyebrow, "Reggie is neither fool nor fop..."

"So I gathered on first impression. Army or Naval Intelligence?"

"Naval. Survived *Queen Mary*. Ah, here he is now." Churchill waved in his aide with an expansive gesture. "You have yet to make any telephone calls, I pray not? Gentlemen, please introduce yourselves."

Introductions complete, without any perceptible shock or even emotion on Lord Elsmere's face, he replied, "I was expecting your buzz, Minister."

"Excellent. General, what gave away our Reggie?"

"Probably the same thing that he will say did me in. The eyes. Cold, clear, hard, in contrast to the costume."

"And you, Reg?" Churchill crushed the remaining half of his cigar, reaching for a fresh one.

"Aside from not being Gunter? Yes, the eyes, of course, but also the ill-fitting uniform. Gunter used my old tailor" – lifting a loose shoulder – "this would not do at all. Plus, the hair, he has not yet learned to properly comb it back. Probably been close-cropped since the womb. You see, my indulgences in dress and appearance belie a scientific study of same. Clothes maketh the man, all that rot. Take Lloyd George, for instance…"

Churchill roared, "Yes! Yes! Take the damned Welsh blighter!" Even the Germans laughed at that one. "Let us return to business. These gentlemen have tidings of uncertain cheer, brought us from afar."

Von Treptow resumed, "Lord Elsmere, among my present duties is the negotiation of a peace treaty with the Revolutionary government of Russia. If you are not aware, a ninety day ceasefire is in place as of 15 December."

"We are, of course, well aware of this armistice, and to be blunt, are profoundly distressed at the prospect of these Bolshies cutting and running, leaving us to face the whole lot of you alone," replied Reggie, archly, Churchill nodding vigorously in concurrence.

"Well you should be, Sir," acknowledged von Treptow. "We all know there are no great secrets between us as to manpower, divisions and the like – you probably know every detail of our every regiment. You may also know many of our Eastern forces are our elites, our very best, remaining there to protect eastern Prussia, not least the estates of our esteemed generals. So, the numbers are only part of the story, and the story is not favourable to you."

"Yes, yes, yes, whether that is a fact or a threat, I care not. Tell me of these Bolsheviks." Churchill puffed away, a Humpty Dumpty wreathed in spirals of smoke.

"As individuals, they are vile, amoral, power-hungry and unclean, to boot. As a group, they are an amœbic mass of thugs, spreading over Russia, grasping control from a chaotic opposition. We are responsible. We gave Vladimir Ilyich Lenin back to the world."

Reggie was intensely interested. "So it was you, yourself, who escorted him through Sweden to the Finland Station?"

"Yes, and I question our, my, judgment to this very day. May I?" he asked, standing and stretching and beginning to pace the spacious office in his distinctive gait. "Our calculation was he and his crowd would take over – he began shouting orders as soon as he stepped off the train, no hellos, nothing else – and within months had seized power and he, personally, ordered the Tsarist-Socialist Army to desist.

"In that sense, our calculus was spot on, as you would say. Despite the creature Trotsky's efforts to build a Red Army, the old Russian Army, the colossus of Europe, is no more. We could take a leisurely stroll all the way to the Urals and Baku on Spring holiday. We may yet do just that."

Churchill looked at Elsmere, then back to the German officer. "Very well, we appreciate you have just divulged plans for a potential offensive. Why? What do you want of us? Allow me my candor, Sir. I hate you Germans for what you have done, the millions dead, the sorrowing families and lovers, the Continent descending into this new Bolshevik barbarity, the inevitable collapse of the world order your ancestors and mine created out of the ashes of Bonapartism. Let there be no mistaking my meaning." These last words were delivered in Churchill's best ringing tones, those used in the Commons to such effect.

"I expected nothing less, Minister." *Von Treptow does not blink, thought Knorr. Or does he?* "But there is no *quid pro quo* on the table. We have come to you, not just to reminisce about the Somme, but because we know you to be the one person in authority in His Majesty's Government who might see the Bolshevik threat for what it is. We ask for nothing but free hands, both left and right." The last was the *quid pro quo,* of course. The Britons could not miss the significance – inaction in the West, acquiescence in the East. "And, to establish a common understanding that in the East there is a greater threat to each of us, and steps must be taken to confound it." He paused, staring intently at each of his English listeners in turn, "Doing so, turning our gaze and our energies to the east, and so turning our backs... elsewhere."

Churchill set his cigar in his HMS *Queen Elizabeth* ashtray. "The enemy of my enemy is my friend? Sorry, chap, I shall not go that far, nor shall His Majesty's Government, nor the British people. Pray do not deceive yourself thus. However," he continued, "on this Bolshevik subject, I am, as I often have been," giving Pieter and Reggie a faint smile, "a voice in the wilderness, a prophet without honor in his own land. I can, and I shall continue to press in official circles for a more restrictive policy toward this new Russian Government, but that is mere talk. Give me specifics, palatable ones, shall we say?"

"A most fair stance. The first specific is, are, Murmansk and Archangelsk. You diverted significant supplies there to support the Tsar. We do not wish Trotsky and his Red Army to avail themselves of same. I can unleash Mannerheim's Finns, along with von der Goltz's Baltic division, now poised to cross from Riga, to seize both."

Churchill glanced at Lord Elsmere, who nodded slightly.

"However, that would involve a conflict with your forces which you would lose, being outnumbered, and we have other uses for those units in any event. Could His Majesty's Government be persuaded to sequester those supplies, secured by force of arms?"

"Secure from attack? We would be free to repatriate those munitions?"

"We would much prefer they remain in the deep freeze."

"Of course you would. No promises, General. Next?"

"Next, Baku and Central Asia."

"Oil?"

"Yes, of course."

"No."

"You have Persia and Burmah, Sir. Could not Britain be persuaded to share the rest of the world?" As Churchill smirked, Von Treptow produced a small map of Europe and the Near East. He pressed his pockets, seeking his pen. Knorr handed him the Montblanc. "Winston, you appreciate a good aide, I take it?"

"No more than three hours a day," winking at Lord Elsmere.

Von Treptow spread the map, smoothing its folds. "Let us not be coy. We propose to establish spheres of influence wherein our respective interests and forces lie. We shall have no interest in your conduct within your spheres, nor, we propose, shall you in ours." He unscrewed the cap and was poised to begin drawing a line beginning at the Arctic Sea when Churchill softly said, "Stay thy hand. You and I have yet to prove we are the equals of Metternich and Castlereagh, master draughtsmen of borders. Mark your interests with a tick, not lines."

Von Treptow paused, then placed marks in the North, on Finland, the Baltics, the Ukraine, European Russia to the Urals, the Crimea and the Don, then east to the Volga basin, and in the south, on all but the east side of the Caspian Sea. "Your move, Winston."

Churchill produced a pen, shook it and scribbled on his blotter to prime its flow. Its ink was red, primary red, to von Treptow's Prussian blue. His tick marks went to the east of the Caspian, three across Russian Central Asia, then Persia, Afghanistan, India and Kashmir, then back to the Persian Gulf, Mesopotamia and Egypt. "Have I overstepped myself?"

"I expected no less, Winston. And this trifle in the middle here?" pointing to Siberia.

Churchill reached over, placed a question mark, then retreated. "Rome was not built in a day."

"Just so." Von Treptow signed and dated the map.

Without hesitation, Churchill did the same. "Pieter," he said, folding the map and handing it over, "please keep this in your safe for posterity's sake. I may have to write another novel to make my debts, and thus need endpapers. Now for all that, Dietrich, you know full well that neither of us carries any authority to make, much less carry out, any agreements on any subject whatsoever."

"Of course, Winston, that is what will make all this work, at least give us a sporting chance at it."

"Reggie, what do you think?"

"Fine concepts, first rate thinking. If these seeds ever sprouted, it would be a good thing, indeed." *In the meantime, we shall grind you to dust and all this blather is of no import.* "It is all very well to carve up a map like schoolboys, but we have lost touch with the main point – how to deal with the Bolsheviks."

"Our blood and treasure, Lord Elsmere, you may put it on our account at the Club of Nations. I shall personally pull the trigger. With pleasure, I assure you. Beyond that, I cannot compromise operations but the Bolshevik threat in Russia, and in Germany, and in Britain, for that matter, will cease, period, with finality."

"We can take care of our domestic factions," said Reggie, sharply.

"Can you, now?" Von Treptow took his small notepad from his pocket. "Coventry: wildcat strike, five days' tank production lost. Allied Aeroplane

Works: strikebound until your government took over. Elswick: machinists slowing production of large calibre naval guns. Portsmouth: stokers' disturbances. Beardmore's Clyde works: destroyers held up. Glasgow, elsewhere: coal miners threatening stoppages." Flipping the top page over, "I could go on."

Nodding, Churchill said, "Labour is looking past the war to taking power alone. I have no doubt McDonald will adopt and embrace any movement and anyone that will help him attain his goal. Labour hates me, as I am threatening to conscript strikers, so I shall be in the wilderness yet again." He tapped his cheek with a finger. "My fear is Cronos' children will turn on him and eat him, and then what?"

"I hate to take the punch bowl away from this party, but time is pressing." Pieter van der Hoek broke the first extended silence of the day. "My guests have other places to go."

"You have your travel arrangements made?" asked Churchill. "Reggie, would you be so good…"

"Certainly. I shall ensure the right people are looking the wrong way at the right times."

"Minister, I cannot express my gratitude for your and Lord Elsmere's audience. I trust both sides will come to see the same goal and collateral arrangements. May I suggest Pieter's services as a conduit for future communications? If, of course, he is willing?" Von Treptow looked at Pieter who shrugged, "I have a choice?"

"General, regardless of the outcome in France, there is a greater threat in the East. Bluntly, if I may," at which von Treptow nodded formally and Churchill continued, "bluntly speaking, we still intend to defeat you soundly and definitively. Make no mistake of our resolve. But, in that event, checking these Bolsheviks will paradoxically be made even the more difficult. Once the Central Powers have been defeated, the clamor to demobilize will ring much louder than even the trumpets heralding the beginning of this damned war. How then do we justify sending our lads east, far to the east, to squelch a former ally? How would Ramsay justify crushing fellow socialists? More to the point, do we want to govern Russia? What would that cost? Better you than us. Let me leave it at that. Reggie, what is next today?"

"Max is on the way – you lunch with him. Our guests should depart forthwith to evade his inquisitive gaze. No news is good news in this instance."

Reggie checked to ensure the coast was clear, then had the Highlander summon the embassy car. Again, Pieter positioned the Daimler to allow the three to enter with their backs to the street behind.

No sooner had the doors closed when von Treptow erupted in the first display of genuine anger Knorr had seen from his superior. Knorr and the driver exchanged glances.

"Damn you, Pieter, how could you lead us into that trap? If I..."

"*Pacem*, my friend. Was it not you that insisted on a meeting at his office? 'A public meeting in a private place,' or the reverse, as I recall? To accommodate you, I had to devise a subterfuge. Had I brought you as businessmen, or diplomats, or clergy, even, our friend Lord Elsmere would have had his agents on you like blowflies on rotting flesh. No, I had to neutralize Reggie, and do so immediately.

"So, I opted for boldness – a subterfuge in plain sight. Reggie and Gunter know each other, not well, but their circles overlap somewhat. So when he saw you two masquerading he knew something was up, and knowing him as I do, his mind was racing to penetrate the enigma posing before him. Why did he not join us to introduce you? He was back at his desk, hand poised above his direct line to Naval Intelligence, running the possibilities in his mind. Fortunately, you broached the matter and likewise Churchill grasped it quickly enough that we brought him into our strategems before he could blunder."

Calming down, twisting his neck in a too-loose collar, von Treptow sighed, "Apologies for doubting you, my friend, that was a scheme beyond my scheming, and only now do I see it. How can we assume this Lord Elsmere – is he really a Lord, or is that another disguise? – how do we guarantee he will be loyal to Churchill, not betraying us before the day is out?"

"No guarantees in this business, Dietrich, you know that full well. Of his loyalty, on that we may rely, of that I am certain. And, yes, he is a Lord, a hereditary one of some centuries, at that. He is an eldest son, heir to a sizeable fortune and several estates, but like so many of similar circumstances, he was a society butterfly, drinking heavily, entertaining constantly though scarcely making a dent in his resources, I gather."

Pieter made a slight gesture to a Mediterranean-looking fellow at a curb opposite, then continued, "His father was a friend of the late Lord Randolph's, prevailed upon Winston to take him in at the Admiralty, and so he had his first job. Very, very bright – drunk or sober – he sufficiently impressed Winston so as to become part of his inner circle. Then Winston was forced out as First Lord, electing to meet his destiny with your Walter on the Somme, but before doing so he secured Reg a commission serving with Beatty in the Battlecruiser squadron. That suited Reggie to a T – easily the most glamorous posting in the entire Royal Navy, and he and Beatty shared the same tailor and style. You should see him when he dresses in uniform, cap tilted across the eyes, just like Beatty's, in crisp, sharp, and non-regulation suiting.

"Beatty recommended him to Admiral Hall – 'Blinker' – at the moment in command of the battlecruiser *Queen Mary*, one of the Splendid Cats, in early 1916. Six months later came Skagerrak, and his beautiful *QM* exploded under the fire of, I believe, your *Derfflinger*. Nine survived, including Reg, blown from the bridge, plucked unconscious from the sea by a destroyer. When Winston returned from the front he immediately took over Reggie's rehabilitation. For six months Reggie lived with Winston and Clementine until he recovered sufficiently to undertake his new duties. Winston cannily arranged the Naval Intelligence connection with Blinker, now at its head – he knew he would be spied upon, so why not by his trusted subordinate?"

"I knew you were good, Pieter, I just did not realize how good."

"You were bound to receive the Revelation eventually," chuckled Pieter, "but I must warn you, Reggie can be mercurial. You saw a flash of his temper, but just a flash. He can be irrational, particularly in his hatred of the Germans who sank his elegant ship and killed a thousand of his mates. Just bear that in mind and consider yourselves warned."

He gazed out the window, "I have known him since his Admiralty days, when I first arrived here as Naval Attaché. We have blazed many a trail in Mayfair and Knightsbridge, all in the name of duty, of course. We exchange gossip and innuendo, and between us have the most complete dossier library in London. Much of our intelligence comes from our female contacts. I have struggled mightily thus far to dissuade him of interest in our Alexandra, she being German, and a commoner, at that. It should greatly impair our operations were he to succeed in wooing her."

Knorr shot von Treptow a hurt look.

"Here we are, please change clothes quickly and come to the service entrance. Alexandra will take you there. You are to be taken in a tradesman's van to another stop unknown to me, thence in a delivery lorry to the coast. You are then on your own. You will not see me again until I contact you, but do ensure I know your forwarding addresses."

He and von Treptow embraced, the latter whispering something, then Pieter turned and walked briskly down the corridor through the shafts and shadows.

* * *

1:15 p.m.
Southeast England

They sat on crates in a van smelling of oils and greases, holding on to the ribs of the filthy canvas enclosure. Bouncing over cobbles and rails and crossing at least one bridge, Knorr was sure, they rode for about twenty-five minutes before squeaking to a stop. He heard the driver speaking to another, then the van moved forward, then backward. The turn could be heard as well as felt, the steering column squealing softly in need of lubrication.

The doors opened into a dimly lit garage or warehouse, they could not tell. The driver said, "Close the tailgate, please, Gents. I don't need to see your faces," as he walked away, hoisting himself back into the cab. He ground the transmission into gear and eased out of the entryway the instant he felt the latch close.

The two Germans stepped aside into the shadows. Along came a small man in a streaked dark suit, vest and collarless shirt with a workman's cap pulled low. He closed the double doors, dropping a footbolt to secure them. "Come along to the office," he said, distinctly Irish. He did not wait and his charges trailed obediently behind.

"Wait here. Make yerselves comfortable," waving at a threadbare sofa, a refugee from the rubbish tip. Knorr looked at his wristwatch, matching it against the wall on the clock opposite. He decided he trusted his timekeeping more.

At length, a door opened and a tall man dressed in tweeds not unlike their own strode in. "Now, then, fancy a little ride in the country?"

"Thank you, Mister…," led von Treptow.

"No names, please. Operational security. You will change into seaman's garb in there," thumbing over his shoulder. "You have delivered a load of fish and are returning to the trawler dock. I'll not tell you where, right? You are taking home some canned goods and bolts of woolens." He smiled, "Which will smell of fish, as will you. Now, look sharp. The driver is ready."

They quickly changed into the slightly rank gear, repacking their cases. "Put those inside these crates here," said Mister Mystery, hammer at the ready to seal same. Then they toted their crates into the rear of the lorry and sat themselves on the wool just behind the driver.

"It's a good four hour to the dock, if we don't get stopped. Get some sleep if you can." The driver was Dutch, with a thick accent and a jerky throttle foot. *As bad as a steamer,* thought von Treptow.

They passed through the East End, dismal and tawdry even in the failing light. Then through the suburban ring of seemingly identical red brick row houses, then detached houses with small gardens, then open country as the dark closed in. Both men nodded away.

* * *

3:00 p.m.
Ministry of Munitions, London

Reggie walked into the Minister's office without knocking. "Well, Sir, what do you make of this?"

"Reg, I am tempted to take it at face value, but what do you know of this person? I know his aide, of course, but only as an officer in battle, a damned fine one at that."

"This von Treptow is an enigmatic figure, it seems. We have very little on him." He opened a slim folder, "Career Army, Army family back generations. High nobility, ancestors were Margraves back when Poland and Sweden mattered, so had border defense responsibilities. Military Academy, staff work, the usual. Always cavalry, never rotated through infantry. His gait may explain that. In cavalry at the war's beginning. Distinguished himself at Mons in that schoolgirl incident in front of one of the bridges, Nimy, maybe Saint Ghislain, one of those. Then dismounted as commander, 24th Brandenburg, his home regiment. Took Douamont at Verdun, 1916. Then, Brigadier, 1917."

Reggie frowned, "Then, invisible. He said Intelligence, correct? That is the first I had heard of him there. I am not sure he is regular, or we should have heard something more in that regard. More likely he is an agent of one or more of the 'highly placed personages' he alluded to. My guess is Prince Max of Baden, purportedly the most 'liberal' of that lot. Probably has the sponsorship of one of the other Princes as well.

"I could not place his age; probably older than the Imperial princes, yet younger than the Kaiser, so I am not sure how a princely connection works. He would be about this Max fellow's age, though, perhaps they were schoolmates."

Churchill was turning the blue helmet in his hands as Lord Elsmere ruminated. "He is something, otherwise he would not have undertaken this mission. I wager you lunch at your club he is on loose instructions, freelancing, as it were."

"Winston, if you think I can get you through the doors of the Carlton Club, you are mad beyond imagining."

* * *

6:00 p.m.
Whitstable Harbor

"Here we are, mates! Get a move on. Take your crates to the boat, that one there with the black stern, then come back for the woolens. I'll get the Captain and crew." He jumped out of the lorry and walked to the public house across the street.

"Extra stevedoring pay, Sir?"

" 'ardly. Put yer back into it and love it, lad!" said von Treptow, affecting his version of Cockney. Three quick trips and the deck was full. They were wiping their hands on their corduroys when the Captain hailed them. "Well done for gentlemen! You might make honest workingmen yet. Well, maybe not!" He and his four crewmen laughed.

"All right, lads, jump to it. No sense in lingering. Gents, come into the cabin where you'll be out of the way. The boiler's lit, just waiting some more coal. You, there, Friddie, make that gear fast, put those woolens in the front hold." He looked at his gauges, then slowly pushed his throttle. The trawler, all twenty meters of it, began to ease away from the dock toward the harbor entrance. As it approached the light, the Captain let loose a blast from his horn, startling his passengers, invoking a return horn from the harbormaster.

Broaching the harbor mouth, von Treptow felt the first swells of the English Channel. *Here we go again.*

"We will be some time reaching our rendezvous; she ain't fast, but she sure is slow." The Captain laughed, his bushy beard bobbing. "If you're going to be sick, do it early. No sense in worrying when it'll come up."

He continued, "We're taking the long way, as if we're headed straight to the Hook, home port for us. Then you get taken home under the water, Sir. We'll look for your people's signal about 0400. When it happens, you'll have only a few minutes – five, ten, maybe – to make the transfer. Best uncrate your bags now if you want to take them – have them at the ready. You can get some rest below. The lower, the easier on the stomach." The Captain was a hardbitten fellow, even for his ilk, and owed no particular allegiance to anyone. Even so, he recognized a person of prominence and power.

"Thank you, Captain," sighed von Treptow, starting to descend the ladder, then turning right around and heading for the gunwales. Relieved of his breakfast, he smiled at the skipper, "That should lighten our load some," then descended for good, he hoped.

* * *

2300 Hours
The North Sea

He settled back on the pile of woolens and dozed fitfully, dreaming of rising hills and falling valleys. He and Knorr both awoke after a few hours, sensing something amiss.

"We're drifting, Sir. No engine vibration."

Von Treptow scaled the ladder. "Captain?"

"Engine trouble. Probably contaminated feedwater. Salt water got in. We need to drain and clean the filter and lines and such. We will be an hour off schedule, though. They ain't going nowhere, I doubt, but it'll be getting light by then – that's the problem."

"How far?"

"Not so far, but we're drifting off course. Seas is good, low clouds. As good as we can hope for, but there's a blow coming in from Scotland. We jes' need to get on with it." The Captain was being well paid for his efforts and risk, but not to fight the Royal Navy in broad daylight.

Von Treptow scanned the horizon to port. "Where do their patrols come from, Captain? The Firth?"

"There, and Hartlepool, sometimes Scarbrough. The light cruisers stay with the big cats, except for one squadron that has the south. We figure to split the difference, but it ain't exact. Besides, it's the destroyers you should worry about. The big ships don't generally fool with us small fry, and the cruisers don't carry depth charges."

"That's comforting."

"Cap'n, 'twern't so bad. We'll have her up and ginning in twenty minutes." The grease covered mate disappeared below to the clanking of tools and much Dutch cursing.

Good to his promise, the engine coughed to life, sputtering, the funnel belching unburned coal dust then the usual sooty cloud. Von Treptow and Knorr stood on deck, getting a little extra coating at the Captain's suggestion. "This stuff'll coat you sure, make you out to be a regular seaman in case anyone drops by to enquire. Won't hurt you none, les' you breathe it," laughing loudly, until he started coughing. "Just a chest cold, it is," with a wink.

Walter looked all around at the surface of the sea, glimmering in the quarter moon's light. "Captain, I cannot fathom, excuse the pun, how the Navy types can fight on this – nothing to see for miles, no landmarks, no hills to take, nothing."

"Just the enemy, if you and he can find each other."

* * *

Thursday, January 17, 0400 Hours
The North Sea

The Captain called his guests back on board. "Time to get ready, lads. Get those nets over the starboard side, short. Get that yardarm over straight out and lash it. Gentlemen, any minute now."

As he and his passengers peered forward in the lightening gloom, his lookout cried, "Cap'n! Smoke on horizon, at nine o'clock." He raised his glass. "Mast, single, twin yards, coming fast. Destroyer!"

As this warning rang out, the Captain pointed, "There! See the light? Bud, flash him to turn it off, we see him. Flash, *'destroyer port beam.'* Turning to his passengers, "I'd hoped to do this in an orderly way, but now we'll scramble. He's only surfacing just enough to get you aboard, and we have to stay between him and the Navy. And the wind's come up. Get your stuff, it'll go quickly."

The trawler approached the submarine whose conning tower was half out of the water; the submarine slowed slightly to match the trawler's speed. "Can't chance Navy seeing us change speed or course jes' 'cause we saw 'em."

Very quickly, the two craft drew together. "Now, Gents, nice and easy like. Over the side on the nets, we'll catch a line – here it is," as a hemp rope landed with a thud – "and lash your cases to it. I don't want them floating away for the Brits to fish out. Now, Sir, you first."

Von Treptow climbed down onto the net, rope looped under his arms, swaying, trying to stay upright. By now, the trawler was directly abeam the conning tower, and two pairs of hands reached from the handrails to grasp first the outstretched boom and then the general, jerking him up and over into the bridge well. Without ceremony, he was trundled down into the bowels of the U-Boat.

Next came Knorr. As he was about to make the transfer, a swell pushed the trawler against the submarine. Knorr lost his grip, slipping from the rope, falling and hitting the rising deck, hard. He rolled off as the U-Boat reversed its swell and found himself being washed down the side of the boat, grasping at the railing, torn away, grasping again, now at slots in the hull. He looked back and saw the propeller guard looming large when a seaman grabbed his collar, stablilizing him. "Grab the rail," he said, looping a line under his chest. The seaman was now leaning all the way around him to secure the line, and Knorr saw he was tethered to the sinking conning tower. Another seaman jumped down and the two jerked a limp colonel against the tower. They hoisted him quickly to the bridge, then down the ladder, closing the hatch just as a wave crested over in a shower.

The U-Boat captain had already waved off the trawler and ordered the boat to dive well before Knorr was out of the water. The conning tower slid below the sea in a few seconds more as the trawler captain did a masterful job of keeping his superstructure between the submarine and the approaching destroyer. "Haul in the nets and the boom! Let's start unlimbering our trawl like we're actually getting about doing something useful."

The approaching destroyer was signalling the trawler: *heave to, prepare to be boarded.* A launch was lowered with a handful of Royal Marines aboard. The Captain had no choice, so turned the boat to port to give the launch a good approach. A few minutes later, a Navy lieutenant and four sternfaced Royal Marines were aboard.

"What were you doing back there, Captain?"

"Well, Sir, you see, we're on our way home, Sir, but the birds looked like they knew something, so we started to set up for a trawl, as you can see. My starboard boom got sideways on us, and tangled the short net there. We're fixed now, and thanks for looking after our health."

"We will check below, unless you object?"

"No, no, Sir, as you wish. Not much to see."

Back aboard HMS *Badger*, the executive officer was standing over the hydrophone operator. "Anything?"

"Mostly just the noisy engine on that trawler. I thought I heard something else, but if it was there, it is masked, Sir."

The XO turned to Signals, "Have that boat cut its screws, our launch, too." The signal was flashed and the engines were stilled.

"Anything, Hydro?"

The operator raised one hand, cupping his headphones with the other. "No, sir, all quiet."

Down below, Knorr was catching his breath, his corduroys and sweater heavy with cold seawater. "Our drowned water rat! Take him to the engine room and let him change where it's warm."

Von Treptow turned to the captain, "That was close, and thank you..."

The captain cut him short – this one's military protocol did not extend below the sea's surface – "I was diving, regardless. You would not find me so hospitable if I had lost two good men saving your miserable asses, but I would not risk my boat and entire crew. Not for the Kaiser, not for that fool von Holtzendorff, not for Jesus Christ himself!"

Von Treptow just looked at him and saluted. "Very well, Captain. Where do you want us, out of the way?"

His mood lightening, Captain Niemöller waved to a crewman, "Put him in my cabin for now, and the other in Koehl's. General, we will be about five hours. These are dangerous waters, even submerged. Seems our High Seas Fleet cannot scare off the British any more. We will sail slowly and quietly, and I will have to take the boat to periscope depth more than I like. We will make it to Zeebrugge, do not worry yourself."

At that moment, a bonerattling explosion rocked the U-Boat. Von Treptow careened into a bulkhead and slipped to the floor. Holding to a stanchion, another explosion sent a crunching shock wave through him, then another. Seamen jumped up to turn valves, stopping sprays of water and steam. "Hold your places, men. Down twenty degrees. Get her to forty meters!" The deck tilted as von Treptow clung to his hold.

Soon the boat leveled out. "He was just playing. Did not know anyone was here, just dropping some cans to see if he got lucky."

"Nothing, Sir."

Badger's XO was disappointed. "Thanks, Hydro."

Niemöller entered his cabin followed by a steward carrying hot coffee. The latter served, then closed the door behind him. "About that scene at the conn, General. Yes, I would have left all three to drown, but that is a command decision one sometimes has to make. I am sure you have been in similar predicaments?" Von Treptow nodded and the captain continued, "The rest of my comments were directed at the crew, a morale consideration, as it were. I know just enough about you and your mission to expect you to understand my meaning."

"I do understand, and I want your unvarnished opinion on the issue," replied the general. "The truth, if you please."

"Certainly, Sir. This crew is one of the best in the entire Navy. We have been through a lot together and have an enviable record. But my men are not immune to, not just grumbling, the seaman's right, but…other influences. The High Seas Fleet is beginning to rot from within, Sir. The submariners are less influenced, being on station for longer periods, and never idle, I assure you. Our *esprit de corps* is unique and justified by the dangers we face. And Ostend and Zeebrugge are far enough from Kiel to distance us from the rabble up there.

"Even so, there are elements in my own crew who have changed, over time, to embrace more radical views. I run this boat with the proverbial iron fist in a velvet glove. Again, Sir, once at sea, the crew is one hundred percent duty; anything less, any loss of focus and we all die. They know that."

He poured himself some more coffee, "Ashore is another matter. I doubt that Hipper and Scheer could raise enough untainted crew to sortie the fleet. Maybe today, but three, six months? My radicals, bless them, are still loyal Germans, and they are willing to share with me what they hear and in turn, I listen to their arguments, privately, of course. You would be well advised to confront High Command with these trends, Sir. I have heard rumour that you, above all others, could make the case."

The intercom crackled, "Sir, approaching point M Three."

"Come to periscope depth. I am on my way." He clicked off the speaker. "Come with me, General, you should find this interesting."

The command center was tense. Every seaman was at his position, focused on his task. The exec was watching the depth gauge. "Periscope depth...now!"

"Up periscope!" The captain removed his sweat-stained cap, handing it without looking to von Treptow. He rotated the greased shaft 180 degrees to get a look behind the boat, then swept to port, then straight ahead. "Fritzie, look sharp. Ten degrees to starboard." He paused until the course change was complete. "Steady as she goes. Care to have a look, General?"

"Of course, always ready for something new." He took the grips from the captain and squinted into the viewfinder. "All I see is water, Captain. Except for this big black wall that says *HMS Dreadnought*."

"Funny."

"Was there something out there? All I see are swells, which are not good for my stomach."

"You'll not be sick on my boat! No, General, you are right. There is a small blue buoy, almost invisible, and totally invisible if you do not know the charts. Marks the minefield approaches to Zeebrugge. We are right on course, thanks to our navigator, Herr Guenther. Normally we would spy this more easily from the bridge, surfaced. Periscope is a bit harder."

"At the dock in one hour fifty minutes, Captain."

"Excellent. General, a schnapps? To celebrate?"

* * *

Thursday, January 17, 1000 Hours
Zeebrugge, Belgium

The submarine made the final fifteen kilometers surfaced, the cold North Sea air flooding into open hatches, sweeping out the interior redolent of stale odors of onions and men and waste. The exec neatly maneuvered along the length of the mole and causeway jutting out the last three kilometers into the sea.

The crew, happy to be home and alive, clambered about the deck and dock, tying off hawsers to cleats, hauling out trash and seabags. Von Treptow and Knorr stepped off the swaying deck onto terra firma, resisting the urge to drop to their knees and kiss the ground, but thinking it, nonetheless.

Captain Niemöller saluted from the conning tower, then shouted some orders to the crew. "Brave man. Brave crew," said the general as the two sauntered, after a fashion, down the dock. "That was a very hazardous task, and he made no mention of the exceptional risk. The Flanders Flotilla had a horrific death rate last year."

"Well, General, I am glad to be on land." Knorr's legs were still swaying with their memory of the sea trip. "A simpler life for a day or so?"

"We certainly have earned it, one would think. But of course not. Will your affair in Hannover be any the less harrowing?"

They hailed a passing cab, directing it to Flotilla Headquarters. Having forgotten their tweeds, they were challenged by the Marine guard at the entry. General and colonel fumbled around in their clothes for proper identification. At one point Knorr had four such documents in his hand. "Pick a card, any card?"

The Marines were neither persuaded nor amused. Just then, out of the vestibule came two admirals, one of them Oswald Boecker. He stopped, looking carefully at his two friends, then motioned to the guards, "Spies! Seize them!"

Before the surprised guards could react, he grasped one's sleeve. "Stand down. A small joke on my part. Well, well, well. Why in Neptune's name are you two here, and traveling together, for that matter? And what is this hideous bourgeois costume? You two have much to answer for, so do come inside. Admiral Altermann, my friends have arrived just in time to force me to purchase their lunch. My regrets to you and the rest of your party."

He led his Dutch imposters into the small trading company building taken over by the Navy. Company insignia, maps and maritime memorabilia still bedecked the pea green walls, lightly grimed with years of soot and cigars. Presently the odd party arrived at a canteen with a half dozen tables scattered about. "Tea? Coffee? Pastry? Strudel? Nothing but the best for my voyagers. That is, I assume you have been voyaging somewhere. Wally, if you have been in this one's tow, there is no telling."

"Oz, you have no idea."

"Wherever you were, it was fishy. Very fishy," wrinkling his nose. "Ensign, please escort these...men...to officer's quarters for a thorough delousing. Then return them to Admiral Altermann's when they are present-able. I will have a proper luncheon delivered there. Quickly, now, before someone thinks salmon is being served. Or the cats mount an offensive."

The ensign doubletimed them through the building and out the back door to one of the seedy resort hotels. "Welcome to the Ritz, Gentlemen. As good as it gets in lovely Zeebrugge. But, we do have hot water and clean towels. Here we are, feel free to use this space. WC's down the hall. I will check back in thirty minutes, if that will do?"

"Just fine, thank you, Ensign. Order some Pommery '06 for our lunch, put it on the Admiral's bill."

"Sir?" cringed the young man.

"Nothing, Ensign. A small joke, very small it seems," responded Knorr. "We require nothing else at the moment. Wait, is there an orderly or valet who can press out these suits in short order?"

The two discarded their well worn tweeds, enjoyed hot showers and dressed. Ensign Wulff returned to escort them to Admiral Altermann's quarters in a French Empire style mansion on the waterfront where Altermann and Boecker were in the study looking over a table full of maps and nautical charts.

"Look sharp, Heinz! A pair of insurance, or worse, war bond salesmen approaching – keep your wallet close!" The two Navy men looked over the newly natty twosome with amusement. "Admiral Altermann, here, and I are going over ideas for our next bee sting on the Royal rump. Our twin flotillas have been rather successfully harrying British shipping and their defenders. My destroyers charge, then retreat, and Heinz's subs take advantage wherever they can. Two destroyers and how many freighters?"

"Eighteen, nearly 150,000 tons in the last four months. Not at all a bad record, especially against no losses, none recently, that is."

"Might your Captain Niemöller be one of these bees?" inquired von Treptow. "We were privileged to a demonstration of your stingers on our way to England three nights ago. Providence had pity on us fools, but not others in our group."

"One of the best. Packs a big sting – one of the destroyers, four freight-ers, including one of those the other night. I am certain he meant to miss you. He had his orders," he winked. "Top notch, one of my most experienced – he has survived since 1915, no mean feat, unmatched exploits in the Med, now here. He undertook a grand risk, he and his men, I hope it was neces-sary. The Channel is no place for U-Boats that close to Hartlepool, at least not solo. Wolfpack is one thing, but alone, not good."

General von Treptow replied, evenly, "I trust it proves to have been worth the risk, but as yet the verdict is cloudy. Colonel Knorr and I were very impressed with his crew and seamanship, and I suppose I owe you for your orders."

"Yes, you do. We shall find suitable recompense, somehow. Meanwhile, your luncheon awaits." Admiral Altermann showed them into the dining room, colored in Wedgwood blue. "I understand you travel with us tomor-row to Hannover? Colonel, your family hails from there as well, yes?"

"Yes, sir, we have been there a while. The family founded Manufacturers' Bank in 1830. My brother runs it since my father passed two years ago. We bank Blohm & Voss and Vulcan, among our navy-type clients, and handle Krupps' trade banking – Gustav has no need of our investment money."

"Excellent," beamed Altermann. "Keep the money flowing to his ship-yards, I am in desperate need of more submarines."

"Destroyers, you mean," objected Boecker with a big smile. "Always pushing his parochial interests, he is."

"At least my parochial interests can get out of the North Sea, Admiral."

"Oof! Touché! I am wounded, mortally, I fear. But it is true. Our surface fleet is next to useless, except in the Baltic. And the Baltic is not a 'High' sea, even in Willy's mind."

"At least we still have a fleet and sailors to man it." This was von Treptow, speaking in a code intended to open a sensitive discussion. "But, enough of metaphysics. We are desperately hungry, Gentlemen. Has my Pommery arrived?"

* * *

Friday, January 18, 10:00 a.m.
London, Downing Street

Churchill and Lord Elsmere were on foot to Number Ten for the War Committee meeting, Churchill with his walking stick in one hand, gesticulating dramatically with his cigar in the other. As he dodged ashes, Reggie asked, "Winston, how much of our recent discussion is fit for ears?"

"Not much, Reg, not much. First, if I say too much, as has occasionally happened in my career, then I have fatally compromised both our newfound friends and ourselves. Next, he cagily gave us nothing on the West, so no inventory to trade there. No, we need a fresh approach. Rack your fertile brain for the missing Delphic revelation, as have I." Churchill walked on silently for a while. "This General, General von what-toe?"

"Treptow, Sir; his home, an outlying region of Berlin. Brandenburg, not Junker Prussia, the east. Which may explain, partially, his attitude."

"Yes, this von Triptoo. Had I pressed him on the Western Front, I suspect he could have delivered my speech of last May word for word. Which says much of his character, of course, but even more about his supporters, do you think?"

"My notion exactly, Sir. If he has any credibility to us, if there is any reason to trust him, it is because someone in high position has anointed him. But that person, persons probably, are independent of the military command."

"And just how have you deduced this?" queried Churchill.

"One, he forewarned us of their intent to take all of Russia. Even though we already expected that course, he amplified the intent and gave us a schedule. A general giving away a timetable and not asking to be paid? No, intimate with command, but parallel, somehow.

"Next, that timetable gave away their plans in the West, and he clearly intended that – do not ask how I know it. Intuition. They commence against the Russians next month. With their von Hoffman in charge and the state of decay there, no more than two, three months to a stop. Then, over one million men and their guns come west."

"So, the hammer blow falls no later than the end of April?" Churchill was now even more dramatic in his gestures. "That is truly priceless information, as I now reflect. Men have died to deliver such, and he simply gave it to us outright."

Lord Elsmere continued, "Which makes your earlier comment even more apropos."

"Which of my words of wisdom would that be, amid the myriad thereof?"

"Your May secret speech. You thought the German could mimic you. Follow that thought. Your main point was to wait until the Americans tip the balance before letting Haig turn the meatgrinder once again. One million new Germans equals four months of new Americans. They attack within two, even three months and they maintain the advantage, increase it, actually."

"Reggie, that is nothing more than the corner greengrocer's arithmetic. Do you think the War Committee does not understand simple maths?"

"Do you think so?"

"Hmmph! Do not get me started. Very well, what do we do, then?"

Pausing at the Downing Street curb to let some passersby past, "A thought experiment, Sir. What is the worst outcome of this meeting?"

"A thought experiment, Einstein? Very well, we lose India."

"Winston, please. Must that be your answer for everything, from collapse of Empire to Berry Brothers' failure to timely deliver the port and cigars for a dinner party? No, seriously, and we have not much time."

"The worst is Germany's momentum for an offensive is unchecked – this fellow, van Ducktoe, fails altogether."

"And the offensive, how would it be successful?"

"Concentration."

"On whom?"

"There you have me. If on us, undermanned as we are, either we get pushed into the Channel, or at best we hold our ground. Unless Lloyd George releases our reserves still here, which he will not."

"Correct. But, follow this logic. If Germany concentrates on France, massively, I have no confidence the French can hold. They would fight, but could not withstand the extra million, probably more, and the Americans cannot get into place quickly enough." Lord Elsmere was unusually grave, for him. "But, even if they could hold, there are elements which would welcome a peace proposal, and I doubt even Clemenceau would be able to rally the common people. Especially if that proposal were both generous and preceded the final attack."

"What manner of peace proposal? Such as the Austrian, Karl, proposed? Chimerical, at best. Or do you mean Wilson's stone tablets?" The current joke at Ministerial level was Clemenceau's observation: *God gave Moses only ten commandments; Wilson has given us fourteen.*

"You see our predicament, then?"

"Reginald, you are the very Sphinx. Get past the preliminaries and decipher your damned riddle!" Churchill consulted his pocket watch. "And be damned quick about it."

"Wilson has stepped in his own dog's mess. The only one of the fourteen that the Germans, by that I mean the ones we are, or might be dealing with would object to would be Alsace-Lorraine, but if they are as shrewd as I think, they will sacrifice that polyglot, or at least French Lorraine."

"What about Russia? That is the single most voluminous of the Commandments."

"Do you not see? Von Treptow told us in a matter of weeks, months perhaps, Russia will not exist, or at least not as Wilson contemplated. Germany will control not only Poland, the Ukraine, Georgia, the Baltics, but the balance of Russia-in-Europe. Wilson's sixth point will be moot. The new countries will be touted as evidence of his notions of self-determination, but in actuality under the German boot. In fact, the rest of the points are tailor-made, no pun intended, Winston, tailor-made for Germany."

"Hmmm." Churchill ruminated, "The Huns can easily make a huge show of rebuilding Belgium, Louvain, that lot. They would carve up the Austrian empire in any event, too incompetent to coexist with Prussians. That much was demonstrated a half century ago. Also, did you note the lack of reparations? Alsace and Lorraine seem to be the only named concession."

"You have grasped it, Sir. Some sweetening of the deal to the French, such as the Cameroons, maybe Tanganyika, what else, I do not know. Both to our disadvantage, I need not add. A non-aggression pact? With that in place would there not be a clamor for peace? On our new Associate's own terms?"

Elsmere continued, playing to Churchill's great love, "Add to that freedom of the seas, free access through the Straits and an easily evaded armaments limitation, and the Royal Navy would find itself on a sticky wicket, indeed."

To which Churchill could only add, "Damn!"

* * *

Friday, January 18, 1200 Hours
Zeebrugge, Belgium

Two staff cars arrived for the four officers and their luggage and off they went to the little train station. The special train had only two passenger cars along with its three freights. Army and Navy commandeered two sleeping compartments and a sitting room between. Zeebrugge to Brussels, then uncouple and wait to recouple the cars to the late train for Hannover.

Settled in, the four convened in the sitting room as the locomotive chuffed away from the station. A porter brought coffee and tea and some bread and jams to tide them over to dinner. Not much to see along the way, not as bleak as the industrial area around Mons, but dotted with the same slag and spoil heaps, reminding Knorr of witches' hats or giant dung hills from some prehistoric creatures.

"So, what can you tell us, Dietrich?"

"There is much afoot, friends. Some concerns your service directly, most is in the East. We have an opportunity, if well played, to exit this miserable conflict on favourable terms. Would that please you? More importantly, would it please your men?"

Both admirals leapt at the answer. "Yes, most certainly," said Boecker.

"Seconded," joined Altermann. "It is all our commanders can do to keep the crews in fighting spirit, and it grows worse each day. We do not run these sweeps of the Channel and North Sea to pad our scores, I assure you. We structure each mission to minimize our risk and maximize the sense of accomplishment. Up the coast" – he meant Wilhemshaven and Kiel, through the canal – "they do not have that opportunity, and the idleness shows in unrest and dissatisfaction."

"Your Captain Niemöller allows grumbling to be the sailor's normal lot, but he says it goes well past that."

"He has nothing to worry about. His crew idolizes him, lionizes him, and for good reason – he has saved their lives several times over. But if even his men are being infected, well..."

Knorr asked, "Can the High Seas Fleet sortie?"

"No," said Boecker, flatly.

"No? Just no?" queried von Treptow.

"No," confirmed Altermann. "*Albion* may have been its last, I fear."

"Excellent." The three looked at von Treptow as if he had lost his mind. The general returned their stares and explained, "You said it best, Heinz. Idleness. A hundred thousand of our best trained men sitting around, scrubbing decks, running drills, without any prospect of engaging the hated Englanders. The Devil's very playground, indeed. Ripe for the revolutionists, anarchists. They need a task, a mission, if you please. Especially one that does not involve being smothered in British cordite and high explosive."

"Care to let us mere mortals in on the Army man's naval scheme?" Boecker looked at Knorr. "Wally, can you interpret?"

"Sadly, no. Story of my new life."

"Gentlemen, Gentlemen, please," started von Treptow. "Nothing extraordinary, I assure you. Merely the construction of a battleship on land."

Rolling his eyes, Alterman said, "Oz, did you not say he had recovered from his dementia?"

"Allow him the chance to spout his twaddle. He knows, or thinks he knows something, even more dangerous. Very well, Dietrich, what have you up your sleeve? To whom have you been talking?"

"Armin Eberhorst, Gustav's right hand man. Special projects expert. Old friend. He says for Krupps, it is a matter of simple construction and reusing existing equipment, hardly any engineering involved. His crews can do his part, if I can arrange the concrete and labor and transport and such."

"To do what? Damn it all, what in Hades are you trying to say?" Boecker could not decide whether to be exasperated or merely impatient.

"Build a battleship on land, of course. But I require your help. Follow this logic, if you will. How many big guns, barbettes, turrets and machinery sets do you think our Navy has in excess? By that, mounted on older ships, or even the newer ones rapidly becoming outdated? My calculation is well over one hundred of twenty-four centimeters or larger, up to twenty-eight. Plus untold smaller guns."

Boecker was counting by fours and twelves on his fingers, "Yes, probably, and were you count the older battleships, another ninety-six if the *Westfalens* and *Helgolands* are included – they were too slow when they were built."

"I thought you Army types had proven fortresses obsolete. What are you thinking?" This was Altermann. "And how could you create such a thing? And how do we help, as if we could?"

"Take Oz's count, including the big guns. One hundred pair with a range – a radius, actually – of twenty thousand meters, average, more for the twenty-eights and thirties. Space at a thousand meters, say. One hundred kilometers of big guns! Thirty centimeters of Krupp steel armor on each turret! Rate of fire five or six times our big siege guns! Able to swivel to any point of the compass!"

"Steady, Dietrich, this is fantasy." Oz was trying to keep von Treptow's arm pinned to the table. "Sheer fantasy!"

Von Treptow wrested his arm free then smiled, relaxed and leaned back. "Of course it is. My special genius."

Altermann shrugged, rose and pulled the service bell. Immediately, an orderly knocked. Opening the door, the admiral said simply, "Bottle of whisky. Four, no, make that three, glasses."

Von Treptow was enjoying himself now. "Make it four, orderly. Big ones, please. And two bottles, if you would."

Boecker raised his hand. "No more storytelling without whisky." Presently their order was delivered with a seltzer bottle. The orderly served each man's preference, then withdrew.

"Now, Dietrich, what really gives here?" Altermann was unconvinced of his friend's friend's sanity. "And where would you put your super-super-dreadnought?"

"Leave aside the practicalities for the moment. Allow me apprise you of recent developments." Von Treptow gave an abbreviated summary of Wilson's Fourteen Points proposal, and the conspiracy to leverage that proposal into a favorable peace. "So, in two or three months, we take Russia, or as much as we wish of that benighted place. At which time we announce to the world we consider these hostilities to be ended. And, as evidence of our...sincerity...we announce a major naval disarmament. No matter that what we propose to scrap is obsolete. The world public will fasten on the headline."

Leaning across the table, "Further, we propose a remarkable act of generosity. We take the armor and armaments from our scrapping program and create an impregnable barrier to future aggression. In Belgium, along the Meuse then over to Ghent, further securing her independence. Able to point either way, toward us or France – those turrets revolve, yes?"

"Rotate, actually, Dietrich," Boecker smiled at his friend's zest.

"Rotate, then. And, the *pièce de résistance,* to be manned by representatives of President Wilson's *'Association of Nations'*. If our adversaries reject this proposal, we position this firepower throughout the Rhineland. We then invite them to invade, if they are so disposed."

"Just one thing, mastermind. Two, actually." Boecker was unconvinced, "Time and actual construction?"

"Krupps demounts the equipment in sequence, first job complete in five months time. Actually, a number of the smaller guns have already been disembarked, is that what you sailors call it? They built it, they can unbuild it. Same time to build the first set of concrete foundations. Twenty thousand Russian labourers, glad to have warm berths and full rations. The demobilized sailors to install the equipment along with Krupps' crews. Keep them busy. Not built in a day, but over time. First deliveries in July.

"But it is not the building that is important. It is the announcement, the intent, the possibilities. The French and British, even with the Americans, could not reach us, either on the Meuse or further back, not in a year, should we mount an intelligent defense. A major unknown, given our High Command, to be sure. But, by announcing, it becomes..."

"A Fleet-in-Being. Even if wholly imaginary. You could build it out of *papier mâché*. Show it off for the newspapermen, they would believe it." Knorr finally got a word in, "Biggest problem in building it is housing and feeding the workers. Next biggest is getting power. Transport? River or rail, I would have to think on that. Concrete and steel, manageable."

Walter wagged a finger at the others, "Main thing is to get the first turrets up for all to see. That ought to show we are serious. Even better, test fire the first one for the newspapermen. Maximum range."

Von Treptow beamed, "Gentlemen, my protégé here is progressing nicely, is he not?"

* * *

Friday, January 18, 3:00 p.m.
Downing Street, London

Churchill and Lord Elsmere stepped outside the War Committee Room, Winston to light another cigar, Reggie contrarily for some fresh air. They were in a small courtyard adjacent to the service entrance. Private enough.

"I confess I rather enjoy the sights and sounds of the arena, Haig and Robertson going toe-to-toe with Lloyd George. Unfortunate nothing gets accomplished," observed Elsmere.

"True enough, but inaction, at this juncture, is superior to precipitous action. Sir Douglas would leap over the trench parapets with but the tiniest encouragement from the Government. David, as purely political as he is, has the proper measure of caution, and good for him. Recoup, recover, rearm. Take the winter to rebuild the divisions, restock the artillery and so forth. And, lest we forget, entrench ourselves as to be impregnable to the forthcoming blow." Churchill let his eyes wander to the eaves above and whispered, "Reggie, I can trust you completely, can I not? With something even Blinker need not know?"

"Of course, Sir." Reggie meant it.

"Our discussion outside, on the way here. Concentration. Us or the French? Herein lies the trick, Reginald. It is one thing to argue with our ally, for our generals to quarrel with theirs. But it is quite another thing to conspire to undermine that ally, however difficult it has proven itself…"

"Winston, do not forget the French have left our flanks exposed in their retreats, have refused to move forces to our support, have walked away from sectors of the front, leaving us stretched even thinner. I, for one, am not sure how much more we owe them."

"So you catch my drift. Excellent. Can our complaints influence our enemy, do you think? What would your new German friend…"

Reggie interjected vehemently, "I know no German friends." A slight leer crossed his face, "Male, that is."

"Very well, your new counterpart, then. How would we…the thought sounds poisonously treasonous…how would we 'persuade' them to look elsewhere down the line for their Spring frolic, should that come to pass?"

"Pieter could pass on a suggestion easily enough to the Germans. That is only the beginning, I rather imagine. Clearly, the group to which our…," he waved his hand above his head, "acquaintance belongs is locked in a struggle for influence with Hindenburg and Ludendorff, and we can only suspect they are the weaker. Let us ponder that for a moment and restate matters. On one level, he, they are trying to forestall their own coming offensive in favor of more mischief in the east. His message was clear in its opacity. Wonderful. If, however, he fails, how can we assist him in steering the onslaught from ourselves? And, at that point, would they care?"

"All very obvious, Reggie. How? What would it take?"

"Again, let us consider the basics. Militarily, we are the target. Fewer men, our backs to the sea. Made worse now that the Aussies rejected conscription. If the Huns knew of our issues with the French, they would exploit them. That, it now occurs to me, confirms the initial thrust."

"Between us, you mean?"

"Quite. Which way do they wheel, that then becomes the question. On the other hand, you made very clear we are determined to win this war. Can you say the same for the French, Minister, as they stand now? I wonder what he knows of their past summer of discontent. Probably as much as the average Frenchman, even with their veil of secrecy. Therefore, we must assume that is not a valuable currency, not new news, you see?"

Reggie paused to think the unthinkable. "Winston, at some point we have to give him something of value. Something he can use internally. Something explosive, something dramatic to counteract the force of authority arrayed against his sect."

"Now we get to treason."

"So it seems, Sir. So I fear."

"Then back to the basics, Reg, a thought experiment, of which you are so fond. Do we even wish to play in this game? I see their clear goal, if not a way, of ending this war on terms favorable to them, but not unfavorable to us, naval issues aside. Is that what we wish, or to crush Germany once and for all as a threat? Not knowing what demons may flutter from her ruptured breast?"

"A marvelous turn of phrase, Winston, I shall jot that down for your next speech. You already know my position. Kill them all. But I am unsettled by the thought of more friends lost, the wailing and keening of womenfolk back home, the hollowing out of Britannia. Particularly of our class, Sir. We, ours, have lost disproportionately, can we continue even now? And we still have enemies wishing to bleed us further, Winston, beginning with the Irish."

"And ending with the Indians. Yes, in winning, we can still lose. But we are simply making matters unnecessarily complicated, Reginald. He already told us what his Germany wants – Russia and the East. That much is plain before our noses. Would we trade our future security for that mess of pottage – which is not and never has been ours to begin with?"

"Do you not think Germany would be made even more dangerous, fueled by those riches?"

"Yes, yes, of course, they would be. But, how to defang them? First, in leadership. Cousin Willie would need to go – maybe these shadowy Princes you refer to could accomplish that. Likewise, H and L – retire them with eternal glory. Second, an agreement controlling, but not limiting our ship-building, guaranteeing the Navy a dominant position."

"Informing our allies?"

"Later."

"Winston, all we – you and I – have are words. There may be no per-suading David or our generals, but we can send messages."

"Through our Dutch friend, yes."

"Certainly, but a more public forum comes to mind. The House of Commons. Another speech like last year's, only well-reported, abroad as well as here. Max can manage the reportage."

"Proceed, Reginald. You plan on writing this address yourself, do you?"

"Only the outline. I am no match for your wordplay. But, to the outline. First, back in Committee – we may already be late returning – announce your intentions…"

"Which are?"

"To signal the Germans that our Ministry of Munitions has far exceeded its goals for 1917 and is doubling same for this year. Quote numbers, exaggerated but slightly. Let there be no mistake at German High Command what they are facing. Our, your new friend, rather, will know what to do with that message."

"Next?"

"Press Lloyd George to give you a prominent speaking time. Your address begins with the munitions message. Having the floor, you continue with observations on the situation in the East. Pieter will have to extract more specifics from our German."

"The point, Reggie, old boy, the point?"

"To shift terms of the national, nay, international discussion. If we are successful in diverting Ludendorff's attention – which is our message to von Treptow – perhaps he returns his attentions to his old campaign grounds, Tannenberg, all that, and spends a few more months doing the job right. More Americans by then."

"Bring the Second Coming to the benighted Slavs and call it a day, Erich, old man?" Churchill puffed away. "On further reflection, will not work."

"Why not, Winston?"

"The Americans are not coming as tourists. The French, Foch and company, will encourage them to liberate France, demand they punish *les Boches*. No general, French or otherwise, can resist a million men-at-arms in place of their own. And remember we do not have them, only the French. Timing is everything, Reggie. Must come to a conclusion sooner than later but I have no desire to let Germany off without much more pain. Much more." Churchill looked up to the leaden sky above the parapet. "We then either rise or fall by the middle of March."

"Treason," murmured Reggie.

"Hmm?"

"Treason. It will take an act of treason. Making a credible offer of peace, without authorization. Turning over some piece, pieces of information to establish that credibility." Reggie had some other purposes in mind.

"Not before dinner, old man," intoned Churchill. "We are not that far gone."

"Not yet, at least."

* * *

Friday, January 18, 2000 Hours
Between Brussels and Hannover

Dinner came, the foursome hardly slowed their discussion. "While you are at it, Dietrich, bring the armor plate with you. Mount it as ramparts, shell protection. Why it was born in the first place." Boecker was growing more enthusiastic about this fantasy.

"I hate to douse your idea with ice water, Gents." Admiral Altermann had a sour look on his face. "I served on *Elsass* in 1905, with the new rifles. Powerful guns, but barrel life was abysmal – a hundred, maybe more rounds before relining or replacement. Longer with a less powerful shell, but shorter range. At one shot a minute, that gives you two hours' bombardment, if the whole thing stays together, no overheating, no jams. Even doubling that, at best a day's worth of shooting, then two months down unless a spare is at hand. And getting it back to the shop, for that matter."

Alterman shrugged, "You see, General, naval guns are designed for but a few minutes of sheer terror, not an eternity of pounding like your field artillery. The newer, bigger guns are much better, but they will be remaining aboard ship. Sorry."

"Trust Navy to dampen Army's spirits. Damn! Is this what one gets when one crosses over?" Von Treptow sulked.

"It is not so bad as that, Dietrich. Go back to Wally's *papier mâché* idea." Boecker had also served in battleships, and was still in awe of the big guns. "Just the sight of the guns, impregnable in armor and concrete, would make a powerful impression. Paris already knows our big guns, and those not so large as these. The few knowledgeable types would raise hell, but the public could be led. You could do it with a few guns and a credible statement of intent, a demonstration."

"Yes, it just could work, but only if you," Knorr, forgetting his rank, pointed at von Treptow, "can orchestrate a peace proposal and persuade High Command to withdraw, not advance. At the very same time."

As dinner was taken away, von Treptow was ready to turn to another proposition. "This has been a very enlightening discussion, Oz, but Heinz, for you, the colonel here and I have something less ambitious but undoubtedly more dangerous to propose." He quickly recounted the core of the meeting with the Irish. "As you see, we can give only limited direct support, paling in relation to their importance to us. We cannot count on gunrunning success forever, at least not under the English nose." He paused, grimacing, "As much as it pains me, Army yet again must request Navy's help."

"...and forgive us our debtors...," laughed Altermann. "What does our naval strategist have in mind?"

"Our Irish allies agree to rise against their English overlords as soon as, or if, we can supply them and protect them from invasion. Navy's role is twofold: hijack a munitions ship and sink the British Army in the approaches to Belfast. Simple, no? No?"

"Dietrich, some day you might consider consulting a chart, assuming, that is, you could even read it." Altermann was not amused. "The North Channel between Belfast and Scotland is about thirty kilometers wide, or less, as I recall. Our submarines would be fish in a barrel for the Royal Navy. Suicide. What was the other notion? Piracy?"

"Yes?" pleaded von Treptow.

Altermann was quiet, turning that idea over. Boecker saw the drift, "I assume you are thinking of an American supply ship. Crewed by American Irish and German supporters. Taken over somewhere on the high seas? Why bother with the cutlasses? Just find a ship owned by a sympathizer. Stage a night torpedo attack, fake damage, wait until the convoy sails on, then go wherever you wish."

"Yes, and we could help with the final approach, keeping any pesky Brits away. I am embarrassed we have not thought of such, Oz. Plenty of Irishmen in America, after all. Back to the first fantasy, General, the Irish Sea. We could afford to waste a few of our older, smaller subs but not their crews. No suicide missions. We would need an Irish port after the raid. The Brits would find empty boats. So be it. My crews might even welcome some Gaelic lassies for company. Minelaying itself would be easier, once we get around the top of Scotland, under the very nose of the Grand Fleet at Scapa."

"If, Heinz." Boecker was sobering up, "How would you get a dozen or so past their Navy?"

"Oh, we would have to think it through, to be sure. A diversion, then refueling up the Norway coast, then over, quiet, moonless, perhaps storm season. Bring the Fleet along. Why not? We can think on it. When did you say?"

"April, perhaps. You would have to tell us," said von Treptow.

"Well, Oz, it would certainly relieve the boredom of war."

After another hour of give and take, the Army men decided to turn in. The ride was slow but smooth, stops were few, and some welcome sleep was had.

The train pulled into Hannover station just after dawn. As it cruised to a stop along the platform, the welcoming committees emerged from the station house, far too cold to mill about outside. Boecker's and Knorr's household staffs bustled about, shaking hands and lifting bags, herding their masters to waiting cars.

The day old snow glistened with a rosy reflection of the rising sun, not yet sullied by coal dust nor turned to slush. All were bundled in the cars against the cold. "Supposed to break the chill today, Sir, get well above freezing, practically balmy." Heinrich was Knorr's butler and general fac-totum. He had been with the family since the 1880's, Walter inheriting him when his father died in 1916. He was legend for his discipline and fastidi-ousness, so Walter tried to tease him, "So, Heinrich, how is the household? Do you approve of the additions I sent you?"

"No, Sir, I most certainly do not. Those hounds are no more disciplined than when they were pups, and certainly less so than when I entrusted them to you. And these human pups? Are they really necessary? And the women? Well, Sir, I grant you they are pretty, but I thought it was the end for you when Rosalie passed. It is somehow not right having them about, in her place."

Knorr was momentarily taken aback by his directness and the path it opened to memory. "Yes, Heinrich, it will be odd. I had not thought of it that way until now. They are merely guests, as I see it. No one will replace Rosalie."

Reinhardt, the chauffeur, broke the chill, "Here we are, Sirs. It has been a while for you, Major, I mean Colonel! And congratulations on your pro-motion, Sir. Anyway, we are all happy to have you back, safe and sound."

"Thank you, Werner. Let us get inside – hot coffee?"

The house was of a mottled red-brown brick, with faintly Dutch gables and a deep entry recess framed in cut Solnhofen limestone from Bavaria, fossils still embedded. When Walter and Rosalie had bought it, not long after marrying, from the estate of a university professor, Rosalie had not had very long to enjoy it, or alter it, so it still had many of the old fittings and touches. Walter noticed for the first time how dark it was. *Needs a woman.*

Frau Rosenblum erupted from the dining room, simultaneously fussing and cooing over Knorr. "A skeleton! I told the girls he would be as death when he came back, and I was right. Here you go, Sir, a proper breakfast to revive you. And not a moment too soon! And who is this distinguished gentleman? He could use a bit of stuffing himself."

"Frau Elsie, he is a general, a very important one, at that."

"Still needs stuffing, if you ask me." She took von Treptow by the arm and dropped him into his seat, holding his shoulders to prevent his escape. She took off his homburg and smoothed his hair. "Starving and in need of a barber, too. Is this what war looks like?"

"Yes, sadly, it is, Frau. General, she has been with me since my birth, and in her eyes I have not grown a whit."

"Certainly not matured any," she sniffed. "Here we are, Gentlemen. I will leave you to eat in peace."

"She will be back, I take it?" asked von Treptow, warily.

"Momentarily," replied Knorr.

And so she was, this time with more sausages. "Must fortify yourselves against the cold. Look at me, I never get so much as a chill." *How could she, the size and shape of a walrus? That was an unkind thought, Dietrich.*

The bustling and trundling of bags had awakened the four smallest inhabitants who came charging into the dining room looking for their favorites. The dogs stood up on either side of Knorr's chair, paws in his lap, giving and getting affection. When he finally calmed them down, he noticed the bulk of his sausage was missing. He began to ring Frau Rosenblum, then thought better of it.

Then it was the children's turn. Knorr's face had healed, so he was no longer the bogeyman and the children had forgotten that fright. Up in his lap they clambered, Sophie picking through his eggs with her fingers, Etienne pinching his cheek. "Have you brought us any presents, Uncle Walter?" Uncle had indeed stopped at the Zeebrugge station shop and bought some sweets, which he unwrapped with great ceremony and gave to each. "Run along now, let us finish our breakfast in peace."

"Perhaps it was a blessing we had no children, General. Just looking at them fatigues me, all that energy."

"All in the dosage, Colonel, all in the dosage. And the timing, of course. Not to mention the duration. And do not forget the volume."

Frau Rosenblum returned. "I have two worthless hounds lolling on my kitchen floor, sausage on their breath. More for you." She was not to be denied.

"Frau Elsie, how are our ladies faring under your regime?" Knorr winked at von Treptow, whose eyes darted to the housekeeper, who, in turn, was facing the doorway, her face frozen in a small gasp. He turned in his chair, then started out of it so sharply he slammed his knee under the table. Rubbing it, he sat back and looked at the apparition in the portal.

"Good morning, Gentlemen. Colonel, I do not have a housecoat for the chill in this house. I found this, I hope you do not mind?"

"Rosalie?" Knorr whispered.

Frau Rosenblum swept past him to the doorway, "Madame Vandenberg, it will be perfectly fine, and should you need anything else, let me know." Close enough to her, whispering, "In advance next time, please. That was, is, his late wife's."

Both officers rose, Knorr still rubbing his knee. Von Treptow took Estelle's hand, guiding her to a seat opposite the colonel. "Coffee?" He poured her a cup. "Did the lieutenant execute his escort duties to your satisfaction?"

Estelle took a sip, never taking her eyes off Walter. Then, breaking away to look up at Dietrich, "Oh, yes. As always the perfect gentleman. Mind you, we saw little of him the whole long train ride. He was in the next compartment with the children and the dogs. Noisy, then quiet, then noisy, then quiet. For hours. He aged perceptibly," she laughed gently.

Returning her gaze to Knorr, "Colonel, I have trespassed on her memory. I am so sorry. I, of all people, should have known better. I shall return to my room to change into something else." She started to rise, but Walter waved her back down. He still could not speak, but fortunately his relief just then burst onto the strained scene.

"Hello, everyone!" Yvette flounced into the room, swirling the pleats of a blue skirt about her legs. "Isabella's sister let me wear this. Isn't it just perfect?"

It was pretty perfect, at that. A sailor-type blouse and pleated skirt, fitting her young figure. Knorr realized it was probably the first fine dress she had worn since fleeing Louvain. He rose haltingly and strolled to Yvette, taking her arm, "We are off to promenade, leaving you stuffy adults behind. Do not wait up."

Yvette giggled, joy in her voice. "Mother, is this, are they not the most wonderful?" Stepping back, she gave her best effort at a curtsey, tipping slightly, then recovering. "Colonel, I regret I must decline. Hildegarde is coming by to take me shopping and to luncheon."

"She has grown up since I saw her last," von Treptow said, not entirely in jest. "Heaven help the young men of Hannover."

"Come, child. If you are going to conquer the big city, you need a little more primping. And a lot less rouge." Frau Elsie shooed her out toward the stair, leaving the three alone.

Estelle resumed, "Did I hear you say Rosalie?"

"Yes, that is, was, my late wife."

"Rosalie Hambrecht, Vienna?"

"Did you know her?"

"Yes, through friends of college friends, that manner of acquaintance. I recall hearing of her death." Estelle rose, "Please Colonel, I will go change."

"No, no need. It is just that, well, I bought that for her in Italy, not long before she took ill. She died wearing it."

"I am so sorry. Please excuse me." Estelle loosed the robe as she walked out, a hand to her face.

Knorr tumbled back into his seat. "Have you noticed, General, Sir, everything we touch seems to turn to dross?"

* * *

Saturday, January 19, 8:00 p.m.
45 Berkeley Square, London

Lord Elsmere hosted a small dinner party at his house, just Pieter van der Hoek and his wife Hildegarde and Winston and Clementine Churchill. And Alexandra Breithaupt as Reggie's guest.

Despite Pieter's misgivings, he and Alexandra agreed to the social liaison as just one more avenue of intelligence gathering. Before agreeing, however,

Alexandra said, "There is something, however, about that handsome German colonel I find appealing, a vulnerability, some loss, perhaps? Shall I have the opportunity to see him again?"

"Alex, dear, I promised your father to look after you, not find you a husband. Dietrich has not told me anything about him as he has just added him to his staff. And, yes, you probably will see him again – I simply cannot foretell when." He paused, then decided to plunge ahead, "He found you not altogether wholly unattractive, I must confess." Alexandra gave him a knowing glance.

Dinner consisted of fresh fish, game and cheeses from the Lord's Northumberland estate, wine from his negociant house in Bordeaux, all the prewar expectations. Within the manse, all might have been as in Lord Clive's day. Clementine was early into her fourth pregnancy, so the ladies retired early to allow her to rest, leaving the men to their customary cigars and drinks.

"So, my Dutch intriguer, what know you of our guests and their mission?" Churchill wasted no time. "Bluntly, Pieter, it is of the utmost importance that we ascertain every nugget, every kernel of information as to their intentions. If this promise of peace is anything but ephemeral, a phantasm, we must know all!"

"Winston, my cigar is barely lit. '*Brandy and cigars first,*' you always say."

"I see a burning ember, old man. No more stalling." Lord Elsmere was equally impatient, simply a bit lighter on the hammer blows.

"Is there no escape? No, I suppose not. Well. I shall impart what I can, what my agreements with General von Treptow allow. You, in turn, must be forthcoming, as well. This is a new arrangement with Dietrich. He encouraged me in the affirmative to open this line. Secrecy is not an issue. If we are found out, I am sent home, taking Alexandra with me." He faced Reggie. "You, and he," waving his cigar at Churchill, "die."

Churchill winked at Reggie, "Our discussions certainly could be misconstrued, I grant you that. And undoubtedly the entire Tory party would lead the procession to the gallows. Lord Elsmere's friends and fellow clubmen will rescue him, so he has little concern." Both knew the risks they were taking, and the possible fate befalling them. Sir Roger Casement was an example, extreme, to be sure, as these two were not to be caught traipsing around in German U-Boats, running guns to the Irish. "Very well, then, Pieter, how do we proceed?"

"Yes. First, our German friends' Russian network has been degraded by attrition and the chaos engulfing the region. As you no doubt gathered, they plan to rectify the universal situation, not merely that nettlesome one, but they are still in want of good observation. He has asked to communicate directly with Francis Cromie. He considers it vital."

Churchill sputtered, "Not only no, but Hell, no! Might as well sign our death warrant as we speak. No!"

"As I expected. Then will you provide him, me, with Captain Cromie's dispatches, and ask him to amplify his observations? Reg, you and Blinker could do so, no? All inside your Naval Intelligence Division? Petrograd – no, such a coarse-sounding name – Saint Petersburg is of such critical interest to them, as you might imagine. And your man, Dukes, his observations, I should not forget."

Winston was unfamiliar with that reference, but not Lord Elsmere. "How?...Never mind. The all-seeing Pieter." Churchill had no time for the others' secrets. "So, we write up that invoice, how will your friends pay? Reggie, what coin would you demand?"

"Weekly updates on Ludendorff's plans, nothing less."

"Will not happen. They are running risks, as well. Dietrich tells me the infighting at the General Staff level is intense. Pro-offensive, anti-offensive. Against yours, against the French. Hindenburg and Ludendorff are the glue, so far insoluble. Von Treptow has played his hand and is the face of the opposition. Even without any perfidy on your part, he may be cashiered or worse, any day. What you ask is impossible. But, if not gold, silver?"

"May we cogitate on same? For a day or three?" Reggie understood when to stand down.

"Of course, but consider the pace of events, the time frame he presented, even if elliptically."

"Of course. Meet me at Crandall and Llewellyn on Jermyn Street, then, ten-thirty day after tomorrow. Winston, if that meets your approval, that is?"

"Be discreet, Reggie, if not with your choice of fabric, in the cut."

* * *

Saturday, January 19, 1100 Hours
Hannover

Rheinhardt drove von Treptow to local Army headquarters to catch up on his various schemes. He had bowed to his Naval colleagues' pragmatism and scaled back his grand land battleship scheme to a demonstration project aimed at the public, not the military. Armin Eberhorst and the two admirals were to meet for luncheon to discuss the matter further, Knorr and Boecker hosting the group at their club.

First, Walter had some catching up of his own to do with Heinrich, Frau Elsie and the staff. There were some repairs requiring his approval, some accounts to bring up to date, the normal run of affairs in maintaining a sizeable estate.

He sent for Estelle at mid-morning when they were done and the motorcar had returned. She came down the stair dressed in her best, not nearly up to a lady's standard here, but her beauty more than compensated. "Wolfie is expecting us at the Bank, and we should have ample time to attend to your business before dropping you at Frost's to meet Isabella. Frau Elsie, she will freeze in that coat. Please bring her the dark fur, if it does not reek excessively of napthalene."

"Colonel, I would rather not…"

"Madame, you are my guest. I am told these things need to be worn from time to time, so please indulge me. Rosalie would have had it no other way."

Estelle looked to Frau Rosenblum for support. "Best do as he says, M'am. Besides, it is a beautiful fur, you will look wonderful. Please?"

She relented, the motorcar was waiting and off they went. At the bank, Hannover's most prominent, every set of eyes was drawn to the couple crossing the marble parquet floor, the colonel in his best field uniform, medals hung, the mysterious beauty, a head of flaxen hair above the fur collar. Wolfgang Knorr turned to see the two and gave his characteristic whistle, further paralyzing the banking hall. "Well, little brother, I thought you had gone off to war, no?" He intercepted the couple in the middle of the lobby, ostentatiously separating his brother from Estelle and escorting her to his offices. "You would think they had never seen a beautiful woman. Well, it is Hannover, after all." He helped her out of the fur, looking at Rosalie's name in the collar, then at Walter.

"So, Brother, Madame Vandenberg, what may the bank do for you today? And I am so pleased to see someone has finally lured this one back to society. Making excuses for him is ever so tiresome, even as I shiver in fear of his behavior, so long out of polite company. Present company excepted, of course."

"Wolfie, I just need to transfer some funds into my household account," pushing a folded sheet of paper across the desk. "Madame Vandenberg has some other business. I shall excuse myself."

"No, please, Colonel, I prefer you stay. The good Lord above knows I have no secrets from you. Herr Knorr, first I need to change some money into marks." She began to open Uncle Isaac's package, "I have some shopping to do while here. Second, I would appreciate your making contact with Barings Bank in London." The two brothers looked at each other. "If that is possible, of course. My late husband arranged to have our resources transferred there at the outbreak of the war. I do not know how to access those funds should I require them."

Colonel Knorr had written his brother with some of Estelle's history, so Wolfgang knew not to bring up Henri or his death, but neither knew of any assets, sizeable or not, in Belgium or England. For all Walter knew, she was destitute, save for her husband's uncle's generosity. *Well. Another surprise.*

"Officially, I have no way to contact an English bank. We are at war, funds have been frozen and all commerce suspended. Unofficially, I can make some enquiries. Would the accounts be in your late husband's name, or yours, or both?"

"Some in Henri's name, Henri Lang, of course. Some in both our names, some in my maiden name. Wolfgang, when I first met your brother, actually the general, it was, I felt I should use my Dutch name, not a Jewish name. I was scared then, but have grown accustomed to it by now. The accounts originated in the Bank of Louvain. Willem de Ruyter is a contact name that may be useful."

"Yes, I know Willem from banking conferences and such, and we maintained a correspondent relationship with his bank. I must confess I knew Henri, as well, through banking circles. I am very sorry. I would be honored to assist you in any manner I can." That difficult business past, he smiled, "You had a precious little daughter, as I recall?"

Estelle laughed, "Not so little, anymore, Wolfgang. Do you have any teenaged sons at home?"

"One left, just fifteen. A hellion-in-training, aspiring to be his uncle."

"Then we have mutual trouble, Herr Knorr. I also have two little ones, three and one."

Wolfgang was doing the sums in his head. He started to ask the obvious question, but balked, and Walter saved his brother, "Time to go, Wolfie, old boy. We have a full schedule today. Let us visit the cashier's cage."

The two doormen at Frost Brothers competed to assist Estelle from Knorr's car, settling on a draw, one opening the lefthand Art Nouveau bronze door, the other the righthand leaf. She turned to wave goodbye, disappearing into a woman's world.

Knorr shuddered at the thought of imprisonment within and quickly brought his car around to the Cincinnatus Club. Oswald Boecker and Admiral Altermann were waiting in the salon. Moments later, Lieutenant von Seeckt dashed in. "Sirs, the General is outside speaking to someone. He will be in shortly."

While waiting on von Treptow, Knorr gave an abbreviated accounting of the young man's heroism on the road from Soissons. "I thought you were infantry, like your uncle. Whence cometh the swordplay and mastery of horse?" Boecker was having fun some fun with his daughter's beau.

"Just raised that way, I guess. Did some fencing at university. Odd, though, killing those Frenchmen was not emotional, not high, not low. Just business. All the others were at rifle range, hardly saw them."

"Not odd, young man. If it were, you would have hesitated and three Germans might have died. No, that is simply what war does to us. Not just this war. War through time. Read your Homer again."

Altermann added, "And think of our war, at sea. Ships, big things, sink, but hundreds of men drown, unseen to us for the most part. We think we sink ships, but we sink men."

"Enough introspection. Ah, here we are, saved by the general." Boecker hailed his friend who had Eberhorst in tow, and the sextet marched into the dining room. Knorr and Boecker had rounds to make. Eberhorst and Altermann immediately began discussing submarine production from Krupps' Germania Werks.

After a time, the social butterflies rejoined the table. "So, Admirals, my friend here aspires to be a shipbuilder. Have you heard anything so outlandish?" Eberhorst patted von Treptow's wrist. "When do you launch?"

"You tell us, you control the process, do you not?"

"We spoke of July, but you indicated outside another idea?"

"A sham. A demonstration. Of our strength and our goodwill, simultaneously." He explained, in brief.

"Which would solve the most obvious problem, one can not just will a completed system into being overnight. Would plywood do?"

"Plywood?" Altermann was nonplussed.

"Yes, of course, plywood. *Ersatz* gun turrets. Only for a few months until the real articles are ready. Which, by the way, we have already started. The oldest equipment was landed beginning last year, much of it sitting dockside or in sheds at Germania, some in Essen, saved from the smelter. Some are smaller, peashooters alongside the big guns, but bigger than most of Army's field pieces. Have you the real estate in hand?"

"Well, not exactly...," stammered von Treptow.

"Might want to get those deeds. Transport needs someplace to stop. Seriously, start between Liege and Namur, history being your guide. East side of the Meuse. Take the commanding heights, increases the range somewhat."

"What about the actual construction, Sir?" The logistics had landed in Knorr's lap. "What do you require?"

"Construction is simple. An excavation seven, make it eight meters deep, a bit more for the bigger emplacements. A little wider. In this weather, we can start the digging. Next is concrete, a slab a meter thick. Nice and level, and give us a good drain. Then the concrete walls, a silo. Gives us something to support the lifts."

Eberhorst gestured, illustrating the process, "Drop the base, the rotating mechanism down, bolt in place. Stack the armored cylinder in sections, each with all the equipment in place or ready. Magazine, shell rooms, then the turret floor above. It is all pretty well self-contained. Need a big crane, and power for the hydraulics, of course. Mount the guns, close it over with a turret top, ready to go. Plywood and sheet metal until the real thing comes. We have some old gunbarrels, too."

"Sounds too simple, Sir," said Knorr.

"Simple? Not at all, but the true difficulty is building the guns and forming the armorplate, takes as long or longer than the actual shipbuilding. One reason the ships are floated out first then gunned up after, you see, Colonel? With the pieces in hand, it is fairly straightforward, if not simple. Still, straightforward." Eberhorst made a gesture, pointing his fingers away from his forehead. "Mind you, we are not doing the construction work, the labourer work. Three firms are ready to do so, using your Russians and the sailors. AEG have to bring power. From your notice to proceed, and labour at hand, the smaller guns can be in place in ninety days, completely operational another sixty or so. 1 July, if we start straightaway. Straightaway, now."

"And the cost? How many submarines will this cost me?" Altermann was deadly serious.

"None. No one will ever see these costs. They will be buried in other budgets. Krupps will earn our customary and reasonable fee, of course, so please do not concern yourself for us."

"Back to the *ersatz* idea, Armin. If you just built the silos, you call them, and topped them with dummy turrets, is that a ninety day proposition?"

"Yes, Dietrich, my friend, essentially so. The silo will be there to receive the real thing at a later date. We can make it realistic, too. You could have a hundred underway, if you so wish."

Lieutenant von Seeckt spoke for the first time at the table, "These newspapermen like to drink and gamble, correct?"

Eberhorst laughed, "As a species, yes. And whore, too. I see where your young mastermind is headed, Dietrich. Yes, a boys' outing would be in order. Nothing like steering the story. Krupps have some experience in such matters."

"I am certain you do, Armin, I am quite certain you do." Von Treptow had started drumming his cheek with his fingers. "I am thinking," he said, "I am thinking!"

Finally, "Colonel, you are to go to Essen with Armin to plan this. Meet me in Berlin on the 26th."

"Five days, General? Why so generous?"

* * *

Sunday, January 20, 1400 Hours
Hannover

The day of the ball arrived and Estelle and Yvette were ferried to Admiral Boecker's home to prepare with the assistance of Isabella and his wife, Maria. The Admiral's household staff would be chaperoning a small party for the younger set whilst their elders were downtown that night. Hildegarde, Isabella's younger sister, was newly fifteen and a blonde version of her older sister. Yvette, still clinging to her geopolitical innocence, was enthralled at the idea of meeting handsome young men like Wolfgang's son Georg; Knorr was completely at sea at the thought of Yvette with *les incorrigibles*, as he was sure they were. *Am I already become a father figure or merely a landlord?*

The four officers convened at Walter's place for lunch, a little bridge and brandy, then a slow run up to preparation for the evening. Von Treptow quizzed his friend, "Well, Oz, what think you of my younger helper? He is one brave young man, ice in his veins, cooler under fire than I. And yet, a clumsy puppy under your daughter's spell."

"She seems fond of him," Boecker grunted, holding his cards closer to his face, adjusting his reading glasses. He paused, then laid both down on the table. "She was also very fond of another soldier, young Graf von Steuben – Willy – called to serve in the Second Grenadiers. Killed at Second Ypres. Posthumous *Order pour le Mérite* for repelling a British company's assault on his platoon's position. Machine gunned fifty or more, then overwhelmed."

He was silent a while. "Family friends. Known the child since birth. Hard on us all, he was our favorite son, as it were, as we have only girls, you see."

"My regrets, Admiral. I did not know. Your daughter gave me the slightest hint of a sadness when we first met." Von Treptow paused a few moments, then continued, "Oz, please do me the honour of presenting these to the lieutenant when he arrives for your daughter this evening. I am certain she would be delighted to stick him." He handed over a box, pulling the lid backward as he did, the contents facing the admiral. Within were a captain's bars and an Iron Cross, First Class.

"Please do not tell me we are now to address him respectfully, General. He will be quite impossible." Knorr was pleased. "Were you planning to share this before the eleventh hour, Sir?"

"Only at the eleventh hour did these materialize. I made the request yesterday, pulled a few strings, and *voilà!* I even arranged a letter from Cousin Willy. Should arrive in the next few days. Meantime, your bodyguard will be dressed suitably, certainly more competitively."

Heinrich had their formal attire laid out when the naval guests were sent home. Walter was in dress uniform for the evening, two Crosses and several ribbons on his chest. He thought of wearing his sword, but he and Heinrich agreed it was superfluous to the outfit, particularly given his service record. *Not after having fought for my life with a French saber; let them think what they will.*

General von Treptow had opted for civilian wear, white tie and waistcoat in grosgrain, a red sash, a black swallowtail cutaway, the entire rig topped with monocle and top hat. A sword was eschewed in favor of a cane topped with a polished catseye, his favorite since a younger man.

He, too, had his medals. Three Iron Crosses, one of them Austrian, and innumerable smaller ribbons, both campaign and honorary. Around his neck he wore the blue cross of the *Order Pour le Mérite* with oak leaves. Prominent on his lefthand peaked lapel were the Bavarian Military Merit Order and the Baden War Merit Cross, bestowed by his protectors.

In such ensembles they marched to confront the cream of Hannoverian society. Von Treptow was impervious to social trepidation, Knorr more than a little nervous. Both, however, were completely on edge at the prospect of introducing, or re-introducing, Estelle Vandenberg to the Swan Ball. Their anchor was Isabella Boecker who continued to have her misgivings, even after Estelle gracefully handled encountering a number of acquaintances while shopping. Nought left to do but face the consequences of their ill-conceived attempt at chivalry.

Reinhardt drove Lieutenant von Seeckt to the Boecker house, Knorr and von Treptow following in the bank's Rolls driven by old Ludwig, another family retainer. The lieutenant was no more eager than the others to face the women, but where to hide? The Boecker's butler met them at the door, followed immediately by the admiral. "Quickly now," he whispered, "into my study."

He pivoted sharply, ducking into an adjoining room, closing the doors behind them. "The only safe place in the house to have a brandy for courage.

The women are on a rampage. Nothing fits, the hair has gone berserk, they simply cannot be seen looking like this or like that. Four women, before Marian was spririted away by marriage, was bad enough. Five, and unrelated, is simply too much. The chambermaids are gasping for air. The housekeeper has the vapors. My valet has holed up in the tower for the duration. It is hell, I tell you gentlemen, hell."

Four exceedingly well-dressed and impressive military types stared glumly into the dwindling contents of their brandy and whisky glasses. Presently, a tumult beyond came closer and the doors were flung open by Maria Boecker with a flourish. "There are my scoundrels! Drinking up some liquid bravado, are they? General von Treptow, so nice to see you again!" She floated across the rug, hand extended for his peck. Standing back to survey the finery, "He is quite the handsomest of all. Please escort me to the foyer."

He followed orders and with Maria on his arm was the first to see the assembly. He did not recognize Yvette, or at least did not at first distinguish her from Hildegarde, so similar were their appearances. Maria swept von Treptow across the room, depositing him in front of the young ladies. He bowed, they curtseyed, then twirled around displaying their party dresses.

"I shall take these two, the rest of you may sort out the others." Yvette laughed, then pulled herself up to the general on tiptoe, whispering, "Thank you, Sir, for all you have done for us." She planted a small kiss on the bottom of his jaw, as high as she could reach.

Von Treptow dabbed at the cinder that had suddenly entered his eye, then turned to the rest: Maria, a more angular or austere version of her daughters, only lightly touched by age; Isabella, flouting convention with her hair completely down, reaching her waist, wearing a rose colored silk dress, rather daring, he thought; Estelle, the mystery woman, smiling demurely first at him, then Walter, in a blue thing recognizable as a dress but easily mistaken for a painting so fitted it was, off the shoulders and puddling on the floor.

Colonel Knorr staggered dramatically and stumbled toward a chair, clutching his chest, mopping a dry brow with his handkerchief. "I have seen the angels. I may now die in peace."

Isabella turned to her mother, "Did I not tell you they are all idiots? What has happened to our men? And you entrusted me to the watchful care of this one," pointing at Knorr, "the very worst of the lot?" She and her mother broke into a gale of laughter.

The general thumbed at von Seeckt, "Yes, and look what that brought."

Admiral Boecker raised his hand. "No more inanity, please. I nearly forgot something very important." He disappeared into his study, returning with von Treptow's black box. "Yvette, young lady, and Isabella, please help me with these." He opened the box to the delight of the young ladies.

"You," said Isabella, pointing to her lieutenant, "Sit!" Von Seeckt meekly complied. Yvette plucked first the insignia, then the decoration, handing them to Isabella to apply. When all were in place, she gave him a small kiss, saying, "Arise, Sir Erich and face your admirers!"

Yvette gave him a full body hug, then Dietrich saluted him, shaking his hand, "Never a more worthy award. Without this young man, we, Colonel Knorr and I, would likely be missing these festivities." The women looked quizzically at him. "A story for the telling when this dreadful war is done."

"Hear, hear," Admiral Altermann added, having slipped into the gathering. "Let it be known he is a man of courage. Enough sentimentality, however. I smell Champagne, or at least Sekt. *Nunc est bibendum!* Shall we?" He saluted Captain von Seeckt and drew Isabella to his side. "Let us not suffer the civilians to usurp our drinking rights."

As the caravan pulled away in the circular drive, in came a load of boisterous youths. Oswald Boecker moaned, "I do not wish to know."

The Swan Ball was held, as was custom, in the ballroom of the Cincinnatus Club. For this wartime edition the decorations were somewhat subdued, but hardly somber. Nor were the attendees; one could hardly tell any difference versus the *ante bellum*, save for far, far fewer young men. The foyer and the anterooms were crowded with well turned out civilians and somewhat leaner military and naval types. Waiters in traditional livery circulated dispensing sparkling wine and chilled schnapps.

Maria Boecker had arranged for a private room off the main concourse to assemble for a relaxed glass before facing the multitude. She knew Estelle's story and shared the men's concerns, so wished to ease her into the maelstrom, stepping out frequently to gauge the progress of the procession, finally deciding the time had come. She arranged the group, leading between her husband and Admiral Altermann, a widower; then came Isabella and her new captain, easily the handsomest couple at the ball; last came Estelle, Knorr and von Treptow.

The herald had no problem with the first two groups. As the third cohort paused at the top of the stair, the enthusiastic applause for Isabella and her escort having died away, the crowd below hushed, momentarily throwing him off his cadence. He recovered, reading the notes Maria had handed him, "Lieutenant Colonel Walter Knorr of the Imperial German Army General Staff; Madame Estelle...Vandenberg of...of...Louvain; Brigadier General Dietrich von Treptow, Margrave of Brandenburg and the Mittelmark." The applause was tentative, then more vigorous, but Knorr noted many still pairs of hands. Certainly everyone's ears had pricked up, especially two pair on opposite sides of the ballroom.

"Well, we have their attention. Madame, there is not a husband's eyes that are not fastened upon you, and no fewer wives with angry glares. Beauty cannot be denied." Von Treptow darted his eyes right and left, acknowledging waves, salutes and not a few winks as the trio waded into the crowd.

"Please do not leave me." Estelle clutched both arms escorting her. "Please." Walter could feel her shiver and put his arm around her waist. Von Treptow stepped slightly in front, deflecting the curious crowd; Estelle was pleading, struggling to maintain her composure. "I feel like an animal in the zoo. Please find me a place to sit."

The officers led her to a cluster of chairs against one wall, smiling and chatting as they went, not betraying their guest's emotional turmoil. Von Treptow snapped his fingers at a waiter, and champagne was produced. Estelle held her glass with two hands, and soon the trembling subsided. Maria came to the rescue with Estelle's university roommate, Theresa. Knorr made room for her after introductions and stood guard as the two hugged and cried, then talked passionately. Maria motioned the officers away as she raised the two women up, leading them away to tend to their faces.

The commotion, such as it was, in the ballroom generated by their entrance had faded. Walter was engulfed in a knot of family friends eager to hear of his war exploits. Erich and Isabella were now dancing, now drinking with her friends, every girl among them wistful, if not downright jealous of her good fortune.

Von Treptow strode back and forth, lighting on one group of officers, now another. He soon discovered he was the only general officer under the age of seventy and rose to the potential of the role. As he strutted about, stopping to meet some friends of Altermann's, a smoky yet dulcet voice behind him said softly, "Dietrich, my love?"

Without turning, "I did not expect to encounter you here, Duchess. Or have you reverted to Princess?" He turned to face the voice, "Hello, Claire."

"Please, Dee, is that any way to greet an ardent admirer?"

"A formerly ardent admirer. You know how sorry I am about Richard, do you not?"

"Yes, I do. You loved him as your brother. It was hard on us both."

"I hope so."

"Dietrich, you bastard! Will you not forget, forgive?" Claire was Berlin's great beauty of her day, and even now gave nothing away to the younger set. Her hair was silver as much as black, cut in a page boy – daring for Hannover, not Berlin – and her face had only hints of wrinkling, mainly from the laughter she was so known for. Her dress a simple sheath ashimmer with silver beads, fitting her fine form, as fine as he fondly remembered it. Eyes of a bluegrey, always cold no matter how warm her voice or passionate her embrace.

Von Treptow took her hand, kissed it, then put it to his cheek. "Can you forget cuckolding your husband, forgive yourself for seducing his best friend? I cannot, no matter how I try. I am sorry."

Claire pulled back her hand. "No, I do not suppose you can forgive, Dietrich, the moralist, the most upright." She placed her fingers on his lips. "I cannot forget the man I have loved since my childhood, have always loved, still love to this very day. You, Dietrich."

General von Treptow looked about them. No attention was being paid to this drama conducted *sotto voce* at close quarters. "Come, Claire, let us dance."

As they waltzed, von Treptow asked, "What brings you here? Did you know I was coming? Of course not, hardly anyone did."

"Do not give yourself such credit, my dear. I was invited unawares."

"Another conquest?"

"Mona, you are acquainted with her, if you must know. You must remember her. My escort is her eighty year old father, still spry."

"Be gentle with him, then."

"Really, Dietrich!" she snapped, bolting away just as the music died down. Dietrich reached out, curling his arm around her waist, pulling her to him. Gazing down at her upturned face, "Forgive me. May we simply enjoy each other's company here amidst strangers?"

"Here, yes, and perhaps elsewhere *sans* strangers?"

"Ever the vixen!" He laughed aloud, "Come, allow me introduce you to my hosts. Wait, now, Duchess or Princess?"

"Vixen will do quite nicely, thank you. No, no, Fritz's Marie is now Duchess, now that Richard is gone. Our cousin the Grand Duke has graciously granted me the return of the old family title." Her wry smilet glimmered then dimmed, "Nice of him, yes, but not that it matters anymore, the way this world is turning upside down." She stopped, a hint of fear in her eyes, "Dietrich, what will become of us, of all this?"

He held her face gently in his hands, "If you knew what I know, my lamb, you would take yourself to a nunnery while there was still time. It is frightening, indeed." He realized where he was, then, "Ah, here we are. Colonel, see what I have found here in Hannover! May I keep her?"

He made introductions all around. Estelle had recovered from her earlier fright, it seemed, and was beaming in animated conversation with Theresa and Maria until she saw the new woman on the general's arm. Since Claire was dressed even more dramatically, more daringly, than the other women, there was an initial stiffness much amplified by the men's stares. Very quickly, though, the women were applauding the Duchess' fashion risk.

All but Estelle, who was searching von Treptow's face for explanation. She took Dietrich by the arm, securing with a glance the new woman's approval to dance with him.

"Who is she?"

"An old friend."

"An old lover, you mean. Attempting to get her claws into you again."

"Yes, I am sure she is. Take care – like a cat's, hers are retracted at the moment. Best not to see them fully extended." He smiled down on her upturned face. "Is there nothing to be concealed from you?"

"Not where women are concerned. Your face is a school blackboard with every emotion, every thought writ large for all to see."

"And what, pray tell, do you see?"

"I see a man of an ebbing sorrow, engrossed in his mission or whatever you term it, attempting to forget. Maria told me everything as we dressed."

"Not everything, Estelle. Maria knows many things and I grant few things escape her, but she is not omniscient. At least not where I am concerned."

"What does she not know, my handsome man of mystery? Some juicy secrets?"

"Just one. Recall the story of David, Bathsheba and Uriah."

"That is it?"

"That is more than enough. Ah, our dance is over, and blessedly so is my interrogation. Do not look – every man's eyes are upon you. As if one could blame them."

He was right. Engrossed in their flirtation, neither had noticed they were practically alone on the floor. Her blue and his black made for a tall, strikingly chromatic sculpture in an unmistakably romantic pose, surrounded by admirers.

He escorted her back to the safety of their little circle. Her breathing had become slightly labored and she sought Walter's supporting arm. "I am allright, merely overwhelmed by our General's charms," giving Claire a lingering glance. "I am sure you have experienced similar?"

"Not precisely so. The breathing always seemed to be heavier, somehow." Before Claire set her tight, sardonic smile, Estelle was certain she had glimpsed fangs.

From across the room, another pair of eyes had not left the figure in blue. For most of the evening Major Walter Honecker had hardly left the company of his fellows, downing schnapps and telling tales, indulging in often obscene and mean-spirited braggadocio. His fellow officer Ernst Ulbricht, playing Mercutio to Honecker's Tybalt, had been prodding and teasing from the moment they heard Estelle's name announced.

Honecker prided himself on his way with women and vilified those who somehow failed to appreciate his charms. Estelle had been one such. "Bitch! I took her to the club's Christmas dance my second year, her first, tried to get her drunk to make it easier on her. Finally had to drag her to the kitchen, put her up against the wall…"

Ulbricht interrupted, "Our master of finesse, you see. The serving girls at the beerhalls appreciated his charms, not so much the highborn college ladies!"

"Shut your face, Ulbricht. At least I conquered, what can you say for yourself? So, I had her up against the wall in the kitchen..."

"And started reciting sonnets, poems of love, *'Spread your legs, damn you. Stop your wriggling.'* He never was one for strict rhyme and meter."

"So help me Ernst! Friends, will you vouch for his provocations when I tear him limb from limb?"

"Just get on with it," said another. "You had her up against the wall, but did you have her?" The laughter only infuriated Honecker further. Taking jokes well was not his forte. He snapped his fingers and brusquely whipped a glass of schnapps off a passing waiter's tray, downing it in one motion.

"Yes, against the wall, then, damn her, she kneed me in the groin. Hard. I doubled over, dropped to a knee. It hurt like Hades. Then, when I am *hors de combat,* the bitch slaps me across the jaw, digging her nails into my skin. I never gave her another chance. Anyway, she wound up marrying that half-Jew Henri..."

Another carouser corrected him, "No such thing as a half-Jew. One drop of Hebrew blood corrupts the same as one hundred percent."

"Thank you, Wilmer, you are quite correct."

Ulbricht was not about to let this end. "Well, now, Walter, there she is, beautiful as ever. This is her chance to correct her past error if you would only be so generous."

Honecker had no choice even had he been sober enough to apply some logic. His *confrères* would not let him live it down if he did not confront his nemesis of many years past. So, he straightened his uniform and strode across the floor.

As he approached, Estelle happened to look in his direction. Seeing him but not yet recognizing or remembering, she was puzzled at the chill in her breast. Then she remembered the tall blond soldier with the dueling scar and tightened her grip on Knorr's arm, who in turn looked up at the oncoming officer.

Honecker stopped, saluting the only uniform he saw, Colonel Knorr's, then bowed and clicked his heels facing Estelle. "You do remember me, do you not? We were at Heidelberg together. You gave me these," pointing to the row of small scalloped scars along his left jawbone. "I have not forgotten, and hoped I could someday repay you." Seeing Knorr, but not Henri, his woozy brain made the connection. "And where is the Jew? Probably dead, executed for some Semitic treachery. Good riddance to him and to you."

He made a sudden move toward Estelle. As Knorr interposed himself, he felt her sink toward the floor, rigid as if paralyzed. He caught her as she fell, then lowered her body gently to the floor. She was not moving a muscle, her teeth and fists were clenched. Her eyes were moving, though, and full of fear. "Get a doctor," he shouted to Maria, the nearest.

"There is nothing wrong with the bitch that a good lay would not cure. She had her chance…"

"Major! That will do." Von Treptow wrenched Honecker's right arm around to face him. "Leave us. Now!"

Ulbricht had trailed his friend as his second and now reached for his left sleeve, whispering warnings, then felt his neck in a vise, Captain von Seeckt's powerful left hand. He made one effort to escape, then relented.

Meanwhile, Honecker's anger rose faster than his senses could clear. He drew his sword and placed it against the general's Blue Max, pushing him backward with its tip. "Who are you to tell me what to do, old fellow?"

"Merely a friend of the family. What unit are you? Oh, I see," looking at his insignia, "Imperial Horse Guards. A show pony. How much did Daddy pay to post you there rather than go to the front as a real soldier?"

Honecker's face went dark. "I'll not be insulted by some dried up, pompous old man!" He drew his saber back as if to begin a slash as another sword came arcing hilt down over his shoulder. Von Seeckt had appropriated his prisoner's sword with his right hand, tossing it to a waiting von Treptow, who grasped it, felt its balance, and took up a defensive pose.

Infuriated, the younger man began hacking away at the general. In but a few moments, however, he realized there was more fight in his opponent than he had bargained for and cleared his mind and reflexes sufficiently to begin fencing rather than slashing.

The two thrust and parried their way across and around the dance floor, von Treptow loudly complimenting his opponent. "A fine club fencer you were, I am sure. Excellent form. Yes, there, fine parry, yes, good counterthrust." He stood back, raising his blade to his nose. "Shall we continue?"

Honecker answered with another attack, effortlessly countered by von Treptow. The older man then backed the younger across the room with a series of slashes, finally drawing Honecker into a clutch.

"More, young man?"

Honecker started to reply with a move, but stopped as his medals clattered to the floor amid peals of laughter from the crowd. Von Treptow had neatly sliced across his ribbons in a barely perceptible move as they parted, creating the desired effect as the other began slashing wildly, quickly exhausting himself, his arm muscles weakening, his coordination losing its precision.

The general turned his back and stepped away a few paces, then turned to confront the brash challenger. "That was fine college swordplay, I grant you that. It is now time for combat." He lunged forward, whipping his blade from side to side in a controlled fury of powerful strokes. Soon Honecker, on the defensive, let his blade tip dip a trifle too much. Von Treptow caught it on the flat with a flick of his wrist, wrenching it away skittering across the floor. Erich stopped the blade with his boot, then released his prey with a quiet warning.

It was not yet over. Von Treptow held the tip of his saber at the underside of Honecker's pointed chin, drawing blood, pushing him back toward his clique. One more push and the major was forced into a chair. "Since you seem to be quite the ladies' man, surely you know they adore a cleft chin," turning his blade and slicing upward. Honecker grabbed his bleeding chin, pressing a handkerchief to the wound.

Von Seeckt walked up, dropping the saber on the floor in front of the wounded man. The general did likewise then turned to a man in uniform, a colonel. "He would make an excellent leader of a forward reconnaissance unit, would he not? I will have his orders to you tomorrow, if you like." The other agreed wholeheartedly and so it was done.

They returned to their women accompanied by a smattering of applause. An elderly doctor knelt by the prostrate Estelle. "She will be fine. She has had an emotional shock causing a form of temporary paralysis known as cataplexy or a cataplectic seizure. It is unusual to be this severe but always dissipates with time and rest. Not just confined to women, I dare say. I see more and more in those returning from the fronts."

Two ambulance men and Colonel Knorr lifted the paralyzed but still conscious Estelle onto a litter. Walter held her hand as they walked her out. Wolfgang Knorr approached Dietrich, smiling broadly, "Between us, I am happy to be rid of that high class Prussian riffraff," winking at him. "Walter told me of your recent scrape and now I see how he escaped. Thank you."

"As your guest I must apologize for that spectacle, Sir. It would appear our evening here is finished. Thank that tall one there with Oz's daughter, he saved Walter, I merely hoped for a draw."

Claire took his arm. "Dietrich, are you allright? You scared us all unto death. Had to play the brave knight, did you?"

Von Treptow started to brush her away, angrily.

"You did the right thing, Dee," she cooed, he relaxed.

"You always do."

Colonel Knorr returned to the ballroom and with his brother and Dietrich sought out the chairwoman of the ball to apologize. She was older, probably late sixties, and every bit the prim overstuffed prude they expected. Until she opened her mouth, after receiving their apologies with a nod. "It was so exciting, young man," taking von Treptow by the arm, "I had no idea one still fought with swords like that. And such a gallant you were, rescuing that beauty. I remember her when she was still in her teens, truly a belle of the ball. I hope she recovers swiftly. Young Walter, I should like to pay a call on her, if I may, that is, if you think it appropriate. Maria has shared her tragic past. And I think it is damned well past time that the younger women dressed in fashions that did not make them look like Mohammedan slaves. If I only were twenty years younger…"

"Perhaps thirty, dear, but then it would have been unfair to the young ladies." Her husband, Herr Hummel, a leading industrialist, pinched her ample rear. "She is still quite the woman," he winked.

The three were trying desperately not to picture that domestic scene when Frau Hummel sent them on their way, retaining Dietrich for a moment. "That woman, Claire, the Duchess from Dessau. Beautiful, but I hear, dangerous. You knew her in your past?" She was prying and knew it.

"Yes, Madame, we grew up together, from pigtails and short pants through university days. We then drifted apart, married different people, were both widowed. We had a pleasant visit here."

"You are not going to give me anything worthy of my bridge group, are you?" Her eyes had a twinkle he was certain appealed to Herr Hummel.

"Not on my life, Madame. Nor hers." With a broad smile, he bowed, kissed her hand, then leaned down and gave her a genuine kiss on the cheek, not the usual perfunctory peck. It produced the desired effect, enabling his escape.

Estelle was in an anteroom near the club's entrance, swaddled in a grey blanket, still immobile. The doctor nodded as Dietrich and Walter entered, "She is fine, breathing is normal. She should remain here until she recovers as I would not put her out in this cold."

Maria Boecker sent her daughter and escort away to their afterparty, and Admiral Altermann rode home with her chauffeur. The rest stayed the next half hour until Estelle began to twitch under the covers. The doctor checked pulse and breathing, then had two of the men lift her to a sitting position. Her breasts heaved a few times as if she was trying to catch her breath and finally her mouth opened to say something. The doctor quieted her with his fingers to her lips.

Another half hour passed before she was mobile enough to be taken to the waiting Rolls, wrapped in Rosalie's long dark fur. She nestled in between colonel and general, finally able to speak. "What happened to me? To you? I could see movement, hear clanging and clattering. What happened?"

"We shall tell you all about it tomorrow. Right now, you need to get into a warm bed and get some sleep." Walter continued, "Do not worry, Yvette will not see you like this."

As they pulled up in the circular drive in front of the house, Walter jumped out to alert the staff. Frau Elsie was staying up late along with one of the chambermaids to assist in undressing and took over once Estelle was safely inside. "Look sharp, you two. She is not a sack of potatoes! Gently, now," she barked at the officers all the way up the stair. At the door to the bedchamber, she shooed them away. "Do not make matters worse by gawking and staring. Go to bed!"

* * *

Monday, January 21, 1100 Hours
Hannover

Walter had earlier invited the entire ensemble to brunch the next morning. Estelle's condition had allowed her to sleep soundly and she looked the freshest of all. The two teenagers were dragging. Hildegarde's girlfriends were allowed to stay overnight, which meant no sleep, of course. Captain von Seeckt was in an advanced state of decomposition having attended an after-after party, Isabella being far too wise for such foolishness.

"So, Ladies, how was your party?" Admiral Boecker knew full well how the party was, based on the bedraggled looks of the girls when their parents' drivers came to fetch them.

"Mmmm. Had fun. Thank you, Daddy."

Estelle pursued the issue. "Yvette, did you meet any nice boys?"

"Mother! They were very nice, yes."

"Walter's nephew, Georg, is quite handsome, I understand. What was he like? Did you like him?"

Hildegarde perked up. "They were sweethearts from the moment he saw her. All my friends are furiously jealous." She glanced mischievously at Yvette, who started to protest until cut off by Colonel Knorr. "I am not sure I am ready for such talk. Certainly not this early." Yvette mouthed a "*thank you*" to Uncle Walter.

Brunch was excessive, consumption closely monitored by Frau Rosenblum. Knorr succeeded in rising from the table despite her objections. "I must pack for my trip to Essen this afternoon. Captain, you are ordered to recover from your indispositions."

The teenagers, newly energized, ran off in search of the little children and the dogs, nearly tumbling Heinrich who was bringing in a telegram for General von Treptow, who took it from the silver tray.

"Not another one," groused the colonel.

"No, no, not official. Of a private nature." Everyone knew instantly what that meant, and who sent it.

Estelle, not looking away from the general, said softly, "Will someone please tell me what happened last night?"

Admiral Boecker tried clumsily to avoid the question, "Aside from your scaring us to death, just a little exhibition of swordsmanship. Nothing dangerous."

Maria swept him aside with a wave. "You did give us quite the scare. That young officer, I do not know the name, practically assaulted you had Walter not intervened. Then you fainted. And you have recovered, so all is well."

"No, more happened. I could still see. General, did you fight him? For me?"

"I attempted to defend you, yes. And your honour. Who was he? His name?"

"Honecker, Walter Honecker. Horribly arrogant student at Heidelberg with me and Henri. Tried to rape me my first year, only a few weeks on campus. I did my best to disable him." She recounted the story. "Apparently he never forgot. He said something awful about Henri last night, it just chilled me."

"Well, my dear, you shall not be seeing him again any time soon. I daresay none of us will, not even his family. He will be on a troop train west this time tomorrow, may God rest his soul."

Walter placed a hand on Estelle's shoulder. "The general is being modest. He could have killed the fellow. And I thought he would."

Von Treptow tried to move the conversation along, "Well, it is past us. Madame, did you enjoy the rest of the evening?"

"Thanks to Maria and Theresa, I had a splendid time, once I…adjusted. Everyone was so very kind. And, of course, the evening would not have been complete without that mysterious woman attaching herself to the general, here." Estelle continued, "Not that I am the least bit jealous. Merely curious." She smiled beatifically at Dietrich.

"Curious you shall remain. An old friend from childhood, is all. Did you notice she was beautiful?"

"So is a tigress," said Maria.

"Or a lioness," said Estelle.

"I long ago gave up trying to understand the feline persuasion, Colonel, Captain. Do not even attempt."

"Sound advice, Sir. Frau Elsie, you will entertain our guests this evening? I hate to leave this gay gathering but I have been posted south for a few days. As a matter of fact, I will be gone for longer, yes?" Knorr looked at von Treptow, who just smiled. "Much longer, likely."

Estelle turned to him, "Walter, I should like to travel to Arnhem. I no longer have family there but I do not want to overstay here as gracious as you have been. If there is a place for me there…"

"We will not keep you, although Yvette is another matter." Walter and Estelle smiled at each other. "I would suggest Reinhardt drive you – three hundred or so kilometers, but a good road – or one of Bruckmiller's military police people could escort you by train. You will not travel alone. Do you have papers? I have only now thought of that."

"I have my Belgian passport. And my old Dutch passport. We keep our maiden names, you know. Of course, I had no problem on the train over with the captain here."

"You could have him," von Seeckt brightened at the general's suggestion, "but I need him in Berlin with me. Erich, contact Major Bruckmiller this afternoon. He will be our best option."

"A German Military Police officer getting into Holland, wandering around?" Heinrich had quietly slipped Wolfgang to the portal. "Surely you are not serious. Come, Estelle, leave these pedestrian thinkers behind. We have business there. Constance and I shall take you. She somehow feels compelled to do some shopping in Amsterdam in the event."

Just then the hall beyond filled with shrieks, laughter and barks. Dogs and children burst in on the adults. Sophie looked at Wolfgang, a new face. "Up? Up?"

Wolfie complied, getting and giving a nose tweak in the bargain, much to the little one's delight. He looked around. "Ah, hah! You must be Yvette. Georg could speak of nothing else this morning. Actually, he could barely speak, but when he did…"

Yvette and her friend giggled. "I see. It is serious, then. I shall have Constance book the cathedral. It is settled. Madame Vandenberg, please be our guest. Day after tomorrow?" Not waiting for an answer, "Excellent. It is settled. Now let these oafs go off and play soldier so we Germans can get back to work."

"Heinrich?" Von Treptow was thoughtfully twirling his telegram, "Please have Reinhardt bring the motorcar around for me shortly. It seems I have a matter to resolve."

Estelle followed him from the room with her eyes.

* * *

Monday, January 21, 10:30 a.m.
Jermyn Street, London

Lord Elsmere took off his gloves at his tailor's storefront, glancing at his new Cartier 'Tank' wristwatch, the first to be delivered to England, of course. Looking down the street in the direction of Green Park, he saw van der Hoek coming his way. He moved on to intercept him. "What ho, old man! I have changed my mind. Let us turn about and walk over to the Carlton Club. An early luncheon is on me should you have the time?"

"Such a beneficence is always welcome on a bureaucrat's meager income, and thank you." As if his income had anything to do with his upkeep.

The two turned down Duke Street, chatting, and then onto King Street, thence to the Club. "Four, my lord."

"I count but three. Where?"

"Bowler hat. *Daily Telegraph.* No brolly."

"Yours or mine?" Reggie stopped to light a cigarette, scanning the street through the smoke. "Yours, I see."

"No, not ours. I thought he was yours. Most interesting."

Both intelligence officers had tails, sometimes as bodyguards, sometimes to see who was watching whom. Reggie had two today, Pieter one, but the fourth was unaffiliated, unknown, and thereby a mystery. And just possibly a threat. Both men made surreptitious signals of their own design as they entered the Club. By the time they finished luncheon, they expected to have the rundown on the interloper, if not the man himself. In such cases it was share and share alike.

Reggie made his way through a clot of Tories, leaders and backbenchers alike, many not at all pleased with his apprenticeship to the turncoat Churchill. One was unavoidable, Andrew Bonar Law, Churchill's chief tormenter. "Lord Elsmere, every day that passes in the company of that blackguard diminishes you. I shall secure you other stations in which to occupy yourself if that is your desire, but you will be irretrievably tarnished by your association."

"I could see how that might trouble a political person such as yourself, Sir, but I do not have to stand for election. I am quite comfortable in Lords. Good day, Sir."

Reggie reached back for Pieter's sleeve, pulling him forward into the dining room. The reception here was much friendlier, the bulk of the members being fellow carousers. The two were led to Elsmere's customary table at a window overlooking the courtyard, a bit safer from prying eyes and somewhat removed from curious ears. A private meeting in a highly public setting.

"So, Your Lordship, have you completed your sums? What will you demand of your co-conspirators?"

"Such unseemly haste, P, old man. Nothing disclosed until third course. Enjoy."

Before that course could be served, the headwaiter brought a telephone to the table, connecting it for his guest. "Yes, Lionel, what do you know? I see. Two of you, and you could not run him to ground? Why do I tolerate you?" He slammed the telephone set onto the table. Heads turned.

Pieter reached over and pried the voice piece from his friend's hands. "Allow me, Sir." He dialed four digits. "Yes, Mary, where? Excellent." He held down the cradle, released and dialed another number. "Vicenzo, what is the word? That far, you say? Did not come out the other side? That is curious. Yes, of course, please make the usual sweeps of the place. A moment, please. Reggie, could you loan us some men? Seems our mystery man doubled back toward Bloomsbury, the Mesopotamian rooms in the British Museum. May still be there."

"Yes, of course. Give me the damned telephone." He dialed, was answered, and growled at his man. Clicking off more quietly this time, "Vicenzo? Your street sweeper?"

Van der Hoek just grinned triumphantly.

"Insufferable, truly, truly insufferable. Why I tolerate you, I know not. Were it not for your late night talents…Speaking of which, where do we begin this evening?"

"Lady Houston's salon. Discussion, probably some crosseyed banana-beaked wraith warbling Serbian love songs or some such."

"Lady Houston? Are we old enough for that crowd? Tell me why, again?"

"You, your never-ending search for mature company. Me, aviation."

"Enough. Lunch continues."

"So it does. The clock has struck third course. Spill it."

Lord Elsmere took several bites, chewing deliberately and slowly. Pieter was smiling, waiting for the fly to spiral into the web.

"Our recompense for such vital information...," he paused for effect, and seeing none, continued, "such vital information, is but a trifle. Pence on the pound. A..."

"Poverty does not become you, old friend. Spill."

"Nothing significant, we wish to show our good faith, not being greedy at the outset."

Van der Hoek was drumming his fingers impatiently on the table. The waiter brought the next course, buying Reggie some time, then he continued, "A simple expression of intent. A commitment. An understanding."

"To what end?"

"When, if, Thor's hammer falls, it falls elsewhere."

"The French. I see. Have you discussed this with them? No?"

"Tell me, Pieter, does the definition of treason include betraying an ally, a partner? As opposed to one's own people or government?"

"Please do not wax philosophical with me, Your Lordship. This proposal itself taxes my feeble brain enough as it is. First, it is a nothing, a mere fleeting point in a longer conversation. Clever. Too clever by half. I secure a reply in the positive, you still have nothing. My friends cannot make that commitment, you know that. So why this approach? What am I missing?" Van der Hoek fancied himself the reigning master of non-Euclidean thought, the more intricate and devious the scheme, the better. But here, simply connecting the points into a straight line was baffling. "Second, the probability of their doing your bidding of their own volition and strategy is high, perhaps not a full fifty percent, I concede you. So why sell yourself short? That assumes you are offering what I requested."

"We are."

"Then explain yourself after the cheeses come."

An extended pause as a tray of cheeses, English on one side, Dutch on the other, was emptied. "There is a thread here, Pieter, if you would cease your analytics. We have on offer something of great value to your friends, yes? Something sufficiently valuable as to meet a specific, urgent request?" Pieter nodded. "We ask something of great value to us, hmmm?"

"Cannot argue with you thus far."

"So. Value great to each side. And the costs? In normal conditions, the Russian information would come with the high cost of betraying an ally, not to mention the risks of gathering same. Russia is no longer our ally. The Minister's opinion, and mine, is that the Bolshevik threat grows daily. '*The enemy of my enemy is my friend*', you recall? Not officially, not as policy, but as a certain, shall we say, unconventional stance? Why not? Nothing is risked, assuming impeccable spycraft. For that matter, how are we to exchange this information?"

"Alexandra volunteers her services."

Reggie leaned back in his chair, a smug grin forming, "All my compunctions evaporate from this moment on, then. Back to the topic of the moment. There is no cost to our Germans, either. They already are attempting to derail the coming Armageddon, so steering the target is not a suspicious effort. And we know from the outset they cannot betray us as they can guarantee nothing. However, you, as an honest broker, shall emphasize the risk we undertake to deliver a tangible good, whereas we ask only for an idea, an argument. Look to the cleat at the end of the hawser, Pieter. Our revelations are useful to them, certainly at a tactical level at a minimum. Our request, if acceded to, is an existential matter for Great Britain. The balance weighs in our favor, I should think."

The telephone rang. "Are you quite certain? Really? Most unusual. I retract much of the calumny and damnation I have visited upon you this past hour."

He looked at Pieter, "They caught him. An American, they think."

* * *

Monday, January 21, 1300 Hours
Hannover

Reinhardt deposited General von Treptow at the house of one Leopold Impelmann, an industrialist of not entirely sterling reputation. His tentacles were in many enterprises, his dealings marked at one level by collusion with government and his fellow oligopolists and at another level by brutal treatment of his workers. For all his newly begotten wealth, Herr Impelmann had been unable to gain invitation to the Swan Ball before its suspension, the oligarchs of the festivities relenting only upon the prospect of his substantial underwriting of the event. His wife Mona, a fragile, porcelain-skinned ethereal beauty, Claire's college friend of many years ago, now was her chief apologist in Hannover.

The butler announced Dietrich and Mona came to usher him into the vast foyer of the equally vast new mansion built on the city's outskirts. Even by the standards of an Elector, this was a house of much substance, if almost grotesquely detailed, no surface escaping some frippery or another.

"Dietrich, darling! So nice of you to pay me a visit!"

"My dear, rampaging Cossack stallions could not keep me from your side. I desperately regret I did not have the opportunity to dance with you last night before that unfortunate turn of events."

The two actually hardly knew each other. They had socialized intermittently for a few years, then nothing.

It was an awkward tableau, the two holding both hands extended, not knowing what else to say until Claire appeared at the top of the sweeping stair, in riding breeches and a soft-looking hunter green sweater with elbow and shoulder patches, her cigarette in a long holder. "Well, darling, I am relieved to see you made it safely home without engaging in another jousting match. Was he not the most glorious thing on the floor, Mona, dear? Certainly more entertaining than all that insipid waltzing about."

Mona was no match for Claire. "As you say, dear. I shall leave you two to reprise the night's events. General, some coffee or tea?"

"Nothing for me, Frau Impelmann, thank you. I am sated."

The two ensconced themselves in a comfortable library, the type populated with books provided by a dealer who bought by the kilo, sold by the gram. Claire curled up on a leather chair, her boots tucked beneath her. "Now, Dee, what are we to do now that we have found each other again?"

"Have we?"

"Have we what, dearest?"

"Found each other?"

"Dietrich, you are the devil! Can you deny what you feel? What you felt last night, when you drew me close to you on the ballroom floor? What you felt when you brought me to your friends, including that beautiful blonde. Your paramour, I take it?"

"You take what you want, Claire. You always have."

She sighed, "Oh, my. So we remain at the nadir of our love-hate relationship? When I saw you, so unexpectedly, I felt as if Providence was
granting me one more chance to redeem myself in your eyes, restore my life
to that shining path to bliss I dreamt of as a child. I am sorry, Dietrich, but
when a girl ties her very being to another, thinks she has entwined her soul
with his only to be left wondering about the man who got away, what is she
to do?"

"That was 1888, Claire. Thirty years ago. You left me, recall? I was not
princely enough for you, or was it your father? I remember it as if it were
last night which accounts for much, as I reflect. In the event, we were children. And then again, under Richard's nose...You always had difficulty
distinguishing lust from love, did you not?"

"And you did not? Please."

"Oh, no. It was always very clear to me."

This time, sadly, not saucily, "Dietrich, you reprobate!" Suddenly she
uncoiled and sprang at von Treptow who was leaning against the intricately
carved spine of a divan opposite. She buried her face in his chest, sobbing
and then sobbing some more. Dietrich held his hands away from her, bracing
her with his elbows, unsure how to respond.

"We only have one life, Dee. I have wasted mine without you. I have
fought and fought and fought yet again to withstand that thought all these
years. Last night I said to myself, *'No more. Not another day. Nevermore!'*
How long will I live? Will you survive this accursed war? And if we do live
on, what will our world be?"

"That is a whole host of questions, Claire. None can answer the first
two. I can say, though, that should the second answer be...unfortunate...
that the last, well, it will not matter to me then, of course, but...well, life as
we know it will be no more. That is not arrogance, but my duty and our little
world's destiny are entwined, bound, inextricably."

Claire whimpered, "Dietrich?"

"When this misguided conflict began, it was reported that the British
Foreign Minister or Secretary, rather, their Lord Grey said, *'The lamps are
going out all across Europe and will not be lit again in our lifetimes.'* Poetic,
yes? Prophetic as well. There are currents, *'tides in the affairs of men'* –
remember your schoolgirl Shakespeare – that are flowing against us and
ours. Even were all our military might to prevail, I still have not for a moment

the confidence we – you, me, Princesses, Counts – and our class will prevail. It will be a tide that draws all down to the depths, the lowest basins, the margins, '*bound in shallows and miseries*', so said the playwright."

He took both her hands in his. "I have a chance to make a difference. A small chance, a sliver. Claire, let me go. Once and for all. I may not pass this way again, as much as I might wish. Let me go, now, while my memory is fresh with you. But forget me, I implore you."

Claire looked up at her general, smiling weakly, eyes of azure and steel sparkling through her tears. "Darling, Mona said I could have this room all day. No one will disturb us."

* * *

Monday, January 21, 8:00 p.m.
Naval Intelligence Headquarters, London

The mystery man had been at Naval Intelligence for five hours without revealing anything. No documents on him, nothing in his clothing, not even labels. Only his shoes, an American brand. Nothing else. And he was very good at not talking, even as Reggie administered a couple of slaps across the face in frustration.

At that, the man finally opened his mouth, "Pretty good for such a Nancy Boy."

Lord Elsmere flung aside a chair as he bolted back across the room toward the table, restrained by Pieter and Lionel Grenville, Reggie's man.

"That's right. Hold him back. Which one of you'll be my friend now? What a load of crap! You guys been doing this long? Seems you would've learned something by now."

His interrogators just looked at each other.

"Well? You gonna ask me something smart, or let me go, or what? You got nuthin' on me. You can't keep me, even with your crummy laws. C'mon, you creeps. You, fancypants, gimme a cigarette."

Reggie, bemused, tossed him his case, followed by a matchbox.

"That's better. Can I get a cup of coffee, American style, please?" He shrugged aggressively, palms up. "Please?"

Pieter stuck his head out the door and made a request. Within the minute, an attractive young woman in khaki brought in some cups with sugar and cream. "Hey, baby, come sit with me – I'm gettin' tired of these prunefaces."

She hustled out as quickly as she could, giving all four something to look at on the way out.

The mystery man's diction and tone changed abruptly. "I have to give it to you, Gentlemen. Your girls always show better in uniform. Out, they strike me as rather horsey. And toothy, come to think of it. Deficient in the chest department, too. As I said, Gentlemen, better in khaki."

He paused for a puff, then continued, "Colonel Robert Wallace Emerson, United States Army Intelligence, posted to General Pershing. Black Jack wants me to get the real thing in British Intelligence, tired of the official bullshit. So, I let you dunces catch me. Is there better coffee on this island?"

Lord Elsmere and Grenville just laughed out loud. Van der Hoek suddenly recalled a pressing engagement and was trying to extricate himself when the American said, "Dutch Boy, how are you mixed up with these escapees from the asylum?"

Pieter just shook his head. *How had they let themselves get caught so easily?*

"I do not expect you to trust me. Have one of yours contact Mitch Cabot at our Embassy. He knows I am here. Just to confirm who I am."

Reggie waved Lionel out to do just that. "So, Colonel Emerson. Of the Ralph Waldo Emersons, I presume?"

"He and my grandfather were cousins, somewhat removed, but yes. Grandfather left New England, went South, to Terminus in 1843 – that's Atlanta, now – he was a railroad man, opening new routes for a succession of lines all over that part of the country. My father grew up in Nashville, that's Tennessee, but I spent most of my youth in and around Saint Louis."

"That would explain the accent, old man, hard to pin down. I trust you normally dress better than this?"

"I should certainly hope so. Learned the haberdashery business while in college – at university, to you – at Wash U. Summer jobs with a friend of Dad's – Harry Truman's shop in Independence – he's now an artillery captain over here. Maybe not up to your standards, Lord Elsmere, but pretty good tailoring back home."

"I see." Grenville walked in, nodding his head. "Well, then, Colonel, what might we do for you?"

Emerson finished his cigarette and stubbed it out on the metal table top. "Appreciate the cooperative spirit, Sir. Allies, after all? Except for the Hollandaise over there, trying to hide. I thought the wooden shoe boys were neutrals?"

"They are, most definitely. Did you not know who you were trailing?"

"I was after you, Sir. I confess I did not know your friend here. But I observed him, to be sure."

Pieter stepped away from the shadows. "Lord Elsmere and I share certain insights about persons of interest to both our Majesties' Governments. And we are friends of long standing, which does not preclude me from accepting his hospitality from time to time. Luncheon, for instance. Your Mister Cabot knows I am Intelligence Chief for our station here and I also have my operatives. It was mine, not his," pointing at Reggie, "who trailed you. I had planned to lord that over him for a goodly while until I just now realized we had been duped." He shrugged, slumping into a chair.

Reggie took over, "After me, you said? Why me?"

"Lady Jenny, of course."

Lionel blurted, "Are all these Americans such bloody riddlers?"

"Easy, old man. His roundabout path to Winston's door. You wish to meet the Minister, discreetly, I take it?"

"Of course."

"Trusting in his fondness for all things American?"

"Trusting in his fondness for several million American boys in uniform. With guns."

"On point, old man, on point. Any specifics?"

"Just one. Will your French friends fight?" Reggie jerked, spitting out his coffee. "Two, actually. Will yours? Black Jack finds French generaldom to be obtuse, obstreperous, obstinate and obstructive. Everything but obstetric. Now, as the signs of a new German offensive mount daily, he wants to make sure we aren't just being used as cannon fodder. That the French will fight 'til the last American, that sort of thing. Obviously, the Froggies won't say so, not to our faces. So, we want the straight scoop. The real news, that is."

"And why us?"

"No bullshit."

"Pardon?"

"No bullshit. Cut the crapola. The real story behind the striped pants types. Isn't your boss noted for his outspokenness?"

"I am daily reminded of that reputation. Several cringeworthy opportunities weekly."

"That's why we like him. That, and a good-looking American mom. Seriously, Sir, that is my sole mission here, to open a backchannel to the real truth. For instance, your Lloyd George fellow is holding back his reserve divisions here in England. Why? Are the butlers and nannies planning a revolt? I don't see the shopkeepers manning barricades of crumpets and marmalade. Can you tell me? After all, two hundred thousand men could make the difference between a fight and a swim, could they not?"

"Pieter, I was hoping it would take our Yankee friends a few years to match our level of underhanded sophistication. Alas, seems they are our equals already. As to the reserves, I shall not answer a question that does not exist, Colonel. Officially, that is. Cocktails tomorrow are at half past five, dusk. Here is the address," scribbling *45 Berkeley Square*. "Come to the service entrance, of course – do not bother to change, old boy. We shall accept you as you are. But beyond that is another matter."

"Actually, Sir, I had been doing some window shopping when you arrived. Perhaps a recommendation?"

"Of course. Pieter, there is hope for him yet. Lionel, please find him a suitable exit from the premises."

* * *

Monday, January 21, 2130 Hours
Hannover

Frau Rosenblum prepared a late dinner for General von Treptow, sitting in the kitchen with the help and the dogs. "Frau Elsie, leave this household, come away with me. I should wither away without your cooking!" He stuffed more schnitzel away, smiling.

"For you, yes, of course, General. But leave here for Berlin? Not on my life. Nought but libertines and revolutionists there. And politicians. Ugh!"

She was just warming up. "And they expect us provincial folk to pay the taxes to support their debauchery. Makes one wish for those days before this so-called empire, when Hannover was independent and free, not just a Prussian subject. You are influential, a man of stature. You can change things, can you not?"

"Sadly, Frau, probably not. I am a mere soldier, one of millions. I ask you, is this opinion of yours widely held? If I spoke to people on the street, high and low, do they share it?"

"Yes, I do think so. Maybe not such trash as your Herr Impelmann" – his afternoon destination obviously was not confidential in the household – "greedy for more war to make more money. But most common folk, yes. To be sure, we all like the idea of a Greater Germany, it's just the feeling we're second class to the Prussians."

"I shall take that under advisement. I must pack now. May I take some with me?"

She patted her meatcleaver against her plump palm. "If you don't..."

In his room, he was putting away his things, clad in a pair of field trousers and a sweater. He answered the knock at the door, "Come?"

Estelle peeked into the room. "May I? Do you need some help, General?"

"No, no help wanted, er, needed. But please do come in. Make yourself comfortable here," moving a case and its contents from a chair to the bed, a less than subtle message.

"Thank you. You will be gone a long time?"

"Yes, that is a good guess. Perhaps some months."

"You will come back here, though?"

"No promises, as much as I might like. No, I truly have no idea when, or if."

"If? That sounds so, so frightening."

"It is frightening, my dear. As a soldier, I put myself willingly in harm's way. That is something I understand and accept. Now there are so many unknowns. So many people out there seeking to destroy all we, you hold dear. And not just the misguided German soldiers of Louvain. I fear the rogue anarchist's gunshot far more than the massed artillery of the British or French. Worse, being forced to live in a Bolshevik regime of terror and subjugation. That is what we face, my dear."

"Is it truly so bad? I had not heard of such, but then I have been cloistered these past few years."

"It is only now fermenting, bubbling to the surface. Began in Russia, but no shortage of true believers in Germany and elsewhere. The idea of these brilliant idiots taking power? Truly frightening when intellect and depravity combine. But you will return to Holland? To Arnhem?"

"I am not certain. I do have some friends there, but they all have husbands and I now have a...," she shrugged, "... a history. It seems harder with each passing day to leave our security here, but I, we, must make our own way. I do not know. Do not concern yourself with me, we are survivors." She brightened, mischievously. "But you, you must tell me of this mysterious woman. Hold nothing back. That is an order!"

He gave her an unexpectedly pained look. She started to speak but he stopped her with a hand, sighing, "Very well, you would have it out of me eventually. But please, this shall remain between you and me? Swear?"

"I swear to the man who saved my children for me."

He sat at the edge of the bed, folding his arms. Estelle thought him not at his characteristic ease. "Claire, once Princess of Baden, then Duchess of Anhalt. She is three years younger. She and her brother Max, my friend, were sent off to boarding school in Berlin as children, the same school I attended. I first saw her when we, Father and I, met them at Zoo station. If there is such a thing as love at first sight, then we, she and I, are its proof. From that day forward we were inseparable. She was a tomboy, keeping up with us rowdies, even after she became a young woman. Accomplished horsewoman and hunter and always effortlessly fashionable. You would agree she is beautiful?"

"Reluctantly, yes."

"Of course. She differs today only in a...not a degree, just a different, mature beauty. The same underlying beauty. And the same, not wickedness, not meanness, just a savage...I do not know. I have never understood it, where it comes from.

"With time we matured and with physical maturity came intimacy, clandestinely, of course. We enjoyed each other's company and bodies until I was twenty-one or so, a newly commissioned lieutenant of horse, full of myself – I realize that may be quite difficult for you to believe," he continued through Estelle's laughter, "and I felt empowered to ask her father to allow her to marry me. Understand, we, my family, that is, have for centuries been considered high nobility – the Margrave of Brandenburg was second only to the Elector or the King of Prussia – but apparently not high enough for her father and her uncle, the Grand Duke, who would not countenance what they perceived as a morganatic union. And unbeknownst to me, the duke and my grandfather had had a falling out over a political issue, an upset with the Kaiser and Prussian generaldom as a whole, my father thereby drawn into the dispute, whatever it was, so long ago now. So I was not in high favor and my proposal was turned down.

"We did not take it well. I accepted a posting as far away as I could go, Tanganyika, for two years. Her father spirited her away back to Karlsruhe but made the mistake of allowing her to return to Berlin to finish university. She expressed her rebellion against her father and, as I realized over time, against me, by eloping with my best friend Richard, Crown Prince, later Duke of Anhalt. You see, she expected me to gallop in on a white charger swinging a sword, rescuing her. I did not and wonder what my life, our lives would have been had I done so. But that simply was not done in those days, my odds of success would have been slim, indeed.

"So, through the years. I married a lovely woman, Louisa, we had one son, Gregor. When Gregor was ten, Louisa caught a fever and died. I had been a typical Army officer, more often elsewhere than home. After her death, my son and I had a difficult relationship. He blamed me for not saving his mother – I was in Windhoek at the time – and as he grew into his teens, we became thoroughly estranged. The winds of social change blowing from the East did not help, of course, and he renounced me, my title, his fortune – all. Took Louisa's family name – Erhardt – and when the war came, enlisted."

He glanced down, then back at Estelle. "He was one of the young men killed in 1914. I found out only because he had kept a medallion with his mother's picture and our family name. So."

Estelle was silent, unable to think of a way to express her feelings.

Dietrich continued, now a little less uncomfortably, "Perhaps that will explain Maria's revelations. But, to Claire, what even Maria does not know. I had kept up with them, of course, we all spent time in Berlin, even if I was there less frequently. Over the years, Claire had been, well, inappropriately friendly for a married woman, shall we say? I managed to deflect her attentions, gently most times, somewhat more roughly others. Our relationship developed into one of alternating affection and conflict, depending on her moods and our most recent history."

He stammered, "I…I should not burden you…"

Estelle reached out for his hand. "I shared my worst, you were kind enough to listen. Please go on."

"Yes, then. Finally, I succumbed to her advances. It was late 1913, I remember it well. My son was gone, I was posted in Berlin and, well, I was lonely, depressed. She came to visit at my townhouse in the city one day, drove herself, of course – Richard was traveling, hunting in the Camargue, as I recall. It was very, very cold that day, and she was immersed in a beautiful fur coat all the way to the floor. I welcomed her into my study, my housekeeper delivered some tea and left us alone. I offered to remove her coat, and as I took it from her shoulders, well, save for her tall boots and her diamonds…you can understand.

"We engaged in frequent and vigorous couplings over a period of nearly a year interrupted, providentially it seems now, by the war. Never found out, but my duty called me away from her. My friend Richard was called up from reserve under my command, and we campaigned together from Verdun through Flanders. We were planning a new offensive against the British after the Somme action, when her brother offered me my current duties.

"I was reluctant, as I knew little of the new post. But also since the operation we were planning required the brigade commander – first me, then Richard as my successor – to take extraordinary risks close to the front lines, coordinating our aggressive tactics. Even though Max commanded me, I still had a choice but accepted. My first posting was in the Balkans, an intrigue of espionage. While I was away in the south, Richard led the operation. It succeeded in its modest objectives but then British artillery counterattacked, obliterating our forward command post. Richard's remains were identified by his tags, an amulet with her picture, and…" Here he stopped, breathing hard, holding himself, rocking back and forth on the bed. Estelle stood and hugged him around the shoulders. "It was a cigarette tin."

"What was that?"

"A cigarette tin. A cigarette tin, something we found on the street at play. Just someone's discard, but to us it was a treasure. We were nine or ten, and the smell of forbidden tobacco was an excitement. We kept things in it over the years, trading possession from time to time.

"I had lost track of it, forgotten about it, but not Richard. When it was found it had a tattered daguerreotype of us in highschool, silly expressions on our faces. On the back we had inscribed our names and ages and the motto '*Siempre Amici*'. Now do you see?"

Estelle said softly, "Yes, I see now your loss, your sadness."

"No!" Dietrich jerked away from her. "No, you do not see!" He alarmed Estelle with his vehemence. "What did I tell you last night?" He was fairly screaming.

"I...I...was it the story from the Bible? What was that again?"

"Yes. David and Bathsheba. And Uriah."

"Dietrich, General, Sir, I am flustered. I do not recall."

"From Second Samuel, '*Set ye Uriah in the forefront of the hottest battle that he may be smitten and die.*' King David coveted Uriah's wife Bathsheba. He sent Uriah into battle in his stead at great risk, to a certain death, in fact. Then married his widow."

"I still do not see. I...."

"No? I am David, Claire is Bathsheba, and poor Richard is, was, Uriah. Now do you see? The only difference is Bathsheba – Claire – was the instigator, the mastermind behind the scheme, but I acquiesced. Sent my best friend to his death. For her. I was away when his memorial was held. I wrote his parents, they were grateful. That was November, 1916. I had not seen her since this damned war began, not until last night." He looked deeply into her eyes, "Now do you see clearly?"

It was Estelle's turn to cry.

* * *

Tuesday, January 22, 1600 Hours
Berlin, Lerhter Station

The general and the captain took the morning train to Berlin, leaving Estelle and hers in the care of the Knorr household. At Lehrter Station, Chief Inspector Helmut Hartwig of the Berlin Metropolitan Police greeted them with several uniformed officers in tow.

"General von Treptow?" Hartwig stiffened, clicking his heels.

"Yes? And you would be?"

"Chief Inspector Hartwig of the Police. Our mutual friend, Major Bruckmiller, cabled me as you were leaving Hannover this morning. He had some concerns as to your safety and, in the event, we have certain developments to report to you."

"My, our safety? In Berlin?"

As they walked down the platform, the policemen took the baggage carts away from the porters. "Yes, Sir. The rabble is stirring. We break up a half dozen demonstrations a day, not counting those we let run on hoping for bloodshed. That is, of course, between the Reds and the merely Pinks. Your name in particular has been reported by our informants to be one of great interest to several factions. I, we, assume because of your involvement with the Russians."

"Hmmmm. I see. Events seem to be accelerating, then. Most certainly on instructions from Russia as a prelude to our renewed negotiations. How many, at the peak?"

"Sir?"

"How many? The size of the mobs?"

"Now up to several thousand, depending on the venue. We expect ten to twenty thousand or more the 28th at and around Brandenburg Gate. A demonstration in support of the Spartacists, those imprisoned."

"The Spartacists? I see. Are they on speaking terms with the Socialists?"

"Not on your life, Sir." Hartwig grinned broadly, "That's the fun of it, Sir. Our agents and informants in both camps are offering encouragement."

"If Bruckmiller learned his trade from you, I am quite certain you are."

"He is on his way, Sir. You may compare us in person."

"Excellent. We have missed his sunny outlook, have we not, Captain?"

"He has accused me falsely, Sir."

"Bullfeathers! Believe nothing he says, Inspector, they are peas in the pod."

Hartwig squinted at von Seeckt and said, "Twins, they are."

At the station gate, Reittimann and a retinue of servants greeted the general. "Sir, you look better, healthier than I hoped. Was it the stay in Hannover?"

"That hiatus nearly spelled the end of me, and my associate, here. Reittimann, Captain Erich von Seeckt, my aide and saviour. Inspector, you will free us to seek our dinner and beds?"

"No Sir, not unaccompanied. Two cars will escort you, five armed men at your gates all night. Escort into the city tomorrow morning. Orders, Sir."

"Orders? Whose orders?"

"Prince Max von Baden, Sir. He awaits you tomorrow at the Foreign Office."

"I see. When does Bruckmiller arrive?"

"0930 hours here at Lehrter, Sir. He is stopping off at Stendal today to visit his mother, short train ride from there."

"The creature has a mother? Imagine that. Very well, you and he plan on meeting us at the Foreign Office posthaste. As I think on it, we may have much to discuss. Thank you for your assistance. Now, Reittimann, let us get this convoy on the road."

They drove through the streets of Berlin, cluttered and empty at the same time. Cluttered with clots of dark-suited, haggard men, at the same time empty of the usual smart crowd in their Mercedes and Horches. "Detour by way of Unter den Linden, if you would, please, Reittimann." He turned in his seat and signaled the trailing police cars. As they passed through the Brandenberg Gate, he noted the signs and banners, some still hanging, most in the gutter. *With the garbage. Where have the dustmen been?* Listless groups of idle or indolent people wandering, it seemed, purposely. *Or lack of purpose.* Past the Adlon, all the way to the Crown Prince's Palace and the Alte Kommandantur, the same. "Reittimann, let us go home."

* * *

Tuesday, January 22, 5:30 p.m.
45 Berkeley Square, London

Just as dusk was drawing day's end, a figure in tweeds stepped into a service alley in Berkeley Square. Staying close to the still-shadowed wall, it stopped, knocked on a door and was admitted.

Shortly thereafter a Rolls-Royce stopped in front of the house. Churchill and Lord Elsmere got out, Winston arguing, "I still do not understand your enthusiasm in this American agent business. Why in the world should we take another, an unknown, into our confidences? I know, I know, he is thinking along the same lines as we, but would it not be more prudent to let him think in parallel, in a less conjoined geometry?"

"I confess, Minister, I am not fully convinced myself. Let us not yield to his advances, but neither should we rebuff him."

"Fine, fine, fine, but what is our ultimate objective in entertaining this notion? And what notion is afoot here, after all? The Americans are, and most certainly will be, on the French side of the front. We, you and I, have no ability to change that state of affairs. Their presence with the French greatly complicates our little plot, does it not?"

"Worse, Sir. It at once increases both the proximity of the coming offensive and its geographic tendency. Sooner, rather than later, and directed away from the Yankees. All wrong, all wrong."

"Drat!"

"Minister, upon reflection that is the justification for more, rather than less, generosity. Do you not see the paradox in our dilemma? We have no influence in our own troop dispositions. General Pershing, contrarily, has considerable influence and this man, apparently genuine, is his conduit."

"Whatever we wish Black Jack to hear…," Churchill chewed his stub, then tossed it to the curb. "Yes, but let us say it inside – it grows rawer by the moment out here."

The two were greeted by Lord Elsmere's butler, shedding overcoats, scarves, hats, and canes. As a chambermaid tottered away with the load, Gresham, Reggie's man, escorted them to the library to greet their visitor. "M'Lord, will he be coming here often, dressed as he is? Not up to our standards, I fear."

"Often, perhaps, but we shall let Jeremy Lewellyn have a look at him tomorrow. He claims more discernment than his garb would evidence."

Gresham pushed open the massive oak doors to the library. At the opposite end past the thirty foot Hamadan rug stood Colonel Emerson, an open book in each hand. "Hello, Lord Elsmere. I was just comparing two of your Homer translations. I confess I do not care for either, your William Morris or our William Cullen Bryant, the mainstay of our public schools. Morris sounds more like a dime novel, Bryant like the Chamber of Commerce. Much prefer the original. 'Οινοψ ποντοξ,' all that. Mister Churchill, Sir?"

"Colonel Emerson, I presume? Reggie here has shared your history. '*Arma virumque canit*', all that. And your mission."

Emerson advanced across the floor to give Churchill a vigorous hand-shake, American style. "Been a fan of yours, an admirer, Sir, from your Boer dispatches onward. All your writings, though as advice, leave off the fiction. You make the real thing come alive, the imaginary less so."

Churchill looked at Reggie, laughing heartily, "Complimented and insulted in the same sentence under one draught of breath. Splendid! You are correct on the fiction, old man. Reggie, have I seen my Hine yet?"

Gresham materialized at his side, silver tray, decanter and snifters at the ready.

The three settled into the leather club chairs fronting the fireplace, backs to the windows overlooking the square. "How many boys do you have out there, Lord Elsmere?"

"Three, Colonel, and one inside. Please do call me Reggie, as do my most insolent friends. And you, Colonel?"

"None, Sir. Just little old me. Cabot is in on it, no one else. I am officially on personal leave."

Turning to Winston, "Sir, I must confess we have a common thread in our lives. Mister Jerome was an investor, along with Mister Vanderbilt, in my grandfather's railroads in the South after our Civil War. He and Grandpa were friendly and your grandfather invited mine to visit in New York several times. Only once was he able to take the whole family with him, my father and his brother and sisters. Dad reminded me of the time, right after New Year's, 1874. He was sixteen, your mother twenty and engaged to your father. He said when he was introduced, he was struck mute, so in awe of your mother's beauty, he was. When I came over here he made me promise I would pay you, and her, his compliments should I improbably find myself an audience."

"Reggie, why is it you say those awful things about this fine fellow? Do please call me Winston as it appears we are related by Mammon, if not blood."

Reggie just shook his head.

"Now, Colonel, what exactly do you want of us? I am briefed on your backchannel notion but have yet to ascertain how to comply with your request whilst evading the gallows. Perhaps you can skip to the end of this novella and reveal what is to transpire?"

"If I follow you, Winston, Sir, just this. We, that is, General Pershing and his staff, hold mounting doubts as to the ability and the will of our new

Associates to fight. Clearly, you, Sir, are of the opinion not to go into the field again without our full strength in place. Sound military thinking, but consider how that plays at Staff and how it will play if our newspapermen wake up to that scoop. Not to be disrespectful, Sir, but you have likened the front, more particularly your Marshal Haig's methods, to a meatgrinder. We just want to make sure we're not the main ingredient in the sausage."

"You are well informed, it seems to me, Colonel. You have no need to worry about the British fighting spirit, old man…"

Emerson interrupted sharply, "Spirit is one thing, Sir, but unless Lloyd George commits your reserves, you might as well be conjuring up the Holy Ghost to hold your positions if the Germans attack as logic dictates they will."

"Hmmph. Gloves off so soon? Cigar? That is a good man," reaching across to light the American's smoke. "Reggie, I have no issue with good conversation over brandy and cigars, opinions only. Concur?"

"I can easily think of any number of other diversions at the moment."

"He can be such a sourpuss, do you think, Colonel? Very well. I, personally, and this is not His Majesty's Government speaking, am desperately concerned about the French, their will to fight. Not their offensive spirit, I think they sacked that altogether last summer. My concern is a wholesale failure of their defensive lines were the Germans to come full force."

"Leaving us to hold the line?" Emerson tapped an ash, then continued, "We understand that much, and are confident our combined resources could stop the Germans. But not supremely confident. Then what? Three more years of trench war? Don't forget who invented that style two score and ten ago, we did. Not interested, Sirs. We want a quick conclusion – this is your war after all, we're just bailing your sorry asses out."

"We thought we would get a quick war ourselves. Everyone did. '*Home by Christmas*,' all that. Several million young men ago." Lord Elsmere was swirling his brandy, looking into the fire. "We cannot prevail without you, we know that now. The Anglo-Saxon bond across the Atlantic, all that yammering means nought unless we bring this war to a successful conclusion."

"Win it, you mean."

"That is not what I said, Colonel. You tell us. How would you have your men home by your Yankee Doodle Day in July? Hmmm?" Reggie was taking a more aggressive tone, needing more from their guest.

"Cease fire. Tomorrow at 0800 hours. Call it a day, everyone goes home, the diplomats go off and masturbate together someplace."

Churchill cackled, "Mother warned me about her countrymen. Direct and often quite crude. Very well, then, Colonel. Who makes that decision?"

"If we're cracking the buggywhips, Sir, Pershing and Ludendorff meet in a pasture somewhere, Black Jack regales ol' Erich with tales of chasing Pancho Villa, they swap lies, shake hands, salute, end of story."

"Heresy!" Reggie cried out through his laughter. "No Haig, no Foch, Clemenceau, Lloyd George? Brilliant heresy!"

Colonel Emerson was now the baffled one. "I actually was serious, Sirs. Ludendorff is clearly their key man, and with time you will see General Pershing is ours, all of ours."

"Trust us, we see that!" Churchill was now agitated, strolling back and forth across the room. "Clearly, we see that! Reggie?"

Elsmere nodded, "Colonel, how many of your divisions are under French command?"

"None. Five of the ten in theater are requested, not amalgamated. No agreements yet as to those still in transit."

Churchill jumped in eagerly, "The other five plus? Why could they not be brought north where they could threaten Ostend, Zeebrugge, Antwerp? The Huns would not favor having their naval bases threatened."

Reggie tried to explain, "Sorry, Colonel, where naval matters are concerned...."

"That's all right, Sir. Tactically sound. What's your strategy?"

"Here, you have to swear secrecy on my dear mother's beauty, Colonel. Swear?"

"Swear I get to deliver my father's admiration in person?"

"Done."

"So sworn, Winston, Sir."

"Strengthen our left beyond attack. Save ours, and yours, in the coming holocaust. Perhaps even prevent it. Our sources – those being Reggie's and my private sources – indicate the Germans will attack late March at the juncture of the British and French Armies. Which way do they turn, once they have punched through?"

"As they undoubtedly will, with a new million from Russia," Reggie seconded his boss.

"I see." Emerson was trying not to betray his feverish mental calculations. "But why not reinforce the French? Paris is the target, after all, isn't
it?"

"No." Lord Elsmere sat down on the table immediately next to the
American. "No, and here is why. The Germans' only hope, despite their
strength, is to divide their opponents, militarily and in the public, civil
arena. If they wheel against us, we are lost. Lloyd George and Haig are
at such loggerheads the reserve divisions could not reach France in time.
The Huns know that. They also know the French will stand by and watch,
so long as their positions are not threatened. And you Yanks are sidelined
in that case."

"And once you Brits are out of play, then south, at their leisure. Not the
most promising scenario."

Reggie stared at him, "Schlieffen reprised, only successfully this
time."

"Aren't you being unduly pessimistic? You still have nearly a million
in the field, a boatload full of guns, and you have tanks, they do not."

"Not so much pessimistic as pragmatic, Sir." Winston lit a new cigar.
"Yes, we could prevail. Or, we might not. With yours we would be assured
of prevailing."

Reggie reinforced the Minister's argument, "Or preventing."

"So, then, the Germans know better than go north, so they go south. You
are unable – or is it unwilling? – to come to their aid, and France is in deep
shit. And the rest of my doughboys, too. We lose either way. So why divide
our forces, the classic risk?"

"Blackjack." Reggie bored in, "The game, not the general. Our way,
you are sitting on twenty. The French option, you are on sixteen. What does
the German dealer hold? Where would you rather be?"

"Not exposing my remaining boys to a slaughter, that's for sure."

"You are missing the point, old man," Churchill's face flared a deep
pink. "Unless you deploy with us, they fall upon us like leopards. If you
are deployed both sides, they are as tomcats. And if you come our way,
I can guarantee, that is, to the extent of my influence, that our reserves
will come to France. Your two hundred, or four hundred, and ours,
together? A daunting prospect, even for such an impetuous fool as
Ludendorff."

"Yes, Winston, but back to the French, Sir. Why are you so sure they will not rally? It is their country, after all."

"I have never contended they would not defend, but there is serious rot in the ranks, and at home. Virtually the entire Army refused to fight last summer. General Pètain managed to quell the mutiny, even mounted their little push this autumn past. Certainly they would defend, but even if fortune favored them, I do not see them pushing forward to counterattack, to crush *les Boches*. So, your three more years of trench war ensue."

Seeing Emerson's frown, Reggie spoke next, "Did your French staff counterparts not mention the mutinies, the dissatisfaction, the like? The government and army did a masterful job of suppressing that news, in the public realm, at least. Privately, the entire nation is depressingly aware, and restive. Did they mention four of their best cavalry divisions being held back near Paris against civilian unrest?"

"They have not been quite so forthcoming as you two. Mention of difficulties, morale issues, and so forth, but Pètain assures us now all is hunky-dory. An interesting variable in our equation. Much will depend on our actual deployments, our designated areas. Hmmm." He paused for a few moments. "There is one problem of gigantic importance you are forgetting." Emerson rose and stretched, then leaned back against the edge of the fireplace. "If we commit to your side of the front, your General Haig's demands for a renewed offensive would become the irresistible force in your politics. Would your Prime Minister still be the unmoveable object? And, the answer being… no, how do we <u>not</u> get dragged into it, having linked arms, if you will? The meatgrinder, you see?"

"Reg, he is too good. Yes, my new friend, that does present a difficulty. One neither His Lordship here nor I can overcome in our present straitened circumstances. I do have David's ear, but that may not prevail. You have the answer, your Black Jack Pershing."

"So, how do I pose your suggestion?"

"Have your staff examine the correlation of forces." Reggie was at his most bloodlessly analytical. "Based on your…sources, General Pershing proposes to shift some of your independent divisions to the coast. For training, say. Not proposed, but certainly intended, is to move more new units likewise, as they are ready. '*A million boys in uniform, with guns*', I believe was your phrase. That would be agreeable."

"And should the French object and withhold their toys, we have more than enough artillery and aircraft to go around," said Churchill, trying to seal the deal.

"Haig would agree to an independent American command, with veto power?"

"Not willingly or happily."

"Would he? That is paramount in your scheme."

Churchill and Lord Elsmere looked at each other a bit forlornly. "We can only do so much, Colonel. Let us give it a whirl." Churchill suddenly blurted, "Please excuse me, I must pay a visit to the loo," and dashed out.

"I confess he is much as I expected," said the American.

"And more, trust me, much more." The two, aristocrat and modern Yankee, chatted amiably for a few minutes. In the meantime, Churchill made a quick telephone call, having consulted his pocketwatch. "Yes, it is very important. Only a few minutes. It is on the way there. It would make me very happy. You, too, I assure you." He returned to the library. Gresham was refreshing the glasses and serving some cheeses to tide the negotiators over.

Churchill resumed, "Would General Pershing accept an offer on that basis? On the assumption, possibly remote, that Haig would do likewise? And would he accept our, Lloyd George's, that is, assurances as to committing our reserves?"

"Quite possibly, Sirs. General Pershing would be the lightning rod between the two, but he might relish that role as I reflect on his character." Emerson laughed genially, "Digging deeper, he is the answer to your Prime Minister's problems, is he not?"

Churchill rubbed his chin at the thought, but Reggie beat him to the punch, "Yes, of course. Brilliant!"

The doorbell rang without, followed by a clamor in the entry. A woman's voice could be heard nearing the study. The doors swung open and in swept Lady Randolph Churchill, dressed for the theater, still striking at sixty-four. "Well, Winnie, darling, now have I made you happy, dear? And why am I here? Hello, Reggie, precious. And who is this exceedingly handsome tradesman?"

"Mother, he is the purpose of your visit. Colonel Robert Wallace Emerson, United States Army. He has something to tell you." Churchill played it up,

"Well, get on with it, man! You brought a message a thousand miles, did you not? Cats have your tongue?"

Emerson stammered, then stopped.

"So it is congenital, is it? Like father, like son? Mother, this…"

Emerson clasped Churchill's shoulder. "I can do it, pal. Lady Churchill, my late grandfather was a friend of your father's," launching into a brief rendition of the story. "So, there you have it. I would be pleased to be able to report my success to my father back home."

"I am touched, truly," said the former Jenny Jerome. "I confess I do not recall the incident, my bridal days were so frenzied. Tell me," she teased, "is your father as tall and handsome as you? And is he still married?" She winked at her son, who shrunk away, seeking the shadows. "You are so kind. Please give him this for me." She embraced him, a generous kiss on each cheek. "Let him know I will always be an American amongst my fellow Americans. Now, I must go. Thank you, Winnie, this was most entertaining but I cannot be late for the seating, as I am not offered much leeway these days. Young man, are you available next Tuesday, formally attired, that is?"

She swept out as she had swept in, a tumult all the way to the door.

"I have created a new monster, Reg, old boy."

* * *

Wednesday, January 23, 0700 Hours
Schloss Treptow, Brandenburg

Captain von Seeckt awoke at his usual 0500, this time with a start. Sitting bolt upright in his bed, he looked around to see where he was. His trousers draped over a chair where he had left them were his only landmark, bringing him back. He then remembered he was in von Treptow's house, not a house but a castle of sorts. Bigger by far than Knorr's or Barton's extravagant country place, bigger than the biggest Junker places he had seen in the East.

Several hundred hectares, he estimated, from yesterday's drive through the winding faux countryside replete with lakes and ducks and geese and bridges, then the schloss itself, an accretion over the centuries from a rough stone keep to a slate-roofed chateau, its limestone façade shining in the late day sun. A series of outbuildings stretched off to the south and east in several styles, all in a rustic vernacular, more Millet than Brueghel, recalling his brief encounters with art history. The drive rose first imperceptibly, then more sharply as von Seeckt recognized the primary prerequisite of the keep, a medieval fortress: the heights, one of the chain of low hills stretching across the southern verges of the city.

The landscape architect had masked the elevation with grading and copses and hedging until it was no longer possible to hide its prominence, then the dramatic climb to the entry. Looking back past the drive, he could see the spires and roofs of Berlin, imagining the Friedrichstrasse slashing through the city. It was a most impressive setting.

As they approached the portico the staff was waiting, waving. The general had explained that upon their father's death, the three sons had taken the unusual step of creating a shared company, a 'GmBH' in form, to own and operate the home estate and its outlying properties as well as the family's investments, including a majority interest in the Albatross aircraft factory in nearby Johannistal, all managed from an office in the city. "A most modern adaptation, do you not think so?" he had asked. His uncle, also a general, died a bachelor, simplifying matters. Both of his brothers were physicians, one a researcher at the University, the other a missionary, now somewhere in Mesopotamia or Palestine, maybe Turkey, he was not quite sure, but certainly not waiting to be ensnared in Allenby's advance.

The arrangement allowed the three brothers to pursue their passions or their duty, free of sibling conflict and the taxman, to boot. There was enough to go around, von Treptow had assured the captain. "*For now,*" was the caveat. Three families shared the sixty rooms, the physician brothers, wives and children and the solitary general. And forty or so servants, another fifty farmworkers, fewer than in the past, now with the young men called to soldier and the girls as nurses. There was still room for more.

Dressed for a day in officialdom, von Seeckt made his way downstairs to the smallest of the three dining salons. Presently the general arrived, greeting him with a slap on the back. "Nothing like roughing it, eh?"

"No, Sir. I mean, yes, Sir!"

"Augusta, what have you here for us?"

"A solid breakfast, Your Grace. We worry about you. All over the world, it seems, and no one taking care of you. Well, you are back for a bit so we will do our part."

When she left them to their sausage and potatoes and coffee, Erich asked, "Sir, I thought one of your brothers was older, yet you have the title. May I ask why?"

"Rudolph relinquished the title in my favor. He is totally dedicated to his research and profession and rightly saw no advantage in it. In my case, it has proved indispensable, so I welcomed it. When I go, however..." He had a thought, "well, it will not be my worry, will it?"

"What is his speciality? And the other brother?"

"Both are fascinated by infection. Rudy began with Pasteur, then studied with Koch. They are quite the pair, Rudy in the lab, Willy in the field. Back in more congenial times, any holiday gathering was trying for their wives – all they could talk about was their science. Willy would use the occasion to return from some God-forsaken morass bringing all sort of horrors for Rudy to obsess about. A miracle we all have not been wiped out as a people by some Abyssinian microbe. The two together are working on the influenza now plaguing the Balkans, Turkey, the Levant, elsewhere. Very, very virulent." He looked off into the expanse of the entry hall. "Most unfortunate they subscribe to Hippocrates."

"Sir?"

"What I mean, is, well, it is a most macabre thought, but searching for a cure or a prophylactic entails propagating the germ itself. As doctors, they have sworn to do no harm to any patient. As German scientists, however, that same germ could be more damaging to our enemies than all our gas or high explosive."

Sensing his young aide's alarm, "Forget my comments, please. But that variety of warfare has its antecedents, does it not, from catapulting plague-ridden corpses over castle walls to distributing blankets infested with smallpox to the American natives. Earlier, even, Apollo sending a plague upon the Achaeans at Troy or the God of the Israelites upon the Egyptians. Not honorable antecedents save the last, but what can we say for our phosgene and chlorine and mustard? You have been vaccinated against smallpox? Pray tell me yes."

"Yes, Sir. As a child. Have the burst bubble to show for it."

"Excellent. Indispensable, in fact, for where we may be going. No, Captain, I do not know. Not next month, not next week, not tomorrow."

The police lieutenant was waiting in the cavernous entry hall, gripping the hot coffee Augusta had brought him. "Good morning, Sir. All quiet here."
    "Off we go, then."

* * *

Wednesday, January 23, 0845 Hours
Foreign Office, Berlin

They arrived without incident at the grey pile on Wilhelmstrasse. Entering through the motor court, they hurried away from the cold toward a suite of offices amid a nondescript wing of the building's main floor. The door said *'Commercial Relations/North America'*, but housed Prince Max's operations.

    A fresh-faced receptionist piped up, "Good morning, Sirs!" With her long braids wrapped around her head and a fully occupied blouse, she reminded von Seeckt of the Hofbrau and other hangouts of his recent youth. Naturally he was interested, making several approbative appraisals as she escorted them through a warren of small offices.

    Finally into Prince Max's office, a cubbyhole for a princely type. Three meters square and as drab as a bureaucrat, Erich figured it was some sort of ruse, a stage set to conceal its occupant's true nature. Sure enough, when Max put down the telephone and rose to greet them, he was dressed austerely, no decorations.

    "I can tell by the look on your face, Lieutenant, or is it Captain now? What has befallen him to be shunted off to such quarters? It is functional, and draws little attention." With that, he motioned to the two massive armed guards concealing themselves behind the entry doors. "No entry, lads." The two closed and bolted the doors, standing in front of each.

    Max sidled over to a bookcase, reaching behind some ledgers and apparently tripping a latch. The case jerked, then stopped and Max pushed it gently to the left, revealing an opening to another room. This one had no windows and no other doors, only a fireplace and some vents along one ceiling edge. Twice the size of the anteroom, and much more comfortably furnished. Max drew the bookcase closed behind him. Ominously, he also drew across a metal door on a slide, closed and latched it.

"Cannot be too careful these days. Dietrich, since we last met, the political activity has stepped up and not just rhetorically. I assume Hartwig gave you a summary?"

"Yes, not unexpected, and the timing clearly in response to upcoming discussions in the East."

"Not just those talks, Dietrich. Whilst you were waltzing your cares away in Hannover, a most extraordinary event occurred in Saint Petersburg, Petrograd. Recall your friend Lenin had agreed in November to a popular election of a 'Constituent Assembly,' a genuinely democratic entity, any number of parties vying for representation? He and his Bolsheviks were embarrassed, badly, less than a quarter of the votes.

"The real question was whether the Bolsheviks would ever allow the Assembly to convene. My bet was never, Captain, and it was ten to one. I lost, in a way. It actually met the afternoon of the 18th, but was shut down by the Bolshies early next morning, the delegates scattered or worse."

He leaned back as he lit a cigarette, "Not that a popular assembly ever had a chance of changing the course of events in Russia, but its thuggish repression has galvanized opinion here among the radical elements. Evenly split it seems, but not along any consistent line. Some Socialists in favor, some against. The far left? Some Communists are blasting Lenin, others are in favor. Those rows are behind the bloodier demonstrations. Most curious of all, Dietrich, your friends Luxemburg and Liebknecht. Rosa, dearest, has been positively scathing in her pamphlets we allow to escape prison. Denounces Lenin as a dictator and so forth. The very heart of the radical Left at odds with her Russian, pardon me, Soviet counterpart."

Von Treptow was stroking his chin. *A bad sign*, thought von Seeckt. "Max, very interesting. Seems only one thing is lacking."

"And what might that be?"

"Someone to light the fuse to the powderkeg the police describe. A real person. Rosa. She is still at Breslau, then?"

"Dietrich, please be serious."

"I am serious, Max. Deadly serious. Can there be a better way to destroy these threats, all of them, than by helping them destroy themselves? Rosa, Karl, that crowd, showing up in Berlin tomorrow? They cannot restrain themselves, you know that. Speeches, pamphlets, demonstrations. Leading to pitched warfare in the streets between factions, aided and abetted by our operatives. Weapons supplied judiciously. Then our Army steps in to restore order, peace, in the eyes of the masses. Some collateral damage, lives will be lost, cannot be avoided, you see. It would take that incendiary voice, voices. Trust me, Max. And also trust me that none of them will see the next New Year. Alive."

Von Treptow knitted his brow and continued, tapping on the desk, "An amnesty. You can make it so, Max."

"General, you are overstepping your bounds here." Max stiffened visibly, von Seeckt observed. "Even should I so wish, I cannot simply act unilaterally. And, damn you, your love of bloodshed cannot be repressed for long, can it?"

"Max, settle down. Think this scheme through. We release them from prison tomorrow, the 24th. Two, three, four days of ferment. We, through our agents, set a date for an outburst – say the 28th, the Spartacist festival. No more than two, three days of conflict, then we put it down. I am in Brest-Litovsk the 1st. Trotsky triumphantly shoves older copies of the *Berliner Zeitung* in my face, trumpeting the revolt of his masses. I slide a copy of that morning's edition across the table. *'Radicals battle each other. Our Army restores calm.'* So much for his uprising. Puts the talks in a different context, would you say?"

"And if it spirals beyond our control?"

"It's like a firebreak, Sir," blurted von Seeckt.

His superiors stared at him. "Go on, Captain," said Max.

"Back home, before the dry season, you start a fire, in a swath. Burn out the tinder, make it hard for a forest fire to spread. But, Sirs, you must have enough water at the ready to keep it from getting out of hand."

"We have the water, young man. And we control the setting of the fire." Max was still wrestling with the risks. "I will not approve anything so bold unless everyone – police as well as local command – are fully informed and prepared. That is your task."

As if on a stage manager's cue, his telephone rang. "Who? Yes, yes, send them down." He clicked off. "The local gendarmerie to the rescue, it seems. Well played, General." He saluted, von Treptow returned the gesture.

Max went over to the armored portal, sliding both closures open. He signaled his guards to allow those without to enter. Inspector Hartwig, Major Bruckmiller, and another man in well-worn street clothes entered, following the Prince into the redoubt, closed tight once again. The stranger was introduced as Captain of Police Brenner, an undercover officer infiltrated into the Independent Social Democratic Party, the USPD, a more radical, antiwar offshoot of the dominant Socialists, so his presence was fortuitous.

Von Treptow wasted little time in outlining his scheme. Hartwig was immediately receptive, "Yes, Sir, if it ever were to work, now is the time before they get even stronger and kiss and make up among themselves. This Russian business certainly has proved useful, flushing them out, as it were."

"Major?"

"Agreed. Inspector, are you confident about our own internal security, since I left, that is?'

Hartwig thought for a moment. "As sure as we can be but one never knows all. We will be careful. But, Sir," looking at von Treptow, "the Army units need to be trustworthy."

"I shall take care of that," replied Prince Max. "Let us plan this extravanza today. I shall have Herbert over at Interior issue the amnesty order. You shall fetch her and hers tomorrow, Dietrich."

The policemen left, splitting up as they went. "Dietrich, before you go, privately, please." Captain von Seeckt saluted and left the sanctum.

"About Claire. I was the matchmaker for Hannover, I hope you do not mind. I know you do mind, so please forgive me. I contacted Mona Impelmann to arrange the invitation. Claire had no interest, of course, and I did not tell her about you, so I had to browbeat her into it. I just thought you two should have a chance to reconvene but I cannot have you seen here in Berlin with her or any of her set."

"Why, Max? Not that I was planning to mingle with those pimps."

"First, there is some danger, I am not sure how much, but clearly there is danger to you and therefore to her. There are enough anarchists out there watching officers, politicians, aristocrats, to fear acts of violence. Second, for a few days at least, you cannot be identified – remember, your name is on the radicals' lists – and certainly not as part of her circle.

Finally, you must maintain some credibility with Luxemburg and company. You had an alter ego during your Bohemian days? Would that still work?"

"Who knows? Josef Borgward, former attorney, then soldier, invalided back to Berlin from Poland. Intercessor with the Interior Ministry, secretly Socialist friends, to gain her freedom."

"That is very thin, Dietrich."

"It is all I have at the moment, but I may simply remain in the Army, as I contemplate the matter. Why not? Sometimes the truth works!" Both laughed at such a radical notion. "Yes, why not? A high-ranking German officer supporting her, in particular, as a pacifist in his conspiracy to bring the war to a close, we settle accounts between ourselves later. '*A subterfuge in plain sight*,' to quote our Dutch friend. It might prove a useful vaccination, a temporary armor against more violent elements."

"And the excitement of having a general, titled at that, supporting their cause. Clandestinely, of course – forbidden fruit being all the sweeter." Max was game. "Yes, it might work. For just a few days, all we need."

He leaned forward, "Still, stay away from Claire. I will do my best to keep her away. So you know, she feels reattached to you."

"So I feared."

"And, Dietrich, this business with Richard. I did not think it through, the notion that I could..."

"Sir, I have thought it through. I know you to be blameless. Your sister and I, on the other hand?" He let that thought sink in. "I am late for my next appointment. Good day."

* * *

Wednesday, January 23, 10:00 a.m.
London, Trafalgar Square

The Minister of Munitions and his private secretary dedicated themselves to their morning work, both straining to keep from discussing last night's events. Finally, Lord Elsmere could take no more of schedules and buffeting Churchill from his detractors and burst in on his chief.

"What took you so long, old man? I cleared my desk of artillery recoil springs and caterpillar treads an eon ago." Churchill waved Reggie to a chair.

"Save for Mother's appearance, that was productive, no? When do the two of you go shopping?"

"Half past eleven. Pity I cannot take him to the club, as tailoring makes me ravenous."

"Truly a pity, most piteous one. Now, where we left off, I have cogitated mightily. Do not give me that vinegary look, old boy, these are first-rate cogitations. To wit, the confluence of two great forces of history."

"Minister, I predict I will shortly have need of some whisky. May I?" Elsmere poured himself a tumbler, taking a generous sip. "And what, or who, pray tell, are these great forces? I suspect the identity of one."

"General Pershing and my oratorical thrusts, of course. I buttonholed Lloyd George on the telephone from home this morning, he buckled to my speaking demands, set for the House session Tuesday next. To your outline, munitions and such, aimed at our German listeners, I add a lengthy dissertation on the Boshevik threat – almost forgot that, did you? – with a coda, no, a finale, demanding that the Yanks be shared. That at a minimum, the next two or three months' worth of new additions be seconded to our front, if not our leadership. In closing, I question myself with a dramatic flourish." He looked at a notepad covered with his scribblings:

'No, I must ask you as I ask myself,
As draw near the dire hours,

Why are not our kith and kin
Shoulder to shoulder with ours?

Despite our past and yet because of it
We are still a common people

Bound by language and ancestry,
Why are we not now brothers-in-arms?

"David will have my viscera fed to the starlings of Picadilly, of course. It shall be worth it, I am confident. Not least for the spectacle."

Reggie shook his head. "Prometheus, bringer of fire! Gad! How will I quench this conflagration?"

"Actually, our First Minister will be secretly pleased behind his outburst of Celtic temper. Your American chum has pounded the railroad spike on its head. Pershing will counteract Haig's insistence on more folly."

"May I suggest tempering your remarks, as a matter of prudence, Minister?"

"And have the entire speech come off a damp squib? Absolutely, categorically not! You are missing the other intended consequence of my remarks."

"Yes, yes, I am quite certain I am." Reggie slumped further into his chair and took another sip. "What now?"

"A bridging of the chasm, the gulf between your favorite former naval person and your very own party. Would not my cherished Tory friends acclaim the exposé of the Bolshevik threat to the propertied class, far worse than anything even Labour could conjure? And the masterstroke for my admirers on the Conservative benches? The return of the prodigal sons, the Colonial rebels to the bosom of Mother Albion, just in the moment to save her from mortal threat?"

"Winston, I believe you have it. An address for the ages, directed to the Holy Trinity – the first part, the nation, the second, the Tories, the last a clarion call of patriotism mingled with sentiment." Elsmere continued, "You will sever any hope of cordiality with Marshal Haig, not that you were particularly desirous of same. He is jealous of his authority as well as stubborn in his demands."

"Pish. We were never fated to build brickworks together. No, your American has brought us trumps should we bid our hand judiciously. Pershing, from what we know, can withstand Haig's fulminations. With ease, knowing Haig as we do."

Churchill was rolling merrily along. "Let us look ahead to the playing of those cards. First, would Pershing cooperate, or would Lansing and Wilson squash this notion stillborn?"

"Colonel Emerson can answer that but I rather suspect Pershing would welcome the challenge."

"Agreed. Find out if Pershing can withstand Washington, then. Next, we have little time to orchestrate this rhapsody. Should Pershing piss on our brilliant idea, well, onto the next one. I pray your poet can persuade him."

Winston was downcast but for the briefest of moments, "No! What am I saying? The speech goes on regardless. Let the protagonists respond to the provocation. Excellent! Finally, place him squarely over the coals on this: What does America know of the Bolsheviks? We must needs convince not only ours, but theirs as to the nature of the next menace to come, lurking malevolently in the eastern mists. We may not have the opportunity to do so in the tumult of victory."

"Or defeat." Reggie started out of his chair. "Gad, look at the time. I must be away. Answers after tailoring."

* * *

Wednesday, January 23, 1200 Hours
Berlin

The balance of the day was frenetic, von Seeckt running sensitive messages all over Berlin, the policemen setting a few traps, Prince and General conferring with General Hentsch, commandant of the Berlin garrison. That meeting was set up as a social event, luncheon at Heller's, just the three of them, a private meeting in a public place.

Hentsch was an amateur actor, a *bon vivant*, a garrulous sort who easily masked his most serious statements with laughter or dramatic overtones as suited to his venue. "Yes, I have enough reliable troops to carry this out – waving, '*Frau Leininger, looking splendid, my dear*' – if it does not last more than a few days. Four battalions in particular will be eager to mix it up, families from Estonia, Courland, Konigsberg. I have separated them for just such an eventuality. Hate Russians from birth, – now standing, '*Herr Grosbeck, you are looking well*' – hate these Reds even more. Tough bastards, hardest part will be controlling them. One or two Landsturm companies in each barracks to watch the others, again, Easterners."

He was quiet for a few moments. "There will need be some subtlety in their deployment, I should think. I shall require exact dispositions of the demonstrations."

"Difficult, Robert." Max was being a bit prickly. "These are mobs, amœbic, unpredictable, chaotic."

"Difficult, but not impossible. I have a mathematician on staff, as a favor to the Rector of the University, keeping him out of the fray. Absolutely brilliant, but a soldier? Hah! However, he picked up on something during maneuvers last year. Something about the flow of people in certain situations, how that flow follows logical mathematical rules, some such. I will have him come in civilian clothes to your office tomorrow. He will require maps and numbers."

His gaze shifted right as he continued, "Can you provide these – '*Hello, Robert!*' '*Elise, my dear, do not tempt me with your décolletage,*' to a young woman who twittered away – so he can analyze? Give him the data, lock him in a room, cannot understand him anyway."

He stood, wiping his mouth with his napkin. "Update me regularly, Gentlemen. It seems that *décolletage* is smiling back at me, an opportunity not to be wasted, no?"

* * *

Wednesday January 23, 11:30 a.m.
Jermyn Street, London

Colonel Emerson had already arrived at the tailor's shop, fingering a few fabric samples, chatting with one of the fitters. His suit, while conservative by this shop's standards, was well cut and fitted, an American worsted, lighter than most on offer. Lord Elsmere entered and was immediately accosted by one of the name partners, Lewellyn, as befitted a major revenue source. "Your Lordship, welcome! And, if I may, on behalf of our little Jermyn Street community, may I offer our appreciation for your generous support of Robert Mathews' family?"

"The least I could do for an old and trusted friend. Too many of whom are not coming back, sadly. You have a new customer, I see. Not draped with your work, Jeremy."

The tailor whispered, "An American, Sir. Not bad craftsmanship, but the fabric is a bit pedestrian."

"An American, you say?" Lord Elsmere sidled past the cases, ostentatiously introducing himself to the Yank. "Welcome, Sir, to our little isle. Are you in any way connected with your Expeditionary lads? Doughboys, you call them? Reginald Collingwood-Tyndale."

"Bob Emerson, Sir. No, not a doughboy, awlman, Oklahoma. Helpin' with our diesel and lubricant supplies. Fascinatin' what comes out of those crackin' columns…"

"Yes, yes, I am certain it is, old man. Here, now, let my friend here show you his best. And his best is London's best, I assure you. Forgive me, I do not mean to force something on you that would fall outside your range."

"Don't have a range, friend. Awl's a good bidness."

"Jeremy, those blues and greys just arrived? Please fetch them for your new customer here." Reggie paused until the tailor was clear. "We have a proposition, old man, based on our chat. Timing is critical, however. Well, here we are. Are my new goods ready for a final?"

Lord Elsmere was led away to the fitting pedestal. Several suits later, he emerged brushing his sleeves. "Well, now, Bob. I may call you Bob, might I? Fancy anything?"

"These three. I'll come back Friday for a fitting, but I think they'll do just fine." 'Fine' came out as 'fan', but was still understood by those cashiering his cheque.

"Excellent taste." Reggie meant it. "Join me for luncheon, old man? A joint of good English beef at Simpson's? You may compare it to your own American steaks. Are you a cattleman as well, Sir?"

"Got me a little spread near Enid. Twenty-five thousand acres. Run some of your Herefords on it."

"Well, you most certainly do know your beef, then." At that point they were on the street. "Simpson's is entirely too public, of course. Take a cab to Rendell's, next to the Metropole Hotel on Trafalgar Square. Go to the loo, then out into the alley, then to the black door next. I will have a Highlander meet you there.

"Well, then, perhaps next time, old man. Good luck." With that, Reggie ducked through the doorway of his Rolls and was away.

He returned to the office, joining Winston in his office for a light luncheon. He picked up the telephone when it rang. "Yes, bring him in straightaway."

Presently, one of the kilted guards ushered in Colonel Emerson. Churchill greeted him, "Here now, please help yourself to some of our trifles. Watching our waistlines, you see. You eat, we shall talk."

"Have you fully recovered from your encounter with Mother?" Emerson shrugged, mouth full. "Is that so? Quicker than most, I must say. Please, to your father, paint her in the most favorable light." Churchill retired behind his desk. "Now, where were we? Ah, yes. Saving the world. Lord Elsmere and I were reflecting on our meeting, your mission, our needs. Cutting to the chase, as we say, we have a modest proposal to table. I am scheduled to speak at the House of Commons the 29th, a few days hence. Much of which jaw-jaw will address matters pertinent to my portfolio, but I plan to add a few blockbusters, as you Americans would say."

Colonel Emerson pushed his chair back from the tea cart. "Allow me a guess. General Pershing figures in somewhere?"

"But of course, old man. Central. But there is another, left at the moment for last. Yes, the doughboys. I plan to challenge His Majesty's Government to demand deployment of America's finest alongside our Tommy Atkins lads. As many as possible. When questioned, I defer to the Prime Minister and the War Cabinet, of course, but the issue will be left hanging, guaranteed to arise at next Question Time."

"So, old boy, do you have your General Pershing's imprimatur?" Reggie asked, tightly.

"Will your dramatic reading specify no foreknowledge on his part?"

"Most certainly!" exclaimed Churchill. "We expect him to express surprise, even shock, that a Member of Parliament would suggest such. Then, upon further thought, admit he is not familiar with Britain's parliamentary traditions. Then, upon even further thought, acknowledge the wisdom of the suggestion?"

"Please fit that script into a telegram, Sirs. Maybe not the wisdom part. I will see if that dog will hunt." Emerson kept close his countryman's desire to shake up the command structure with just such a proposal. "You will be making that statement naked, you understand. I need the writing immediately to present it to General Pershing. Handwritten and unsigned will be fine, never mind the telegram, I will deliver it myself. What time on the 29th? This I need to see in person."

Reggie replied, "Noon. I think we could make an exception in your case."

"So, that's simple enough, Gents. What's the other?"

"Understand I am saving your proposal for last, due to its sheer incandescence. Immediately preceding will be a jeremiad warning of the threat of Bolshevism in Russia and Eastern Europe. Are you familiar with these blackguards? Are your countrymen?"

"Barely, Sir. It's in the newspapers some, but not on people's lips. Certainly not the Army's, nor many politicians', for that matter."

"It should be, Colonel." Reggie was tumbling ideas. "It should be in your newspapers. And ours, Winston. We are grossly underutilizing our most effective propaganda asset."

"You mean Max, I take it. And his ties to the big city papers in America?" Reggie nodded in assent. "We are still bereft of details, photographs, stories. Cannot very well publish our diplomatic dispatches."

"Gentlemen, do not forget you have a stranger in your midst," said Colonel Emerson.

"No longer," smiled Churchill. "You are now one of us. So says Mother."

"That being the case, you need to meet Bertie. I'll bring him back with me."

"Whootee?" sputtered Churchill. "Another of Mother's American admirers?"

"No, Sir. But he might be, come to think of it. Robert McCormick. Editor and publisher, along with his cousin, of the *Chicago Tribune* and its Paris paper, the Army edition. Family owns it. Coincidentally a major on my, General Pershing's, intelligence staff. Been with us off and on since Mexico. He's the one you want. About as rock-ribbed conservative as they come. Says it makes his skin crawl to be in the same room with a French Socialist. Yes, indeed, he's your man."

* * *

Thursday, January 24, 0600 Hours
Berlin to Breslau, Schlesien

The train to Breslau left in the cold blackness, the two officers taking a private compartment. The trip was long, about three hundred fifty kilometers, five hours at reduced speed enforced to save fuel. From the station, a staff car took them to Breslau prison, dark and forbidding on the sunniest of days.

Commandant Albers met them in the *porte cochère*, "Hello, General. Here to return me to Berlin, my most fervent hope?"

Albers was wasted here, but numerous injuries on the Russian Front had retired him to more sedate duties. "Franz, stow away with us, assuming you can stomach the company. Please meet my aide, Captain Erich von Seeckt."

"Pleasure. Related to Hans and that bunch of squareheads? If so, my sincerest condolences."

"Yes, Sir, that is us. Big family."

"Injury?" noting his cramped shoulder.

"At the Somme, Sir."

"Note the decorations, Franz. One of our best."

"Glad to have the both of you here. Overjoyed to be done with this pompous so-called intellectual rabble," jerking his thumb toward the interior of the prison. "Did I note your not so subtle touch in our Prince's communiqué?" Von Treptow shrugged. "Of course I did. Well, not a moment to waste. Guards!"

There were to be five of them, Luxemburg, her current lover Paul Levi, Karl Liebknecht and two others von Treptow did not know and did not care to know. They were assembled in an interrogation room, the former operating theatre of the prison's hospital. Von Treptow was able to look down on the group as their release orders were being read. Rosa, never the most beautiful of women, with her strong features and prominent – *very large, remembered von Treptow* – nose, was disheveled, unkempt, not surprisingly, her full head of hair now going white, whiter than Claire's. Liebknecht, with his pince nez and upright shock of wavy hair – *to look taller?* – had not changed much in his two years in prison.

The group was separated, male and female, given their street clothes and personal articles, then brought back together. That was the signal for the two officers and Albers to depart in advance, to greet their guests in the privacy of a railway coach.

Each prisoner was to be sequestered separately in a guarded compartment, in Rosa's case, alone with von Treptow. He saw her limping along the platform, squabbling with one of the unknowns, then giving Liebknecht a push. *Not cooperating? Another schism?* He lowered the shade as she passed. Then he heard her distinctively authoritative voice telling the guards where she planned to sit, and with whom. No sound from the guards, even when they slid the door open, shoving her into the compartment, sliding the door closed and latching it loudly.

"Damn you, you tools of the imperialist classes! Cannot you see your oppression in front of your face? Idiots!" She turned, facing a figure in an Army uniform, face hidden by the morning newspaper, a curl of smoke rising. "And who are you, another fucking guard?"

Von Treptow lowered the upper half of the paper down to the fold, smiling. "Hello, Rosa, my dear."

She gasped, her hand at her collar. "Josef? You, here? What is this?" She dropped onto the bench opposite.

"Sorry, Rosa. Not Josef anymore. Never was, actually. Cigarette?"

Luxemburg was frozen for minutes, it seemed, moving only to grasp a handrail to brace against the forward lurch of the locomotive. "Cigarette, my dear?" von Treptow repeated, now rising, lighting it, taking it from his lips and placing it in hers. "May I explain?"

She held her cigarette with trembling hands, trying to maintain her composure. She and the general, as Josef, had been acquaintances, then lovers, during Dietrich's brief flirtation with Berlin's underground bohemian counterculture. He had showed up one Spring afternoon in 1912 at a café frequented by radicals and artists, taking a seat outside in the sun, watching the crowd with amusement. Arguments rising, egos bristling and deflating, posturing and posing. Amateurs trying to reconcile their academic theories with reality, their sterile fabrications with the lives of real people.

Dietrich, then a colonel, was taking a leave of absence, a sabbatical at his request. He had let his hair and beard grow for two months and no longer looked the part of a Prussian Army officer. For another three months he was a habitué of cabarets, salons, workers' meetings. Rosa could not fail to notice him, tall, handsome and quiet, all contrasts with her comrades and fellow travelers.

She had taken the initiative in front of her sham husband, Lubeck, to begin an intimacy. At the same café at lunch – 'Josef' was paying, of course – she took his hand and held it at length. "Gustav, Josef and I are going to take a walk down to the Tiergarten. I will see you this evening." Without waiting for a reply – there was none forthcoming – she pulled a hesitant 'Josef' out of his chair and down the street.

Down the street meant to a flat several blocks away, a place used by her crowd alternately as a meeting place, a safe house and a trysting nest. She wasted no time undressing and mounting him. This went on over the next months until one day 'Josef' was nowhere to be found, failing to show for an assignation. Rosa sought after him in cafés and among acquaintances, until a few days later the safe house's doorman handed her an envelope. Within was a note:

> *Dearest Rosa,*
> *I can never thank you enough for entwining your life*
> *with mine these past few months.*
> *But it was not enough, as much as it was,*
> *to rescue me from my depths.*
> *My past will not free me to embrace our future.*
> *Your Josef will be no more when you read this.*

"Well, may I?" His voice broke her concentration, his spell.

"You were dead."

"Josef was dead. He is no more, remember? I became myself again, the man, the officer you see before you. Dietrich von Treptow."

"Von Treptow!" she shrieked. "The imperialist? A general? You?"

"Yes, yes, but calm yourself down. I am the one setting you free."

"What? How can that be?" She shrunk back, whispering, "Why? And why you?"

"Because I know you, Rosa. Because I have been at your side ever since."

"You make no sense. By my side? Ever since when?"

"Since Josef…'died.' When we met I was struggling with family issues, had separated myself from my position, my rank, my duty, in an attempt to see if my life was destined elsewhere. I recovered over time, no small thanks to you. Mainly I saw you and your ilk, please, no personal disrespect meant, as diametrically opposed to my beliefs and values. So I returned to my former existence.

"I watched you over time. Admittedly, I, we, spied upon you. I worked with Military Intelligence setting up the infiltrations of your and other groups. We provided some of your financial support." He paused to let that sink in. "Do not bother trying to identify our people – you cannot, and most are no longer involved. Our efforts were designed to allow your radical elements just enough strength to rise to the surface, to make themselves visible so we could observe them. We succeeded. Now we require your assistance, your cooperation."

"Assistance? Go fuck yourself."

"No, no, no, Rosa. That will not do. Here is the gist. Your movement, whatever you call it these days, is in danger of being swamped, crushed by the Russian Bolsheviks. They have infiltrated far more deeply than we ever could. You, you and Karl, must rally your group to combat them. We are still opposites, enemies to be honest, but we have a common enemy in the Russian Reds. This Lenin is a dictator, your very word. I have seen him in action and you are quite correct. Unless they are crushed, we cannot end this war."

Her jaw dropped at this last comment. "End the war? Please, do you take me for an idiot? Your imperialist class can only survive on a steady diet of war and subjugation!"

"Funny, I liked you with the moaning more than the sloganeering. Still do." He smiled, raising his left eyebrow slightly. "Rosa, only you can inspire your comrades to confront this evil. The Army would only throw more petrol on the fire, even as it crushed all of you. All of you. And the Army can crush you, easily, totally, I assure you. It now shall be your choice. My choice is to end this war. I am actively doing so in my own way, my own methods."

He crossed the compartment, sitting close to her. "When this war is over, you shall be free to raise your voice, compete at the ballot box. But a misguided attempt at revolution will destroy all. You are a born leader, Rosa. You must lead. You step off this train free to pursue your own ends. Just remember who the true enemy is. Or the most immediate enemy. The enemy of mine enemy is my friend. At least for now."

Rosa replied, "That is a slogan, Josef, General, whoever you are or once were. I, too, preferred the moaning." She smiled mischievously.

* * *

Thursday, January 24, 1700 hours
Berlin

The train chuffed to a halt at Zoo station. Von Treptow gave Rosa Luxemburg a kiss on the forehead. "We make a most unusual couple, Rosa, dear. We are class enemies as you say. We hate each other, do we not?"

"Speak for yourself, General. How hard it is for me to use that word for my Josef." She straightened her collar and scarf, "Will I see you again?"

"Yes, but allow me the watching. You have work to do, urgent work. Your comrades have been alerted and will be waiting to whisk you away. A word of warning – have nothing to do with the Reds, the Russian variety and their sympathizers. For your safety. Absolutely do not find yourself in their company or I shall soon find myself fishing you out of the Spree. For that matter, your socialist friends, Ebert and Noske, the others, Kautsky. They are dangerous, at the very least unreliable. The first two are jealous of you, afraid of your persuasive powers, your charisma. Even your friend Kautsky, well, you broke with him, he has not forgotten, I should think. There are enough fervid, violent spirits abroad in the city to mask one more murder. Please be most careful."

"Josef, Dietrich, whoever you are, this has been the most unusual morning, day of my life. Will the rest of my life pale? I know not, but I suppose I must thank you for my freedom, if not my safety and success. So, thank you, and *au revoir*, my dear." With that, she kissed him full in the mouth, then spun and exited.

The German officers waited until the revolutionaries had left the station altogether. Albers gathered up von Seeckt and the general as they left off the other side of the train to a waiting staff car. "Well, General, how was your guest? Mine sucked lemons the entire trip or so it seemed from the looks I got." Albers was happy to be back in action, of sorts.

"Mine could not have been worse," von Seeckt interrupted. "Clara someone. Smelled worse than any whore. Would not stop lecturing me on the class struggle, that crap. I finally pulled out my member to see if she would shut up and suck on it for a while. No luck. Seems she prefers the ladies." He was not making it up. "Sir, I simply thought I should take matters into my own hands, as it were."

Albers looked at von Treptow. "I see that discipline has broken down completely in your unit. Why am I not surprised?"

"I encourage spontaneity, Colonel. Here we are, now." Imperial German Army headquarters was another of the forbiddingly grey piles of stone dotting the otherwise bright and vibrant streets of Berlin, or once bright they were in 1913. "Franz, join us for the day. Your experience will prove useful, unless you desperately need to return to Breslau forthwith?"

"Immediately, next week, if not sometime next month. Glad to be of any use here, thank you, Sir."

"Excellent. Max will be happy to see you, I am sure."

To avoid undue exposure, the car drove through the sentry station into the motor court. The officers disembarked in a light mist into the building, a captain escorting them to the War Room, Eastern Front. *Machineguns, too, everywhere, a nice touch,* thought von Treptow.

Two guards threw back the double doors into the War Room. At the end of the dispositions table, facing a map, his back to them, was General Max von Hoffman, a stocky, bullet-headed figure gesturing to his aides. "I detect the footsteps of one General von Treptow, a distinctive gait, indeed. Welcome, my friend, not a moment too soon. You have paroled Albers? Hello, Franz. And who is this Siegfried? Is he quite big enough to shelter you, Dietrich?"

Introductions to his staff followed. "We have much to do. Your Colonel Knorr is quite voluble, do you know that? We have received reams and reams of papers from him. Useful, but, gad, the volume!"

"He is very thorough. Shall we begin?"

"Indeed. Turn here to the map table. Captain, where are you from, did you say?"

"No, Sir, I did not as yet. We hail from Freidenberg, Pomerania, right here. Estates are much reduced from the old Teutonic Knight days, but we still have several thousand hectares here," pointing, then dragging a finger down to Posen, "and here. Once owned all this here," now pointing into Russian Poland.

"Perhaps we can see our way to returning it to you. Now, to our dispositions. Army Group Ten is here, Nine here, and Eleven over here in this salient. The keys to a lightning advance are rail and telegraph, not horses and boot leather. Accordingly, these lines in red are our Day One targets. Colonel Knorr has done the calculations based on our estimate of Russian rolling stock within reach, and we will not be able to push quite as many troops through as we would prefer, not in the first two days. After that it will go more quickly."

"Sabotage, Sir? Irregulars and the like?" Von Seeckt had soaked up much in a month. "No rails, no advance."

"Just so, Captain. Words of wisdom, indeed. And do not forget, the Russians will not have their locomotives on our borders at full steam, waiting to load our luggage. No, we have several infiltration units forming at each railhead ready to advance quickly, by horse if necessary, to seize stations and stock. And the telegraph. They will be in place a day or two early, hidden."

"And what of this Trotsky and his Red Army? I take it these are their dispositions?" Von Treptow was pointing at a series of circles wax pencilled in red. "Why have they withdrawn like that?"

"They are going home, Dietrich. Can you blame them? We move these marks eastward every day based on our aeroplane observations. Those with stars, however, are serious threats, but, as you can see," von Hoffman waved his hand across the entire front, "they are scattered, and not all are connected to rail. We have some of our best units ready for shock assaults, but isolating rather than destroying them is sufficient for the initial few days."

Max continued, "The main thrust continues along the rails. Each train we overtake or capture goes back west to pick up more troops. By Day Three, we are into our Landsturm and Landwehr occupation troops – eager, by the way, to see some action, maybe some looting, whatever keeps them happy. Colonel Frederikson of the Rail Corps will explain the next aspect, rather clever, as I reflect."

It was said the best brains produced by the War College went into the railway section and ended up in lunatic asylums. Frederikson was one of those geniuses of the Rail Corps, probably the most efficient unit in the entire Army. At the outbreak of war, after some intitial stumbles, the nation's rail network had proved to be an efficient mover of men, materiel and horses, of course, a thousand trains every two days, over two million men in ten, on two fronts hundreds of kilometers apart.

"Yes, Sir. As you should know, the Russian rail system is itself designed to thwart exactly the type of movement we plan by the simple expedient of a wider track gauge. Our stock simply cannot roll across their tracks as they now exist. We are planning on steady attrition of captured stock due to breakdown or the captain's sabotage. So, we plan to install a third rail on their tracks, inside theirs, which will allow us to run our stock. That way we are sure of consolidating our advances with occupation troops, supplies and material. We have already completed these rails where we control territory and we regularly push the general here to acquire more trackage."

He smiled as von Hoffman made a gesture, "There you have it. Thank you, Colonel."

Von Seeckt asked, "How quickly, Colonel?"

"Quicker than the Army can move on foot, certainly. I have little wagers on it with several division commanders. It is easy work so long as the road-bed, crossties and the lefthand rail are intact. We have been producing new rails around the clock. Bridges and switching stations are more difficult, so seizing and protecting those are critical. But in ten days or less, it is all over."

"Ten days, Sir?" von Seeckt was skeptical. "What happens when a key link is blown up, or little patches of rail here and there are chopped out? Or worse, a dynamite charge blows a train?"

"More prescient observations, young man. It is, after all, a line, composed of many points, yet must be continuous to be of use. Speed is the best anti-dote, speed and security."

"That, and the saboteurs have to come to you, so we know where to look. I see, but it still seems risky to gamble so much on one system." Von Seeckt was fascinated by this new warfare. "And the ten days?"

"Ten days takes us six hundred kilometers into Russia." The newcomers whistled in unison. "With a margin, Gentlemen, this is a conservative time-table. Each successive day increases our forces along each line by four divisions, two attack, two occupation. Forty divisions, five hundred thousand men, half guarding the rail lines and stations. That should do it. Oh, yes, four prongs: Riga to St. Petersburg, Minsk to Moscow, Warsaw to Kiev and on, Lemberg to Odessa and on to the Crimea, eventually beyond. It is a big operation, Sirs."

"The Austrians?" Von Treptow was thinking of his global strategy.

"Romania, Moldavia, Bessarabia. Keep them out of the way. Cannot muck things up that way." Hoffman did not attempt to conceal his contempt.

"Now, what about this Czech Legion? We need to find our way to them at the earliest."

"Yes, yes, Dietrich, we know. It is not that easy. Hardly a matter of strolling up with a white flag. Even if you bring a couple dozen schoolgirls with you. And of course, there is the small matter of persuading the Austrians to allow free passage to the force that will wrench Bohemia and the rest away from them. Have you thought that through, my friend?"

"Masaryk will have a way of contacting them, I hope. As to Austria, well, *c'est la guerre?*"

"Too cavalier, horseman. Prince Max has a daunting task. I should not want Conrad's men shooting at mine."

"Of course not, but we should elude the Austrians if possible. What about this line from Kiev to Brest-Litovsk, down to this point above Kraków, then Breslau, then Prague? Cannot reroute through Hungary, the Magyars would not stand for it." Von Treptow had traced a line running above the Austrian army's positions, thence down through Germany into Czechland. "Colonel Frederikson, could we use the returning trains?"

"To Brest, certainly. Three days' worth of capacity, quick enough? From there, it will be a question of availability, going the wrong direction, you see?"

"Yes, and I would prefer they did not linger about on our territory. Still, that would do. When do we reach this point?" Von Treptow put his finger on a railway junction about a hundred fifty kilometers southwest of Kiev, closer to Kharkhov.

"Is it a priority, Sir? That is well over eight hundred kilometers from our forward positions. Six days, maybe eight. Getting them back will be longer. It would be a great help if they could be persuaded to bring some equipment our way."

"Of course, Colonel." Max von Hoffman slapped the table. "Dietrich, if you and the Princely one can get through to these Czech supermen, let them pirate the Russian trains, fight for us, to clear our way back to our lines. Seize the most forward points. More trains, more men."

"Max has the Ukrainians lined up already, for the most part. Any Red forces would be pinched from two directions. I approve. Captain, recall I asked about your Ukrainian? Do you now see the wisdom of my ways?"

"Mysterious ways, Sir. Still mysterious."

* * *

Friday, January 25, 0800 Hours
Foreign Office, Berlin

Hartwig and Bruckmiller met the officers for breakfast in Prince Max's hideaway. "Sirs, your little gamble seems to be paying off already. Our informants report the Spartacists and the UPSD are well and truly stirred up by Liebknecht and Luxemburg. Someone in the Russian front groups is really pissed off at our friends, and the plain old Socialists aren't much happier."

Von Treptow asked, "What next? The 28th meeting still on?"

Bruckmiller replied, "Definitely. Some are pressing to move as early as tomorrow. Our dear Rosa counsels caution, but other factions chafe at their bits. The smart ones realize they need to get better organized – that's weapons, as well as people – but Liebknecht is hell bent to turn the get-together into a full-fledged uprising. Seriously, Sirs, and he will carry the day according to our men."

"And the others?" Prince Max was now alarmed. "What else might issue from Pandora's box, Gentlemen, having prised open the lid? Are we truly prepared?"

"Yes, Excellency, what will I be facing?" Robert Hentsch was not alarmed so much as calculating, confident of his forces. "How many of my men, and where?"

"As many as you can muster, Sir." Hartwig understood the mob dynamics better than the others. "We'll be giving you the locations, but it all centers around Brandenburger Tor. By the way, Sirs, we baited some traps with your announcement yesterday. One of our inner circle, Theodor Grunwald, was caught forwarding a copy to the outside. That plugs one of our most persistent and perplexing leaks. Two other traitors were exposed hawking inside information within their groups."

"They won't be hawking, or cooing, or chirping again." Bruckmiller was smiling morbidly.

"Don't gloat, Ernst. Yes, we discreetly disposed of those two. More importantly, the heat of the moment is boiling off caution and covers. The pickings will be plentiful."

"Yes, Hartwig, I am sure you will be overbooked at gaol. But, I need dispositions – this is still a military operation." Hentsch turned to von Treptow, "My mathematician sits outside. May I introduce him to this séance?"

Von Treptow asked, "Is he reliable, General?"

"As reliable as the Western Front, General." Everyone understood the simile.

Prince Max said, "Bring him in, then."

Presently one of the Prince's stormtroopers escorted in a tall, gangly, bespectacled figure with multi-directional hair, wearing an ill-fitting suit. Hentsch announced him, "Gentlemen, I give you Herr Doctor Ernst Thesiger." He rattled off the names of those around him.

The guest looked around, first at the setting, then at the august company. All he could do was nod.

"Do not mistake his shyness for a lack of mental acuity, Sirs. Ernst, allow me show you what we have so far." On the map table was a large scale layout of the area around the Brandenburg Gate, scaled out to a kilometer or so. To the west, the Tiergarten park, to the east, the Pariser Platz then Unter den Linden with buildings hemming the curbs. Two main crossing avenues, Königgrätzer Strasse and Wilhelmstrasse.

Thesiger looked over the map, then took an oblong black case from an inside pocket from which he withdrew a pair of calipers and a slide rule. Spreading the calipers, first across the map scale, then over the map's dimensions, he took up the slide rule. "Am I to understand this is an exercise in crowd control?"

"Of sorts, yes," said von Treptow.

"Of sorts. Hmmm. Then, at an average density of one person per point-four-six square meters, centered on the gate, approximately twenty-two thousand, four hundred twenty-seven are to be accommodated on the hard surfaces and verges within this area. That is, within earshot of the gate. Now, am I to assume there will be chaos at some point during this assembly?"

"Yes, so we anticipate." Prince Max was both amused at the genius and fascinated with the slide rule.

"Multiple points of chaos generation?"

The group nodded.

"Well, then. Understand a crowd such as you expect is similar in many respects to a gas of a known density contained within a vessel of a known volume with the obvious difference that the initial state of the particles, your individuals, is more or less static, not in true Brownian motion. Follow?

"No? I suppose I need not elucidate the applicability of Bernoulli's theorem in describing the flow of the collective mass?

"No? I see."

He drummed his long fingers on the map. "Allow me an attempt to explain. Assume the crowd is predominantly on the Tiergarten side of the gate, the west. No, no, perhaps we should assume a significant cohort is clustered behind the gate, approximately…forty per cent of the total. Now, an event of chaos generation occurs here" – pointing to a spot twenty meters to the west of the Gate. "Assume further that amygdala-driven responses predominate."

The stares grew glassier with each comment.

"I see. Panic, Gentlemen. Which triggers a predictable pattern of flow not unlike a gas being released from pressure." He looked at his audience. "Perhaps I should simply take this information and report back with the results of my calculations?"

Faces brightened expectantly. He continued, "I assume weapons are to be used. Mausers only, or machine guns? Which? And where along the spectrum from reluctance to enthusiasm?"

"Both weapons classes, Doctor. Initially with restraint, then more… aggressively. A graduated response, rate of which cannot be known beforehand."

"Thank you, General Hentsch. That is all I require at the moment. Would 1700 hours be convenient for my exposition?" The good doctor gathered his things and slipped out.

"I feel as if my head has been squeezed," von Seeckt said, holding each side of his cranium. "At least I could sleep during lectures at Heidelberg."

* * *

1400 Hours
Foreign Office, Berlin

Von Treptow and von Seeckt returned to the Foreign Office after a hurried lunch only to find a smiling Colonel Knorr waiting, casually reading a newspaper. Annie, the buxom receptionist, presented a message to the general and her chest to the captain. "Come, lad, we have more news to digest along with that horrid sausage. Colonel, you are a day early?"

"Yes, Sir. Krupps did most of the work, I finally was just in the way. Engineering begins as we speak. No niceties such as deeds and the like required, according to the Adjutant. Besides, I have a few things for General von Hoffman's staff," pointing to a bulging briefcase.

"He will be overjoyed. Lieutenant, Captain, that is, please watch where you are going, not where you have been or would like to be!"

Knorr piled on, "You were left in my care by the ladies of Hannover, Captain. Were I to allow you somehow to get lost in Berlin, civil war would be surely break out between our house and the Boeckers. That must not be allowed to happen. Understood?"

"Yes, Sir. Merely windowshopping, Sir."

"Which leads to purchasing. And maintenance, endless maintenance."

"Enough, you two." Reading his message, "Our Herr Masaryk arrives tomorrow morning. Just in time. We are to discuss Austria with Max, then back to our other Max with your scriptures, then back here for our maths lesson. Much to do."

Entering the sanctum, General von Treptow stopped and gave a small bow to a tall man in morning dress. Richard von Kuhlmann, the Foreign Secretary, gave von Treptow a perfunctory bow in return then strode off at high speed. "Hmmm. Must have had the same sausages we had, Captain. Excellency, what gives with von Kuhlmann?"

"Seems he would have control of foreign policy returned to him. Imagine. I suggested he take up the matter with Ludendorff. Caused a fit of dyspepsia, I fear. Well, such are the ways of diplomacy, no?"

"He is in a difficult spot, Sir. Have a little sympathy."

"Yes, I suppose you are right. Sympathy does not change my methods, however. Now, down to business. Good news from Kiev. The Ukrainians have finally screwed up their courage and issued their declaration of independence. Much to be done to keep it and their heads, but it is a start. It also relates to the note about Masaryk. Max is harassing me about your obsession with Gadja and his Legion, but he concedes they could be useful. Putting two and two together, our efforts should be aided, I should think. Kuhlmann fears we will precipitously dissolve the Hapsburg Empire, that relic, which we most certainly will. He recognizes its inevitability, but wonders if we could show a little decency toward our Germanic brethren?"

"That is your area, Sir. We are but the spears of your will."

"Dietrich, enough. I have to steel myself to pulling the rug from beneath a perfectly fine young man, perhaps the most well-meaning of all of us, if naïve. The young man would gladly yield the burdens of Empire with the prospect of retaining the crown of a German Austria. He simply does not have the strength of will to keep the *ancien régime* intact, if such a thing were yet possible."

"Are you, in your roundabout way, granting us permission to secure the Czechs and return them to Bohemia and Moravia?"

Prince Max slumped back in his chair, folding his arms. "Yes," he sighed, "against my good judgment. Only because you will be needed in Kiev thereafter. It there the slightest possibility you could be discreet in their extrication and avoid bloodshed in the process?"

"Doubtful. Colonel, Captain? No? Three nays, Excellency. The people have spoken. A plebiscite."

"Out, all of you."

General Hoffman's office was abuzz with activity, the staff sensing new action ahead. Colonel Knorr was greeted by several of the staff demanding his time, disappearing with him as ants toting a grasshopper back to their nest.

"Max, we are onto the Ukraine, we have learned just now. Simply a matter of fixing a date. When will you be ready?"

"Anytime after the next ten days. My shock troops will be in place by the first. Max cabled me about the Ukrainians – we have been in contact with the Tsarist remnants there, they look to us as their army to defend against the Reds. Mindful, I am sure, that it is much easier to get us in than get us out." He smiled broadly. "If we can coordinate, that will get us another hundred kilometers or more as an advance point without a fight. Your Czechs may prove useful before returning home, Dietrich. Think about that, please."

"Certainly, Sir. I still have little concrete notion as to their dispositions, both geographic and mental. Appears it will take a personal audience," looking at von Seeckt.

"So it seems, Dietrich. My focus is now on Saint Petersburg. The Reds took the Finnish government by surprise this week, but by mid to late February, Von der Goltz and Mannerheim should be on the very cusp of driving them and the Russians out, so we will be positioned that much closer. Let me show you." Hoffman faced the wall map. "We need detach only part of Mannerheim's force to block the Reds from reaching Archangel without unduly weakening him. Gustav and the remaining Finns then wheel south, blocking access to Saint Petersburg from the east. We squeeze the city from the west with our troops in Riga, and via naval blockade and landings at Reval. We shall at least give the Navy something to do with their big guns."

He pointed on the map to the south, "Kornilov, Kerensky's former military minister, claims to be raising a hundred thousand, mostly Tsarists, to invest the city from the southwest, basing in Minsk. I question his numbers and his ability, but we will give him materiel and some men, if we can punch through fast enough. Your Colonel Knorr has offered several suggestions for redeploying some of our artillery units. I confess neither I nor mine had realized the difficulty in moving them along with the shock troops, but he showed how to move them into supporting positions for Saint Petersburg."

Von Hoffman smiled slightly, "So, it can be done, we think. Oh, the South will be sheer improvisation. Supply lines, distances, time for the Reds to recover, all that. Several other 'Whites', as the anti-Bolsheviks call themselves, are grouping in Crimea and east of the Don. Captain, I am sending your uncle back to Turkey to coordinate the whole Black Sea theater. He is overjoyed, I am sure."

"Thrilled, Sir."

"Now, Dietrich, here is the catch. Your man keeps adding little factors to the analysis – food to here, ammunition to there, new boots everywhere. All of which slow us down."

"Apologies, Sir. Cannot be helped if we are to fly like the wind." Colonel Knorr had rejoined the conversation and was unapologetic in his new position of authority. "Theory is on point, execution depends on those little factors."

"Just so, Colonel, just so. Accordingly, we are moving more units closer or beyond the original ceasefire lines."

"Do not tip our hands, Sir. The Reds have eyes and brains, too."

"We are well aware, Dietrich. So, we are sending some…irregulars… to contact the Tsarists, where we can find them. Point in fact, I can think of three no more irregular than you. Not just the Czechs. You will find yourselves sleeping with Cossacks before you know it." Looking at the clock, he snapped, "Damn! The time! We are due at Max's for our maths lesson."

* * *

Friday, January 25, 1200 Hours
Somewhere near Chaumont, France

Colonel Emerson hitched a ride in a DeHavilland DH-4 being ferried to the American Army Air Service at Bar-le-Duc, the original Lafayette Escadrille's forward base. Mitch Cabot had cabled HQ to arrange transport down to Chaumont, a seventy kilometer drive, and a few hours out of Biggin Hill aerodrome he was on the road south.

From time to time the road became crowded with French detachments, their little blue helmets bobbing along. "Always away from the front, Sergeant? That's the fourth group now going south. None coming north?"

Seargeant Westmoreland had offered the colonel the passenger seat for the ride, displacing his corporal to the lorry bed with part of his platoon, the others in two lorries trailing. "No, Sir, I only seen one or two the last weeks going that way. Many more heading away from the fun, it seems. But then, this is only our fourth run, so maybe we've missed them."

"Do you think they move up at night and down during the day to confuse Fritz? Hiding their strength?"

Westmoreland looked about, conspiratorially, past Emerson's window, the rearview mirror, leaning forward to peer across the windscreen. "My opinion, Sir? They ain't got as much strength as they and we would like. They are packed like sardines in their rear area trenches and dugouts, seem pretty darned comfortable. But when we done a recon, like last night, seems we're pretty well alone in the dark, up front."

"See action, did you, Sergeant?"

"Not much, Sir. Weren't supposed to. Just testing the Heinies' positions. Curious, though. They saw us coming across No Man's Land, crouching and crawling, but didn't open up with machine guns, just a few random rifle shots. When we got to the trenches, we could hear them scuttling away, then they opened up from another line. We found the connecting trench, moved up, same damn thing. It's like they were practicing getting away. We finally just came home. No papers, no maps, a few helmets and such as souvenirs. No heroics, leastwise, not yet."

"That is interesting, Sergeant, very interesting. I will relay that to General Pershing, with your permission?"

The sergeant just gulped.

* * *

1400 Hours
American Expeditionary Force Headquarters, Chaumont

Emerson walked into the entry hall of the wing housing Signals and most of the Intelligence staff. "Hello, Captain! Anything happening here?"

Captain Daniels stood and saluted, then sat back down at his desk as his superior waved him off. "Quiet for the moment, Sir. How was your London visit?"

"A nice break from things here, that is certain. Do I have a stack? And is Major McCormick back from Paris?"

"Yes and no. Due back tomorrow night, late. You'll see him Sunday dinner with General Pershing. Major Schroeder wanted to see you upon your return, something about signals or such."

"Buy me some time, if you would. I'll be in my office."

He went down the hall to a spacious sunlit room. He carefully removed Winston Churchill's letter from the inside fold of his jacket, setting it to his left. *I wonder what Black Jack will say?* He riffed through a pile of telegrams, memos and notes in front of him, prioritizing them in his piling system. The trifles he slid off into his wastebin. The merely important, he piled in a corner. The three of interest he laid in his lap as he leaned back in his chair.

The first was a letter from home. His father, only sixty-two, was not well, some digestive upset. His sister back in St. Louis was worried about him. Could he come home? *Clearly not. Maybe I can lift his spirits.* He took a telegram form from his drawer and began to compose:

> *Dad*
> *Met Lady Churchill as requested. She is still a looker, Dad.*
> *She gave me a kiss for you. Asked if you were still married!*

Why not come over to England. I can arrange quarters, first
class. Let me know.
Love
Bobby

Maybe that will help, he thought. *Doctors won't be any better in London than at Wash U, though. We'll see.*

He shouted out the door at Daniels, handing him the draft as he came in, then returned to his second piece of paper, a memo from a Signals man pointing out a series of coded and clear messages between Hannover and Berlin, the source being an unnamed neutral. *Probably the Swedes, maybe the Swiss,* he thought, *wanting to sell guns to the new boys.* His task, without being told, would be to divine the reason for that traffic given that Hannover was not a major Army center. *Okay, maybe this is what Schroeder wants to talk about. Not so important?*

The best was saved for last. A still perfumed letter from home.

* * *

Friday, January 25, 1700 hours
War Office, Berlin

"General Hentsch, I trust your savant here has solved your deployment quandary?" Prince Max was inclined to be indulgent of the odd character unfolding his plans. "Without too much Einstein to traverse?"

"Let us see what he has on offer without prejudgment, shall we?" Hentsch was prepared for as much befuddlement as the others; all he had done was hire the magician for the birthday party.

"Please, Sirs, it is not that difficult. Do not trouble yourselves with the theoretical underpinnings, just focus on the manifestations." Looking at the faces, "The marks on the maps, Gentlemen."

Seeing nothing but blank slates, he commenced, "So, from this morning's sessions, these circles represent claques – sympathizers of one hue or another, arranged in exclusivity. Very important, that exclusivity. Spartacists here, Bolsheviks there, Socialists of several stripes – here, there and over here. Understand, these are labels only, but it is essential to maintain the segregation of each group from the other. So, my Gentlemen from the Police, place them wherever you wish, but in groups. Understood?"

Bruckmiller replied for the department, "Of course, Professor, that is their natural inclination. We will reinforce it with our operatives."

"Excellent. Do you understand why, my good man?"

"Let me try, Prof. Birds of a feather, to start. But mostly friction along the edges where the scum can shout and push. Mixed and mingled, it's just a mess."

"Precisely! Were you one of my students, Sir? No, I suppose not. They seemed unable to grasp such elegant concepts."

"No, Sir, just one of the unwashed." Bruckmiller beamed at the recognition.

"Then let us proceed. We posited an act of disruption here," pointing at the same spot as the morning's session. "May we accept that as a given?"

"Bomb or pistol shot?" Bruckmiller enjoyed being the teacher's pet. "Tell us, which is most effective?"

"Pistol normally would do, but not in a crowd this large. What is required is something with a blast radius equal to half the displacement from the main locus, the speaker's platform. A bomb, Gentlemen, approximately five million five hundred thousand joules effective energy – one and a quarter kilos of trinitrotoluene – would do the trick, allowing for dissipation of energy due to destruction of bone and tissue intervening. Can you arrange same?"

Hartwig spoke up, "Let us assume so. What happens next?"

"Back to my perceptive pupil's observation. The explosion casts a shock wave, literally, into its surroundings, repelling all objects, but rapidly exhausting its force. Then, the human factor prevails. A shock wave of panicked humans replicates the chemical force. Then, and only then, does it get interesting."

His audience was thinking in terms of shattered bodies and blood flying about. That was interesting enough. More? "Yes, Gentlemen. Then friction becomes the dominant physical force, the same force that slows your horses' hooves or your motorcars' wheels. You have a remnant of the demonstrating population fleeing circumferentially, all directions, but, as we noted there will be pockets of one faction or another upon which another tribe will find itself hurled. Think back to your days of old, the collision of two lines of ancient warriors, Romans against Carthaginians, Athenians against Spartans. Physical displacement meets ideological or tribal resistance. No greater disruptive confluence in all of society. Need I add that this all follows the basic thermodynamics of an expanding gas, in this case explosive?"

"No, Professor, you need not add to our confusion. How many casualties, and where do I deploy?"

"Ah, yes, General. I always seem to forget the client. First, casualties." He fiddled with the slide rule. "Deaths, four hundred, forty-four per cent due to the original explosion, the balance to…frictional effects. Significant injuries – use maiming as a standard – no more than two times the deaths. Total serious, twelve hundred or so, give or take a few hundred unfortunate individuals. Deployments, thank you, General for allowing me to exercise my creativity in this regard. Policemen, have your insiders set up barricades at every major entrance. Then, at your signal, your men and General Hentsch's retire to the outside of same. To hold these fast against the pressure of the crowd. Doing this can increase the casualty count twofold. Very efficient. Finally, the mass bulges here, and here, spilling to the west. There should you deploy your machine guns for maximum effect – a screaming mob charging your troops, if you have that picture."

He packed his things. "Is there anything else? If not, Max Planck and I are at work on something far more important than this mere trifle. May I be excused?"

Prince Max likewise excused General Hentsch and his staff and Chief Inspector Hartwig and his colleagues. Max was a devotee of compartmentalization, of need-to-know strictures, and those excused certainly did not need to know the contents of the Dutch Embassy's memo.

"I am not quite certain I know what you did or did not say to our British counterparts, but I am equally certain I do not wish to know with any degree of exactitude. Officially. Whatever bait you laid before them, they have bit and swallowed. Read this, Dietrich."

A few moments later, "Much of this is our Pieter's brokering a deal, Sir. The Saint Petersburg dispatches were as much as we could hope to procure, and we shall have them." General von Treptow lifted the memo to the light, squinted, shook it and looked for a shower of debris. Finding none, he replied to Max, "For nought, it seems. Our good will. Use of our persuasive powers to divert HL from the Brits. Nice to see Pieter trumpets our influence, meager as it is, in truth."

"Too good, too easy, Dietrich," Max replied as von Treptow handed the memo over to his aides.

"*Claro que sí.*" Von Treptow had a catchphrase from every civilized language. "Of course it is, Sir. Question is, why?"

"Either it is a honeytrap or they truly mean it. We need the truth from our friend, Dietrich. Face to face, man to man, look him in the eye. Pieter may well be the only true friend we have in Europe, and beyond, for that matter, but he is not one of us."

"Yes, Excellency, and he needs our word of honour, our bond in return. I have no problem with the response, we certainly agree to bend our will as they request. That is the message; who is to be the messenger?" His and Max's heads swiveled in tandem toward Colonel Knorr.

"London? Again?"

* * *

Saturday, January 26, 1000 hours
Foreign Office, Berlin

Not a particularly small man himself, Tomas Masaryk was towered over by the two stormtroopers ushering him into the inner sanctum. His bushy walrus moustache and full van dyke along with his stiff wing collar and plain dress set him apart from his German counterparts in their uniforms and trim, or no facial hair. He spoke a fluent south German with only a bit of an unidentifiable Slavic or similar accent, in a precise and courtly manner.

He and Prince Max had met several times, von Treptow once, briefly. So, the preliminaries were dispensable at the expense of Colonel Knorr and Captain von Seeckt. Von Kuhlmann had not been invited, nor would he have attached an official benediction to the proceedings by his presence. This was to be the dissection of a dying, wheezing empire, its polyglot composition only exceeded by its nominal predecessor, the original Roman Empire.

"So, General von Treptow, you spoke for my friend Prince Max here? '*Terms acceptable*' was your terse response. Am I to take it the German Empire, Kaiser Wilhelm and all, are consenting to the creation of a new state in Bohemia, Moravia and Slovakia? With its significant German population? Please make yourselves completely clear on this point."

Max stepped in, "Please remember, esteemed friend, we are giving you this new state. You have not yet earned it. Our Sudeten brethren will be accommodated, whether by borders or by reservation of rights within your new constitution. They are, after all, about a quarter of the cadaver before us. Understood?"

Masaryk had no option but to nod his assent.

Max closed, "Well, then, shall we carve?"

By the time Masaryk was to be shipped over to von Kuhlmann for the diplomatic rituals, such as they could be between a Foreign Secretary and a stateless exile, the new Czechoslovakian state had been sketched, if not completely formed. A buffer carved out, twenty to forty kilometers deep, at most, around the business end of the Bohemian dagger pointed at Germany's underbelly, bringing Prague closer to the German Army, but giving the concentration of Germans therein a properly German province of their own. In return, Masaryk got a piece of Carpathia, most of Ruthenia, some additional plots around Bratislava from Hungary. And the draft of a treaty closely binding the new nation to its benefactor, economically and politically, as well as militarily.

As they escorted their guest to the fortified door, von Treptow reminded Masaryk of his obsession with the Czech legion, briefly outlining the 'railroad pirates' scheme. "I will send a message to Gajda immediately, General. That suggestion benefits both, immensely as I reflect upon it. I still fear Austria's reaction, but the enigma is the response of the Poles and Hungarians. All my contacts with their leaders in similar circumstances to mine indicate a great pent-up demand for territory as well as their freedom. I must have his Legion in country posthaste. I cannot be too emphatic." He pounded his fist against his palm. "Besides, radical influences are seeping into Prague and Bratislava from Russia, and Gajda is reliably, no, allow me amend that, rabidly anti-Bolshevik. A raw and ruthless man, but precisely what a fledgling needs guarding its nest."

Alone, the four officers relaxed with a light meal. "Not a bad morning's work, would you say, Gentlemen?" Max was glad to have that business behind him, with satisfaction. "Not everyone can conjure up a new country in Central Europe before luncheon. Do not forget old Bismarck, *'Whoever rules Bohemia holds the key to Europe.'* We shall let Masaryk think he rules Bohemia, but we know otherwise, do we not?"

Captain von Seeckt piped up, "President Wilson will chide you for copying him, Sir. I have been studying our dispatches, Sirs. Perhaps it would serve our purpose to allow him to take credit for this development when it transpires? Ease the pressure from the Foreign Secretary and the Austrians?"

Max inquired slyly, "Studying the American dispatches? Are they not in my Annie's area? Is she helping you?"

"Only with the big...words, Sir."

"What were your courses at university, Captain? Not limited to carousing, it seems?"

"Law, Economics and some Physics, Sir. And Music."

"I see. Continue your analysis, please."

"From my readings, here and back at headquarters, it seems this Wilson fellow is one of those who thinks he is far away the smartest in the room, has a thin skin for criticism, is motivated by rigid political theory and, most importantly, would not hesitate to stoop to stealing an idea or an accomplishment. I could be describing the Bolsheviks, Sirs, or any number of German or British politicians, but this man will be the main figure astride the world. Or so I am told," he smiled. "So, how do we turn what we perceive as his personal weaknesses to our political strengths?"

"Max, I choose my acolytes carefully. Let us think how we can toss the man a bone. Music, Captain? Really?"

"Yes Sir, just an excuse to play some American Negro music on school time."

"Negro music...? Never mind. What else may we glean from your review?"

"Speaking of Negroes, Sirs, President Wilson is apparently quite the bigot. Yet, when a suggestion was made to organize an elite Negro unit in their Expeditionary Force – with white officers, of course – he reversed course. Named them the 'Harlem Hellfighters', trumpeted them about the French countryside. Outstanding regimental band playing their Negro music, jazz, they call it, according to the French newspapers. A small example, Sirs."

Colonel Knorr added, "The Captain is correct on all counts from what I can gather. If we spring a very unexpected surprise, he may well be disposed to reject it as inauthentic, or coerced or the like, and certainly not of his creation. On the other hand, if he thought he were the instigator, no, not just the instigator, but the inspiration for such a development..."

"Offered as a token of good faith by both Austria and Germany, with effusive praise by the Czech and Slovak beneficiaries – our late guest." Max was warming to the idea. "An escrow deposit on the entire Fourteen Points. Von Kuhlmann gets to play in the backchannels. We must watch carefully to ensure he does not bollix up the thing."

Von Seeckt had thought it through rather carefully. "Kept in confidence, or we must manage the timing, Sirs, very carefully. He could not be trusted to keep it under his top hat very long, when he could reap great political advantage and personal acclaim. And, it would have a deleterious effect on our Russian effort – all the Hapsburg nationalities would soon be agitating for the same, thus ending their participation in combat. They would turn the other direction, toward home, the very next day."

"We would needs have the southern flank well in hand. Ukraine has offered us that key, so we may have more flexibility. Very perceptive, Captain. Your fearless leader's deviousness has rubbed off. On both of you." Max looked at Knorr and von Seeckt. "I am glad of it."

"Osmosis, Sir," offered von Seeckt.

"What? Never mind. Dismissed!"

* * *

Saturday, January 26, 9:00 a.m.
Ministry of Munitions, London

Churchill and Lord Elsmere awaited their breakfast guest at the Ministry. "Reggie, are we quite sure this is what we wish to do? Tangible evidence and all that?"

"Sir, if there is one thing of which we may be certain, it is Pieter's judgment. And circumspection, for that matter. What we are to show him will have been purloined by a German agent. That is, if found out, that is the story. His courier, the lovely Alexandra, is German by birth. She holds a Dutch diplomatic passport, but even Mansfield Cumming could see through to her German identity."

Reginald had ever only had one employment in life aside from his present position, and that was the Navy. Accordingly, he had little brief for the intelligence amateurs outside Naval Intelligence, including the new boys at MI Five and Six. "Our fingerprints will not, repeat, not, be on these dispatches. I personally, with Blinker's full backing, will commence a witchhunt within NID should this be exposed, searching for traitors, you see."

"In that event, what would happen to the lovely Alexandra, as you so knowingly call her?"

"We would interrogate her, obviously." Reggie allowed a leer to escape his mask.

"Obviously. Then what?"

"I think we could see through to expulsion."

"Expulsion then, not execution?"

"Possibly."

Churchill was silent, twirling his cigar. "Reggie, it is quite one thing to speak in our detached manner of the deaths of hundreds of thousands of anonymous Russians or Germans. It is quite another to contemplate a young life extinguished for the sake of our machinations. Do not place me in that position."

"I am sorry, Sir, truly sorry. No, I should not have her placed in such jeopardy myself. We, Blinker and I, have some means at our disposal should things go awry. She will not be harmed, you have my word. I have my own word, as she is one alluring thing. Married, with children, you may have forgotten such exhiliaration, and if not, no need to confide. No, she is special. Nought will happen to her, I assure you."

Fortuitously, Pieter van der Hoek was announced and ushered into the office. "Just in time, Reg, old boy, comes our guest of honor. Always a pleasure, Pieter."

Van der Hoek made a show of suspicion at the too-exuberant greeting. "To which of the circles of Hell am I being led this morning? If the eighth, I can accept the company of Ulysses and other frauds. Consistent with my existence here, it would seem. No? The ninth it is, then, the pit of treachery." He pursed his hands together in prayer, looking to the ceiling. "Well, Alighieri, old fellow, it was nice up here while it lasted."

Churchill suppressed a giggle, "Can your friend not accept anything at face value, Reginald? Accept us as the simple, sincere plodders we truly are?"

"You know him right well yourself, Sir. The straight and narrow has never been his path."

"Enough, my friends. What are we having for breakfast? English, I see. Perhaps some Russian tarragon?" He sat at his place, tucked his napkin and attacked the nearest banger. "Affinity in sausages is a clear sign of brotherhood among nations, I always say. These would be held in high esteem at home." He lifted an eyebrow. "As would most German wurst."

"Really, Pieter, this is serious business. But, I grant you we both have an interest in keeping the sausage manufacture away from the unwanted eye, do we not?" Reginald had brought the goods, which he placed on the table, concealed in a canvas bag. "See for yourself, but you might wish to handle it gingerly. Sausage-free, certainly."

He extracted a paper envelope, untied its lacing and pulled out the contents for the Dutchman to peruse. He tapped his left hand with his right, reminding Pieter.

"Yes, of course, Lord Elsmere." He snapped his leather gloves on, then accepted the file. A quick review and it was returned. "I cannot speak to the content, but the form is authentic. Thank you."

"The form is authentic? Authentic?" Reggie was beyond bluster. "Are you telling me you have been reading our Naval dispatches?" Van der Hoek nodded, then brought another slice of sausage to his mouth. "Then why ask us to risk all for these?"

Pieter pointed to his mouth, furiously masticating. He swallowed the unchewed remainder, then gulped some water. "All things in time, my lord." He patted his chest. "Including sausage, always. No, Reg, all I have seen are lower level, harmless messages, and those several years ago, at best. But the form persists, part of the institutional memory. I swear I have seen nothing from Russia."

"Reggie, he is what he is. We cannot change that. Accept him at his word." Churchill was not entirely able to comfort himself. "Sir, we are trusting you to do the right thing. Do not betray us or we traipse down through the circles together."

"Fear not, Gentlemen. Now as to the details of spycraft. Alexandra will acquire these from you tomorrow night at your house, at your cocktail soirée post-Philharmonic. Presuming, that is, you would be willing to detain her after the last guests have departed, hmmm?"

Lord Elsmere arched his eyebrows expectantly. "Must I, old man?"

"Force yourself, you roué. She is scheduled to return home on leave next day. We have coordinated our, her, shipping schedule with our friends in the German Navy. A strictly neutral cargo and passenger manifest. The exchange with German Intelligence will occur in Amsterdam, not The Hague. Too many prying eyes. You shall not know the location. I travel on to the Ministry of Foreign Affairs, routine consultations and the like. A diversion, you see."

"All this rigamarole for one packet?" Churchill was increasingly impatient with the convolutions this subterfuge was assuming. "Why not merely cable the contents?"

"Are you telling me your boffins have not mastered our codes? Thank you, Sir, if that is true, but let us not chance it. I prefer the old fashioned courier approach. With diplomatic immunity, to be sure."

"So be it then. With the risks you impose on your young lady?" Churchill clearly was not yet mollified.

"The transit is a routine matter, Sir. We both are protected against your very own attempted searches and intrusions. Are you suggesting you cannot guarantee Great Britain will observe each and every convention of international behavior regarding the safety and inviolability of diplomatic personnel?" Pieter had used this speech many times before, merely substituting one offending power's name for another. It had always worked, save that one time in Turkey.

Churchill, glowering over his reading glasses, relented, "No high and mighty folderol here, Sir. Not among friends. Yes, damn you, you have made your point. Just be damned careful! Now, off with you, then!"

As the steward rolled the trolley away, Churchill returned to his desk in search of his first, no, second brandy of the day. He leaned back in his chair, swirling, not drinking. "Reggie, does he have anything on you, old man? A question that fairly begs to be asked, you see?"

"Our dossiers on each other are easily the most voluminous of all, save for such as Shaw, Russell, the Bloomsbury set, that sort. No, Winston, he is in far greater danger of my revelations than I may be from anything he might hold against me. He finally got himself married, after all." He gave Churchill a lurid grin and a wink.

"Reciprocal annihilation. Sound and foolhardy at an instant."

Lord Elsmere struck a pose. *"Si vis pacem, para bellum."*

"Our motto from this moment forward, then."

* * *

Saturday, January 26, 1600 Hours
Foreign Office, Berlin

"Sir, I am trebling your household guards from now on." Hartwig caught up with von Treptow outside the Foreign Office along with Bruckmiller.

"Orders from Max?"

"No, Sir, common sense. We hear things, you know. Things that are rather volatile, Sir. We are bringing reinforcements in from the other boroughs. We will need to string up a telephone connection between your front gate and the house and recommend blockading the countryside entrances. Trouble is, Sir, you've got too nice a place. Too big, too much perimeter, too tempting." Hartwig was clearly troubled. "Dozens of references to you by name in every garret meeting, every street corner gathering. Recommend you send the brothers' families away. Don't think they'll follow them to Sonnenberg, your Kirchsee place."

"Can you trust your servants, Sir?" Bruckmiller was similarly on edge. "They are of an impressionable class, Sir, the younger ones may come under some charlatan's spell. The footman, Martin, the landscape brothers, Gerald and Ragnar, the chambermaid, Christine. All seen in questionable quarters, with unsavories. We would not put it past the Communists and others to engage in a spree of aristocratic bloodletting, perhaps a night of a plague of bullets and blades. Would not want your own to aid and abet, Sir."

"Just those, you think? Anything more concrete on them? You know all three lads suffered gas injuries at Ypres and the Somme. One would think them loyal. What if we send them away to guard Rudy's and Willy's? They would not harm them, I am certain. With Christine, she is Charlotte's girl, anyway. You could assist, of course?"

"We could spare a few, not many. Let me see about that," said Hartwig.

"Ernst, come join us. The quarters are not half bad, despite being several hundred years on."

294 James Emerson Loyd

"How's the food, Sir? Wouldn't want to trade potted meats and boiled turnips for just any old fare. You understand, I am sure?"

"Ask our captain here. He seems not to have suffered under Augusta's regime."

"Retract all your false accusations and I might be persuaded to share, Major, Sir."

"Done. I will come out with one of the shifts, as a regular officer. Seems I am getting a little popular, myself. My reputation precedes me, not that I ever discouraged the making of my legend."

"Let us hope you two are being alarmist. Colonel, what is next?"

"Your cinema friend, Wegener. Not until 1900 hours, at Kranzler's. Inspector, Major, a private room, entering from the alley. We are not fools."

Hartwig said, "You should know then, his, his...associate, Lorelei – Major, her last name escapes me? Has she one?"

"Just Miss Lorelei, but we call her Big Tits." Bruckmiller had few opportunities to leer lately.

"Yes, this Lorelei. She is a Red Russian agent, did you know? Been active in the Marxist groups since 1913. It is common knowledge, after all."

"Hard to hide them, Sirs," offered Bruckmiller.

Von Treptow twisted his face, "I now recall meeting them, er, her. At a premiere or two, perhaps. My acquaintance with Wegener amounts to little more, well somewhat more. This complicates matters. I suppose Paul cannot be persuaded to abandon her, Ernst?"

"You'll have to ask him. Might be more than a trifle difficult. Could your colonel or captain here distract her? At the bar, perhaps? She is known to sun herself there."

"There is another possibility, Sir." Hartwig was a bit uncomfortable, loosening his collar with a finger. "She may be a double, perhaps a triple, for that matter. For all we know, that is. Circumstantial evidence points to her as the source of several embarrassing, if not incriminating photographs of not just movement leaders, but some of the more established Socialists. We have received six of these since early 1917. A female voice called in to a different precinct each time, left directions. No followup, no desire to meet, no demand for payment. Nothing."

Von Treptow asked, "The evidence?"

"Several inconclusive lines. The voice. The quality of the photographs. Our camera personnel think several may have been taken from a motion picture, there being certain marks that mean something to them. Finally, smudgy fingerprints and some powder residue. A woman's, we think, but whose?"

"Why cinema films? Could not be taken surreptitiously, could they? So what value, if the subjects knew of the filming? How embarrassing?" Von Seeckt was very curious now, "Miss Lorelei could not be missed?"

"Sadly, not in the pictures. No, three of the photographs, normal, we think, are of men cavorting together. The others of meetings, speeches, that sort."

Knorr pressed Hartwig, "Anyone other than radicals in these photographs, those who would not appreciate being linked to the movements? Police officials, high politicians, clergy? Surely there are many faces? Perhaps the message is in the background, not the main players. That would be consistent with your double agent theory."

"Perhaps," Hartwig replied. "We see the faces of our agents, but only because we know them. No, no other notables. A few staff types in some of the ministries, but they are being watched, if not already dealt with. Otherwise, the images are obscure. It could be a warning to them, but we think not. That is the mystery. Aside from the compromising photographs, nothing we did not already know. And the lovers, well, that is not the least bit unusual behavior in those circles."

"Nonetheless, this scuttles my thought of having Wegener film the festivities at the Tor." Von Treptow let his gaze wander to the disorderly clouds above. "No, cannot take the chance if this Miss Lorelei is on the other side. For that matter, the same for the East. So, no need to buy him a dinner."

"Might still want to do so, Sir. Just a social visit. See if you can find anything about her, and him for that matter. Might bring one of the photos to see what he thinks of their cinematic origin. Check his reactions." Major Bruckmiller saw an opportunity, and another. "Captain, do you have civilian dress here? Go early, sit at the bar. See if you can attract the butterfly."

"I shall take that as a compliment. Yes, we all have business attire, had planned to change regardless. Colonel, have I your express consent to chat up this...suspect?"

Knorr placed his head in his hands, shaking it slowly. "Lord have mercy on fools such as us."

A police detachment escorted the officers to the von Treptow estate. Two layers of police officers in stahlhelms with Mausers greeted them at the main gate. Just beyond the second group was a small tent, a power cord running down from a lightpole. Inside was a telegraph set and a telephone, its line sneaking under the skirt of the tent and on to the house a kilometer away.

Once in the schloss, von Treptow summoned Reittemann to his study and recounted the concerns about threats from both within and without. "I am not rushing to accuse any of them, you understand, but we are in dangerous times, Reittemann. Your thoughts?"

Reittemann cleared his throat. "Among the staff there is always a current of grumbling, some dissatisfaction with something or another, Sir. To me, it is like the soft hissing of one of the radiators – always there, never changing in volume and tone. Just the background noise of a large household, Sir. I am inured to it, I fear. But when there is a spike in the volume, as it were, it is immediately noticeable. There have been such spikes in your absence, I must admit. Not outwardly rebellious or endangering any of the household, Sir, but distinctive in tone. And secrecy. I have my own secret police, such as it, they, are." Von Treptow's expression evinced no surprise at that admission.

"Yes, any Master of the staff has his favorites, his stalwarts and the like. I have many pairs of ears, Sir, upstairs, downstairs, in the stables and fields. More reports than I like, but nothing, again, Sir, hinting of imminent danger. Mostly youthful foolishness, infatuation with a different *Weltanschauung* than prevails within the estate."

Von Treptow scribbled Bruckmiller's four names on a sheet of paper and slid them across his desk. "Yes, all these and," scribbling three more names, passing it back, "these." Pointing at three of the seven names, he said, "Harmless, Sir. Lack of wit and spine. These three" – the two gardeners and one other new name – "could be more serious."

Dietrich balled the sheet and tossed it into the fire. "We expect trouble, major trouble on Monday. You need not know the details, but by midday there will be disturbances in the city. And I am a target of many groups, some harmless, some potentially murderous. Hence the police presence. I do not wish to expose Rudy and his and Willy's to that danger. I shall ask them to spend the next few days in Sonnenberg. A nice Sunday drive tomorrow, do you think?"

Reittemann nodded his assent. "Yes, Sir, I think that is a capital idea. And not necessarily suspicious, it is the childrens' winter break. I would send..."

Von Treptow interrupted, "Why not our conspirators? Would keep them out of trouble in the streets, away from the newspapers and pamphleteers. We would have police units at the ready, nearby – they could quarter in Baumgarten."

"Hmmmm. Risky, Sir? The foxes amidst the fowls? *Wenn der fuchs predigt, so nehmt die gänse in acht?*"

"Who would you add as counterweights? Reliable ones?"

"Gerhard, Emile, the two grooms, just here from the Posen estate – I trust them. Otto and Marie-Therese, and their children, as I think on it. Otto is an ox, and would take any trouble as a threat to his little ones. Christine, Charlotte's maid, and a couple more. Get those featherbrains out of here. One or two more will do. I will have Otto brief the staff at the lake place."

"Excellent. I knew I could count on you. Keep your ears open, reactions to the police presence, you see? And we will be hosting a Police Major here the next few nights. May prompt some more grousing. Is Rudy home yet? I would discuss this with him."

The three officers, now in fashionable civilian attire, returned to the city in the estate's Mercedes-Benz cabrio, a special order made for the three brothers' love of speed. Under the bonnet was a modified racing engine, potent but temperamental. Captain von Seeckt was let out for his early rendezvous in a garage forecourt on a narrow sidestreet four blocks from Unter den Linden. Von Treptow drove on to his townhouse's carriage court, through a seemingly unconnected alleyway, safe from prying eyes. They would walk separately to Kranzler's, to the second service entrance invisible from the street in a pee alley accessed only from another twisting pee alley between two medieval buildings.

Von Treptow knew these meanders from his youthful escapades with Max, Richard and his brothers. The bakers and restaurateurs had given up trying to secure their pastry kitchens from their depredations, having no hope of catching the urchins as they escaped through the warrens.

So, they eased into a storeroom, then through another into the butler's pantry serving the private dining room. They were half an hour early; Roehmer, a preferred, and discreet, waiter served them and reported on the captain's fortunes. "Oh, yes, she is at the bar. When your young giant strolled in, she noticed. Definitely. He first stopped at a table of very attractive young ladies…"

"Shit!" exclaimed Knorr.

"No, Sir, I think he was only framing the scene. They are an attractive group, I must say. Regulars at that time of day. Wealthy, spoiled and beautiful. They perked up at the sight of him, shedding their bored faces, seen-it-all attitudes. He stopped as I said, surveyed the scene then apologized with much hand kissing for taking his leave. *'Later, perhaps?'* Then straight to the bar, confidently, and secure in his mysterious anonymity, I think. Leaned over right next to her, smiled, then turned to the barkeep, ordered his whisky. Smiled again, turned back to scan the dining room. Still silent. Turned back her direction…"

Both officers were leaning forward at his every word. "Get on with it, man. Then what?" Colonel Knorr's foreboding was exasperating.

"She started the conversation. Still going on. I will check on the two lovebirds."

He turned, leaving the two alone. But not for long. Captain von Seeckt poked his head through the butler's pantry door, "Just taking a WC break, Sirs. Must get back to duty." He ducked out, then back in. "Wagers, Sirs?"

"On what?" demanded von Treptow.

"Your prospects for success?" Knorr cringed.

"No, Sirs. Her sex." He vanished.

"What now?" Knorr slunk back into his chair.

Paul Wegener came into the dining room like a normal person. "Hello, Dietrich, old fellow. Have you been ill since we last saw each other? You are looking so thin."

"Just the effects of this war. You, clearly, have not been affected. Where is your assistant, that blonde? Surely, we do not have to stare at you the entire dinner? Oh, yes, Walter Knorr, my associate from Hannover."

"A pleasure, Herr Knorr. I saw her in the bar with some younger fellow. Weaving her web as usual. A handsome lad, just her fancy."

"Will she be joining us, then? Let us hope?"

"I did not realize the invitation extended to her. Let me fetch her and hers, if that is allright?" He started to rise.

"No, no, not yet, Paul. I have a few things to discuss with you before-hand, although we will tell Roehmer here not to let her leave without our knowledge."

"As you wish. Roehmer, my good man, might I have a Manhattan – Canadian, please? Gentlemen, are you well placed?"

"For the moment. Walter?"

"I think I probably need another drink. Whisky, neat."

Roehmer slipped out the door, but not before von Treptow could issue instructions for another update. "Well, Paul, are you making motion pictures these days? Given our sad circumstances here in Berlin?"

"Sad? Here? In Berlin? Dietrich, I never know when you are being ironic or merely attempting humor. No, of course, we are quite untouched by this war. My, Lang's, Murnau's actors simply vanish underground to avoid con-scription, then show up miraculously on the screen. UFA takes very good care of us, although the propaganda mishmashes they demand are most demeaning to an artist such as myself." He leaned back in his chair, waving his long cigarette holder about. "But, they pay well. So, we are good. And you?"

Von Treptow replied, "Soldiery is difficult these days, Paul. Even for generals, and colonels like Knorr, here." Wegener stiffened a bit, as if he had forgotten his friend's occupation in their good-natured reunion. "We have been battered about these last two years to make life here in Berlin tolerable." He set down his snifter and stared at the cinema man.

"General, my apologies. I meant, well, I certainly...what I am trying to say is, yes, certainly, I honor your service, of course...but, well, what have you been doing?"

"As I said, getting battered about on the Western Front. I shall relieve you of your discomfort if you will aid us in resolving a small mystery." He slid two of the police photos over to Wegener. "Could you help us identify these?"

"General, Sir, please. I am not a snitch nor an informant of those dread-ful police fellows. No, I cannot help you." He tried to push the photographs back but von Treptow held them in place.

"Perhaps our recruiting officers could help focus your attention. On patriotic matters. You do understand, do you not?"

Wegener got the message, "Very well, Sir, but I thought we were having a friendly dinner here, not an inquisition."

"Oh, Paul, do not be such a stiff. Of course it is friendly. Here, may I be more specific? The crowd picture, could it have been taken in a motion picture camera? One...what do you call each little picture?"

"A frame. Or a cell. Yes, I believe you are right, Dietrich." Wegener quickly forgot the perceived affront. "Here, these streaks, barely visible? Part of the mechanical process of threading the film forward – tiny abrasions, you see. Here, at this edge, just the slightest hint of a sprocket hole. Whoever provided this photograph must have taken a reel of film and shot just this section, then blew it up to this size – see how poorly the faces and details read? The blurriness is the result of magnifying an already poor resolution. This is interesting, Dietrich. Sir, I mean." He was already back in the fold.

Knorr chimed in, "Would that person have intentionally produced this? With all the hints you so quickly found? That is, was this photograph and others we have been intended as a message, despite the poor content?"

Paul was quiet for a few moments. "The medium, itself, is the message? Announcing that motion picture films of these meetings exist, that there might be more, while not revealing anything at the outset?" He stroked his smooth upper lip, then stroked it again. "Yes, Colonel, you may have hit on the truth. The next question is not who delivered this, but who was the original cinematographer? I can tell you categorically it was not me or my studio."

Both von Treptow and Knorr blurted, "How?"

"We have largely eliminated the source of those little abrasions. New equipment generously supplied by UFA. And the German people, of course!" He knew when to curry some favor. "And that sprocket? We use newer cameras and AGFA films with a smaller sprocket, more numerous, hence smoother in operation. Compare *The Student of Prague*, from 1913 – you were at its premiere, Dietrich – with my work from, let me see, from late 1916 onward. A vast leap in cinematographic quality. So either these are older films or a less sophisticated photographer. I would wager on the latter."

"Why?" pressed Colonel Knorr.

"UFA, again. Why use old technology when the latest thing is delivered to your door, updated regularly? No, someone outside our little preferred circle of cinema men."

Knorr was thinking ahead. "Russians."

"Yes, quite possibly, or their fellows. May I have this photograph to examine with a glass? I promise to return it. There is something about the composition I cannot put a finger on. Something familiar. General von Treptow, Sir, you doubtlessly are aware of my political leanings, my associations?"

Dietrich waved his hand dismissively. "Of course, Paul. We miss nothing." Which was not quite true. He and Intelligence knew of his 'associations' with the Socialists and the near left, but were unaware of others further out on the spectrum. He bluffed. "Paul, everyone is entitled to the mistake of consorting with the Socialists," he paused for a few seconds, "but these Spartacists, Communists and the ilk, surely you have not thrown in with them?"

"I have more sense, financial and political, than to do so. No, I have limited my exploration to Kautsky and his group. Do not look askance at me, Dietrich. His passion to end this war is what draws me there, not his mainstream Marxism, too theoretical and philosophical for me and for most. Of course, within the strictures of my devil's bargain with UFA, I hardly can propound his views on film, you see?"

"Colonel, shall we share?" Knorr nodded, and von Treptow gave a brief overview of his little cadre's efforts at ending the war, hinting at the cinematographic aspect, hoping Wegener would take the bait, and the initiative.

"Dietrich, General, Sir. I am floored! I never, ever thought I should find myself in this position, able to perhaps partake in events, not merely record them. Please, Sir, let me do my part. I could envision a magnificent documentary – no, a whole series of films – the subject of which being the winning of this war! Wait! One moment, please, do you plan to do anything about these Reds, the Bolsheviks? Tell me you do. Kautsky, my current guru, mentor, what have you, despises Lenin and Trotsky as parvenus, heretics, power hungry, I could go on and on. I share his views, completely, having encountered the Bolshevik true believers in my rounds, as it were. They are a mortal threat to all of us, Sir..."

"Stop, Paul. You are prosyletizing the original disciples." Both von Treptow and Knorr were laughing heartily. "That is what we came to discuss with you. These police photographs were just trifles, a favor to our friends. Yes, we have grand plans, first in the East, Russia, then in the West. But this is not something to brag about in salons and saloons, Paul. We must have political reliability, not just in script and plot. Do you understand?"

"Of course. That may take some doing, as I seem to attract the more radical types to my work. Let me consider that."

"While you consider, what about Miss Lorelei? Big Tits, as the police lovingly call her." Knorr was deadly serious. "She is a Russian agent!"

At that moment, before Wegener could respond, Captain von Seeckt chose to bring his conquest into dinner. "Gentlemen," he slurred slightly, "allow me to introduce Miss Lorelei. Is she not quite beautiful and well turned out?" He made a lewd gesture at chest level.

"Paul! Whatever are you doing here, sweetie? And these serious, yet handsome faces?" She was perfectly made up, long eyelashes, blond hair piled atop her head, a nearly sheer netting covering her neck, shoulders and the beginning of her ample cleavage. And the breasts were spectacular, with more than a hint of nipples protruding from her yellow silk dress.

Wegener made the introductions. "Gentlemen, as I was about to say, she is not quite what she seems…"

"Oh, Paul, I hardly need you to add to my air of mystery, do I, dear Erich?"

Von Seeckt was grinning broadly. "No mystery, really." At that, he reached over and grabbed and twisted one of her breasts. She just looked at him and started laughing in a slightly lower register, then adjusted the offended breast.

Knorr was shaking his head, von Treptow making a *'What gives?'* look at Wegener.

"You are a smart boy, I concede you that. How? I have been very successful up until this very moment. Only a few know. Paul, did you expose me? Not that I care in the least, of course."

Wegener shook his head as von Seeckt said, "Three things, Miss Lorelei. Your shoulders are a bit too broad and the joints too substantial. Your knuckles, likewise," holding her exquisitely manicured hands for all to see, pointing, "too large, at the base and the first joint. Finally, your Adam's apple, still a little large for a woman, whatever, your size, cannot be completely hidden."

"He wins the prize! Damn! Where did you learn these observations?"

"My brothers let me tag along when they came into the city for some fun. We were at a cabaret, the old Schilo's, I was fourteen. Rainer, sixteen, my brother's friend, got taken backstage for what he eagerly anticipated would be his first experience. He came running out, buttoning his fly, bolting out the door. Ever after, we made it a point to study the transvestite talent before moving on to more conventional outlets. Poor Rainer, I am not sure he ever recovered. Last I heard he was a homo artist somewhere in Austria."

Knorr and von Treptow were still dumbfounded. "Please, you silly men. Have you never heard of a transvestite? Homosexuals? Thick as thieves here in gay Berlin. Do you get about at all?" Miss Lorelei looked at them, "Of course not. Would do you some good, I should think."

She turned to von Seeckt. "You have omitted one thing, my dear. Or did you not deduce it?"

"I did not wish to be indelicate, Miss, Sir, whichever. If performed some years past puberty, I was told, those masculine features would not entirely fade away."

"Paul, did you find this one? Are you a physician, sweetie?"

"No, Ma'm, er, Sir, just a soldier."

"A soldier? Now, that is a delicious prospect."

Von Seeckt shrunk away involuntarily.

"Please, what in the hell are we speaking of here?" demanded von Treptow.

"*Sono uno degli castrati, caro mio. É un tradizione molto onorevole.*"

For once, von Treptow regretted his familiarity with languages, instinctively covering his crotch. Knorr looked at his superior, then reading his body language, "No!"

"Yes, but of course, dearie. Just a logical extension of my basic nature. It was a leap of, well, certainly not faith, but it has paid off handsomely. I am the former Loren Reifenstahl, once destined for a mediocre career, a chubby wife and three or four snotty children in some dismal provincial town. But I recognized I was different, and through the taunting and the bullying stuck with my inner core, came here, saw an opportunity and seized it. In a manner of speaking, of course. Oh, I see you brought my photographs. I was wondering if those police dunces would ever wise up."

She flipped over the crowd picture and picked up the intimate view. "Do you recognize these two?" she asked the officers, who were not eager to look too closely. "No, of course not. That one, receiving, is yours truly. That one, giving, is one Boris Krulov, also known as Herr Doctor Theobald Dittmar, the Communist theoretician. Sufficiently compromising, do you think? Especially as he has a wife here. And one in Russia, but she is a revolutionary, so approves as a doctrinal matter."

Knorr begged, "May we return to the crowd picture? Quickly, please?"

"Soldiers, you say, Paul? So squeamish? Yes, now the crowd. This is a Bolshevist meeting from last spring. I made it from an outtake from Orlov, Eisenstein's man, who filmed the affair. Clumsily, I might add. I made the print just clear enough to show the Police informer's face, but not so well for the others. Did your police friends make that connection?"

"Yes, they did. Three police types, if you must know," Von Treptow replied, then continued, "and why this meeting? Those other faces?"

"For me to know and you to find out. Three, you say? Hmmm. Better than I thought."

Roehmer and a squad of waiters brought in trays of dinner. "Your little party was so engrossed, General, I took the liberty of bringing your favorite dishes. For each of you, although the new fellows will have to settle for the general's fare. Enjoy!"

"So, I understand you are friendly with the Reds, my dear? Lorelei or Loren, which?" The general was trying to be polite, yet casual; Wegener dragged a palm down his face and nose.

"Paul?"

"Nothing, my dear. I said nothing."

She looked long and hard at von Treptow. "Yes, I suppose I did let that bit about the meeting slip. Actually, I intended it, of course. So you would ask me that very question. And it shall be Miss Lorelei to you, Sir."

"So, you are friendly with that crowd. Out of conviction or perhaps another motivation?"

"Cigarette, please." Von Seeckt beat Dietrich to it, lighting it for her. "Damn, Paul, are all your friends so direct? I do appreciate a take charge type, but, well, you get the idea. Let me just say that Paul and I share certain political views. There is more to me than that, Sir, but there are still things mere generals were not meant to know."

Von Treptow tried to shake several thoughts out of his head. "I see. We have been intrusive enough. And Roehmer presents the bill. I detect no hands reaching out to grasp it, so it befalls my lot once again. Paul, Miss Lorelei, we have much to discuss. Could you come to my place in Treptow tomorrow afternoon? Safer, more discreet."

Wegener nodded, then elbowed Miss Lorelei. "Yes, I suppose so."

"One last question, for both of you. Surely the world assumes you are, were his mistress," looking first at Miss Lorelei, then Paul. "How do you keep up the masquerade so effectively?"

"Have you met my wife, Lyda Salmonova? Do not bother counting, General, she is my third. If so, or when, you will understand. Unlike my colleague here, I have no desire to sing soprano."

* * *

Saturday, January 26, 2300 Hours
Schloss Treptow

By the time they drove up to the gate, passed through the security and made it to the house, Major Bruckmiller was finishing up his second light supper. "Am I glad to see you fellows! I am lost and forced to eat to maintain my stamina in search of my bedquarters."

"Always a pleasure, Major. Before we retire, Gentlemen, let me address the matter of firepower, heaven forfend it should come to its use. Please follow me." General von Treptow descended a staircase, then strolled in his gait down a long corridor, eventually coming to the rough round walls of the keep. "A suitable place for an armory, do you not think?" He drew a pair of keys from an inconspicuous niche in some elaborate metalworking and opened the thick oak and wrought iron door. Passing through heavy stone-work walls and arches, he opened another door, this time solid steel plate. Inside was a gunner's paradise, Mannlichers with custom scopes, Purdeys and Hollands of every gauge and type, even two elephant guns, explaining the paucity of pachyderms in Brandenburg.

"Here we are." Von Treptow cleared some shell boxes off a wooden crate marked '*Samuel Colt, London, UK*' and '*Model 1911*'. Opening the box, he took out a handgun wrapped in oiled tissue and presented it to Colonel Knorr. "One of the Oerlikon salesmen persuaded me to buy this case, eager to make use of their new agency for the Colt factory. In American parlance, it is a 'forty-five calibre', about eleven and a half millimeters to us. So, heftier than a Luger. Nearly twice the grains, much greater stopping power in close quarters, if you get my drift." He gave two pistols to each and a pair of cartridge boxes. "We shall try them out tomorrow at the range. And choose a shotgun, as well."

Von Seeckt thought, *The range?*

Returning to the main floor, they were met by Reittimann. "Sir, it seems we have a visitor at the gate. The guards are requesting guidance. They are on the telephone in your study." Von Treptow gave the others a quizzical look, shrugged his shoulders and followed his butler up the grand stair.

Inside, he took the receiver. "Yes, von Treptow here. Who is it? A woman? Her name? No?" He motioned Reittemann out. "What is she wearing? Yes, I will wait." Two minutes passed. "I see. Ask her if she will open the fur for inspection." Two more minutes. "No? I thought not. Let her enter, and lead her in your car, please. She may not remember the way."

He rang Augusta. "Frau Augusta, I am sorry to trouble you at this hour, but we have a refugee from the city. Female. No, you need not speculate. You will see her soon enough. Please prepare the suite adjacent to mine for feminine occupancy. Thank you, Augusta."

Stepping out into the concourse, he motioned Reitimann over. "Break out the troops. Our visitor's car will need garaging and I predict no shortage of luggage to be toted upstairs." He shook his head.

Reittimann whispered, "Is it her, Sir?"

"Yes, old friend, it is. Prepare to have your life upended."

Princess Claire of Baden entered to the astonishment of the staff, astonished they were by her familiarity with their General and with Augusta and Reittimann. Seems in the old days, there were few secrets kept from the trusted retainers. She greeted each of the other eight assembled servants with a compliment, a smile, or a kind word.

One chambermaid whispered, "By Our Lady, has the master gotten married?"

"Oh, no, dear. Do not worry about your general here. He is impervious to my charms. No, just a few days relief from the big city, fresh air, all that. Is that not right, General?"

Von Treptow had long since passed his astonishment at anything Claire would say or do or think. He approached her, gave and got cheek pecks, then asked, "Claire, that coat looks so terribly heavy. Shall we take it?"

She smiled that dangerous smile of hers. "No, dear, I am still chilled. Perhaps in front of the fire in your study. A brandy, perhaps, to warm me?"

"Reittimann, will you please do the honours? The rest of you may go about your duties. You will see more than enough of her the next few days."

* * *

Sunday, January 27, 0930 hours
Schloss Treptow

Augusta and Reittimann had gotten the other families away earlier in the morning, the wives and children happy to leave the cold stone pile for the bright skies and skating at the lake. Rudy, as usual, was oblivious to all but his work and had been driven to the University early as was his custom. So it was just the four officers at breakfast in the small parlor off the main kitchen, warmed by the ovens within.

"So, Colonel, any news from Hannover?" The new additions to Walter's household had not been forgotten, but were not at the forefront, either.

"Yes, two messages. One from Wolfie. Holland did not work out so well. She is not disposed to relocate, which is fine. She and Yvette and the children will keep my staff on their toes, a good thing." He was still reading the telegram for the first time when his eyebrows arched in surprise. "Wolfie spoke to a contact at Union Bank in Zurich, who called in Baring's man. Barings contacted their Willem fellow in London. Turns out she has on deposit in London three millions in English pounds, Dutch Guilders, bonds and gold."

"Three millions what?" asked von Seeckt. "Marks?"

Reading on, "Yes. Marks, the equivalent. No, more? Damn!"

"Damn!" said von Seeckt.

"She is too old for you, Captain, and her daughter too young, that much has been established." Von Treptow stubbed out a cigarette. "Good for her. Takes a bit of a weight off your shoulders, Walter."

"Yes. I suppose it does, in that regard. If she could access the money, she could set up in Lille with her uncle…"

"No, Colonel. Never. I cannot see clear to place her in a war zone ever again. That is the least we can do. The risks are too great, especially knowing Ludendorff's schemes as we do."

"I agree, Sir. Alone with that Jew family? I shudder." Major Bruckmiller was right.

Von Seeckt settled matters, "Your generosity has created a new world for the children. They need, deserve some stability, Sir."

"I see your…" Knorr turned his head to see what the other three were looking at.

Claire had slipped in to breakfast, dressed in a riding outfit. "Good morning, Gentlemen! Yes, I was listening. Talking about that beautiful Belgian girl? Did she recover fully from her fright? Please sit down, all of you. Who is this fellow? Have we met before?"

Major Bruckmiller beamed, "Yes, Miss, er, Princess. We were never properly introduced at the Clarion that night a few years ago, but your identity was made clear to all of us on the force."

"Oh, dear. My past catches up with me. Here," holding out her wrists, "place the manacles, lead me away to gaol. I was a bad girl, Dietrich, if you can believe such."

"I can believe anything about you, Princess. Anything. Major, allow me a surmise. She was the epicenter of some disturbance at a fashionable night-spot?" Bruckmiller nodded. "With artistic types abounding?" Another nod. "Intoxication?"

"At a minimum, General, Sir. Our chemists were kept busy for a week, finally had some Farben fellows help us. Cannot divulge the results, Sir."

"Thank you, Major. Claire, please join us, now that you already have." He rang for Augusta. "Another place if you would, please. Coffee, my dear? Sleep well, did we?"

"We did, did we not, once we got to sleep?" Claire's expression was impishly dimpled.

Von Treptow flushed slightly, then held his head in hands. "Any other personal matters to reveal to my guests?"

"Well, yes, dear, of course..."

Knorr interrupted with a clearing of his throat, "Madame, Princess, I have a message from that beautiful Belgian girl. Would you not prefer to hear its contents rather than further embarrass our host?"

"Oh, yes, please. I can embarrass him any time. Pray read on!"

"Very well." He started reading the letter silently to himself, then aloud, "They are all well. Yvette is taking lessons from Wolfie's and Constance's tutor – it had not occurred to me that she had lacked proper education these past few years..."

"Yvette? That is her name? I thought..."

"Her child. Fourteen. They were...in bondage for several years. She is beautiful, herself, Claire. Competition." Von Treptow sought small victories.

"Please, you two. Yes, she is quite bright, they hope to catch her up by next fall. Arnhem, Amsterdam do not seem to work, we heard that already. Maria and her friends Theresa and Mona are helping, as is Constance. She is still reluctant to engage in larger company. But as long as her children are secure she will manage. Hmmm. She and Frau Elsie – my housekeeper, Your Highness – have become fast friends. You see, there was a *contretemps* over my late wife's clothing, allow me leave it at that. Elsie helped smooth that over."

"She will be difficult to dislodge, Sir," said von Seeckt.

"He is on point, Walter." Von Treptow looked at Claire.

"Are you hinting that I have nothing to fear from her? That her attentions are directed to another? That you are all mine, dearest?" She slipped her free hand into the crook of his arm. "Is it not a beautiful day, Gentlemen?"

* * *

Sunday, January 27, 1500 hours
The Treptow Meadow

The men were finishing their shooting exercises, getting comfortable with the heavier handguns when Claire came riding up on one of the estate's mares. Martin, the suspect footman, took the chestnut's reins as Claire dismounted. Von Treptow wanted the lad to be fully aware of the firepower and skill in the house.

"Dears, what on earth are you doing?" She approached von Treptow, gave him a lingering hug, then turned to look downrange. "Were you trying to hit those targets? Then why did you miss them? May I?"

She took von Seeckt's Colt, and as he showed her how to chamber a round, press the safety and the like, she kept up her badinage. "Major of the Police, let me guess. You use one of those little snubnosed gangster revolvers, do you not?"

Bruckmiller nodded, "In close quarters, yes, Madame, Princess, Ma'm."

"It shows." She had to hold the big gun with both hands, bracing her legs, but managed to put all nine rounds on the target, four respectably. Bruckmiller had but two in the rings. "A nice toy, Dee. May I have one?"

"Perhaps at Christmastide, Claire. I shall place it, and you, at the top of my list."

"See that you do, dear. If you know what is good for you."

"Well, then, Gentlemen, we know when we have been bested. In every aspect of life. Back to the house, then, our afternoon guests should be here soon."

"Guests? Are we having tea, dearest?"

"No, it is a matter of business, not concerning you I must say. We should not be long, I would think. Did you bring something to read or otherwise entertain yourself?"

"But, Dietrich, you are my entertainment. My sole entertainment. Can these guests – I am sure they are frumps – can they be stalled a few hours?"

"Enough, Princess. My authority crumbles each time you open your mouth. No, it is important business of a rather sensitive nature. I should very much appreciate your permission to conduct my affairs as I see fit."

"You said the magic word, Dee."

"Word? What word?"

"Affairs," she cooed.

Wegener and two others were announced by the police guard and motored up to the entry. One of the chauffeurs took their car away as von Treptow met them at the door. Once inside and out of the weather, Paul introduced his companions, "Matthias Groening, my best camera operator, particular adept at exterior shots. He is really the cinematographer, not me. And you met my other friend last night."

The other friend was an unassuming, nondescript, mid-sized, middle-aged man, clerkish, except for his stubble free, unusually smooth cheeks. Before either could reach the other to shake hands, that familiar voice came lilting down from the top of the grand stair. "Paul, dearest! What a surprise! Dietrich never tells me who is coming to visit, sadly. Shame, shame, Dietrich! And Herr Groening, hello to you!" Looking past the small crowd to von Treptow, "Dee, have you met Loren Reifenstahl? He is the most interesting man in all Berlin. Loren, dearest, did I get that right? Are you a still a man? How shall I refer to you?"

"Person will do, Claire. We met his group last night. Had a most interesting visit. How do you do, General?" Reifenstahl looked around. "Where is that gorgeous giant? I could think of nothing else last night."

Knorr and von Seeckt had been approaching the gathering from beyond the staircase. Hearing this last, Erich did an aboutface and hid behind the stair.

Von Treptow, able to look over the heads of the group, covered for his aide. "I sent him into the city this morning. Have no idea what trouble he has gotten himself into, but trouble always seems to find him." He made a quick 'NO' sign to Claire, who winked back.

"Pity. With this war, the truly outstanding specimens seem to be mouldering away somewhere in France."

Von Treptow looked down at Loren's face with its smug grin and restrained himself, just. "Mouldering away to allow you your libertine ways. Why have you not volunteered to serve, Sir, Miss, whoever you are? No shortage of lusty young men in the trenches. Is that not attraction enough? No, you would much rather prance about in the cabarets, sucking cocks? Is that your idea of service?"

The group, even Claire, was shocked into silence at his outburst, but Loren was calm, brightening as Major Bruckmiller came from the adjacent study, a concerned look on his face. "Ah, General, Sir, I have something important..." He stopped, looked at a beaming Reifenstahl and stuttered, "Paragon? What are you doing here? What gives, General?"

"You tell me, Ernst. What gives here?"

Bruckmiller continued his stammering, "I…I…well, I cannot…"

"Oh, stop it, Inspector. Are you not amongst friends here? Out of place to be sure, but you are here. Let me spare you the misery. No, General, he and I have not coupled, at least not how you think. Paragon is my *nom de déception,* General. Ernst was my chief contact in the Metropolitan Police before he went to war. I am a snitch, a stool pigeon, a cheat, an informer. My speciality is the political left. You saw the photograph last night. I had doctored it to blur my features so my friend here would not have a shit fit. I am proud to say most, if not all the intelligence the Police have on the far left is my product. That is worth anything, I might add. You may imagine how I obtain it or you may not," looking at the other's pained expression, "but I come by it honestly."

Von Treptow turned back to the Police Major. "So, you two have met. Bosom friends, it appears. Yes, yes, of course, bosom friends. Ernst, I present you Miss Lorelei. Big Tits, you call her?"

As Bruckmiller staggered back to a chair, Loren started in on him in mock high dudgeon mode. "Big Tits? That is the respect you pay me? For all the valuables I have procured for your sad, incompetent excuse of a police force? Yes, procured! I pimp for you and Hartwig, and what do I get?" He was convulsed with laughter at his own words, as always, the cleverest person in the room. "You, you…" Reifenstahl was now giggling like his alter ego.

He paused, catching his breath. "Well, at least the costumes seem to have worked. Ernst, are they too big? Should I cut them back? I should hate to call attention to myself."

As the entire group erupted in lusty laughter, Bruckmiller attempted a comeback, "No, no, they are your signature. You might dim the headlights, though."

"And let the *dummkopfs* miss the point? The points, that is?"

"No, no, of course not. Carry on, Miss."

"If you two are over your infatuation, we did ask Paul here to discuss an assignment. May we regain our composure? Is that too much to ask?" Von Treptow was amused, now past his irritation. "Please, Gentlemen, Person, this way." He led the group to the rare books library, the middle of three such rooms in the house. As he entered, Major Bruckmiller caught his sleeve. "Sir, one matter of great importance. May we speak privately?"

They retreated to an anteroom across the hall, closing the door. "Yes, Major? Surely nothing to do with your girlfriend?"

"No, Sir, but I must confess to a great shock. And realization of having been duped, completely and totally. But, on the bright side, if he, or she, could fool us, think of the darkness shrouding our targets. So on balance, not such a bad day?"

"I am so very pleased you do not feel permanently emasculated. What is this matter of such urgency?"

"Telephone, Sir. Your lady friend, Her Grace, has been making a number of calls to the city. We rerouted your connection through ours, of course, and we can identify the destinations. It takes a while to crosscheck but more than half her calls have been to, shall we say, persons of interest? The balance to her brother, friends of no known radical connections, the like, but I am concerned she could bleed some sensitive information to the outside."

"What steps do you recommend? Shut down the connection? Render the estate *incommunicado*? How would we manage?"

"I would not recommend cutting the outside connection. Were we to do so, she would immediately be suspicious if she is engaged in some, ummm, activity. We do have the ability to listen in on any conversation and obtain a stenographic record. On the other hand, merely recording her conversation allows her information to reach others."

Von Treptow sensed the risk and demanded a solution, "Again, Major, what do you recommend? This is not an area of my expertise."

"Limit her access to the telephone, obviously, by suggestion or failing that, disabling her set and other easily accessible sets."

"By suggestion? You do not know the woman. Too obvious, as well. Can your man degrade the connection, selectively? When a suspicious call is made?"

"Yes, Sir, that was my alternative. We can introduce a crackling noise – static electricity sound, the Telekom people call it, makes the call unintelligible. You can tell her the outside lines are at fault, ice or wind, tree limbs, something. You will have to tell her that story, Sir, just plead ignorance."

"That seems to come easier to me with each passing day, Major. But you bring up another difficulty. Tomorrow. If she attempts to go to the city to the festivities. She could meet her contacts directly or get caught up in the action."

"We have already thought of that, Sir." The major had indeed. "Her car will be incapacitated, most untimely it seems. My chief mechanic and yours will be able to fix it by late afternoon, not before."

Von Treptow smiled. "Excellent. Return to our meeting, then?"

Back with the cinema types, General von Treptow laid out his long term plan. "Paul, we will provide all the transport, logistics and the like. My main concern is the earliest dissemination of the films and photographs to the newsmen, whoever can present them to the world. Speed is of the essence, ideally within a day of the event if that is possible."

"Processing can be tricky, sir. Cannot just set up a tent and create a masterpiece. Editing, titles, the like, you see. Kiev and Minsk should not be a problem, I had contacts there at one time, with facilities. Tallinn, Helsingfors, the others, cannot say the same. We will just have to get there and see."

"Paul, we can use the wireless photograph transmission. Would need the *Zeitung* boys to come with us, bring one of their Belinos. I do not understand it, they do. But the quality? Hmmmm." Groening was thinking through his options. "We know the story, do we not? The outcomes, I mean? We could prepare the titles in advance before we leave, then match to the film as it is made. '*Premier so-and-so embraces our General such-and-such here*' and so forth. Can we count on express trains back to Berlin?"

Wegener was considering his cameraman's ideas when Reifenstahl interrupted, "Make believe. Just like me. Make believe, a…a confection!"

"A concoction, you mean." Wegener continued, "Loren and Matty may be on to something, General. We can lay out the standard UFA newsreel format, then splice in our new footage. I know we have some stock footage of Warsaw, perhaps Kiev. We can ask around for others. I cannot think of another way to accelerate matters, but…"

"Splicing would do it, Paul." Groening had thought it through. "Yes, that is the way to do it. General, you are not seeking anything new other than the signing ceremony, the toasts, that sort?"

"We will want to document our progress across the countryside, Gentlemen." It was Knorr's idea after all. "But, once you have seen a Polish country scene, you have seen them all, no? Do you have artists who can draw maps, maps that show our progress across the East?"

"Not only that, we can animate them. A cartoon showing a wave of our brave soldiers marching against the Reds. We can do that in a week, no?" Groening nodded. "Give us the plan, Sirs. We can be ready in ten days."

Von Treptow brought the group back to a more serious tone. "What I am about to show you is of the utmost secrecy." He took out a paper from his jacket, unfolding it, the same edition of the little map he had marked up with Churchill. He noted dates for each capital, then a series of lines or waves indicating the German advance. "If this scheme or the information here escapes our tight little circle, I shall have each and every one of you executed. I am deadly serious. If you choose to withdraw, now is the time. Otherwise, you may join us in making history. The choice is yours.

"Oh, yes. One more thing. Stay away from the Spartacist demonstration tomorrow. That is an order."

* * *

Sunday, January 27, 1900 hours
American Expeditionary Force Headquarters, Chaumont

The weather having turned cool and dry, Colonel Emerson decided to walk the half a mile or so from his billet to main AEF Headquarters. At the sound of hoofbeats from behind, he turned to see Robert McCormick riding his way. McCormick stopped and leaned over to shake hands. "Mind if we trot along? Want to ride up top, here?"

"No, walking will do. How was Paris?" Emerson took the bridle in his hand as he walked alongside McCormick's big roan gelding, brought over from his stable. Looking the tall horse in the eye, "And, you, Buster? How is life among the *chevaux*?"

"He has it made. Too bad he isn't interested in the mares. Some of the French lads brought their own, some beautiful horseflesh. Oh, well, big boy," patting the speckled neck, "saves you the heartache of parting."

"If we ever do part this place."

"Bobby, that's no way to talk. Home by Labor Day, if not before. You can ride down Michigan with me in the victory parade. Maybe even Fourth of July – five months is all, should be wrapped up over here by then. That's what I promised the readers."

"Even you know better, Bertie. Blinded by your optimism, as usual."

"You have me pegged, Emerson. No, my disenchantment grows daily. Paris, you asked? Three days listening to chubby-cheeked French generals telling us – US, Bobby – where and how we are to fight in their defense. Considerably less precise in their hows. And, I am beginning to suspect, their whethers."

"Really?"

"Really. Something is wrong. These are the bravest soldiers – well, maybe add the Tommies – the bravest in Europe, they have withstood the Huns for over three years, thrown back time after time. But, you wouldn't think that from listening to their generals. Almost like they would stand pat, as long as it takes for the Germans to decide to play elsewhere. Not even a word about Lorraine or Alsace, much less Lille and Picardy. Just sit tight. At least until we are upwards of two million, by their calculation."

"Let me guess. Feed us into the meatgrinder first?"

"Something like that. Or just hang around rotting in the trenches. How long? Well past Independence Day, that is certain. Between you and me, Bob, I am thoroughly disillusioned. Three months here and I am ready to pack up and leave this bloody mess to those who caused it. '*Avoid entangling alliances*', Washington's words, or close enough. This war is old Europe's problem, not ours."

"Be careful what you wish for, Bertie. A new Europe might be a lot more dangerous than even this old one."

"Food for thought, Colonel, Sir. Speaking of food, I hear we're having steak tonight. May not be Kansas City, but at least I can see what I'm eating."

Finley greeted them at General Pershing's dining room, saluting then shaking hands vigorously. "Glad to see you back, Mister Bobby, and you, too, Mister Bert. Get you your usuals?"

"Yes, thank you, Finley. It is not as if I disappeared from the Army. Just a few days off," said Emerson as he took his whiskey.

"It's war, Sir. If I sees you, you're alive. You takes too many risks for this old man." Finley was not an old man, maybe mid, late fifties, still lithe and muscular. His father was a freedman in Kentucky at the end of the Civil War and became one of the first Pullman porters. When his son left school, he pulled some strings to get him one of the coveted jobs, but James only stuck with it for a couple of years, '*tired of babysitting white folks,*' he once told Emerson.

He enlisted in the Army, becoming a Buffalo Soldier in the Tenth Cavalry, serving ultimately as a sergeant all across the West in the Indian Wars. In 1892, with then Lieutenant Pershing out of Fort Assinniboine in Montana, he took an arrow, then a bullet in a skirmish with the Cree, remaining mounted long enough to dispatch three more warriors before collapsing. He recovered, but not well enough for immediate combat duty. Lieutenant Pershing thought sufficiently of him to keep him on as his valet, through his days at Nebraska, then again in the Army, now as his steward.

He got to be a soldier again in Cuba in 1898, the Phillipines in 1901, and in the chase into Mexico after Pancho Villa, with stops in Tokyo and Paris in between. He was fiercely loyal to his General, protective, even, and extended his care to his Mexican expedition mates. "General will be along shortly. Mister Georgie is coming, too. Just the four of you; got some nice steaks for a change. Made a little trade with one of the Frenchies. Don't say nothing about that, now. Oh, don't forget this is the 27th. He may be a little quiet tonight." He winked conspiratorily just as General Pershing strode in.

"At ease, Gentlemen. Welcome back to the both of you, not that you deserved such cushy assignments. We may need to sharpen you up in the trenches." McCormick and Emerson just smiled at the general's casual humor. "But, maybe, just maybe we can put you to some use around here."

"So, George is joining us, Sir? I stand on my offer to write a recommendation for his promotion. He has taken on authority well above his rank," said Emerson.

Just then, Major Patton rushed in, breathless. "Sorry, Sir, my machine broke down, with not a horse in sight. Had to hoof it here myself. Those Renault tanks look pretty good, but we are having the dickens of a time keeping them running."

"Hello, Bandido," said Pershing. "We figured you had gotten yourself in another fight with one of our allies." Patton's flawless French extended throughout the entire range of expletives and insults, particularly those relating to distaff heritage of which he was the undisputed master.

"No, Sir, for once I have a legitimate excuse. Finley, I am dry to the bone. Some of their bottled water in the house tonight? Then my Scotch."

"First things first, then. Finley, aside from his hydraulic needs, are we ready for dinner?"

Finley had traded a case of Kentucky Bourbon to a French counterpart for several pounds of Charolais beef and five cases of red wines. The foursome appreciated his resourcefulness, to be sure.

General Pershing was a little quiet, as Finley had predicted. It had not been so long since that 27th of August back in 1915 for him to relegate the date to an annual memory. His wife and three of their four children had perished in a fire at quarters in the Presidio when he was off on duty in the Southwest. Only Finley's quick action had saved Pershing's son Warren. It changed him fundamentally despite his stoic manner, according to Finley and others who knew him before Colonel Emerson, Major McCormick and then Captain Patton joined him in New Mexico and Texas in 1916. These three were now his family along with the other million men of the AEF, but none closer than these, and Finley, of course.

Midway through dinner, he started to come around. Looking at Patton, "So, Major, is General Garrand more forthcoming since I sent him that letter?" The French were keeping their new tanks pretty close to their vests, particularly after Patton literally drove circles around one of their training units then burnt out an engine pursuing a cavalry squadron at maximum speed.

"Some, Sir. He realizes he has to play ball with us. I try my best not to show them up, Sir."

"I am sure you do, I am sure you do." The table was engulfed in laughter. "But enough of you, thankfully. Major McCormick, a briefing on your Paris stay, please."

"More of the same, Sir. They want us posted hither and yon, filling in their gaps, providing stuffing to their ranks. Why, General? It is the simplest of questions. Are they so depleted, or is it a case of presenting fresh troops to the enemy? Your brigadiers are positively chafing at the thought of being seconded to Foch and Pètain, losing their operational control."

McCormick took a drag on his cigarette. "Sir, you tasked me to divine the essence, the real truth behind Foch's posturing and lecturing. Here it is, as far as I can tell, we are the junior partner, to be sure, in numbers, training and experience, but also their saviours. It's their nervousness, their body movements, facial expressions, Sir. Every time we question a deployment, a trench position, anything, they go goofy on us. Our officers press, theirs dissemble. Why, we say? They reply, it must be so. That's just not the American way, Sir. Something is wrong, not just militarily..."

Emerson interrupted, "General, Bertie and I started to discuss this very matter on the way over. My London expedition uncovered the key, Sir."

Pershing and the two officers looked at him expectantly. "Well, Colonel, that is why I sent you there at such expense. The key, of course. What is it?"

"Mutiny, Sir."

"Mutiny? If it were mutiny, the roads would have been lined with the crucified!" Patton was his usual restrained self. "We have not heard of any such mutiny." He paused, reflecting, as were the others. "But, you know, it seems to me there is an acceptance of the status quo, a comfort, as I reflect on it, born of an expectation of not having to expose oneself further. We have seen that before, Gentlemen. Blessed is the man who expects nothing for he shall not be disappointed."

"Beatitudes notwithstanding, George, the French are about to be sorely disappointed and us along with them if we do not play our cards right. Because it is not nothing they should be expecting, but in fact the furies of Hell about to descend upon them."

"Bobby, get to the damned point." Pershing's patience was not infinite. "What did this Churchill fellow have to say? It was your idea to contact him. I hope he was forthcoming."

"Well beyond my expectations, Sir. Only these three things, Sir. One, the French are covering up the Nivelles mutinies of this past July; two, they are, as George said, secure in their defensive posture, unwilling to retake the offensive, a direct consequence of those mutinies; and three, when the Germans do attack, as we are sure they will, the Brits hope, pray, cross their hearts and fingers that Fritz will fall upon the French. That would obviously mean against us. And we are not ready, Sir."

"No, we are not. That much is certain. When and where?"

"Churchill and his aide, Lord Elsmere – Naval Intelligence – expect the next blow by the end of March. Very, very high confidence in that timing."

Pershing interjected, "Way too soon. We will be nowhere close to full strength."

"Yes, Sir, exactly, which explains the timing. Plus, what we feared is fact: Germany's campaigns in Russia will be drawing to a close, freeing up their extra million or so. They, Churchill and Lord Elsmere, that is, confided the mutiny information and confirmed the standoff between Lloyd George and Haig over the Home reserves and for that matter, renewed offensives. I had Mitch confirm with his sources. Put those all together with George's and Bertie's insights from the field and we are well into the briar patch, it seems."

"Conclusions, recommendations?"

"Before mine, let me me present his." He reached into his jacket, retrieving Churchill's unsigned, though hardly anonymous, letter. Handing it to General Pershing, he said, "This is a sensitive document, Sir. Not just in the nature of its contents – you will each see that as a truth – but in the offer contained therein. Once read, the reader is tainted." He sat back to allow the general time to read and reflect.

"He is bold, Bobby." He handed the letter over to McCormick and Patton to read together.

"More like desperate, I would say, General. Sufficiently desperate to jettison their ally to save their own skins. Leaving the weakest to the pack of wolves to assure their escape."

"Not exactly chivalrous," intoned Patton.

"Apropos to this miserable excuse for a war," rejoined Bertie.

"But sound, I give him that. Tactically, strategically sound. I like it. I always have, but the politicians…" Black Jack was fully engaged, the 27th long forgotten, thankfully. "We, I, can deploy the next ten divisions to the north if I choose. That is within my discretion, free of interference from House and Lansing. Rawlinson and the Australians have already each requested a division. We will have staff game that scenario this week. Did you assure your new friend that I might even enjoy the political fireworks?"

"I hinted as much, General."

"Excellent."

Finley cleared away the scanty remains of the beef and served coffee. McCormick still had Churchill's letter in front of him. "Bobby, what about this Bolshevik business? Seems your Briton is more afraid of them than the Germans."

"They, these Bolsheviks, are the devils Churchill and his Lord Elsmere fellow don't know, at least not as well as the devils they do know, the Krauts. The latter, they know what that war is like. The former, a huge question mark. They do know that Russia under these Reds is no longer an ally. The old Tsarist army is crumbling, allows the Germans to come west. I think much of it is a class thing, Sir. Their upper class would suffer, even be destroyed if events mirrored those in Russia."

"So, what do they want of us? We cannot send men to bolster the Russians, that is clear. Even if we wanted to. I don't understand their position." McCormick fiddled with the letter until Patton slapped it down on the table.

"More a matter of education. Bertie, you're coming back to London with me tomorrow. Churchill makes a big speech next day. Permission, General?"

"Yes, why not? Finance officers are already harassing Wilkins over your trip," said Pershing. "But to what end?"

"Again, Sir, just education. These Russian Reds are the most radical, ruthless form of Socialists according to our newfound friends, yet we and America know little of them. The upheaval in Russia is only a few months old, after all. Bertie, I thought of you immediately when he mentioned Max Aitken, the newspaperman."

"Haven't met the man, but certainly know his reputation. Sensationalist, maybe less so than Hearst. Lord Beaverbrook to you, now, Bobby. A propaganda campaign? Is that what they're getting at?" McCormick was getting interested.

"Yes, exactly. That's why I suggested you come back with me. We have much to talk about with this Lord Beaverhat."

* * *

Sunday, January 27, 10:00 p.m.
45 Berkeley Square, West End, London

A very well-dressed covey of prominent London socialites of all stripes descended on the house at 45 Berkely Square. Lord Elsmere, the ringleader of this eclectic band, exited his Rolls, extending his hand to his companion for the evening, Alexandra Breithaupt. The Royal Philharmonic's program had featured English music, German having fallen into disfavor. Tonight's was an Elgar fest, the *Enigma Variations* and his *Violin Concerto*, with its own Windflower enigma.

"All this nonsense about enigmas and mysteries and elliptical references, all a bunch of well-rotted manure," said Churchill as he walked up the stair with Bernard Shaw. "Sir Edward has never discussed any of this with me. An enigma wrapped in a riddle inside a shepherd's pie. Hmmph!"

"Winnie, you are, as usual, devoid of that exquisitely tuned sense of the appreciation of the finer things. Of course it is an enigma." Shaw's beard shook with his laugh, "Sells more concert tickets!"

"That much is certainly true, GB. As usual, you have scored the bulls-eye." Churchill brightened at his odd friend's wit, which he considered second only to this own. "But you are blinded by your friendship with our esteemed composer. He could be writing lewd monosyllabic drinking songs in the Cockney argot and you would be lauding him to the heavens, old man!"

"You may be assured of it, Sir. I am loyal to my friends, even two conservative curmudgeons like the twain of you. You each have at least one redeeming virtue justifying my esteem, if not your well-fed upper class existence."

As Churchill started to say, "And pray remind me…," he was accosted by Reggie. "A moment, Minister? Mister Shaw, we need but a few minutes to produce more implements of death, if you do not mind? His lovely bride may not last much longer in our company in her state, the unfortunate result of Winston's failure to heed your eugenics theories."

Pieter van der Hoek had arrived earlier as surreptitiously as possible. He, Churchill, Elsmere and Alexandra convened in the library. "I shall not linger here long, my friends. No need to allow a connection to be drawn by some inadvertent glimpse or contact. Reggie, you have the package, I assume?"

Elsmere swung a Gainsborough on its hinges, fiddled with the lock and withdrew the package from his wall safe. "Here. Handle with care, please," handing it to Alexandra, who slipped it into her handbag.

"Excellent. Now, some payment in kind. First, there will be disturbances in Berlin beginning on the morrow. In some fit of beneficence, the Imperial German government saw fit to release Luxemburg and Liebknecht, the Spartacist leaders. I would have said it was an inexplicable fit of insanity but the release was promulgated by none other than Prince Max von Baden. I shall leave it to you to draw the appropriate inferences."

He faced Churchill, "Those disturbances will be fomented by the two aforementioned, but also the various Red factions. Does that not suggest an expansion of the Bolshevik menace? A subject for your address to the House of Commons?" Darting his eyes left, "Do not ask, Reggie. The source was female, as you might expect.

"Next, and this is not for your speech, nor any other dissemination. Absolutely. Agreed?" The Englishmen nodded, Churchill holding up the three finger Scout's honor salute. "Good. Apropos of our cartographic exercise, the Ukraine independence gambit is in play as we speak. A new nation of the Czechs and the Slovaks, likewise. The Baltics, and Finland, as well. The Poles are being obstinate, why are we not surprised? Von Treptow returns to Brest-Litovsk on the first. If, by the eighth, he does not achieve his heart's desires, the onslaught begins. You may place that date, coded, please, in your daybooks. Make your own estimates of the Eastern campaign's conclusion and expect troop movements west the next day. Do not place that date too far into the future. That is all I can say."

With that, he headed for the butler's pantry, turning only to say, "Have the young lady home by her curfew, if you please, Sir," then through the swinging door and on to the service entrance.

"Well, then. He was to the point, as usual. Reggie, we now have more clarity of the threat, do we not?"

"Yes, Minister. We need the Yanks more than ever, but in no wise will they be on line in time."

"All we have, then, is their potential. Pershing's acquiescence. Six weeks? Seven?"

"No more than six, Sir. Count on no more than that."

Winston whisked Clementine away as she had reached the limits of physical endurance and patience with her husband's intrigues. Lord Elsmere and his beautiful consort enjoyed their roles of host and hostess until the last guests departed just past midnight. They sat in his study, Alexandra guarding her handbag, Reggie finishing his fifth or sixth or seventh brandy.

"Reginald, where do you collect these people? Or do you grow them on one of your estates? That dreadful Warfield-Winstead woman. Surely she was manufactured somewhere? No one could be so pompous and clueless, and constantly self-referential, combined in one body, I mean."

"The cream of London society, I would have you believe. Actually, I do manufacture my guest lists carefully, selecting equally for comic effect as for wit and conviviality. The trick is not to combine all characteristics in one – separation heightens the effect." He leered, "My dear, in my position, I do as I please, as you have no doubt noticed. And it would please me to get to know you more intimately. There. I have said it." He placed a hand on her thigh, she allowed it to rest there.

He suddenly pushed her against the arm of the sofa, trying to kiss her. She pushed him away with unexpected strength, then followed to give him a light kiss on the lips. "Reginald, you have made me so very happy these last few months, and your company has helped me so much." She had been involved with a handsome RFC captain shot down over Flanders the past September. "But, I am simply not ready…please, do not take this the wrong way."

Reggie extended his right arm to trap her against the arm of the sofa, aggressively attempting to kiss her, his hand still heavy on her thigh.

Alexandra pushed him away again and bolted from her seat. "Please, my lord, do not spoil things for me, and just perhaps for us. I must go."

Reggie sprang to the double doors, blocking them. "So, is there another? One I could best in a fair fight? None wealthier or more highly placed, that much is certain. Another of those dashing flying chaps? You prefer those to a mere sailor like me?" He had imbibed entirely too much and his acquired resistance to the wave of intoxication was crumbling. He grew silent for a few moments, eyeing her figure. "A fellow countryman? That German friend of Pieter's? That handsome colonel, Winston's fellow man-at-arms? Is that it?" By now, he was nearly shrieking. "Is it?"

Poor Alexandra was seeking any way out of the trap. "Yes," she murmured.

"I cannot hear you!" He took a step toward her, but was no longer quick enough as she retreated out of reach behind a chair.

"Yes, it is." Her voice was quiet, yet firm, "Are you happy now?"

Lord Elsmere felt himself start to spin and braced himself back against the doors. He turned, flung open both doors and yelled, "Gresham! Gresham! See this young lady home. Immediately." He turned and looked at her. "Later, my pretty," and bolted unsteadily up the stair.

Gresham hastened to the doorway, having already summoned the car. "My apologies, young lady. He sometimes gets this way. Since Jutland, it is worse."

He helped Alexandra into her fur and escorted her to the street. She clutched her handbag close.

* * *

Monday, January 28, 1:30 a.m.
Dutch Embassy, London

Alexandra rang Pieter's quarters, still shaking from her encounter with Lord Elsmere. Hildegarde answered the ring, "Yes, dear? Whatever is the matter?" As Alexandra started to stammer out her account, then stopped, she said quietly, "Please come up right away. Yes, he is awake, or soon will be."

Pieter was tying his robe as Hildegarde let Alexandra in. "Please, dear, sit down. What on earth happened to you?" As she was settling in, trying to calm herself, Pieter turned to the teakettle, staring at it until it whistled back at him. He poured her a cup, then one for his wife, and then for himself. "Now, then, what can you tell us?"

Alexandra managed to give a coherent account up until the very last, then buried her head in her hands, then looked at them both and blurted out the part about Knorr.

"Please tell me you did not say that, young lady." That was as stern as Pieter had ever been with her.

"Please, Sir. I knew you would be cross with me. I had to say something to get away from him."

"Yes, of course you did, my dear. Pieter, she had to defend herself. You would not understand." Hilde put her arm around Alexandra's shoulders, "Then what, dear?"

"Then he screamed at me some more, then left me with his butler. Then home. Then here."

Pieter gazed into his teacup for a long while. "Well, it is done. I do seem to see that side of His Lordship all too often late in the evening. So, then, we have to get you away from London at first light. Certainly before he rings me up or comes to offer his apologies. Pack your things, Alexandra, you travel on your own. I shall have to catch up to you."

* * *

5:30 a.m.
Dutch Embassy, London

Pieter sent Alexandra off by car to a halfway house, a country manor in the Kentish countryside belonging to one of his nocturnal female friends and her Lord Husband. Secluded there overnight, safe from her suitor, she would be taken next morning in the estate's shooting brake from the forest gate to Dover where she would be spirited aboard *SS Edam* early and hidden away.

Van der Hoek breakfasted on his own, it being a tad early to rouse the staff and he being too awake to return to bed. Besides, he expected his lordly friend at the earliest. He was not disappointed as one of the Dutch Marine guards knocked at his study door at 6:45. "Lord Elsmere, is it?" he asked the blueclad marine.

"Yes, Sir, and in a bit of a tumbledown state, I would say, Sir."

Pieter slapped the guard on the back, "Well, not the first time, is it, lad?"

The two took their time in their walk to the main entry. There they found a very peeved and agitated lord, disheveled in face if not in his perfectly turned out dress.

Before Pieter could even enter the foyer, Reggie began shouting, "Where is she, damn it? And damn you, Pieter! Damn all of you Germans! Damn, damn, damn!"

Pieter stopped at the doorway into the smaller reception chamber. "Perhaps you would care to address your curses to the cherubim and seraphim on the ceiling, old man? This way," extending his arm to the door.

Giving van der Hoek a fiery look as he stripped off his gloves, Reggie acceded, Pieter closing the door behind him.

"Brandy, Your Lordship?"

Reggie turned pale at the thought. "Do not think you can needle me, old man. Where is she?"

"Miss Breithaupt returned from her evening with you quite distraught, as you might imagine. You do remember, do you not?" Despite his friendship and professional association, His Lordship was not getting a pass from the Dutchman. "You threatened her, made improper advances, what else am I forgetting, Reginald? I sent her straightaway within the hour to Portsmouth. There is an early morning steamer," consulting his watch, "leaving dock as we speak *en route* to Rotterdam. I have made the necessary requests of the German Navy via The Hague, I just hope the message gets through to the submariners."

"Gone? I do not believe you for a moment!"

"Would you care to examine her quarters, Your Lordship?" Pieter adopted a formal tone and posture. "To see for yourself?"

"No, no, you know I will not. Why, Pieter? Why?"

"Why what?"

"Why did you allow her to link with that German colonel? She admitted as much, surely she told you?"

"Of course she told me. She was deathly afraid I would be cross with her."

"And you were."

"Was what, old man?"

"Cross with her! Do not play games with me, you, you, of all people should know better!"

"Oh, I do, believe me, I do. Green tea or coffee? Please seat yourself anywhere." He turned his back on the fuming aristocrat and walked over to the service bell, then opened the butler's pantry door to the surprise of the four young women of the kitchen and chambermaid staff who were hanging on every word. One of them, Gretchen, sweet but simple, nearly toppled into the room. They scurried away like mice and presently Gretchen returned with a laden tray.

"Good morning, Your Lordship! And you, Sir!" She was still blushing as she backed out of the room, bowing repeatedly.

Lord Elsmere relaxed a little at the spectacle, one of his own creation he reminded himself. "Yes, Pieter, I thought I could trust you on most every matter. But to have my contact, my courier, my...my..."

"Girlfriend?" offered Pieter.

"Yes, damn you! No! No longer!"

Elsmere paused to catch his breath to start again when Pieter interrupted, "No, Reggie. They are not lovers. They have seen each other twice, for a full total of perhaps five or six minutes, in the officers' comings and goings here at the Embassy. She thought him attractive and he likewise. But that is the alpha and the omega of their affair. No, she said what she did in search of an escape from your unwanted attentions and your drunken fulminations. Really, my friend, and I hope to remain your close friend always, you must think of the other at least from time to time. Have you ever thought of women as anything other than objects of desire, the quarry in the hunt? And please remember she is not one of the jaded sophisticates we flirt with in the course of our nightly business."

He let that sink in, then, "No, there is nothing there. A ruse to escape your clutches. With your precious information, do not forget."

At that, Reggie sunk deeply into his chair. "May I take you at your word?" Pieter bowed. "Very well. I shall ask you to deliver her a note of apology." He took out an envelope and notecard from one inside pocket, his fountain pen from the other, and commenced writing. Finished, he signed it with a flourish, sealed the envelope with a lick and handed it over.

The two said in unison, "What is next?" They laughed at their little inside joke.

Lord Elsmere was thinking of other things as well.

* * *

Monday, January 28, 1000 hours
The Brandenburg Gate, Berlin

Von Treptow had reserved the entire west side of the top floor of the Hotel Adlon as an observation post. Below, the crowd was already gathering and it was clear it would easily exceed Professor Thesiger's calculations. Hartwig's men were at work marshalling and segregating their respective groups. In addition to Rosa's Spartacists, the hosts of the affair, Kautsky's brand of Socialists, Ebert's mainline Socialists, Mensheviks and Bolsheviks and dozens of other factions were milling about, their positions marked with flags, banners and signs.

The larger groups were fairly well disciplined, the UPSD on the south fringe, the Russian follower groups in the center rear behind the gate, closer to the Tiergarten, thronging Königgrätzer Strasse, closed to traffic. The Spartacists held center stage facing the stage set up in the shadow of the Tor. But at every fringe there was pushing and shouting, sporadic fisticuffs, angry men and women. More were flowing in by the moment preventing the Police from setting or keeping the barricades.

Major Bruckmiller was on the telephone. "Hans, have the northern barricades moved back, further up the Friedrichstrasse. Send a runner over to the other side, same message." He looked at von Treptow, who was dressed in a dark suit, no necktie, much resembling the uniform of the protesters below.

The general turned away from the window, "Ernst, have Hentsch's men move away from the rear of the crowds, both sides of the Gate. We do not wish a premature confrontation. Have his men smile and joke with the crowds. All friendly, you see?"

"Yes, Sir."

The time passed slowly as the crowd below coalesced into a seething mass. Then the factions grew more agitated, rippling from east to west. From the south along the Wilhelmstrasse below the Adlon's windows came a small convoy of three open cars. Von Treptow could see Rosa Luxemburg's distinctive head and face in the middle car, next to, he thought, Liebknecht. Brownshirted strongboys pushed the way clear with their batons, holding both admiring and castigating crowds at bay. The convoy stopped at the east end of the Brandenburg Gate; its occupants exited and made their way to the stage erected just to the front of the passage.

Stage hands were fooling with the loudspeakers and microphones as the speakers waited seated on the platform. Chants arose and subsided, taunts hurled between groups like unruly football fans at a match. Finally, the first speaker, a University professor of law, said Hartwig, unknown to von Treptow, made a halting start at the microphone, the speakers buzzing and crackling. The crowd alternately moaned and roared, swaying back and forth, new groups jockeying for positions in front of the Sparticists and being rudely hurled back.

Finally the speaker resumed. "Didn't ground the equipment. Idiots," murmured one of the police cameramen. The law professor droned on and on, leaving the crowd seething with frustration and anticipation. Then, another speaker, and another.

Knorr was nodding, von Seeckt yawning, the policemen raptly attentive to every detail. "See, there," pointed Bruckmiller, "that is Dieter, stirring up the Kautsky crowd. And Wiggy, doing the same with the Mensheviks. Here comes the star of the show" – von Treptow perked up – "not Rosa, General, but our delivery man, Gerhardt." He pointed down at a man dressed like all the others, with a cap pulled down to his brow, carrying a lawyer's case. "See his beanie, Sir?" Von Treptow noted the cap's button, painted yellow. "That's how we track them from above, Sir."

Gerhard had an armband on each arm, white with red stars. He pushed his way through another group – "Martini's anarchists," said Hartwig – then was gathered in by some of the young Bolshevists. He gradually moved toward the center of the group, then a little more to the rear. He was now closer to the Bolshevik and Menshevik factions, about thirty meters behind the speakers. He leaned down slightly, coming back up with both hands clapping. "The package is armed now," said one policeman clicking a stopwatch. "Twenty-five minutes."

Then a roar, and another roar, followed by yet another. Liebknecht had risen to speak but Rosa brushed him aside. The crowd erupted again. "This is getting dangerous on its own, Sir," said a police lieutenant. "Let's start moving our men back."

"Agreed, but slowly, now. Give the signal." Hartwig nodded. The lieutenant edged to a window, waving a yellow cloth or handkerchief across his chest as discreetly as he could. Von Treptow noted the movement of the colored buttons – first five, then another three, then six or seven. Several remained in place. "Again, Lieutenant." Two more, then the last, the bomb carrier. Some slipped through unobtrusively, some covered their exit with pushing and fighting, but all were soon at the perimeter where they remained.

Rosa's voice was by now booming through the speakers and the crowd had quieted to a low rumble, like distant pealings of thunder. Feedback and interference between the front and rear-facing speakers garbled her speech, so the observers up high could only distinguish fragments and snippets – "*...the usurpations of the dictator Lenin...*" – furious shouts from the Bolshies, the Spartacists shaking fists – "*...this Imperialist war...preserve the oppressor class...*"

"Sounds like your girlfriend is giving them right hell, Sir," smiled Bruckmiller.

"Fifteen minutes," called out the timekeeper.

In walked General Hentsch towing Professor Thesiger along. "Is our little picnic proceeding as expected? Oh my, Professor, look at the size of the crowd."

"Yes, most impressive, most impressive," he said impassively. "My density assumption was obviously faulty. I should have accounted more aggressively for the compression effect. And the sheer numbers of interested parties. Would someone point out the location of the explosive?"

The lieutenant of police described the crowd in the immediate vicinity. "Yes, that will do nicely. Perhaps a bit farther away, but still adequate." He turned to Hartwig, "I trust you had no difficulty obtaining the necessary quantity of explosive?"

Hartwig puffed up, "Not at all, Doctor. We are the police. Even five and a half kilos is but a trifle for us."

Thesiger blanched, his pasty face now completely drained of color. "Did you say five point five kilograms?"

"Yes, five and a half. Your calculation was for five thousand five hundred grams, so five point five kilos. Very clear, Doctor."

"My calculation was five point five million joules of energy. One and one quarter kilogram. Gentlemen, I suggest we step as far away from the windows as possible. It will be dramatic."

"Twelve minutes."

The open telephone crackled. It was one of the snipers on the roof, "...package may have moved...yes, someone has picked it up. There seems to be some struggle."

Down below, a drifter, in for the fun, perhaps a lifted wallet or two, had spied the case. He looked around and tried to pick it up. Too heavy for a casual lift, he bent down and used both hands. A man standing next to him grabbed his shoulder but he wrenched away and took a few steps to the rear, followed by a shout of "Thief!" alerting a couple of sizeable lads who blocked his path.

Hentsch said, coolly, "Can he get a shot? Stop him?"

Before anyone could respond, Captain von Seeckt grabbed von Treptow's arm. "Look, Sir. At the rear, toward Tiergarten." It was one of his estate's motorcars, stopped by the soldiers manning the perimeter. Von Treptow took the field glasses, training them over the flanking pavilion's tile roof. "Claire. Damn!" She was arguing with the young soldiers, then wrenching her arm away from their grasp and plunging into the crowd's rear.

"Ten minutes." Rosa was still fulminating.

Erich turned, "General?" He was already out the door and down the hall to the stair.

Two minutes later, Bruckmiller spied von Treptow emerging from the hotel, fighting his way through the crowd then freeing himself toward the margins.

"Seven minutes." The drifter had been knocked down and was struggling to regain his feet, still clutching the case. "Too difficult a shot, General Hentsch," said Hartwig.

"A shot would spoil the entire dynamic, disrupt the fluid mechanics potential of the set piece," intoned the professor. The others turned and looked at him as if he were mad.

Meanwhile, von Treptow had lost sight of Claire even though she was as tall or taller than many in the crowd. He looked back to the Adlon, saw Knorr frantically waving both arms to his right. Von Treptow turned that direction, jumping up and down until he saw Claire's salt and pepper hair veering into the crowd yet still sixty meters or so from the center. He shoved and bulled his way on an interception course until a burly worker took exception to being pushed from behind.

Von Treptow found himself flat on his back in a knot of surly types. He sprang up, moved toward the big man and buried a knife deep into his chest, his thrust hidden by the throng. He sidestepped the staggering man and made a dash toward Claire.

"Four minutes, General Hentsch, Sir. Not much time."

"May God shine his countenance upon them, then," Captain von Seeckt said. "In the next world to come."

Von Treptow was now close enough to shout her name. She looked around, first away, then toward him. "Dietrich?"

"Come to me, Claire! Now!"

They met midway, and he took her by both arms, hustling her toward the perimeter. He stopped, looked back at the hotel, and saw what he thought were two fingers in Knorr's outstretched hand. "Let us move more quickly, dear."

"Dietrich, what is going on? Why are you here? Dressed like that? And where are you taking me? You are hurting my arms," she spat. "Let me go, damn it!"

Von Treptow's eyes were fixed on a statue of a crouching lion, ten meters ahead, just visible over the heads of the now very agitated crowd. He turned Claire around, now dragging her as he pushed with his back then suddenly broke clear, almost falling. He recovered their balance and made for the safety of the massive plinth.

"What..?" spurted Claire.

"Dear, I saw you from afar and was possessed with the overwhelming desire to make love, to ravage you. Lie down and let me cover you with my passion."

"Ooh, Dee, you brute..."

Just then the whole scene was enveloped in a brilliant flash, then a shock wave, then a terrific noise. Dirt, dust and cobbles were hurled past the statue. He looked down at Claire, her eyes wide with terror. He hugged her tightly, then heard a cracking noise. He looked up at the statue above them which tilted their way then rocked back the other direction and was still. Dietrich felt a soft rain or mist on his upturned cheek, touched his hand to it and drew back bloody fingers

He started to rise, then saw the approaching stampede. Like Knorr's cattle, the crowd flowed around the plinth as if choreographed, first converging, then dispersing randomly. He heard the rat-a-tat-tat of machine guns behind him, far in the distance. Then a crawling plume of dense, foul-smelling smoke enveloped them. As he lifted Claire and made for the safety of the nearby wood, another huge explosion nearby rocked them, nearly knocking her down with its concussion. Then, another, and another, more distant.

They reached the safety of one of the Army formations, the general flashing his insignia pinned to the inside of his jacket. He looked Claire over for any obvious injury, then stepped back and smiled. "I think you will be fine..."

She slapped him hard. And hard again. Two soldiers standing nearby started their way but von Treptow waved them off. "What have you done, Dietrich! This was your doing, yes? How many have you killed? How many of my friends are lying dead back there? You! The moralist, the upright? Monster!" She broke away, turned and ran across the debris field, dodging stones and bodies and fragments.

"Let her go. She, of all Berlin, can take care of herself. Sergeant, give me five or six of your best. To see what we have wrought here."

Königgrätzer Strasse was a clutter of cobblestones, heaps of dirt and bodies. Many bodies, some unmarked, some horribly burned, most quiet, some moaning piteously. As they moved toward the Gate, they passed through zones of increasing devastation. Ahead, Dietrich could see a blackened area; closer, he could see the outline of a crater, apparently the point of detonation. Looking around, he could make out the radial pattern of death and destruction, then several patches or heaps of bodies further away. *The professor was right. Those mark the collisions between groups.*

Knorr hailed him from the Gate. The stage was still standing although the chairs and equipment were scattered about. The Tor itself had a faint demarcation in soot about halfway up, the lower part cleaner. He turned back to the crater and made a mental line tracing the lower part of the blast, angling upward. *So, Rosa and company survived, after all. Good. I am beginning to think Claire is right. I have killed too many, too easily. Unthinkingly.*

"General, you found her?" Knorr was anxious, justifiably.

"Yes, we managed to shelter in time. Just in time. After, she decided she wanted no further part of me. Can you blame her, Walter? We have gone too far."

The policemen and the professor came over to survey the scene. Neither von Treptow nor Knorr were in uniform and General Hentsch and his men were staying away from the scene. "This is at once most interesting and most unfortunate, Sir. My instructions were misinterpreted," looking at Hartwig and Bruckmiller, "and the power was disproportionate."

"Disproportionate, man? Disproportionate? Is that all you can say? Did this not fit within your tidy little equations?"

"General, respectfully, Sir, was it not your description of this as a matter of crowd control? An incident, calculated to set one group against another? You gave me a problem, I gave you a solution. A proper solution, ruined by incompetence. Respectfully, Sir." He buttoned up his jacket, turned and loped away.

Ten meters on, he was met by Police Lieutenant Schnabel carrying a sheaf of papers. The two conferred briefly then turned back to the general and his group. "Respectfully, Sir, we have some new information that may change your opinion of this exercise. Lieutenant, here, has counted the bodies that might reasonably be attributable to the initial blast, I emphasize initial, Sir, and he estimates," looking at the crude site diagram, "he estimates less than sixty deaths, despite the excessive quantity of explosive deployed," looking at the senior Police officials.

Walking over to a pair of bodies, "Observe the orientation. Head up, away from the point of origin. Note the damage to the anterior crania." He walked to the other side of the crater, pointing at three more. "Head first, but face down. Damage to spines and posterior crania. Their backs were to the blast." Looking around, "You see, a rather limited number of bodies following that pattern. Let us accept the Lieutenant's count, add a percentage for disintegration – fifteen percent would suffice – and the blast's direct toll was no greater than seventy. I believe the highly compressed packing of the crowd acted to absorb both the blast and the debris, equally fatal effects."

"Further note these other bodies." He strolled further away, almost casually, save for the need to sidestep bodies and bloodpuddles, "random in their positioning, it would appear, except for this tendency for those closer to the blast to fall away, those farther, to fall toward. Obviously not blast caused. This was a confrontation, Sir, as predicted, when the inner group fled onto the lines of the outer group. You see, Sir? Here a bullet wound to the skull, there an obvious slashing wound. Not blast caused." Waving his hand, "Many, many more out here. I stand by my original design, ignition by explosion, death by confrontation. Do you require anything further of me?" Seeing no response, he turned and walked away.

Von Treptow and his colleagues could merely gaze at the departing figure, mute with shock. The police lieutenant spoke up, "Sirs, be aware there were at least three, perhaps four, other blasts following closely on ours. Two were to the east of the Gate, both grenades. The other," pointing to the rear, "was a substantial explosive, much larger than a grenade. Obviously a planted bomb, perhaps carried. Just inside the leading edge of the Bolshevik – Menshevik junction here," pointing to his sketch, then to their rear.

"A reasonable guess, Sirs? This bomber hastily caused its detonation shortly after the initial blast, surprised at that blast and the dispersal of his targets. He, or she, may not have survived. A similar pattern of destruction to this. Clearly, Sirs, others were intent on mayhem. It is not unreasonable to conjecture that even more bombs were planned, simply pre-empted by the initial explosion and the ensuing chaos. Also, here are messages from our outlying observers. There are pitched battles ongoing among factions and fragments of factions. I do not have all the details. Some storefronts ransacked on Unter den Linden and other streets, some building fires. Looks like a general riot, our people are staying out of it."

Von Treptow's gaze lingered over the devastation. "Be careful what you wish for…"

* * *

Monday, January 28, 1700 Hours
Calais, France

Colonel Emerson and Major McCormick had made their way by car and train across France to the British embarkation quay at Calais. As they sat on the hard benches in the midst of a group of boisterous Irish Fusiliers looking forward to a bit of home leave, McCormick lit a cigar, Emerson opting for a French cigarette he had bought off a pretty street vendor outside. "Should be a special category of marriage for those posted in combat zones. Temporary disengagement of responsibilities or some such."

"In your fantasies, Colonel. And when you return home and your wife asks if you brought her something from France, you surely do not want to answer, '*I hope not.*' She was very pretty, Bobby, I grant you that, but sufficiently to upend your domestic bliss? I think not."

"Back to earth, then. I wonder where these Tommies are bound?"

"Not Tommies, Sir, Micks! And proud of it!" A gangly Irish soldier, clearly well into his cups, responded as he swayed to and fro. His mates were laughing at him, poking at him to see if he would topple. "No, Sir, we're proud Irishmen, County Donegal volunteers. We're done over here, Yank. Not coming back, no way."

The smiling lad was a good-natured drunk and soon the Americans were laughing along with his friends. "No, Sir, I'm serious, deadly so. We're all going home. Getting out of here. No place for the Sons of Erin. Ireland is dangerous enough since the Easter rising, but here in the trenches lies certain death."

He poured himself onto the bench next to McCormick, leaning over to make his point, fragrantly, "The lads and I went over the top south of Passchendaele last fall, I looked back at our British captain, I swear I saw Death in khaki – smiling skull face, long bony fingers, cutting our strings as we moved ahead. A snip here, there went Patrick, face down in the mud. A snip there, another good man spins around, blood spurting from his temple. I looks back, the Captain of Death still smiling. He looked down, picked a string, grinned at me and took his shears to it. Just then, a German shell blew the post to perdition, Death with it."

He stood upright, suddenly and unsteadily, and shouted, "And that's why I am alive today, going home with my mates, to see my Bridget!" He stumbled and was caught by a couple of his fellows. They lowered him to the pew in a crumpled heap, now just murmuring to himself.

"Sorry, Gents, don't mind him, please," said one of the Irish. "He's harmless as a kitten. Not one of those heroic Irish drinkers we're supposed to be. Two pints and he's silly. Give him a third, and he gets all dramatic, like you see. A fourth, and he's asleep. We dinna want to carry him all the way home, so he dinna get that far."

A group of Tommies, Cornwalls this time, came along. One of them, a corporal, said loudly, "Typical Micks, lads. Drunk and useless. Useless at the front, too, damn them."

Immediately the two cohorts bristled and glowered at each other, awaiting a spark. Colonel Emerson stood up to his full six foot three and saluted. The British corporal and the drunken Irishman's minder snapped to attention with crisp salutes. "You will stand down, soldiers. Now. You," pointing at the Cornwall, "take your men over there," thumbing over his right shoulder. "You," pointing to the Irish, "manage your boys. Everyone to their seats, and no more of this bullshit. Am I understood?"

The two leaders shouted, "Yessir!" in unison, and motioned to their mates.

"You two," Emerson was pointing first to the Irish, then to the Brit. "Shake hands. That's an order." The British corporal scowled, then broke out in a big grin. "Yes, Sir. As you say, Sir," extending his hand, which was hesitantly grasped. "You Yanks just say the word, and we'll do what it is you want, Sir." His Irish counterpart smiled, gave his man a stronger, lingering grasp, then released.

The Brits moved off and Emerson took his seat. The Irish corporal moved his somnolent mate over a bit to squeeze in next to McCormick. "Thank you, Sir. Not least for reminding us of proper discipline. Those Brits expect us to be rowdy and uncontrollable. And drunk. We have to be on our guard at all times, just to disappoint them."

He and the Americans introduced each other. McCormick said, "I'm a Scot. Can we talk as fellow Gaels?" The Irishman, nodded. "Back home, the English-Irish divide narrows all the time. My friend here married an Irishwoman, flaming hair and all."

"And temper. Scots-Irish, actually. Same difference, at least to me."

McCormick went on, "With you over here, it just gets wider, it seems. I'm from Chicago. Loads of your type there. Everywhere – politics, business, labor, everywhere. Big advertisers in my paper, too, so I don't have time to be a bigot, even if I were so inclined. My question, when will it end? Will it end? And will you go back to fight in Flanders for the United Kingdom?"

"Them's three very nice questions, Sir. Answers to which could land me in gaol, my fellow Gael. May I enquire as to why you enquire, Sir? Who are you, respectfully, Sirs? Fit like, Sir?" gesturing to McCormick.

McCormick replied, "United States Army Intelligence officers. Scary enough? And clan MacCorquodale, Argyll. Can't trace the MacCormack part. Fit like?"

"Donegal O'Connors. Might be able to understand your grandfathers. And, yes, Sir, plenty scary, Sirs. But we've been through worse. You Yanks, you just don't yet know the terrors awaiting you. No one can, not 'til you've been in it, Sir. And the British, and surely the French won't be telling you aforehand, 'struth.

"But honest answers to honest questions. My people's way. The matters back home will only end with a free Ireland. Nothing less. All of it, and send the Ulstermen home. All due respect to your forebears, Sir, and your wife's, Colonel, Sir, but there's no place on the Isle for the Protestants. Not just as a matter of religion, tho' that friction is undeniable, the tribes just never will reconcile. Best a settlement fair to all, and get 'em gone. And then it will be all over, Sir. Just like that. Me, I'm well past them what grew up as famine slaves to the English. Me and mine, we manage, but now it's our time. Your own President says so, Sirs. Self-determination, he says. Why should we be any different from the Finns or the Poles or the rest of that scurvy Slavic lot? Any good reason, Sirs?" Looking at the Americans, "I thought not."

He looked about him and softly said, "Now grant me amnesty, on your oaths, Sirs, for what I am about to say, and please draw closer. Will you?" Emerson and McCormick looked at each other, then nodded. "Return to fight for the United," he said with a sneer, "Kingdom?" He took a deep breath, "No. None of us will be coming back. And not the next thousand. And not the next. By summer, we'll all be home."

A long pause, then, "What's left of us." O'Connor stared down at his feet. "The Tenth, not really Irish, not anymore. Some of the boys still in Palestine, but those of us still over here, they'll melt away. My Fifth Royals, and the rest of the Sixteenth? If Haig had had his way, all us Irishmen would be hanging on the Huns' barbed wire, still. Well, he won't be having another chance at us. The half of us that's left after Passchendaele, maybe, that is. We'll be home and they can't get us back once there. The rest of our boys scattered about? Dunno. Thirty thousand, forty, maybe? Dunno. They've been given the message. They'll come home, too, somehow."

"New men? Conscripts?" asked Emerson.

"No conscription in Ireland, Sir. They wouldn't dare try. No, we're all volunteers. Thought we'd get a proper shake by fighting for England. No such deal, Easter and all."

So the Irish are out of the line, probably by the time the Germans strike. Thirty thousand, he said? Maybe more, counting these? Experienced, tough fighting men? Not good. Emerson added that to his ongoing equations. *Black Jack won't be happy. He needs to know, though.*

Just then, the loudspeaker called out for boarding. The two officers took advantage of their priority and bade their Irish friends goodbye.

On board, they laid their duffels down and bundled themselves against the cold breeze coming down the Channel. "Too cold, Bertie. A fine spring Chicago day for you, maybe, but not for me. Let's go back inside."

They found the officers' lounge more to Emerson's liking. Settling into their chairs, they were immediately joined by a ramrod stiff British officer. "Lieutenant Colonel Chauncey Wollstonecraft Yarmouth d'Eyncourt, Gentlemen. I have the pleasure of addressing Colonel Emerson and Major McCormick, I presume?"

"British Army Intelligence, I presume? In return, of course?" asked Emerson.

"Actually, Sir, MI Five. Counterintelligence."

McCormick asked impishly, "Counterintelligence? Since you surely know us to be intelligence officers, are you countering us, Sir?"

"Encountering, Sir, not countering. Welcoming you to Merrie Olde. Have you been here before?"

Both nodded.

"Right answer, Gentlemen. Would not do to dissemble on first acquaintance. Mister, rather, Colonel Emerson, you enjoyed the hospitality of Naval Intelligence without deigning to pay us the courtesy of a visit? Did you have some warship business to discuss? The arrival of your dreadnoughts at Scapa, perhaps?"

"Did I? The Navy is beyond my understanding, Sir."

"Are we being interrogated, Colonel?" McCormick was at heart a fighting bull terrier and quickly warmed to a conflict.

"No, of course not…," started d'Eyncourt, but McCormick interrupted, "No? Will we be followed? If so, please be assured we will raise the issue at our Embassy and a protest will be lodged with His Majesty's Government. Really, Sir, is this any way to treat an ally? Particularly one that will be instrumental in preserving your precious way of life?"

"Do not be so presum…"

This time it was Emerson who cut him off. "Cut the crap, Colonel. You know it, and we know it. But, Bertie, we should not get off to such a rocky start with our new friend. Yes, Colonel, I was here last week. On leave. Did some shopping, bespoke suits. Met an old friend of my father's, too. Made him very happy that I could renew their acquaintance, pass on his best wishes, that sort of thing. But, about this Naval Intelligence business, Sir? That part I do not follow."

"We noted you entering the Ministry of Munitions at 0945 on the sixteenth in company with the Dutch Chargé, who is, of course, their intelligence man, Sir. You were disguised as their Military Attaché. Not very well disguised, I might add. But not you, Sir," nodding to McCormick, "his companion was shorter. Why? Not to meet with Mister Churchill, that is not your brief, I take it?" He looked first at Emerson, then McCormick. "I thought not. So, it was Lord Elsmere, who is, of course, Naval Intelligence, Blinker's boy. We have the full story on him. Rich, independent, does as he pleases. And his nighttime rounds with van der Hoek, your Dutchman. Then on January twenty-third, just noon, outside the tailor's," now fumbling with his notes, "Llewellyn and someone or the other, again with Elsmere. So, Naval Intelligence again. Why not Army? And why use the Dutch as go-betweens? Are we not allies?"

"Are we not spying, one on the other? Allies?" Emerson queried softly. "And on your own?"

D'Eyncourt stiffened. "Necessary, Sirs. In time of war, every connection, every thread must be scrutinized. We have been very successful with the Germans here, give us credit for that."

"All credit due, certainly. And what other contacts, my good man? Surely that is not all?"

"Sadly, yes. You left two days later from Biggin Hill aerodrome...," started the Brit.

"Royal Flying Corps aerodrome, not Naval, you might concede. Professional courtesy?"

"Very well, yes, RFC it is. Then back to London this trip. It is London, is it not?"

"It is."

"And who are you seeing?"

"You will find out, I have no doubt." Emerson was done with forthrightness.

"Please, please, Colonel. Let us not play games. You have a connection. Why? What are you about here?"

Emerson looked slyly at McCormick. "Shall we let him in on it?"

"I suppose we must, Bobby."

"Well, then. Colonel...d'Eyncourt, is it? French, or Norman, is it not?"

"Yes. Dates back to the Conquest. And well before, of course. Please, you are evading. What were you on the cusp of revealing? We dock in Dover shortly."

"Our mission? To withdraw the AEF from France. Go home, forget the whole thing. Our meeting is with the Ambassador, giving him General Pershing's reasons to convey same to His Majesty's Government." D'Eyncourt's stiff mustache twitched as his head rocked back ever so slightly. "Sorry, Chaunce, old buddy, old pal, nothing so dramatic. Regular debrief with the Ambassador and staff. Chance for comfortable beds and better food." He smirked at the Briton, "But back to this Naval Intelligence connection, the Dutch Attaché? Serious case of mistaken identity. You might have a real spy on your hands, not just a couple of American jokers. The tailor shop, that was your man? Said his name was one of your hyphenated British concoctions, cannot recall. But first name...," he snapped his fingers, "Rupert, Russell, Reginald. That's it, Reginald. Nice fellow. Very well-dressed. Check with the tailor. Got three suits to fit while I'm here."

McCormick interrupted. "Thanks be to a merciful God. We're here." The steamer was easing into Dover harbor. "Well, Chauncey, old fellow, it was a pleasure, I'm sure." He picked up his duffle and headed for the exit without a backward glance. Emerson followed, turning his head over his right shoulder to give the Five man a wink.

Mitch Cabot met them at the station, handing out their tickets. "Let's board right away, friends, too much curiosity around here."

"We were made straightaway, Mitch." Emerson recounted their session with the counterintelligence agent. "Hardly had time to settle in before the inquisition. Might as well be carrying signs."

"MI Five? Those clowns? That means Army Intel is still out there somewhere. Well, your newfound friend and his men will be on your tail. Did us a favor, really. Shows off their lack of skill. Still a new group, mostly aristos and ex-India officers – your man probably fits both – and they haven't yet created that institutionalized sense of good procedure. Smart, though, some of them are really sharp, but they have work to do. Starting at the top. Kell, their headmaster, is competent, but the ranks thin considerably below him. Plus, the British have, well, let's just say they've created an odd way to run a railroad."

Walking down the aisle of the First Class car, Cabot made a switch. "This cabin is a bit closer to the loco and the tender, a bit noisier. We'll settle in and generously give up the more desireable spot to their Worships, whoever they might be. No listeners about, see?"

Sure enough, when a group of dowdy dowagers came along, Mitch played the chivalrous American, oozing Brahmin charm from every pore. "Yes, ladies, we would be delighted to take tea with you at the Savoy. My friends here have many a harrowing war story to tell, I am sure."

As the door closed, McCormick said sharply, "Surely you do not mean it, Cabot? We have no time for babysitting the superannuated!"

"Actually, Bertie, I did mean it. I was thinking of defeating the expected surveillance. The Savoy has several very private quarters off the lounge. Private for trysts of a different sort, to be sure. Churchill favors it for luncheon. Your friend Chauncey just telegraphed we cannot meet at the Embassy, nor at Churchill's Ministry. Too many eyes."

"Lord Elsmere's?" suggested Emerson.

"Likely watched. The Secret Service has a particular problem with NID. The Navvies have outshone them throughout the war, and Elsmere – your Reggie – is in especially bad odor. Rich, arrogant, supercilious, all that. Sounds like you got a hint of that from your man on the boat. Remind me, without fail, van der Hoek must also be warned."

"Max's place?" Bertie was thinking ahead to a newspaperman talk.

"A possibility. His office? Fleet Street is too busy, too many union lads about, as well. But he and Churchill are fast friends. Nothing to keep them from a visit or lunching there together. Reggie might be included, but would be a bright lure for the trout." Cabot thought on it, then, "Major, you could go by yourself as a fellow newspaperman paying a courtesy call. Easy enough. Before the Commons speech. That's how we get you in, Max's guest, a newspaper type. Then to the Savoy? We'll figure something. I'll make some calls tonight."

* * *

Tuesday, January 29, 0900 Hours
Foreign Office, Berlin

"No, Dietrich. No excuses. A disaster. And how did you let my sister escape? How did she get there in the first place? Why in Heaven's name did you take her in?"

"Yes, Sir. We were too bloodless, if that is possible, at least in our analysis. And your sister? Do your questions assume I have any control over her? Ever had any control? And how did she know I was back at the schloss?"

Prince Max unclasped his hands from behind his back and turned to face von Treptow. The old friends looked tautly at each other. "No, I did not tell her. Not in so many words. She can read my face, if not my mind. But how could you let her leave, knowing the danger?"

"We cut off her telephone privileges and disabled her car, if you must know. She took one of my cars and forced her way through the gate, giving two of the policemen sound bumps, fortunately for her not serious. I reached her just in time, Max. She would have been right on top of the second bomb, the one for the Bolsheviks, or by them, we may never know."

"Harrumphh." Hartwig and Bruckmiller had also been called on the carpet. "Your Excellency, Sir, we at the Metropolitan Police acknowledge mistakes were made. Honest mistakes, Sir, yet not as devastating as we feared." Hartwig was defensive, but not yielding. "We all were agreed on the course of action, Sir. Let us think on the aftermath, which is proceeding exactly, no, well in excess of our expectations. The Socialists have made the most of the chaos. Their Freikorps allies were well prepared, as our men predicted. They have pummeled the smaller groups badly. The USPD leaders have taken refuge behind their labor thugs, so will survive, if not prevail, as matters proceed now. The Spartacists may well be extinct."

"Sir? General von Treptow, Sir?" Bruckmiller was uncharacteristically formal.

"Yes, Ernst?" Von Treptow was not paying much attention, still focused on Claire's fate.

"The Freikorps captured Luxemburg, Liebknecht and the other Spartacist leaders. Planning to hold their own tribunal."

Von Treptow shifted his focus abruptly. "How can they do that, Hartwig? Is this not your jurisdiction? This will be murder, worse than us!"

Hartwig was discomfited, to place matters mildly. "Well, err, …"

Max rescued him. "Yes, they can. Ebert and Noske have been granted a certain latitude regarding security in these troubled times and authorized the formation of these units from returning soldiers. To absolve the Army of a repressive role wherever possible."

Max noted von Treptow's louring face. "At the appropriate time, we shall crush them in their turn."

* * *

Tuesday, January 29, 10:00 a.m.
Fleet Street, London

Mitch Cabot had made the setup the night before. Churchill and Lord Elsmere would walk over to Aitken's office at ten. Shortly after, Major McCormick, in civilian attire, would take a cab from the Embassy to Aitken's in his role as a prominent American newspaperman paying a courtesy call. All in plain view. Emerson and Cabot, in contrast, would be concealed in a *Daily Express* delivery van and driven to a separate entrance at the newspaper offices screened from the street, arriving at eleven.

Churchill noticed his companion's uncommonly laconic mood. "What, ho, my Spartan friend? Sparing of words this morning, are we?"

"Too much liquid enjoyment the other night, Winston, pursues me yet. But, a splendid time was had by all, yes? You missed the sparring between Shaw and Chesterton after you and Clementine departed. Dueling scriveners at a pace and a half. Chesterton said, '*To look at you, anyone would think a famine had struck England,*' to which Shaw replied, '*To look at you, anyone would think you had caused it.*' Spectacular. Clementine held up well, I hope?"

"Well enough. I should have half the energy, and she has three others about. She needs to rest, but between her canteen work and Lord knows what else, she hardly stops."

Up the steps to the building housing the *Daily Express* and the *Evening Standard*. Max's secretary met them at the door, as usual. "Miss Adelaide, my dear, you are looking your usual wonderful self," gushed Lord Elsmere for effect if not sincerity. "Has your day begun well, I hope?"

"As well as one could hope, working for that man in this place." She gave a sour look, then smiled. "He was off on a labour tantrum even before I arrived this morning, has not let up. Please calm him and failing that, muzzle him, please?"

"We shall do what we can, Adelaide dear, but remember we are confronting one of the great untamed forces of nature!" Churchill guffawed as he flung open the office door, ushering Reggie in ahead of him to collect the first barbs.

"No, secondly no, and finally, NO!" Max Aitken slammed down the telephone receiver on his desk and waited for his adrenaline to subside. As the blush receded from his domed forehead, not unlike Churchill's save surmounted by a proper head of hair, he turned to his friends, "You may have them all, Winnie. Every last one of the lot. Pressmen, typesetters, all! Put them to productive use elsewhere, making bullets or such and let me find someone who wants to work!"

Reggie, the stalwart Tory, saw his opening, "Not exactly the Liberal Party line, old man?"

"Oh, hush. And you, too, Winston, before your jaw goes agape and commences to flap. So, what are these matters of such urgency? Is it not enough to be expected to sit through your droning at the Commons? I can read the text at anytime, in my own papers, of course. Or as you hinted, Reggie, some propaganda? How I do love it!"

"Yes, indeed, Minister."

At the moment, Lord Beaverbrook was the Minister of Propaganda in Lloyd George's coalition government, subject to the Welshman's whim or an excessively critical editorial. But there was only so much extolling of Commonwealth soldiers' valor and pillorying of German excesses that held the public's imagination these days. Something new was needed, and needed now. "Good. I have papers to sell and a public to inspire. What have you?"

Churchill, settling into his chair, replied, "Max, old fellow, we have discussed the bits and pieces about our former allies in Russia. But just that, bits and pieces. Until now." Aitken perked up. "Two new sources, one within, one without. The clearest picture to date of the villainy beyond the Vistula. Reggie, note the alliteration. Old Charles would be proud, *'Who often, but without success, have pray'd for apt Alliteration's artful aid.'* Excellent!" Churchill withdrew his script from his coat, jotting down the phrase. "A picture that must needs be presented to the British people in its starkest clarity. I begin today in the House, with this," waving his papers.

"I thought you were speaking of boots and bullets, old man. What is this damned dynamite, Winston? Alliteration, Reggie." Lord Elsmere rolled his eyes at Aitken's jape.

Churchill was warming to his topic, "Bolshevism. A greater threat to all of us, certainly our ilk. Germany is as weary as we, but if we can grope our way toward a conclusion, an armistice, even a ceasefire, however flimsy or precarious, we have a chance to rebuild the world we knew. I prefer to crush them once and for all, but we must recognize realities. Should we continue knocking seven bells out of each other, stumbling and clutching like two drunks in a East End pub, we will stagger and fall together, our energies spent. Then these Bolsheviks will have the clear field."

"So far, sounds like a decent headline, but elaborate, please. These Reds, your Bolsheviks, took over Saint Petersburg. We have reported that. Their war seems to have stopped, according to our correspondents. No news is definitely not good news on Fleet Street. What gives?"

Reggie responded, "Let us save one of our sources for our American visitor's benefit, the part we have some right to know. We have another source, no, not for your eyes, Max. We have fresh information, up to the minute, as it were." Pieter had given Reg his government's latest news and analysis of the events in Berlin, courtesy their German friends, and certain intelligence scraps from within Russia itself. "First, these Reds have given in, cut and run. A ceasefire with the Germans, now peace treaty negotiations. If that were not evidence enough, they issued a proclamation yesterday disbanding the Russian Army." As Reggie spoke, Winston scribbled, having heard only parts of the Dutch messages. "It was a disintegrating entity as it was, the peasant soldiers simply heading home. Now they have made it official. The Minister will be making the case that Russia is no longer an ally in our fight with the Central Powers."

Max raised both eyebrows at that. "Taking over at the Foreign Office, are you, Winston? Have you informed David or Arthur?"

Churchill kept his head down, marking and scratching. "No, just raising some issues." He looked up and grinned, "Delicately, of course, as is my wont."

"Delicately? I see. Continue, Reggie, continue."

"Moving ahead, then, to their doctrine of a world revolution of the masses, to overthrow of the existing order, including, I need not add, the House of Lords. He will add murder, oppression, dictatorship, all hallmarks of their variety of brute."

A knock on the door intervened. Miss Adelaide stuck her head in, "Sir, your Mister McCormick is here. And Jenkins needs to lay something before you. Cannot wait, he says."

"Show them both in. The *Chicago Tribune* shall see how the *Evening Standard* makes the news."

She escorted Bertie in by the elbow. Jenkins, Max's editor, dodged around them both to reach the desk first. He laid out two wire photographs and a rough galley proof of a story. "Berlin, Sir! Massive disruptions and disturbances!" One of the photographs was of the Brandenburg Gate before the blasts, the other in their aftermath. "More rioting, fighting amongst factions in the heart of the city! Looks like the Prussian Revolution, Sir! What a headline! What a story! "

"Yes, yes, Jenkins. Very interesting. Could be a good story, I grant you that. May I think on it until after luncheon?"

"Sir? This is monstrous in its proportions! Could be decisive in the War! Cannot let the other boys get it out ahead of us!"

"Agreed. Prepare the headline. 'Berlin in Flames.' 'Reds and German Army in conflict.' Leave it thus until I return. Do not worry, old chap, we shall make your reputation and the *Standard's* with this story. There is more to it as I am now learning. We will make deadline, I assure you. Now, these gentlemen demand my time. Please leave this," gesturing to the proof, "with me."

Jenkins was bewildered at his boss' lack of customary aggressiveness, but knew when to yield. McCormick, though, was his usual direct, Midwestern self. "Sir, Robert McCormick, *Chicago Tribune*," leaning over to shake Aitken's hand, and without pause, "my London correspondent, Adcock, left yesterday morning to cover USS *Texas'* arrival at Scapa Flow, would otherwise be here. I need this," pointing to the photographs and the story, "sent to Chicago at the earliest. If, of course, you are willing to share the scoop?"

"Jenkins, that will be all. Please be so kind as to give this man every assistance as he requires." When Jenkins had closed the door behind him, he continued, "Normally, your request would be out of the question. You would say the same to me. But you are bold, and I admire boldness, and you are United States Army Intelligence after all." He winked at Churchill and Lord Elsmere, "As a Canadian I have other opinions of our oversized adolescent neighbor, but we are at war together, finally, not a moment too soon. Major, please retrace your steps and meet Winston Churchill, Minister of Munitions and Reginald, Lord Elsmere, his aide."

"Sorry, Gents, I got carried away with the news story. How do you do? I have heard much of the two of them, Lord Beaverbrook, so am somewhat prepared."

"Never can be too prepared for this duo, trust me. Well, please sit down. I assure you you may share this story, however it plays out. Apropos of same I was just being apprised of recent developments in Russia to which this Berlin business is tied, to be sure. Your Lordship, Minister? Continue?"

Churchill took the lead, "Mister McCormick, allow me begin by posing a query. What have you told your readership of events in Russia since the Tsar's abdication and the Kerensky government's overthrow this past November?"

"Besides confusing them with the Russians' October and our November? Not much, frankly. Our correspondents have been prevented from visiting the war front, or travelling far outside Petrograd or Moscow. Clearly these Bolshevik fellows are in league with the Wobblies and Debs and his Socialist ilk, but we can't get straight stories even from them. Dangerous, we must assume, but how so?"

"Dangerous, yes. Very dangerous. Take the worst of your anarchists and Haymarket bombers and combine them with the oratory and theorizing of Debs, and then give them an army, of sorts, and a country. A very big country."

Miss Adelaide stuck her head in. "Your other guests, Sir. Will you be retiring to the dining room?"

"No, we shall remain fixed here. Please show them in."

Colonel Emerson and Mitchell Cabot entered with short introductions, Cabot knowing all, only Emerson having not met Aitken. "Find yourselves a seat, Gentlemen. Winston and Reggie, here, are trying to scare the Holy Infant out of us with their tales of…what was it, Winnie, '*Villainy beyond the Vistula*'? Always fresh with the phrase, old man. He intends on igniting the dozing backbenchers with his incendiary comments."

"And so I do, Max. Colonel, before I forget, I am to invite you to Lord and Lady Halifax's tonight for dinner and what passes for conversation in the Holy Fox's dreary London upper crust circle. Oh, as Mother's escort, of course, she mentioned it the other evening. What is that? Cannot attend? Pressing duties require your return to the Front? Neglected to pack your formal dress? Oh, dear. Mother will be so disappointed. Well, I tried."

"Not so fast, Sir. Intelligence duty requires the gaining of understanding of allies as well as enemies. Might I consult my calendar and give you a later reply, Winston?"

Churchill gave Lord Elsmere a pained look. "Reggie said you were obstinate. I wash my hands of the whole affair. Make your own ill-advised decisions."

Max frowned, "I thought we were gathered here together, beloved, to discuss matters of somewhat greater gravity than your dear mother's infatuations, Minister. Please continue, as you have a speech to make, and make shortly."

"Yes, and not much time," said Churchill, looking at his pocketwatch. "Much to be said about the Bolshevik threat, but much more by you two to your readerships," pointing at Aitken and McCormick. "We shall resume these discussions afterwards, but now to the *piece de résistance*, the culmination of my remarks."

Aitken interrupted, "By now we are an hour and a half into your speech and you are just getting to the point? I have a newspaper to run, old fellow. Deadlines!"

"Then another headline for you. '*Yanks to be deployed with our Tommies?*' That is my point, Sir. Why allow the French to monopolize the growing American strength? They are after all, of sturdy English stock…"

Emerson raised a finger, "Except for the Germans and the Irish and the Italians and the Scots and the Negroes and the other hosts. Be careful with your comment, Winston, Sir. A shrewd opponent can throw it back in your face."

He is not being entirely helpful, Reggie thought. *Bad news from their headquarters?*

Churchill paused a few moments, taken aback at the criticism of his pinnacle, his crest. Uncharacteristically subdued, "Yes, Colonel, yes, I suppose there is truth to that. And I can think of any number who would seize on it to distract from my point and personally besmirch me."

"May I offer a suggestion, Sir?" This time, Emerson was trying to be helpful. "United by language. Shakespeare, Milton, Scott, all that."

"Excellent! But with a twist, a clever one, of course." He scribbled on his script. "Now, since you are being so impertinent, what says your General Pershing to my missive?"

"Run with it, Winston," eliciting a broad smile from Churchill. "With the caveats we discussed, but he warmed to it immediately. Especially when I brought up the French mutinies. Put five new divisions in your hip pocket for your speech. More on good behavior." Emerson smiled back.

Reggie consulted his wristwatch. "Your speech, Winston. We must be off."

They left the complex the way they had entered, Mitchell Cabot walking Colonel Emerson down the Strand, Aitken and his three proceeding by limousine. The House of Commons was packed, every bench and seat full. Many of the members were expecting a reprise of Churchill's secret speech of the summer before, unaware of the even greater controversy the speaker aimed to foment. Both lords and their American guests found places in the public gallery, just down from the Dutch Chargé d'affaires who briefly acknowledged Reggie and Emerson. After comments from the Speaker and the Prime Minister, the main event began.

As Churchill stood, the murmurs and rumbles from both sides increased steadily. Churchill was equally despised by Labour as an aristocrat and by the Tories as an apostate, and his Liberal support was none too solid in the event. Not that it mattered to him as he took his time to fumble with his waistcoat, then his reading glasses and finally his draft. A voice from the right rang out, "Is the Right Honourable Member finished?" answered by shouts of 'Yes' from the right and applause from the left.

"Finished? Polished, I should say. Finely honed."

His speech started tamely enough, a relatively calm reading of statistics pertaining to Britain's impressive increase in output since Winston's advent at Munitions, especially of his brainchild, the tank. From time to time he punctuated the drier recitations with references to the Kaiser or Ludendorff or unrestricted submarine warfare, proudly touting the benefits of his insistence on adoption of the convoy system and its restoration of Britain's lifelines. He finished this chapter with a flourish:

Astride the far reaches of the Earth
Britannia now stands fully girt
Woe to those so blind
To confront her so inclined.

The House, friend and foe, stood and cheered. Even his most bitter detractors could not gainsay the Ministry's accomplishments, even as cries of '*Conscription*' rang out from the Left. Churchill raised his head, swiveling it left to right, not really looking at any of the Members, and then nodded toward the Speaker, informing him he would be making additional comments. The Speaker nodded back, the Prime Minister gave the Chancellor a quizzical look as Churchill launched headlong into his second chapter.

Freddie Guest, Churchill's cousin and Lloyd George's aide, leaned over to Reggie to ask, "Did you temper his remarks? Tell me yes, I pray?"

Lord Elsmere's face gave all the response Freddie required. "So be it. Off to the races then, old man."

Churchill began in the same measured tones as his earlier remarks. "We face an implacable foe to our east, as has been our fate through the centuries, a fate not just a figment of our Divine mapmaker's wisdom in separating us from the Continent, but of a fundamental divide in civilization. Geography dictates, yes, but Civilization creates, and at this moment, the British civilization our forebears created, our cherished way of life, is under siege, facing a threat not seen since the end of Bonapartism." Warming to his subject, he continued in his distinctive cadence,

Yes, we are holding fast, Yes, we are armed as no other, Yes, our
Navy protects our shores and our lifelines, and our doughty yeomen
Shoulder arms again as at Blenheim and Waterloo, their Enfields
Striking as did their forebears' longbows at Agincourt.

Standing fast against the Eastern eagles, whosoever they may be,
Now as we approach another year of this senseless war,
Yet another menace begins to shed its rough cloak
Presenting itself to a sorely ravaged world.

A threat greater even than the Teutons across the trench, yes, clearly
Far, far worse than the Turk, the Bulgar, the Magyar, the Czech
Yet, once friends in arms as were the Prussians against
The Corsican, but now in cowardly retreat and
Quitting the field in the East – the Russians.

A murmur from the left rose to a rumble, then encouraged, to a roar. Ramsay McDonald rose to challenge Churchill, "I can certainly understand the Minister's aversion to any expression of Socialism as he considers the will of the people a trifle to be smiled at and dismissed by himself and his fellow aristocratic elites. The Socialist revolutionaries in Russia have only paused to gather their resources and their not inconsiderable strength in anticipation of a renewal of their deadly conflict with Germany. To our advantage, I might add." He turned to his backbenchers, his glib smile an expression of his satisfaction with himself and his remarks. "I have this from unimpeachable sources in which I have the highest confidence." His Labourites acclaimed these comments with loud applause.

Churchill looked over his reading glasses and began his rejoinder, "I do not resent criticism, even when, for the sake of emphasis, it departs from reality. But perhaps the Honourable Member for…for Labour should recall Drayton's words,

'Ill news hath wings, and with the wind doth go,
Comfort's a cripple and comes ever slow.'

"If, of course, he is the least familiar with English poetry." The Tory benches, packed with public school products, roared back across the chamber at the Left. McDonald began to rise to respond to the rebuke, then thought better of it, and Churchill improvised a further riposte:

Your desired Comfort is past crippled, now and future lamed,
immobile
Whilst on wings of bats doth ill news fly on a strong easterly wind,
Not just Petrograd do we see bathed in blood and terror
But Berlin itself in flames, a new conflagration set
By Labour's Socialist allies themselves.

No, my friends, do not spring to hope Berlin's agonies will bring down
The hated German regime, the Kaiser foremost, his Generals.
No, that regime will prevail, and against commonsense
We must wish it so, for who knows what demons
Might flutter from its ruptured breast?

And to the east? Trotsky announces the end of the once vaunted Russian
Army,
And a cowardly policy of disengagement, freeing our German foes
To fall wholesale upon us and our Allies in Flanders,
Rescuing Germany from the noose, our blockade,
As they pursue peace on Teutonic terms.

Pausing to let his imagery sink in upon a suddenly quiet House, he
returned to his prepared script:

We know not the depths of the villainy beyond the Vistula, but can
imagine
The bestiality of the Russian Bear now having discovered
That immoral and debilitating philosophy called Marxism
And twisting and turning any scrap of logic therein
Into a creed of iron control and repression.

Russia is being rapidly reduced by the Bolsheviks to an animal
barbarism
Maintained by bloody and wholesale butcheries and murders...

Suddenly a shout of "I spy strangers!" rang out from the Labour benches.
Reggie thought it came from Henderson, or someone near him. *Is Cromie
right about him, already?* Emerson and McCormick leaned over with questioning looks. "Any Member may call for a secret session, and that was the
ancient cry therefor. We are required to leave our seats, and when the House
is cleared, Winston shall resume without us. Here," handing several sheets
of notes to Beaverbrook, "these are his impromptu comments to add to your
carbon."

"Thank you, Reggie. Now I can get my newspaper out, to maximum effect. Major McCormick, you will return with me and we will give you use of our modest facility. Do let me know, Freddie, old man, if he goes off on another tangent or two?"

When the House had emptied of guests, Churchill prepared to resume, unruffled by the commotion. He poured himself a glass of water, conspicuously downing half then turning toward Bonar Law, "I think it a great surprise to the Leader of the Conservatives to see I do drink water." His Liberal colleagues gave out shouts and peals of laughter at Churchill's jibe. He then started again,

Russia is being rapidly reduced by the Bolsheviks to an animal barbarism
Maintained by bloody and wholesale butcheries and murders
Civilization is being completely extinguished over vast areas
While Bolsheviks hop and caper as troops of baboons
Amid ruins of cities and corpses of victims

No longer can we count Russia as ally, however inconstant we thought her
No longer can we hide behind her millions at arms, now disbanded
No longer can we see her as an anachronism of feudalism,
A monarchy perched atop one of history's dung heaps
Glittering above, fetid and festering below.

That day has passed. And with its passing comes another mortal threat,
Devoid of even the misguided, docile Christianity of Germany,
Harnessed in its contortions to the service of that regime
For there is no Divinity, no Grace, no Compassion
Promised by the atheist, this wretch Lenin.

I shall not go so far as to proclaim 'The enemy of mine enemy is my friend'
Any more than I would embrace Cousin Willie as our prodigal son.
But we must make our British people and the world at large

Aware of the mortal threat arising once again
From the nightmare lands of the East.

The House was a seething cauldron of voices, hoots and harrumphs. Lloyd George allowed himself the smallest of smiles whilst furrowing his bushy brows. Churchill paused briefly amid the tumult, turning again to the Speaker, then began again as the Members settled in their seats, still abuzz.

No, forewarned of the Red Menace, let us not take our eyes from the West,
Remaining locked, indeed deadlocked, in deadly combat with the Hun,
Resolved to once and for all lay that mortal threat to rest, yet
Knowing the fearsome blow sure to come this Spring,

We have committed Isles and Empire even unto to the smallest parish
English, Welsh, Scots and Irish, Canada, Australia, India and Africa,
And why? The Belgians? The French? Certainly not Russia.
No. We know why. Blake's green and pleasant land.
Britannia, Albion, a notion, our nation.

But let us acknowledge the reality alongside the ideal. Russia, gone to us.
And as she goes, freed are the very best of the Hun, in their millions
To fall upon our lads in France as the leopard upon the doe.
And whence cometh our succor? We, fully invested,
Having paid a grievous toll, are near spent

So to counter the East we must look to the West across the broad Atlantic
To the return of the prodigal sons, the Colonial rebels, to the bosom of
Mother Albion, in the moment to save her from mortal threat.

In their strength, bolstered by their Italian and Pole, Negro and Spaniard,
And, yes, even their German, at full flood, arriving by the thousands
Raw, untrained, ill-equipped, yes, but fresh and fervid and
Ready to serve. But how? And to the point...where?

Members, consider those two most vital questions. In France, of course.
But, are they coming to our aid? Are they deploying to our thin-held
Lines, to the trenchland so dearly paid in blood and treasure?
No, they are somewhere deep in France, and I defy a
Member among you to show me on the map.

He paused for a draught of water, surveying the Chamber, quiet, rapt, every bench. He measured the silence, then returned to his closing, short and pithy:

Now I must ask you as I ask myself,
As draw near the direst hours,

Why are not our kith and kin
Shoulder to shoulder with ours?

Despite our past and yet because of it,
We are still a common people

Bound, not divided, by language and ancestry.
Why are we not <u>now</u> brothers-in-arms?

The House remained silent but a few moments until even the Tory benches erupted in cheers alongside the Liberals. Labour's leaders had not let their scowls fade from Churchill's scarifying critique of their Bolshevik brothers, but a backbencher cried, "Send us the Yanks!" At that, the other parties picked up the chant and continued until the Speaker managed to restore order. "Has the Right Honourable Member fully concluded his remarks?"

"Yes, Mister Speaker, I am finished. Sufficiently polished. Finely honed. Good day." He left the front row, encountering as he did Lloyd George. The Prime Minister remonstrated with his hands and scowls for public consumption but his words told a different story. "Well, Winston, now you have well and truly done it. Next time you usurp our policymaking, do please give me but a minute's notice? But," drawing closer, "well done. You have put the ball in play at the most opportune time. Haig and Robertson have become quite unbearable. Knowing you, you have more arrows in your quiver. Do please drop by Number Ten and let us discuss what lies beneath your oration. Scintillating, it was. Your best ever."

Lloyd George brushed by him to take on the brunt of the simmering Chamber, leaving Churchill to make his exit, luxuriating in cheers.

On Fleet Street, Max Aitken was simultaneously proofing and editing Jenkin's galleys, drafting an editorial by hand and listening to Lord Elsmere's briefing on his and Churchill's clandestine intelligence sources. Aitken stopped, eyebrows up, when Reggie mentioned their German intelligence connection. "I am not sure I wish to hear any of this, old man, as I am entrusted with a portfolio. Yet…" Just then, Miss Adelaide rang. "Yes? He is where? The Savoy? Tell him some of us actually have work to do. Tell him…tell him I shall send him some of his beloved Yanks." He hung up and turned to Reggie. "Winston. Luncheon. Now that he has slain his dragons, says he is famished. Mister Cabot, would you please take your Americans with you to the Savoy. Seems the Minister requires an audience even at mealtime."

McCormick waved his fellows off, "Max and I have editions to make. Will catch up later. After, repeat, after teatime."

Churchill was well into his meal when the Americans arrived, but had hardly eaten, such was the stream of wellwishers drawn to his table. Seeing the two, he rose and beckoned them, nodding to two others in conversation with him. "Come along, Yanks, join me for a light repast. Allow me, James MacKay, our Lord Inchcape, and General Sir Peregrine Smythe-Bonham. At first glance, typical examples of the Tory species, yet beneath the surface, typical examples of the Tory species."

The two Englishmen laughed, MacKay replying, "At the hands of such we are hoist? I think not. The fact is, Gentlemen, we are not at all typical inasmuch as we actually converse with this reprobate, this renegade, against strictest party orders."

Cabot and Emerson introduced themselves, in bare breaths truncated by Churchill's continued bantering. "This one," pointing to Emerson, "demanded to meet Mother the other night. She and his father were acquainted in America, it seems. As were a great many other Americans, I am now reminded. Pray tell me you did not bring your formal attire, Colonel?"

As MacKay and Smythe-Bonham gave each other quizzical glances, yet without evident surprise at whatever issued from Churchill's lips, Emerson took great pleasure in replying, "Of course, Sir, my dress uniform. I was invited, after all. You see, Gentlemen, we Americans are playing catch up, as we say, in this whole war affair, so every opportunity to ingratiate ourselves with our newfound fellows is welcomed. Mitch, can your valet press some things?" Cabot nodded and Emerson continued, "Mister Churchill, would you be so kind as to so notify your dear mother?"

Churchill placed his fist against his chest, the variety of indigestion unknown but likely related to his new Yankee friend. He waved at a waiter and barked out a short message for immediate delivery. "He dines at Halifax's tonight, then. On such experiences have alliances been sundered and monarchs deposed. Enough. These two were critiquing my speech and I was listening as they were exceedingly complimentary of the sentiment and the delivery, but felt I had been much too timid in my prescription."

"Yes, Winston, yes. Colonel, your General Pershing has some bal... audacity to keep his force under his command. Can he respond to the Minister's pleas?" Smythe-Bonham was a retired Major General, one with a commendable record in Africa and South Asia. "I toured the front just this past week with Haig and Plumer, on Herbert's return, and we are thin. Winston, your guns and limbers are piling up in the rear for a lack of crews. Same with every trench and dugout. Dangerously thin."

"He has made his position clear, an independent American command. The French still do not see it that way. There is some friction." Emerson paused to let the last sink in a bit. "Our problem, as we see it, is simply getting the boys here and trained. Every Cunard and White Star ship is packed with doughboys with four or five weeks' basic training. Right now, the French are taking the lead in polishing them up. We lack enough senior NCO's and junior officers to do the job, just on the sheer numbers. Perhaps, General, Sir, the British Army could spare such?"

"Which would bring them to the north, of course. Closer to Calais, for that matter. Allow me some inquiries." General Smythe-Bonham had been offered a Corps in 1914, declining the command as he felt himself too old at eighty-two. Since then, he had been advising the Government behind the scenes on the British Army's senior officers' competence. It had taken him a year and a half to be rid of French, a million casualties, a like period with Gough, another half million, and he was wrestling with Haig at the moment.

"Please do not forget my ships, Colonel. P & O has lost nearly eighty hulls thus far, though I commend our host, here, for his convoy system – our losses are cut dramatically. None of the troopships lost, thankfully." MacKay was Chairman of Peninsular & Oriental, now with well over half his ships requisitioned. "Hence my conviviality, despite Party dicta."

"Bobby, stay out of their interparty squabbles. Make ours look like your daughters' tea parties. Crap! Speaking of tea parties..."

Just then two of yesterday's dowagers came sweeping across the crowded dining room, ignoring all but those clustered around Churchill. From several tables away the lead tank let loose a salvo. "Lord Inchcape, Sir Perry, how can you possibly consort with this turncoat, this traitor to his class? At least your American friends can plead ignorance but there is no such excuse for you."

"Good day, Lady Postlethwaite, Lady Entwistle. Such an unexpected pleasure. No, I fear you have us dead to rights, Madame." MacKay wore his amusement openly on his grinning face. "Please assure us neither of you will reveal our transgressions to Andrew lest we be banned from the Carlton Club and your lord husband's company." He lifted, with some effort, Lady P's hand to kiss it, then turned to Lady E's more willingly proffered hand.

General Smythe-Bonham gave a formal bow, "My sentiments, precisely, Ladies. Please forgive our all too public indiscretion. Jimmy, we must be away. Good day, Ladies, Gentlemen." He tugged at MacKay and slipped beyond reach with a parting wave.

Lady Postlewaite then turned her florid wrath on Churchill, who swirled his brandy ostentatiously for her benefit. "Drunk again at midday! Your long suffering darling wife shall once again be disappointed when you stumble home."

"Sadly, in confronting your Ladyship I am not drunk, but if I were, and were to stumble home, it would be this afternoon, not in the wee hours tomorrow morning." Lord Postlethwaite was known for closing down the Carlton Club in preference to spending evenings with his wife.

Before she could reply, Cabot played the diplomat. "Ladies, we are here for tea, as advertised. Shall we?" He turned Lady Postlethwaite around, signaling Churchill behind his back to flee. "Colonel Emerson and I are delighted to see you again."

"Unfortunately, I have pressing appointments and must depart. Mister Cabot, here, you should know, was a dashing young cavalry officer with us in Mexico, chasing Pancho Villa and his bandits. He has many tales to tell, I am sure." Emerson made his exit pursued by Cabot's murderous looks.

* * *

Tuesday, January 29, 1700 Hours
Foreign Office, Berlin

Max and von Treptow had dispatched Knorr earlier to Amsterdam, not London, to his immense relief, to meet with Pieter and his assistant to take possession of the Saint Petersburg dispatches. The police came in from time to time with reports of the unrest, confined largely to Berlin and environs, satellite disruptions in Munich, Frankfurt and Dresden already quashed. Hentsch's men were just now being deployed, already proving his prediction of their ferocity.

"Dietrich," said Max, looking at the latest message from outside the sanctum, "if you have any ideas about your friend Rosa, you must act now. From Noske," pointing at the paper, "tribunal this evening, 1800 hours."

"My instinct is to let her swing at the Socialists' hands – she has played out the part we wrote for her. Yet I hate to waste a resource such as she. There may be another role for her in the future. Max, I am thinking of her opposition to Lenin and her credibility as an ideologue and intellectual. She may be worth more to us alive than dead. I cannot say the same for her colleagues."

"Do you think you can control her?" Max smirked at Dietrich, "More so than my sister?"

"Your sister is beyond any measure of control. Always has been, you know that. Rosa we can control, back in Breslau. We try her for treason but incarcerate her beforehand for as long as we think she might be useful. If she proves otherwise, well, she is dispensable, is she not?"

"Bloodshed. Well, all our hands are bathed in blood, and she is a traitor, that is a certainty. I shall write a letter," he began scribbling on his princely letterhead, "and have the warrant issued. All of which will have no effect if Ebert and Noske get their way. We will have to fetch her away from that danger. Call Hentsch, get a company or two of his men to go with you."

"No, no time and unnecessarily provocative. Captain and I will go, along with your two sons of Ajax, if I may have them."

"Then be gone. Here, take my letter. The warrant may, or may not, arrive in time, but you would have disregarded it regardless, yes?"

"Yes." He turned to von Seeckt, "Ready to use the Colts?"

"Yes, Sir!"

Passing Police Lieutenant Schnabel, he requested three cars' worth of officers to rendezvous a discreet distance from their destination, Socialist Party Headquarters.

* * *

Tuesday, January 29, 1730 Hours
Hannover Station

Wolfgang met Walter as he stepped from the Berlin train, changing to Amsterdam. "Well, little brother, now you are onto spy work?"

"Diplomacy, dear brother, diplomacy. Merely banker's work in the geopolitical sphere. Nothing so intriguing. How are my houseguests getting along?"

"No change. Yvette and Hildegarde parade themselves whenever the weather allows, trolling for boys, my Georg included. We see Estelle from time to time, but do not impose on her. Frau Hummel from the Swan Ball did pay her a call, went well, I am told. I believe some of your youthful indiscretions were revealed, so be forewarned."

He handed over a stamped visa and a commercial activity permit. "Here are your entry documents, fresh from the Dutch Consulate. And, if you have not forgotten these, your business cards as Managing Director of the bank. Kept in the unlikely case of your return to the fold. Your cover, following on my last business trip."

"My cover? Are you reading espionage novels now? Nothing so dramatic as you can imagine is fated to happen. This is a simple meeting, nothing else."

"Of course. Do you require a weapons carrier? I have a few hours to spare."

"Enough. Give my love to Constance. I am gone."

* * *

Tuesday, January 29, 1800 Hours
Berlin

Von Treptow and his three bodyguards stopped in front of Socialist Headquarters, an undistinguished former insurance company building on a nondescript street between working class and lower bourgeois neighborhoods. Monocle in place, he stepped out of the idling staff car and strode forcefully to the entrance. Eight armed guards, several in *stahlhelms,* blocked the entry until their leader recognized the general and stiffened into attention, holding a salute. "General von Treptow!" he exclaimed, setting his fellows on alert, "You, er, ah, you are not expected, Sir."

"No, I daresay I am not. Sergeant...Sergeant Moelcke, is it not? 24th Brandenburg? Company Delta? Were you not with Colonel, rather Major Knorr at the High Wood? An Iron Cross for you?"

"Yes, Sir, on your recommendation, Sir, and thank you, Sir! You, men! Shape up! This is one of the true heroes of this war! Brigadier General von Treptow! *Achtung!"* His little detail did shape up, more or less, a pair of grumblers at one end. Von Treptow performed an impromptu inspection of the line, ending at the obviously disgruntled pair with a withering stare. The two shrunk away.

"Now, Sergeant, if we may?" Von Treptow pointed to the door, his meaning clear.

"Yes, Sir! Boys, let the general and his men in!"

Once in, the little group brushed past several dozen surprised and unfriendly men in the foyer, some in semblances of uniform, others in working men's garb. Von Treptow slammed open the double doors into the Party's auditorium and continued striding in his distinctive gait toward the speaker's platform. Friedrich Ebert was berating his captives on the stage when he turned toward the commotion effervescing in the officers' wake. "What? What is the meaning of this? Who...Ah, General von Treptow. Did your master, Prince Max, send you to plead clemency for these vermin?"

Von Treptow continued, silent and unchallenged, until he bounded up the steps to the platform coming face to face with the Socialist leader, drawing his Colt and placing it atop Ebert's nose. The latter looked crosseyed up at the barrel. The crowd responded angrily and von Seeckt and his mates turned and drew their pistols, presenting a 'W' of gun barrels to the rabble. Von Treptow withdrew Max's letter from his coat with his left hand and handed it to Noske, commanding simply, "Read."

Noske did as ordered, then gave him a little smile. "Sorry, General, you have no sway here. These are our prisoners, subject to Socialist justice alone. You may leave now."

Von Treptow cocked his pistol. Ebert pleaded nervously, "Gustav, I think he means some serious business. Reconsider? Please?"

Noske sighed. Expressions of weakness disgusted him. "Very well. General, will you at least lower your weapon? We will talk, I assure you."

Von Treptow lifted the barrel, releasing the hammer. "Captain, stay alert. Yes, then, thank you, Gustav. Do as I say and we shall be on our way. No bloodshed. There has been enough this week as it is."

"Just Luxemburg?" asked Noske, rereading Max's letter. "No warrant, no Police? Just you and your supermen?"

"And our persuaders, yes," waving his Colt in Noske's general direction. "Yes, just Luxemburg. A warrant follows, all perfectly legal."

"And the rest of this sorry lot?" asked Noske.

Von Treptow walked across the platform past each of the prisoners. He turned back and stopped in front of Liebknecht, placing his pistol against the unfortunate's trembling forehead. "I am tempted. Sorely tempted, I am." He paused, "But, no." He lowered his gun, holstering it. "I wash my hands of these. We take our leave. Unshackle her. Now!"

Noske turned to one of his aides who had already leapt to carry out the order. Rosa rubbed her wrists as they were released, then stiffly, haltingly, attempted to rise. *She has clearly been abused at their hands,* thought von Treptow. He helped her up, then covered her shoulders with his left arm as he led her back up the aisle without looking back. They proceeded together, the tall officer and the slight radical, through the doors to the waiting staff car, stopping only to salute Sergeant Moelcke and shake his hand, then away they went.

A few blocks away, Major Bruckmiller flagged down the car. "Let us be quick, Sir. Too many eyes about tonight." Moments later, gunshots were heard from the direction they had just come. "Let Socialist Justice be done," said von Treptow, his irony clear. Bruckmiller just nodded, Rosa still too stunned to respond.

"Rosa, you are alive, but not free. You are to be returned to Breslau immediately to stand trial for treason. A fair trial, not the rude judgment just rendered on Karl and your friends. Good night. Major?..."

"We will treat her with every consideration, Sir. Count on us."

"Good night, then."

As von Seeckt climbed back into the car, he asked, "General, Sir, may I ask why we went to pistols so quickly, Sir?"

"Captain, to abridge Ecclesiastes, profanely, there is a time to kill and a time to heel. I do not heel. Have you noticed this?"

"Yes, Sir, I have. Regularly. It has entered my daily expectations alongside dawn and dusk."

* * *

Tuesday, January 29, 2100 Hours
Amsterdam Centraal

Colonel Knorr stepped off the First Class carriage onto the platform wearing one of Frantz's British business suits he rather fancied. Diagonally across toward the station a cigarette lighter flared. Knorr and the smoker walked along converging paths, the latter passing behind, saying, "Black Renault, end of the taxi line. Morten."

Walter stopped at the WC, then bought himself a hard roll at a kiosk, then exited the station. Seeing the taxis, he stopped to tie his shoe on a bench, then picked up his cases and walked with purpose past the cabbies' calls. The Renault's driver was polishing the car's canted grille. "Morten?"

"Where to, Sir? I can suggest a hotel, several, if you like. Other diversions?"

"Your recommendation will be satisfactory, I am sure." Knorr handed his cases to the driver and entered the enclosed passenger cab.

Not ten minutes later, the driver looped his car around a block of flats a street back from one of the canals, then turned sharply into an alley, stopping with a sharp stab on the brake. Knorr had only a moment to leave the cab before it resumed its motion, 'Morten' tossing his cases to a shadowed man just inside a darkened doorway.

"Welcome, Colonel, to our little hostelry. All the comforts of home as you shall see." He closed and bolted the steel door behind him, then led the way down a dimly lit hallway. Opening a door, he led Knorr into a well lit room with three soldiers, two at wirelesses, one reviewing some papers. "Captain Schoenig at your service, Sir. Privates Schmidt, Schimpff, and Lieutenant Dettweiller, Military Intelligence. And cashiers at Dresdner Bank, all. Hard to keep their fingers and thumbs from getting sticky."

Knorr saluted, then went round shaking hands. "Captain, will we have the meet here, or is there another safe house? My briefing was precisely that, brief."

"Next door, actually. Our Dutch counterparts' establishment. Delicatessen in front. Connecting doors, concealed, so no need to expose yourself. Unless, of course, you would like. Our front is a fully functioning brothel. Pretty girls, really, Sir. Great cover."

"Really, Sir," piped up Schmidt. "A great duty posting."

"Whose idea? No, no, let me guess. General von Treptow?"

"No, Sir, you know the man. Pieter van der Hoek. The entire setup was his idea. Of course, he has others for the French and British, but not so well located, nor," he cocked his head toward the front, "...so well stocked as ours."

"Considerate of him, truly. Speaking truly, I am truly fatigued. I will retire, solo, if I may?"

"Of course, Sir. This way."

* * *

Tuesday, January 29, 2345 Hours
Port of Rotterdam

SS Edam eased up to the quay, longshoremen and sailors swarming about like a tribe of ants, securing hawsers, opening hatches and lowering the gangway. A dozen or more passengers of all stripes and shapes descended from the little steamer, chatting and jabbering, looking for taxicabs. After a good fifteen minutes, two more emerged, one male, one female, hurrying down to dockside. From a warehouse entry came an automobile, quickly pulling up to the two and their porters. In seconds the two and their luggage were securely within and the car lurched away. Moments later another car turned onto the quay, following the same path. And another, stopping alongside.

From the bridge, the Captain and a well-dressed businessman watched the promenade. "Sir, my protest still stands. I have missed my schedule, risked U-Boat attack and inconvenienced my passengers. Regardless of any official business you may have."

"You have been well recompensed. Do not trouble me with your trivial complaints." He flicked his cigarette over the side, gathered his cane and coat and left the bridge, disembarked and entered the waiting car.

"Your Lordship, we have three tails on their two cars to ensure no switch is made. We will be calling attention to ourselves, so I trust this is a matter of vital importance?" Captain Wingate of Naval Intelligence, aka the British Naval Attaché, had been alerted late into the matter, cobbling together his operatives and driving up from The Hague.

"Would I be here were it not? Yes, vital. Ask no more questions, please." Lord Elsmere was in a foul mood, having spent several hours in what he considered steerage, after having terrified Gresham in his dash to Dover in his Mercer Raceabout. Lionel and his NID agents had tailed Pieter, quickly divining his destination and alerting Reggie at Aitken's office. Reggie in turn had Gresham bring the Mercer and a suitcase to Fleet Street and he simply stepped out of the offices and was gone.

With the Dutch tricolor painted on its side for the U-Boats' benefit, NID had no difficulty in identifying the ship and buttonholing its Captain, informing him of a delay to await another passenger to be secreted aboard at the last minute. The last was the tricky part as every porthole had eyes within. One lifeboat was removed for repairs, its substitute hauled up by the davits just at dusk with one Reginald, Lord Elsmere under its canvas cover.

* * *

Wednesday, January 30, 11:00 a.m.
Ministry of Munitions, London

"No, Miss Linthicum, I have not seen him! I seek the cad myself! Notify me immediately the instant he appears!" Churchill slammed his telephone set down on his desk. "Where is that man? He knows we have important discussions today."

"Perhaps a little too much entertainment last night?" asked Cabot. The Americans themselves were late, as Colonel Emerson had stayed out past curfew, having squired Lady Churchill first to Lord Halifax's for a delightfully splendid dinner and equally stultifying conversation. "Then your mother could take no more, abruptly announcing we were departing for some club or another. Lady Cunard saw her chance and joined us. By now, both ladies had imbibed professionally, if you catch my meaning, and decided to walk at least as far as Lady Diana Cooper's house where they were assured of obtaining more wine.

"A beautiful night it was, until the searchlights came on. Four Gothas cruised toward us – miles away in the spotlights, actually, but seemed right on top of us – so we detoured. The ladies were in a tizzy, sure the Huns were following them and them alone in all of London. Sure enough, the bombs came down not so far away, just as we reached safety at the Cooper house. I thought they were done, leaning back in the drawing room chairs, fanning themselves. No, sadly, just recharging their batteries. Three hours and two clubs later, I managed to get them both home. Sorry to have disturbed you, Winston, Sir."

"He is married, is he not, Cabot? Tell me she did not propose."

"No, Sir, I suggested she and my father would be more compatible, as my Emily would not countenance an extra wife, even if set apart by the entire Atlantic. I have invited Dad to visit, but may ask you to provide the necessary disclosures, if you get my drift."

"Your drift, your tides, your entire damned ocean. Yes, for my own and Clementine's sanity, I will gladly furnish fair warning. Your father was widowed when? Or divorced, if I am not prying?"

"Widowed, Winston. Mom passed in 1910. He is doing okay, a few age ailments, but is much in demand as an escort in what passes for society in St. Louis and Clayton, if not yet as a second or third husband. Whether he can handle your mother, well, that would be his problem, no?"

"You fail to grasp the enormity of it all, Robert. The enormity." He rocked his head side to side, his jowls shaking. "Well. When do you report back to your General Pershing?"

"We are to head back tomorrow, but I seriously doubt I will be able to pry Bertie away from your friend Lord Beaverbrook. I'll have to cable over to gain him additional leave, but as you can see," pointing at the newspapers on Churchill's desk, "there is important stuff here."

"Yes, this 'stuff', as you say, is dynamite, again as you Yanks would say. Max's editorial in the *Evening Standard* was positively unassailable on both counts, your deployments and the Bolshevik threat. Even if he relied heavily on my poetry. At least he published my remarks in their whole. Even the *Guardian* was in grudging agreement. Your McCormick's editions will be similar, yes? Is his readership so inclined to such serious topics?"

"Not so much as the seaboard informed classes, but his paper cannot be ignored," said Cabot. "I have already seen to it that the *Globe* and the *Times* will pay attention to your comments."

"And I thought I was the one who moved the presses to print. Hmmm." Churchill leaned back, twirling his cigar, "What would it take to move your President Wilson, Colonel?"

"I will defer to the diplomat, Sir. Mitch?"

"Well, Sir, Tommy is an obstinate...."

"Tommy? Our soldier's moniker?" Looking at the others, "Moniker. An Irish usage. Nickname!" Churchill threw up his hands. "Goodness!"

"Very well, Thomas Woodrow Wilson, Sir. Tommy among us Princetonians. As I was saying, Tommy, President Wilson, is self-assured, borderline arrogant, no, not borderline, just plain arrogant and a rigid ideologue to boot. That is not just opinion born of my Republican ancestry, but is widely held among thinking Democrats if not the machine nonentities and the masses. With that in mind, he will instinctively resist favorable comment on the Max and Bertie line. To move him, as you suggest, would....Hmmmm."

"Hmmmm? That is my line. What have you in mind?"

"A private conversation, the contents of which he could adopt as his own. Then promote as his own Revelation to the benighted world. That last is particularly important as he considers the rest of humanity beneath him. Smarter than the whole lot of us, you see. Every speech a jobation. Except he falls well short when it comes to impromptu or unprepared repartee..."

"Repartee? My speciality indeed!"

"My suspicion, confirmed. Could you secure your Lloyd George's approval of a message, a long telegram really, setting out not only your position but some intelligence intimations such that he could recast in his image? In your words, Sir, to give at least the illusion of sparkling repartee?

Unofficial, of course, as I would have to bypass Lansing. And Colonel House, for that matter. Much more difficult. I do have one other pathway."

"Of course! I relish the challenge and shall put pen to paper."

Reggie's absence had been forgotten, at least for the moment.

* * *

Wednesday, January 30, 1200 Hours
Amsterdam

Her parents let Alexandra Breithaupt sleep in after her early morning arrival but she managed to reach the family offices by 0930. There, Father and brother Bertrand wasted no time in cajoling her to come home to join the family business again. "You are far away the most perfect, most stunning advocate of our furs, my dear, the very exemplar of their elegance. If you wear them, everyone will want to wear them."

"Father is right, Sister. You might even find a husband, who is to say?"

"Hush, both of you. I have important duties in London, and here, too, I would have you know. If I could, that is. I do want to look over next winter's line, though..." She spent the next few hours trying to make things more *au courant,* less matronly, a bit more dashing. Not a skilled artist herself, she nonetheless could communicate her notions and those she picked up in London to the staff designers. *But, one could only do so much with fur...*

At noon, she gathered her brother for lunch. "You run your errands, I will stop at that delicatessen behind us. Come back for me there in twenty or thirty minutes. Do not stop next door. I will be watching." The two walked along the canal promenade, then turned back onto the street behind.

Pieter had picked this location for its proximity to Alexandra's family business, a convenient and credible excuse for being in the neighborhood. The deli had a deep enough seating area for the rear tables to be inconspicuous, hard to see from the street. Alexandra took the rearmost table, one that had been held for her, and ordered for her brother and herself. The staff knew to take their time, allowing her an extended visit to the facilities.

The women's was at the end of a narrow corridor, next to the rear entry. As she approached the loo, she continued straight out the rear, then to a blank metal door adjacent. She gave a coded knock, it opened and she disappeared instantly into a small storeroom, stepping straight into the back of a Dutch officer who had turned to slide a hidden wall panel. As they apologized to one other, Colonel Knorr appeared on the other side of the new opening. She stifled a small gasp as he greeted her, somewhat shyly. *He is even more handsome than I remember. And this is a dangerous mission for him. Did he come because of me?*

"Miss Breithaupt, you have met Colonel Knorr. I understand you have something for him? Commander van der Hoek should be along shortly. We will be up these stairs," sliding back yet another panel. Walter took Alexandra gently by the elbow as the two ascended the very steep stair, she clinging to the rail with her free hand, he carrying his valise. At the top was a low-ceilinged open space with no front windows, boards across the narrow rear windows.

"Captain Gruber, Miss, Sir. One of Pieter's aides. This," waving about, "is a mezzanine level tucked in between the ground and first floors. No other access. Not apparent from the street."

"Clever. Almost as clever as the girls' school next door. Are they yours, too?"

"Absolutely not, Sir. They are professionals!"

Outside, Pieter walked down the alley behind the building, secure in his invisibility and anonymity. Then another entered the other end of the alley, not at all what he was expecting. He thought briefly of reversing course, then decided to brazen it out, estimating he could reach at least the delicatessen's rear entrance. The other figure seemed to accelerate and soon his identity became clear. Van der Hoek stopped. "Reggie, what is the meaning of this? Why have you violated our accords?"

"I might ask you the same question. Why did you lie to me?"

"Aside from putting an end to your rantings? To protect Alexandra, of course. You put quite the fear into her."

"Enough. Enter, I shall follow."

"Your delicate constitution could not tolerate the food here, but it is convenient to my rounds today. What sort of Dutch food do you prefer?"

Lord Elsmere drew his Webley from the folds of his overcoat. "Enter."

Looking down the barrel, Pieter knew better than to banter. "Very well." He stepped beyond the deli entrance to the next door, rapped four times then keyed the bottom lock. Shortly, the top lock responded and the door opened.

"He is armed, Captain. My failure to anticipate his intensity. No resistance. Hand him your revolver."

The three ascended the stair, Reggie pocketing the Dutchman's gun. Pieter thought of abruptly stopping and shoving his friend down the steep flight, but he was his friend, after all. At the top he stood aside to let Lord Elsmere step out upon the floor. Alexandra cringed, but Walter Knorr, unaware of the controversy, smiled and walked over briskly, extending his hand only to confront a pistol levelled at his chest.

"Quite a way to greet an acquaintance, Sir. Have I displeased you in some way?"

"Your entire nation displeases me. From your idiot Kaiser all the way down." He turned to Alexandra, "Including you, my pretty."

Trying to tamp the tension, Pieter said, "His Lordship does not tolerate rivals, Colonel. For her attentions, that is." Seeing Knorr's puzzled look, "How long have you known our Alexandra, Colonel? Five minutes, perhaps ten? And when is your return train? Five hours hence? Hardly time for an assignation, let alone an affair. Reggie, he is here for the stated business. With some... "

Gruber lunged for Reggie's pistol hand, trying to knock it to the floor, but the Briton was too quick, sidestepping then smashing the barrel against the other's temple. Gruber staggered down to one knee. Elsmere waved the pistol around the room, then placed his foot against the Dutch officer's shoulder, shoving him back toward the stair. Unable to check his backward motion or grasp a rail, Gruber tumbled head first down the stair, landing in a heap.

Van der Hoek flashed a dark look, then made for the stair. Reggie shouted, "No! Do not move!" Pieter paused and looked his erstwhile friend square in the eye then turned toward the stair, his back to the pistol. Reggie took a step, aiming, when a metallic click resounded plangently in the confined space. Knorr pressed the American Colt hard against the back of Elsmere's head, hammer back, trigger lightly squeezed, his left hand around the other's neck.

"Well, hoist by my own petard, am I? Not gentlemanly to conceal one's weaponry, old man. Hardly sporting." He began to raise his hands in surrender, then dropped below Knorr's aim, swinging his pistol around. Knorr had not relaxed and he slammed a knee into Reggie's ribcage as it presented itself, then brought the heavy gunbarrel down hard across the lord's head.

As Reggie collapsed to the floor, his Webley discharged on impact.

Pieter looked across the room at Alexandra. She was holding the right side of her abdomen with both hands. Blood began to seep between her fingers.

As Knorr rushed to cradle her slumping figure, Pieter picked up the Webley, then the telephone set on a table a few steps away. "Hendrik, bring the cars, quickly. To the alley, now! Unlock the door yourself. We have injuries. Gruber and the young lady...No, no time to wait for an ambulance. Alert the military hospital...no, cannot have the police. No further attention here, you see. Move! Now!"

He dropped the Webley into Knorr's open case then the German's Colt likewise. Alexandria had fainted, but her breathing was only slightly irregular. "Need to get her out. Can you carry her?" Knorr nodded. Van der Hoek took Knorr's case and Alexandra's purse, leading him down the stair. Reggie lay still, crumpled upon himself.

He checked on Gruber, moaning on the floor below. "He is a tough one. Served in the Indies with me. Here, no time – step over him, if you can."

Knorr did so – Alexandria was light, at least against his adrenalin-fueled muscles – as the first of the Dutch officers opened the door to a brilliant sun in its brief daily survey of the narrow alley. He laid her gently into the rear seat of the first of two cars, then went round the other side. Then three unknown men came running down the alley and two gunshots rang out, startling all as the bullets whizzed high. The other Intelligence officers began to return fire, but Pieter stopped them after two or three shots, waving his handkerchief. Two others had already bundled the bulky captain into the other car. "Back down the alley, quickly. I will join you. Go!"

He stepped in front of the receding cars, blocking the view and, he hoped, more gunshots. He took Lord Elsmere's Webley out of the valise at his feet, breaking the top as he raised it, emptying the cylinder. "Your man's, I believe?" He tossed it at the feet of the leading intruder, and as attention was diverted, brought out the Colt, pointing it at the three. "Automatic, Gentlemen. Please do not force me."

The leader stopped short, lowering his pistol. "Captain Percival Wingate, British Naval Intelligence. Where is he? Have you killed him?" He raised his gun again.

"No. He is up that flight. He will have a headache equal to the very worst of his mornings after but is otherwise intact. His psyche is most deranged, I fear. We must get him out of the country immediately, as he has attempted murder. His two victims are on the way to hospital and questions will be asked. He fomented this, you shall clean up after him."

As the Brits dashed up the stair, he shook his head. *Such a perfect setting, among all my creations. A shame to have it go to waste.* He looked down at his case, then back at the exit from the alley. Stepping inside, he rapped sharply on the connecting door. Almost immediately it was opened by Captain Schoenig, asking, "What just happened? Gunshots?"

"Later, old man, later. Here," handing over the Cromie dispatches from Alexandra's purse, "these must be in your General von Treptow's hands at the earliest. I fear our designated courier will not find himself free to depart, not before his chivalric duties are done."

1500 Hours

Pieter greeted Alexandra's parents and brother at the entry to the small military hospital on the outskirts of Amsterdam. She had only been in surgery for less than an hour, so he had no news. What he could impart was shock enough, to say the least. Her family had entrusted van der Hoek with their daughter on nothing more than a girlfriend and an escape from the impending doom of war and Alexandra had not confided any hint of exciting, much less dangerous duties.

"Johannes, Anna, Bertrand, I am so sorry. A simple diplomatic errand has taken a most unfortunate turn. An accidental gunshot. Not at all what is expected in my profession. I take full responsibility, but I assure you she is in the hands of the finest surgeons, trained for exactly such conditions."

"Surgeons? Will she die?" Anna Breithaupt was frantic. "Pieter?"

"I wish I could explain, but I am equally at a loss. Perhaps…"

Herr Breithaupt cut him off. "Who did this? Has he been apprehended? What have the police to say?"

"Hans, we are well beyond that point. Please trust me to set matters straight. If I am able."

* * *

Thursday, January 31, 1500 hours
Schloss Treptow, Berlin

Von Treptow and his associates had retreated from the abating strikes and disturbances in Berlin to the seclusion of the estate. By now the Army and Police had largely put down the main activity, having waited for the various factions to batter each other to exhaustion. And into visibility. General Hentsch's barracks on the city's fringe was full of detainees, those who had survived the confrontations. Many more had not.

Prince Max, though indisposed to bloodshed, was nevertheless satisfied with the last few days. He and von Treptow spoke repeatedly on the telephone, its normal functioning having mysteriously been restored.

"Yes, Max, the Saint Petersburg dispatches arrived just now. Annie brought them in," looking at von Seeckt, who studiously kept his head down. "Amsterdam? Apparently there was some confrontation, several injuries. An unexpected guest caused the fracas, Winston Churchill's aide, one Lord Elsmere. What? Yes, I have met him, that most recent London visit. Van der Hoek warned us of his engrained hatred of us. It is a long story. No, he will not be back immediately. I have granted him a few days. Hoffman has his plans, I have a few days of ennui amidst the Bolsheviks, he will catch up to us in Russia. What is that? No, I would not dream of denying him. Yes, of course, Sir. Good day."

"Denying him, Sir? Denying him what?" Von Seeckt was flipping through more dispatches, part of Annie's special delivery.

"Taking tea with Trotsky, mmm, caviar with the Cossacks. Cannot think of anything with the Ukrainians. Fear not, we shall not create mayhem without him."

The estate was an island apart from the wider world in normal times, now a fortified redoubt amid troubles elsewhere. Treptow and the outer boroughs were mostly residential with a few industrial pockets here and there such as the Albatros factory in nearby Johannisthal. There had been disturbances and a major fire fueled by the highly inflammable dope used to seal the canvas and linen coverings for the wings and fuselages. That conflagration and the small rising responsible had swiftly been extinguished. Military justice at a key weapons factory was swift, rough and final.

Dietrich's eight year old nephew, young Willy, had developed a fever so Otto, the estate's engineer, brought him home with little sister Gracie and their mother Adele, the rest remaining in the country. Willy adored his important uncle and was fascinated by the big captain in his impressive uniform. A remarkable recovery ensued once he was allowed to sit with the officers and tag along with Major Bruckmiller and his squad on their rounds of the schloss and grounds.

Then a call came from the gate. "Sir, for you. You might wish to go into exile, Sir. I can tell them."

Willy looked at Dietrich, then Erich. "What does he mean, Uncle? What is exile?"

A look of illumination crossed von Treptow's face. "It means to go to a faraway country and not come back. Ever. A most enticing alternative, Captain. Well, nothing to do but admit her. Warn Augusta if you will, please."

He looked down at his nephew, "Come, Willy. Let us greet a real live princess. Go fetch Grace, but do not tell your mother."

Dietrich gathered his little protégés at the top of the grand stair. Soon enough the sound of motorcars and doors and orders came from without.

"Is she a beautiful Pwincess, Uncle Deet?" asked the not yet three year old Gracie.

"Oh, yes, little one. Very, very beautiful. See, here she is."

Below, a company of maids and footmen had assembled to greet the visitor. She brushed her way through them, "My things are already here, thank you. You may go. I have no need of you."

Gracie clung to her uncle's trousers. "Is she a wicked Pwincess? Willy tells me scawey stowies. If she is wicked, I shall be vewy afwaid."

Von Treptow lifted her up. "No, she is not wicked. I sometimes might think so, but she is not. Let us greet her." They met Claire at the bottom of the stair, Gracie clinging to his tunic, Willy in awe of the tall, striking woman dressed in austere, almost military fashion.

"Willy, dearest," leaning over to give the lad a kiss, his eyes tightly closed. "I have not seen you since your christening, seven, eight years ago?"

"Eight, Ma'am, Princess, Ma'am. I am eight." Von Treptow snuck a peek down to see if there was a puddle forming, fortunately not.

"And this precious little girl? What is your name, dear?"

Gracie buried her face in uncle's tunic. "Gwaycie," was the muffled reply.

"What was that, dearie? I could not hear you."

The little girl suddenly faced Claire and blurted, "Gwaycie! I am Gwaycie! I live heah. Wheah do you live? In a castle? With a Pwince?"

Claire laughed heartily, inducing both children to laugh along with her. Even Uncle Dietrich smiled. "Here, sweet child, come to me." She took Grace from Dietrich and sat on the bottom step, balancing the little girl in her lap. "I do not live in a castle at the moment, but I would very much like to live in one again. Like this beautiful castle," waving her hand at their surroundings. "You live in a beautiful castle, Gracie. That means you must be a Princess! Am I right?" The little girl nodded shyly. "I thought so. I can tell a Princess from leagues distant. Alas, I do not have a Prince. I have not lived happily ever after, dear child, but you will, I am certain."

This was a bit much for Gracie's understanding, but she smiled at the beautiful woman who was being so nice and said, "Uncle Deet is a handsome Pwince. I would vewy much like you to be his Pwincess." She looked up at a bemused General.

"As you wish, my little bunny rabbit. All your wishes shall come to pass. Pwincess, what think you?"

Claire started, "If that is a proposal...."

Gracie interrupted, excitedly, "Here comes the giant, Pwincess." Now very, very gravely, "please do not be afwaid, Pwincess. He is a vewy nice giant."

Von Seeckt motioned to the general. "Something new, Sir. Needs your attention. Now."

"Children, time to return to your quarters. You will see the Princess again at dinnertime. Augusta, please see to Claire's every need." He turned and sprinted up the stair, as if fleeing impending doom.

"Really, Captain? Or was that a rescue attempt?"

"Both, Sir. Whenever I hear the word proposal from a girl's lips, it stirs my flight instinct. Bruckmiller has some disturbing news."

Major Bruckmiller was standing in the upstairs study used as the schloss' command center. "Ah, General. It seems the worms begin to turn. Several reprisals attempted by the remnants of a number of groups, some successful.

Three assassinations, several fires. Two firebombs thrown at the Foreign Office, Prince Max's wing. Cannot be happenstance. One at the Reichstag, one at Army Headquarters. Most disturbing, apparently coordinated attacks. A car exploded in Unter den Linden, then another just as the ambulance arrived. A dozen or more dead. Another crazy walks into Zoo station, pulls out a cluster of dynamite sticks, lights it and holds it until it explodes. Most had time to get away or at least down. Three deaths so far, more injuries, not to mention the property damage."

"You cannot control this? Your infiltrators?"

"Most have been exposed in the actions, rendered useless. We have actually stopped several more attempts, which may mean progress, may not. The best news is the diminished ranks, only so many martyrs left for the cause, you see? Army is posting guards, redoubling patrols, and for our part, well, Sir, heads are rolling." The Berlin Police had a semi-secret cadre of tough guys, originally to fight gangsters on their own terms, now diverted to the political sphere. "The message has been sent to the various leaders. We will see."

"Except for the Anarchists, who have no leaders. Are you hinting we might face danger here, Major?"

"Yes, Sir, it certainly is possible and I have no more men to go around. And, then, well, Sir, she arrived just now."

"Do you have something to tell me, Major Bruckmiller?"

"Please, may we sit down, Sir?" He gestured toward the fire. "Greta, please make sure we have no eavesdroppers." The policewoman stepped outside, closing the doors behind her. "Your Princess Claire, Sir. She has been known to consort with rather dubious characters. Mostly cabaret types, artists, debauchees..."

"And Miss Lorelei, in both her incarnations. Yes, I see. And these characters, these pimps, she has been attracted to them for years. Gets into trouble from time to time. There is more to it?"

"Only this, Sir. Our plants and informers, 'Paragon,' Miss Big Tits, being a main source, have seen her in company of the leaders of several factions. Mostly socializing. Maybe, ahem, lovers, Sir. Have not uncovered any evidence of significant financial support, other than picking up the tab at the cabarets, but she is well acquainted with them, to the exclusion of polite society, shall we say?"

"Cannot blame her for this last. Your point, or points, Major?"

"Just these. Her presence and then her reaction at the Gate. Her disappearance, complete, the last two days. The, er, attrition among her Socialist friends and contacts. And now her appearance here."

"You think she might be a Trojan Horse? To unlatch the gates for some murderous Achaeans? Or, something more direct? Me?"

"Cannot say, Sir. Maybe each of those, maybe nothing at all. Your telephone system has already broken down again. Telekom types cannot seem to get it right, if you catch my meaning. We are running another wire up here to this connection alone. After dark we will withdraw from the front gates to a perimeter outside the schloss itself, well concealed, and add more men inside. But, Sir, that is all I have."

"We are alerted, then. Thank you, Major. Carry on." He saluted, surprising Bruckmiller, who stood, clumsily returned the salute, spun on a heel and marched out.

Damn it all. We could use Walter here tonight.

* * *

1800 hours

"Hiding behind children and giants, are we now, Dietrich? So cowardly for such a legendary killer? The blood of hundreds still fresh on the hands cradling your little princess of a niece?"

Claire had been sitting on a chair opposite the study for the last two hours, glowering at Greta and her replacements. Being denied entry had only stoked her fire, now at blue heat.

Von Treptow glanced at von Seeckt, then turned to his tormentor, "You are free to go at any time, Princess, if you find the company so revolting. Apologies, not the word of choice this week, is it? Let it be so. Yes, my dear, I am a killer. Many thousands more than just those few misguided unfortunates you saw at the Tor. Pointblank or artillery range, it is all the same to me. Atavistic, savage, ravening. Look into these eyes. Cold, cruel, call them what you will. Yet they have seen every decapitation, every mound of spilled intestine, every gushing fountain of blood. The men, boys, really, pleading with me to end their misery with one breath, then mewling for their mothers with the next. Yes, these eyes have seen them all. Every one."

He took a deep breath, then, "But these eyes grow weary, dearest Claire, as I grow weary of dealing cards with Death. I have cheated him time and time again, but I may well find I have no more aces secreted in my cuffs. Should I survive this night or any night to come, it will only be because Death is not done with me. He shall have a great and awful business with me yet, I fear. If not, well, I shall be discarded like a cold cigar in a stein of stale beer.

"And yet I regret none of this. I am not the monster you would have me be, Princess. I no longer control my destiny. Not since I crossed the Belgian border, certainly not since I sent Richard to his fate. I am caught between my bridge partner, Death, and an ephemeron, a fleeting vision of a life, our life, Claire. A life from whose roots I cannot wrench myself free. You only think you have, Claire, but you have not, never will. I never will, but only because I myself will wither before the roots themselves crumble away."

He glared at her, "Death has showed me the Socialist future, Claire, and it does not work contrary to your friends' wet dreams. No, that Red future will make Hobbes' nasty, brutish and short existence seem a carefree holiday. That is why I kill, Claire. I do not expect you to understand. If there is nothing else, we have other matters to attend. Dinner is early at 1900 hours so the children may join us." He did not wait for a reply.

* * *

1930 Hours

Claire smiled her way into the dining room, apologizing for her tardiness. "I hope you did not keep the little ones starving on my account? And you, Adele, dear? Your children are so precious. Hello, Rudy! Cure anything today? Major, Captain," rounding the table to the chair Dietrich held out for her, "My Pwince, Miss Grace. Is he not the handsomest, even moreso than the ones in your picture books?"

Gracie leaned her mother's direction, whispering loudly, "She is a pwincess, Mother."

"Yes, she is," whispered back her mother, "she reminds us so from time to time." The two women exchanged those knowing glares exclusive to their amalgam of gender and class.

"Well, now, Claire, this is a pleasure for these old eyes." Rudy had arrived from his laboratory just in time, innocent of the domestic intrigue and barely aware of the tumult surrounding the university. "There was a row of some sort between some of the older boys and a rabble outside the gates. Our boys had their swords, I hear. More shouting than anything else."

Claire started to object, but Dietrich interposed himself. "Rudy, tell us of the influenza. Well, perhaps not now," glancing at Willy and Gracie. "Then perhaps...."

Major Bruckmiller entered the lists. "Sir, thank you and your laboratory assistants for the diagnosis of that curious disease affecting our dogs. Most of them pulled through. We even have a healthy litter of puppies. Children, would you...if I may, Frau von Treptow?"

"It seems you already have, Major. Proceed."

"We have some Alsatian puppies. One very small one, she will be too small to walk with the policemen. Would you like a new puppy?"

Squeals and cries of 'yes!' rang out from the children.

Claire said mischievously, "And the Police will clean up after them, children. As they do elsewhere," the last not so cheerily.

Dinner over, children off to bed, the von Treptows retired to the study along with Bruckmiller and Captain von Seeckt. "The influenza, you asked, Brother? And why?"

"For us, it is a matter of mass infection among our troops. They are weaker than we would like, and I cringe at the effects of an epidemic."

"Willy noted it last year in the Balkans, or so he thought. We call it influenza, because he could not detect typhus or cholera in the patients there, or in Palestine and Turkey. So, it may or may not be similar to the Russian disease from twenty or thirty years ago, but we do not think it one of the bacterium-caused ailments as does Pfeiffer. We are puzzled as to its nature but not its existence. I have no intent or desire to publicize our findings, but for us in research, medicine has no borders, admits no censorship. I receive telegrams daily from Copenhagen, Zurich, Belgrade, Boston, Madrid, Oporto, Salonika, elsewhere."

Rudy shrugged and continued, "Whatever this is, it is in America as well as Austria-Hungary and the Balkans. It is now in Brest. Clearly brought by the Americans. That is where your concentrations are, or will be. Curiously, though, there may be two strains about. The southern European version attacks all ages and constitutions, not just the old, infants and the weak, as we have seen before. The American version, on early diagnosis, affects the young and strong preferentially. Soldiers, you see?"

Bruckmiller and von Treptow conferred briefly. "Yes, General, we are as prepared as possible. Spread thin, though, now having to cover the children's and their mother's wing." The massive house's first floor, aside from the ballroom and supporting rooms at the center rear, was divided into four wings within the remaining rectangle, four corridors off the central concourse. Rudy's and Willy's families had the left, Dietrich and the senior servants the right. The massive entry stair front and center, an equally imposing stair at the rear of the ballroom. Bruckmiller's men were concentrated around the front entry, rear accesses secured and locked.

"Reittemann?"

"Yes, Sir?"

"Everyone accounted for among the staff?"

"All but Martin, Sir. Nowhere to be found."

"Trouble stalks us then, General," opined Bruckmiller.

"So it does. Reittimann, keep the staff well away and out of sight. You included."

* * *

Friday, February 1, 0200 hours

The first shots rang out in the center of the ground floor, from the rear of the house. Bruckmiller's men were surprised, two going down immediately, the rest seeking cover. Three rough-looking men charged forward, using military tactics to pin down the police.

Upstairs, the ballroom doors were flung open and a dozen men poured out. They were met with a hail of fire from the top of the stair opposite, four going down, four taking cover, the remainder scattering into the wings.

The officers had not slept, Colts at the ready. The three raiders sent to find the general soon were under pistol fire from behind doorways and overturned furniture. The first was surprised with a round in the forehead, the second with two to the chest. The survivor dashed back across the concourse, evading the crossfire, and into Willy's wing.

The three officers edged forward when suddenly one of the intruders crossed into view, backing away from a too-exposed position. All were surprised, but Major Bruckmiller and the other traded shots. The invader went down with finality, but the Major had taken two bullets, one in the left thigh, and spinning around, one in the buttocks. In pain, he grimaced, "Damn! Butt shot. Do not tell Big Tits!" He crawled back to a secure position, waving the others away. Captain von Seeckt eased his head around the corner, summoning several shots. "Three or four, Sir. Well armed. Carbines and pistols. Is there a way around them?"

"My study, opposite. I will go. Covering fire."

"No, Sir, you will not." Von Seeckt took his arm. "That is an order. You are not quick enough with your leg."

Dietrich looked at his aide. "Very well. Have to cross into the open. Go all the way across to the butler's pantry shared with the ballroom. You are on your own from there. Godspeed, Erich."

The captain smiled, gave his stub salute and hurtled low across the concourse, rolling into the corridor opposite before the startled shooters could correct their aim. The general eased to the edge, firing twice, then signalling the police what to expect.

A shot rang out, then silence. Von Treptow was as puzzled as the intruders. Then one of the ballroom doors opened with a very dead invader shielding von Seeckt, who popped off two rounds; the general fired three times, the police a few, fearful of hitting the captain. This threat was gone.

"Major?"

"Could not be better. Might need a bandage. Captain, your status?"

From below, "Controlled, Sir. Three criminals down." A pause. "Volckert and Schulte also, Sir. Dead, Sir."

Von Treptow was standing in the center of the concourse, surveying the carnage. *At least the Old Masters were spared, if not the furniture and porcelain. Inappropriate, Dietrich.* He became conscious of someone coming from his right, from his wing. It was Claire with a Colt in her hand. "So that's where the oth...."

Claire raised the pistol with both hands, aimed it at von Treptow and fired.

Twelve meters down the hall opposite, one of the brigands spun around and crashed into the wall, then slowly slumped, painting a swath of blood on the plaster and silk.

Claire walked on to von Treptow, still aiming the pistol at his head now speckled with powder and wadding. "Killer of men, of my friends, you let your guard down? Shame. Such a mistake could be your last."

Just then, a scream pierced the new calm. "Grace! He has my Gracie!" Adele's cry came from the doors beyond the fallen revolutionary. Von Treptow waved to the study, "Claire! The door!" She dashed into the room, leaving a door just cracked. Out came the last intruder, Gracie in his arms, pistol to her head. Adele was frozen at the door behind them hugging little Willy.

"Let me go now, and she'll be just fine. Get me a car. Do as I say!"

Von Treptow stood impassively at the head of the corridor, tapping his chest, "Would you rather not have me? Dead, alive, as you please? Here. A rather large target, do you not think?" He made a theatrical gesture of dropping his automatic. "Take me. She has a full life ahead of her."

Gracie had stopped her terrified squalling, staring in unison with her captor at the general, tall, outwardly calm. "An even trade I should think. You are, if you would only realize it, a dead man. So am I. You see, an even trade. What could possibly be fairer? Here. Need I place the barrel to my own heart? Man, were you a soldier?"

Now thoroughly baffled, the captor answered softly, "Yes."

"I cannot hear you. Come closer. Were you a soldier?"

"Yes." The gunman's voice caught in a small choke, "Yes, Sir."

"Then you can shoot, can you not? What unit, what regiment?" He turned his head toward his captain, "Probably one of von Bruckow's. I shall wager you one hundred goldmarks, Erich."

"Yes. Yes, Sir, I was."

"You were what?"

"Third Hesse, Sir. Brigadier General von Bruckow, Sir." He shifted his little load. Gracie was in shock, frozen, unresponsive.

"So I win my wager. What are you going to do, soldier? Did you not come here to kill me?"

"Yes, Sir," his grip getting a little weaker.

"Who else?"

"Anyone who got in our way. And the Royal, Sir."

"Your were going to kill servants, children, women? For the pleasure of killing me? I am flattered, man. The Princess, too, you say? Why her? I thought she was your friend?"

"Not ours, Sir. Not the Bolsheviks', not ours."

"Well, well, well, that is so very interesting." A pause. "Very well, back to the topic at hand. My death. Are we to get on with it or not? Come closer. Your hands are shaking too much to aim true, even at this range. Here, use this Iron Cross as your target. Here," pointing. "Do not hit it, of course! They will pin it on my corpse for the funeral."

The man muttered something.

"What?" Cupping his ear, "Come closer, man, I cannot hear you."

The Bolshevik took the last fateful step that placed him abreast of the study door which quietly opened. Claire pounced catlike, levelling the pistol mere centimeters from his head and pulling the trigger. A shower of blood and brain painted the wall opposite as von Treptow lunged forward to bat away the dead man's pistol and catch little Gracie who finally was able to howl and scream.

Clutching the little girl close to him and away from the grisly scene, "Thank you, Claire, I am forever in your debt." As Adele came rushing forward to scoop up her daughter, Claire said in a chilling tone, "We are not finished yet, Dee." She raised the pistol to his forehead. "Back."

She pushed him across the concourse toward a set of chairs, backing him down into one, Colt pressed against his forehead. "No, dearest, we are not finished." Several policemen came toward them but were waved away by von Treptow.

She cocked the hammer. "Not yet finished, Dee."

* * * * *
* * *
*

Who Desires Peace...

Notes and Attributions

Date	Notes

January 1

Crown Prince Rupprecht of Bavaria's Northern Army Group advance headquarters was in the town of Mons, near the French border. The convent is fictional as a matter of architecture and atmosphere.

Main Imperial Army Headquarters was in Kreuznach, Germany, later moved to the resort town of Spa, Belgium. Lieutenant von Seeckt's reports from the fronts reflect the status quo of the war at the beginning of 1918.

The Verdun incident actually happened as described; Sergeant Kunze was a real person.

A note on the characters: General von Treptow hails from the Berlin suburb of Treptow, the 'von' meaning 'from' or 'of', denoting nobility. 'Treptow' caught my eye while examining an 1860's map in my collection. Lieutenant von Seeckt derives from his real uncle, Hans von Seeckt, whose career is as described. After the war, Hans von Seeckt led the surreptitious rebuilding of the Wehrmacht.

January 2

Colonel von Lossberg, Major Niemann and the unseen Captain Geyer are historical figures, prominent tactical experts in the General Staff.

Von Treptow's premise – that Germany had the war won if it did not throw its strength away in a futile last offensive — is, besides being the basis of this narrative, a "grave mistake," as Churchill describes Ludendorff's decision in The World Crisis.

Prince Max of Baden was heir to the Grand Duchy of Baden, and a leading liberal voice in the German hierarchy, later Chancellor in the last days before the Armistice.

"Truth...," Senator Hiram Johnson, 1917.

The Nivelles/Chemin des Dames mutinies were among the most important events of 1917, next to America's entry into the war (triggered by Germany's unrestricted U-boat warfare) and the Russian collapse. Many French soldiers — the poilus or "hairy ones", for their beards and moustaches, the equivalent of the British Tommy and American Doughboy — simply refused to advance, to 'go over the top'. John Keegan's The First World War gives an excellent account, pp. 329-331 and 356; also William Manchester's The Last Lion, p. 639, especially the "bleating" of the poilus being herded to battle. France was essentially on defense only on the Western Front for a year until July 1918.

The French 'veiled in secrecy' the true extent of the mutinies, keeping the truth from their Allies and also kept four of their best divisions away from the Front, near Paris, in the event of civilian unrest. Britain began unloading her dead at night to hide the true human costs of 1916 and 1917.

Operation Michael was the first and largest component of the planned Spring offensive, aimed initially at the British.

Armenius is the Latin name for Herrmann, the German hero whose forces destroyed two Roman Legions in 9 A.D. in the Teutoberg Forest in what is now western Germany, ending Roman rule east of the Rhine.

The 1916 Battle of the Somme was a bloody misadventure by the British, with terrible casualties on both sides, for little strategic or territorial change. The first day of the offensive was the bloodi-est day of the war for the British, 29,000 killed or wounded. Major

Knorr's escapade is grounded in fact, geography and time – there was/is a High Wood, the 24th Brandenburg Regiment was involved, the British and South Africans advanced, with cavalry charges and an early use of tanks. His narrative is an amalgam of history and fiction – there were only four tanks used, not a dozen or more, the cavalry did charge, but the final battle is an imagined version of the day's events, with the British finally taking the ground for good. Winston Churchill was not present, having returned to England in May, 1916, but had been Lieutenant Colonel in command of the 6th Royal Scots Fusiliers in the trenches not far from the battleground, sporting a blue poilu's helmet, a gift from a French general.

Looking at the site of the High Wood and its surroundings in a Michelin atlas, one is struck by the sheer number of British cemeteries, one every quarter mile or so along every road in the area.

Phosgene, chlorine and T-stoff were gases used by the Germans, along with mustard gas. The Allies responded in kind.

Cambrai was a 1917 British/Canadian offensive with the first massed tank attack. The Germans quickly adopted anti-tank artillery tactics and blunted the British attack after its initial gains. Kurt Krueger was the German artillery hero of Cambrai, dying after reputedly knocking out 16 tanks.

Churchill's dagger would have come from the Duke of Marlborough, his ancestor, given him by Prince Eugene of Austria to commemorate the British/Austrian victory over the French and Bavarians at Blenheim, 1704.

The Belgian soldier account recounts the German sweep through neutral Belgium, assaulting the fortress towns of Liege and Namur.

Stahlhelm: literally, "Steel Helmet," a term applied to German soldiers.

Franc tireur refers to partisan or guerilla snipers, the excuse for German atrocities. The *brassard rouge*, or red armband, was worn by the Belgians sent to Germany as forced labor.

Schrecklichkeit was the German term for their own policy of terror and repression. Louvain, a beautiful medieval town near Brussels, was indeed torched by the Germans, a horrendous loss and filmed by the arsonists, to boot.

The General's dissertation on the strategic situation, the effects of blockade, the death tolls, the changed makeup of the British Army, all reflect the reality of the day. His comments about Mons, the first battle the British fought upon landing, likewise. The 6th Royal Scots were actually raised in 1914, a transition between the Old Army and Kitchener's New Army.

January 3   The pamphlet, "The Attack in Position Warfare" was real, a systematic effort to deal with the deadlock of trench warfare. The November 11 reference is to a meeting in which the Final Offensive was first proposed by Ludendorff and his staff, subsequently approved by Hindenburg, the 'Wooden Titan,' hero of the battle of Tannenberg in which Germany threw back the first Russian offensive of the war. See Barbara Tuchman's The Guns of August or Alexandr Solzhenitsyn's August 1914. The Hindenburg and Siegfried Lines reflected the considerations of strategic retreat, a recurrent theme.

Colonel Walther and Department IIIb were real, part of German Army Intelligence as was Count Wittenberg.

The Swan Ball is the premier social event in Nashville. I attended once, but was not asked back. Hmmm.

The reference to the battlecruiser names is fictitious, except for SMS *Mackensen* – the ships' keels were laid down, but never completed. Teutoberg was Armenius's victory and Tannenberg was Hindenburg's victory over the Russians in 1914.

Hindenburg and Ludendorff reflect their descriptions in several publications. Hindenburg was commanding Field Marshal of all German forces, Ludendorff his chief of staff, but by 1918, effectively military dictator of Germany. Von Kluck and Von Bülow were the two generals commanding the war's initial sweep into France, checked just short of Paris in the 1914 Battle of the Marne. Both had been invalided out of active service by 1918.

Ludendorff's comment, *"We will punch a hole..."* is a direct quote, cited extensively.

General Bruchmüller was an artillery commander who created a means of pre-setting individual guns to eliminate the need to adjust their aim, to surprise defenders with accurate fire rather than give them time to take cover and regroup.

The overwhelming threat to Germany — since Russia was crumbling, the French were not leaving their trenches, and the British were undermanned — was the advent of the Americans. British and French divisions had been steadily reduced in size by attrition and manpower limitations to the 10,000 man range. The American divisions were of 28,000 and millions were on their way. However, the Yanks were not fully trained and had to rely on their Allies for almost all their weapons, including aircraft. American soldiers and Marines did not see really heavy action until early summer, 1918, only a few months short of the November 11 armistice, but were the looming threat to an increasingly depleted German Army.

Food supplies, for both civilians and soldiers, were tight for Germany and Austria-Hungary due to Britain's effective naval blockade. Unrest was simmering, but not just in Germany; France in particular was frothy, particularly after the 1917 mutinies.

The German Army delivered Lenin from exile in Switzerland to St. Petersburg, with the results described. Churchill later described him as a plague bacillus infecting Russia, exactly as the Germans hoped. Lenin was subsequently badly embarrassed by the disclosure of his substantial German financial support. The strategic situation favored Germany as the Russian Army crumbled and the Reds struggled to consolidate power. The ninety day armistice was signed December 15th, with peace treaty negotiations to start again in February. The comment about the Russian soldier is a direct quote from Lenin.

Landsturm and *Landwehr* were reserve units. Crown Prince Rupprecht was a real person, heir to the Kingdom of Bavaria as preserved under the German Empire's structure, also (tenuously) to the British throne through his mother's descent from King James I. He was one of Germany's most capable military leaders, but also a realist about the futility of the war. After the Canadian success at Vimy Ridge in 1917, he said, *"The further question arises. Is it of any use to pursue the war further under such conditions? Only if a peace with Russia is speedily concluded. If not... we must admit ourselves to be conquered."* (Terraine, The Great War 1914-1918, p.292).

Lebensraum, or 'Living Room" refers to the subjugation and colonization of the lands to Germany's east.

Rupert von Spandau's reference to the rarity of lung cancer is drawn from a George Will essay quoting a medical professor at Washington University in St. Louis during an autopsy in 1908 for a rare such case.

Estelle is fictional, but her tale of escape from Louvain and the Germans is all too typical. German reprisals against real or perceived provocations were brutal and commonplace; her husband's fate was not uncommon, and her sister's unknown fate in the village of Dinant, likewise: over 600 were shot there in one incident.

The Battle of Mons was Britain's first engagement soon after its first landings in France. The Germans were caught by surprise in old-fashioned marching tactics by the British Army's very effective rifle fire. The British, however, were vastly outnumbered and forced to retreat. See Terraine, <u>Mons – Retreat to Victory</u>.

The incident at the bridge with the schoolgirls actually happened, appropriated here for our General von Treptow's character. His (fictional) title is Markgraf, literally, Count of the Central March, the 'Mittelmark', the area containing Brandenburg and Berlin between the Elbe and Oder rivers.

Estelle tried to flee but was surrounded by the Germans and their reputation for terror and thwarted by her captor's threats against her daughter. Then, her pregnancies.

January 5   All the French characters save Barton are real. Laval was executed after World War Two for his treason as leader of the Vichy government. Malvy was indicted for treason for his newspaper support, convicted only of negligence and exiled for five years. Maurras was as described, a potent reactionary force of the times. The Camelots du Roi, literally, *'Streethawkers of the King'*, and Croix de Feu, *'Cross of Fire'* were rightist/monarchist groups often engaged in street violence. Joseph Caillaux, a former Premier, was arrested in January, 1918, a week after von Treptow's comment, accused of 'plotting against the security of the state', that is, treasonous relations with German agents. Until then, he was a 'rat such as that,' living comfortably in Paris. He was convicted in 1920, but released for time served and later amnestied. See William Shirer's <u>The Collapse of the Third Republic</u> for an excellent description of the conflicts and tensions in France before (and after) the war.

Offensive à outrance, Élan, Le Cran: Offensive to the limit, Fighting Spirit, Guts. France's dominant military posture was the offensive, always the offensive.

The fifty-five were the executed ringleaders of the 1917 mutinies.

Georges Clemenceau, the French Premier (*Président du' Conseil*), had taken over in late 1917 after a succession of largely ineffective leaders. His motto was "I make war".

The Deuxième Bureau was France's military counterintelligence agency.

January 6   Handley-Page was the manufacturer of the largest British strategic bombers of the war; their last version could reach Berlin.

The conversation among the Princes and the General reflects events unfolding in the East, a work in progress, the Germans determined to control the outcome. Max von Hoffman was German chief of staff in the east, the mastermind in that theater.

January 8   Woodrow Wilson makes his first appearance via the publication of his Fourteen Points. The commentary reflects views of the day, but, unfortunately, both the Allies and the Central Powers were too hardened in their positions to immediately grasp the proposal. The situation in the East was understood only in the abstract by Wilson, understandably since Russia was a failed state in opaque confusion as he wrote.

"*...vain ass...*": General Henry Wilson, British Army Chief of Staff, quoted in several sources.
"*...Today's words...*", Prince Max's <u>Memoirs</u>, Vol. I, p. 219.

January 9   Germany made several efforts to enlist the Irish Republicans as a fifth column threat, pinning down up to 50,000 Tommies. An early gunrunning exercise succeeded, but one in 1916 failed. Sir Roger Casement, a prominent British diplomat, was caught working with the Germans (booking travel on their submarines, even) and executed.

Tomas (or Thomas) Masaryk was a Slovak patriot, a founder of Czechoslovakia and its first President. And he did shop around for the best deal for his new country. The Czech Legion and Radola Gajda were very real, the center of one of the more bizarre episodes of the war. All the warring powers wanted this large unit in their service. Gajda despised the Bolsheviks but was more than willing to fight the Germans in France. To do so, his Legion had to take the Trans-Siberian railway to Vladivostok, then by ship around the world to France. They actually got as far as Chelyabinsk in western Siberia, when a chance incident caused them to rebel, taking over the railway and fighting the Bolsheviks. The last units finally reached the Pacific in 1920.

Syurzhyk: A rural combination of Russian and Ukrainian.

The Laramie connection just occurred to me, and took little embellishment. It crops up again later at a very opportune time.

January 10 Humbert Grosz is fictional, meant to look like the grotesque caricatures of his namesake, George Grosz.

January 13 Charlotte Despard (Sir John French's sister), Emmaline Pankurst, Michael Collins and Liam Lynch were real people. Collins was assassinated by anti-treaty Irish rebels in 1921 during the Irish Civil War.

"William" Butler Yeats, Ireland's foremost poet of the time.

"I imagine... ", a quote from Yeats, 1925, referring to his mystical "Daimon' spirit and the gyres of history.

"Eleanor" Marx, Karl Marx's youngest daughter. The quote and references are from "The Second Coming", written 1919-20 referring to the war-brought disruptions of civilization.

January 16   Reginald, Lord Elsmere: Not to be confused with the Earl of
                  Ellesmere, his name and its spelling comes from the street on
                  which my wife's mother grew up.

                  Oberbefehlshaber Ost: Supreme Commander German Forces
                  East; Leopold was Rupprecht's uncle.

                  Churchill presented a map of Eastern Europe to Stalin at Yalta,
                  1945, marked with his prospective "spheres of influence" in vari-
                  ous countries.   Stalin marked his assent with a tick, or
                  checkmark.

                  Martin Niemoller was a highly decorated U-Boat captain in the
                  Mediterranean, later a prominent Protestant minister imprisoned
                  by the Nazis (*"First, they came for the Socialists..."*).

                  HMS Dreadnought, the first 'all-big gun' battleship, rammed and
                  sank a U-boat, the only such sinking in the war.

January 18   'Albion' was a High Seas Fleet operation against the Russians in
                  the Baltic.   Gun sizes: 28 centimeters = 11 inches (diameter);
                  30(.5) centimeters = 12 inches; these two were the smallest guns
                  then mounted on battleships, newer ones up to 15 inches. The
                  "24's" refer to a large gun (9 inches) mounted on cruisers and
                  older battleships.

January 20   The *Order Pour le Mérite* is the famous Blue Max.

January 21   *"The lamps are going out..."*: Lord Edward Grey's words.

                  Andrew Bonar Law was leader of the Conservative (Tory) Party
                  in Lloyd George's coalition government and Chancellor of the
                  Exchequer (Treasury Secretary).

                  Harry S Truman started his store in Independence after the war;
                  he was an artillery captain in the Argonne Forest battle.

Max's real (older) sister was Princess Marie, married to Friedrich, Duke of Anhalt-Dessau.

January 22 Οινοψ ποντοξ: "The wine-dark sea" as often translated from *The Iliad*

January 23 General Allenby commanded the ultimately successful British Army campaign in the Middle East, assisted by one T. E. Lawrence.

The Constituent Assembly in Russia was as Max described, the last chance at democracy before the Bolshevik dictatorship.

"Damp squib" – a dud fireworks.

January 24 Franz Albers: Not the artist.

January 25 Ernst Thesiger: a favorite actor of the 1930's. Played Doctor Praetorius in *The Bride of Frankenstein*.

January 26 *"Whoever rules Bohemia..."* one of many quotes from Chancellor Otto von Bismarck, the unifier of Germany.

"To which of the Circles of Hell...", Dante's *Inferno*

"Wenn der fuchs predigt, so nehmt die gänse in acht?": When the fox preaches, look to your geese.

January 27 Paul Wegener was one of Germany's foremost theater and film directors; Miss Lorelei is a 'confection'. UFA: consolidated German film producer, primarily propaganda. (Fritz) Lang (*Metropolis*), (F. W.) Murnau (*Nosferatu*): film directors.

Reifenstahl: from Leni Reifenstahl, Nazi-era director and propagandist (*The Triumph of the Will*). Matthias Groening: let no reference go unexplained - *The Simpsons*. Enough said.

"An enigma wrapped in a riddle... ": Churchill's famous description of the Soviet Union, here tortured. Sir Edward Elgar's work featured the enigmas mentioned.

Pershing chose the town of Chaumont as HQ, establishing offices in a large public building there. Pershing's career is depicted through Finley's history. He lost his family, save his son, as described.

House: 'Colonel' Edward House, Wilson's confidant; Lansing, US Secretary of State; Rawlinson: British General, field commander in Flanders..

January 28   The Spartacist 'festival' and mayhem following reflect the real-life workers' strike and aborted uprising of January, 1918 (not the Spartacist uprising of January 1919), fostered and directed by Russia, specifically Trotsky. He expected Germany to collapse into revolution, thus sparing Russia from the German Army. The uprising was short and unsuccessful.

M(inistry of) I(ntelligence) Five: MI5— British counterintelligence (domestic), run by Vernon Kell. Mansfield Cumming ran MI6 — James Bond's foreign spy outfit. See Ferguson, <u>Operation Kronstadt</u>, Chapter 2.

January 29   Charles Churchill: 18th Century poet and satirist, if related to WSC, only through distant cousinry?

'Ill news hath wings... ': from *The Barron's Wars*, 1596. Public School = Private (Prep) school.

"Russia is rapidly being reduced... ": Address to his Dundee constituents, 1919 (first paragraph only, the rest is mine). <u>Manchester</u>, p. 676.

"I think it a great surprise...": WSC to Nancy Astor, the first woman MP, 1919.

January 31   *"...scawey..."*: lifted shamelessly from *The Son of Frankenstein.*

Sources

Barry, John M. The Great Influenza, London: Penguin Books, 2004.

Blucher, Princess Evelyn. An English Wife in Berlin, London: Constable, 1921.

Breyer, Siegfried. Battleships and Battlecruisers, 1905 – 1970, Garden City, Doubleday, 1973.

Churchill, Winston S. The World Crisis 1911-1918, Abridged, London. Free Press, 2005.

Dallas, Gregor. 1918, War and Peace, London: John Murray, 2000.

Eisenhower, John S. D. Yanks, The Epic Story of the American Army in World War I, New York: The Free Press, 2001.

Ferguson, Harry. Operation Kronstadt: The Overlook Press, 2009.

Forty, Simon. Historical Maps of World War I, London: PRC Publishing, 2002.

Gilbert, Martin. Churchill, A Life, New York: Henry Holt and Company, 1991.

Gilbert, Martin. The First World War, New York: Henry Holt, 1994.

Harris, Stephen L. Harlem's Hellfighters, Washington, D. C.: Brassey's, 2003.

Hayward, Steven F. The Age of Reagan, New York: Random House, 2009.

Haythornthwaite, Philip J. The World War One Sourcebook, London: BCA, 1992.

Hochschild, Adam. To End All Wars, New York: Houghton Mifflin Harcourt, 2011.

Johnson, J. H. 1918, The Unexpected Victory, London: Arms and Armour Press, 1997.

Johnson, Paul. Modern Times: From the Twenties to the Nineties, New York: Harper Collins, 1991.

Keegan, John. The First World War, New York: Alfred A. Knopf, 1999.

Lattimore, Richmond (translator). The Iliad of Homer, Chicago: University of Chicago Press, 1951.

Liddell Hart, B. H. The Real War: 1914-1918, Boston: Little, Brown & Company, 1930.

Lloyd George, Robert. David & Winston, New York: The Overlook Press, 2005.

Ludendorff, Erich. Ludendorff's Own Story, August 1914 – November 1918, Vol. II: New York, Harper & Brothers Publishers, 1919.

Manchester, William. The Last Lion: Visions of Glory, Boston: Little, Brown & Company, 1983.

Massie, Robert K. Dreadnought, New York: Random House, 1991.

Massie, Robert K. Castles of Steel, New York: Random House, 2003.

Max, Prince of Baden. Memoirs, Volume I and II, New York: Charles Scribner's Sons, 1928.

Mee, Charles L., Jr. The End of Order: Versailles, 1919, New York: E. P. Dutton, 1980.

Neiberg, Martin S., et al. The Eastern Front 1914 – 1920, London: Amber Press, 2012.

Palmer, Alan. Victory 1918, New York: Atlantic Monthly Press, 1998.

Pershing, John J. My Experiences in the World War, Volumes I and II, New York: Frederick A. Stokes Company, 1931.

Shirer, William L. The Collapse of the Third Republic, New York: Simon and Schuster, 1969.

Stevenson, David. With Our Backs to the Wall, Victory and Defeat in 1918, Cambridge: Harvard University Press, 2011.

Terraine, John. Mons, Retreat to Victory, London: Wordsworth Editions, 2002.

Terraine, John. The Great War 1914-1918, A Pictorial History, Garden City: Doubleday and Company, 1965.

Toland, John. No Man's Land, 1918, The Last Year of the Great War, New York: Konecky & Konecky, 1980.

Tuchman, Barbara. The Guns of August, New York: Macmillan, 1962.

Tuchman, Barbara. The Proud Tower, New York: Macmillan, 1962.

Warner, Philip. World War One, A Narrative, London: Cassell Military Classics, 1995.

Watt, Richard M. Watt. Dare Call It Treason, New York: Simon & Schuster, 1963.

About the Author

James Emerson Loyd is a recovering architect and retired real estate executive, hardly apprenticeships to becoming an author of historical fiction. As an amateur historian of the twentieth century, he had long been fascinated by the First World War and how Germany's collapse in 1918 led to Europe's descent into totalitarianism. So, after reading and re-reading some Clancy and Crichton and Furst along with his histories, one day he decided to write his first novel. With a rough idea of a subject – how that collapse could have been prevented – he sat down at the keyboard and began writing. Before long he found himself simply taking dictation from his characters as they grew into the storyline, and a thousand pages later, he was done.

A San Antonio native, he spent twenty-five years away from home then returned after marrying his high school sweetheart. They live with their two dogs (one French pointer, one German schnauzer, appropriately) in their old neighborhood.

www.ingramcontent.com/pod-product-compliance
Lightning Source LLC
Chambersburg PA
CBHW071148250626
47159CB00001B/27